THE NAMELESS STORM

THE STARS AND GREEN MAGICS
BOOK 5

NOVAE CAELUM

For detailed content notes, please see:
https://novaecaelum.com/content-notes

1

REST

> *I have had two fathers. And at times, I've found myself both exasperated with and immensely grateful for both of them.*
>
> — ARIANNA RHIALDEN, MELESORIE X IN *THE CHANGE DIALOGUES*

Iata woke to soft light, soft sounds, soft blankets. He was propped up, which was odd.

He wasn't in his bedroom, or his own bloodservant's bedroom, and that realization made his heart-rate spike. And *that* made a monitor nearby chime.

Haneri was curled in an awkward position in a chair beside his bed, her eyes closed. Her clothes, for once, disheveled.

He inhaled and smelled antiseptic, and...rust.

A pile of rusted metal flakes lay scattered across his lap, his left hand resting in the mess. His right hand was tied to an intravenous hookup. His torso, beneath the blankets, was stiff with med patches and healskin bandages. He didn't have a shirt on.

"Ungh," he said, which was about the most sound he could manage.

Haneri jerked and sat up, peering at him through bleary, golden-brown eyes. Her flawless brown complexion wasn't dimmed, not even a little, by the wan overhead lights. And was it horrible—Adeius, yes, it had to be horrible—that his thought at that moment was how beautiful she was when waking up beside him?

Even if she was in a chair, and he in a bed that wasn't his own.

Haneri's eyes darted to the pile of rust on his lap—that had to have been a metal bar, and who had supplied that?—and then back to him.

He shuddered and broke into a cold sweat. If he had rust in his lap, if someone had given him metal to pull strength from, then his aura was showing. Who had seen it? How many, and could they be contained?

Iata was in the palace infirmary, not in a public hospital, but even so. He took a breath and tried to push his aura back inside himself, but gasped as his whole body repulsed his attempt. Adeius, fire was boiling in his blood.

Haneri jerked forward. "Don't—Homaj, don't. They already know. There wasn't time to get Dressa or the bloodservants to take you through the back corridors. We had to take you through the main ones."

The infirmary was on the floor beneath the royal residence, near the back of the palace. Accessible through the back corridors, yes, but also through a service staircase and lift. He wouldn't have been paraded through the court—at least he hoped not. Who had seen his—his unconscious body? His bleeding body?

Iata looked down at his chest again, trying to make out the colors of the med patches beneath the light blanket. Trying to assess the damage.

He focused inward—he remembered that he could focus inward, and took a bodily inventory. He'd had surgery. He'd been sedated and was still feeling the haze from that. He knew not to smooth that post-surgery haziness away—he'd need that energy for healing.

The injury. He blinked hard, and what had happened snapped back into memory.

Lesander.

The hug. The knife.

He could feel with his Change-trained senses the edges of the wound inside him, the most aggravated parts. He measured the precise fix of the surgeon's intervention. His body had an influx of stored blood, so he had lost much.

The injury might have killed him if he hadn't managed to call for help. If he hadn't been a magicker, pulling strength from the wood of the floor around him to let his Truthspoken training maintain his body and heal. He had an automatic heal command set for when his body was in a dire state—that had kicked in. Now, he was pulling from several nutrient patches to replenish his system reserves, but he knew it would be several days before his body would make a full recovery.

Iata lay back again, his breaths coming short.

"You will recover," Haneri said.

He nodded and smoothed away a burst of nausea. Maybe he would need that energy, too, but he had no wish at all to throw up.

"How—how bad is the court taking this—I'm still—"

"Homaj, I don't know."

Right. Yes, he was still Homaj. He was still, from sheer habit, speaking with Homaj's intonation, using his gestures. He reassessed himself with that in mind, made small adjustments. If he was Homaj now and others had seen his aura, then he had to keep being Homaj for the time being, no help for that.

"I've been here," Haneri said, her voice gathering steel.

"Someone had to make sure that you got the proper care. Ceorre is tending to everything else."

"And Dressa?" he asked.

"Dressa is distraught." But there was more there she wasn't saying. An anger that boiled just beneath the surface.

Was he reading that through her body language? Or, with his aura out, feeling it?

He gingerly reached to brush the rust on his lap. "Did you bring the metal?"

Then he sucked in a breath, looked to her. "Are we safe to talk?" That she was calling him Homaj made him think they were not, but maybe she was being overcautious.

Haneri rolled her shoulders, tilted her neck to either side to work out the kinks, then reached into a hip pocket, pulling out a compact combination dampener-scrambler. It was one of the models, he saw, that obscured visuals, too.

Haneri flicked it on, nudged it in beside him, then pulled her chair closer.

"You're asking, I think, if everyone thinks you just manifested? There is speculation. Oh Adeius, there is speculation. We're not going to get around that. But I talked briefly with the First Magicker. He said it would be best if we all broadcast that this was your manifestation, this injury. It's a trauma, that's plausible."

"Haneri, my rank isn't low—"

"And neither is your social rank. I think that follows."

"But Imorie's rank—"

Her hand closed around his. The monitor beside him was chiming again, and his heart hammered in his chest.

He closed his eyes, damning the stabs of pain that his breaths were bringing, and separated the pain from himself. Iata slowly, slowly brought his heart-rate back down, but the effort left him sweating.

He opened his eyes and squeezed her hand, unable to stop tears of sheer frustration.

"Imorie will be fine," Haneri said with her usual bluntness. "I need to know that you will be fine. You're Homaj. Can you continue to be Homaj?"

He turned up his other hand, his rust-covered hand, and she frowned, standing to pull the soiled blanket off of him. He finally got a good look at his exposed torso and grimaced. Yes, that matched what he felt inside.

Haneri brushed off the remaining rust, grabbed another blanket, and covered him again.

There was a pile of blankets beside her chair, and how many times had she done this? How many metal bars had he crumbled?

"Mariyit brought the metal. He said it would give you more strength, but not to use more than he brought."

"How many bars?"

"Ten."

Fuck.

"How long—"

"It's afternoon, day after."

Startled, he tried to push up.

Haneri pressed him firmly back down.

"*Homaj.* You will absolutely rest until the physicians say you can safely leave the bed."

"But—"

"Ceorre has the kingdom in hand for the moment."

"But Dressa, my Heir—"

Haneri tilted her head. And even though the dampener was on, she lowered her voice.

"Where is Iata?"

He looked between her eyes, but knew that if he was Homaj, she was asking after Maja. And her question earlier about if he could remain Homaj might plausibly be asking if he could Change or not. Just in case every other security precaution was failing, because no dampener or scrambler was ever one hundred percent secure. Nothing was ever totally secure. Not even his study. Not even his judgment.

"Hestia," he croaked, and she grabbed a bottle of water, put it to his lips.

He coughed before managing a few sips. "Haneri—you don't need to—"

But she waved him off, recapped the bottle. "So, is this a temporary thing? It's already been almost three weeks." Three weeks solid of being Homaj, barring his Change when Imorie had arrived.

He swallowed again, clearing his throat. Okay. So now she was going to throw security to the wind, but she wasn't wrong that she needed to know.

And at that moment, he was too fucking tired to really care. The dampener would have to be enough.

"It was supposed to be temporary—I was supposed to step up fully—"

Haneri's brows shot up. "Am I still married, then?"

Asking, then, if Maja had abdicated yet, which would follow that he had to abdicate if Iata was to rule. All of which was...complicated.

He turned his hands up. "Legally, yes. Technically..." He tried to sit up straighter again, and this time, she didn't stop him. "Haneri, my magics—my *manifestation* of magics—what is Ceorre saying? How is she handling this?"

"She's saying you were attacked. We had to"—she made a face—"we had to blame it on Iata. That got out first, unfortunately. Some of the staff or some of Jalava's people saw Iata going to your apartment before this happened. It got out too quickly, though Jalava is trying to find the leak. I've tasked Vogret with that, too, and she is effective." This said with a tight nod. "But the danger, too, was that Imorie would be blamed. As a magicker associated with the deaths of other nobility. Or Eti, though I'm sure it would have been pinned on Imorie."

Iata groaned and sat back, closing his eyes until the room stopped spinning.

"So, you're publicly a magicker," she said. "You're being painted as the victim by everyone on your side—which you *are* a victim—and that the attack made you manifest. You'll need to be clumsy in your magics at first—"

"I know how a manifestation works," he snapped.

At her sudden and eloquent silence, he opened his hands.

"I am the Seritarchus," he said, and didn't know if that was a declaration or an apology.

Haneri, her mouth tight, nodded. "And you'll remain as such. You're not going to abdicate just now, if you were considering that. Not when Dressa's associations are...in question." She narrowed her eyes.

"Dressa didn't do this," he said quickly.

"Oh, I know. Ceorre is sorting that out."

"I want to see Lesander—"

Her eyes glinted. "No. Not yet. Not until I've had the chance to talk to her."

He opened his mouth, was going to say that Lesander hadn't wanted to do this to him. That had been painfully clear. She'd been crying. She'd embraced him.

Unless his senses had been so locked down, his magicker senses too frayed to tell the lie in that, too.

He was having trouble keeping his eyes open. "Tell Ceorre. I want to see her. When she can."

Haneri laid a cool hand on his brow, and, startled, he opened his eyes again.

"Do I have permission to touch you, Husband?"

She'd called him that before. But here, knowing she knew who he was, knowing she knew now that even Maja wasn't truly her husband anymore, it made his back and neck prickle.

He nodded. And he knew that she was trying, in whatever way she could, to give him strength. He wouldn't take it—but he knew he already had, when she'd offered. When he'd been dying.

He took her hand, pulled it from his face, gripped it tightly.

"Thank you."

She nodded. "Just rest, Homaj. Please. Rest."

2

PERMANENT

I'm sure people would like to hear that when I was first sealed as a magicker, I rejoiced to join the ranks of magickers in service to the kingdom. The reality is that it was a sign of permanence for a life I hadn't yet asked for, and closure for a life I was leaving behind.

— FIRST MAGICKER MARIYIT BRODEN, AS QUOTED IN *THE CHANGE DIALOGUES*

The second time Iata woke, Haneri wasn't in the room, but First Magicker Mariyit Broden sat next to the bed, reading a paper book.

He glanced over at Iata, his bushy brows lifting as he smiled. He shoved a folded tissue between the pages to mark his place. Mariyit looked determined to be cheerful, but his face was a little too pale, too flushed in the reading light.

"How are you feeling?"

Iata unfocused, delving within again. His body had made progress—he was sure someone had replaced the nutrient patches since he'd last been awake. He would have used up the others.

"What day—what time is it?"

"Late night, one day since you were injured."

Iata noticed how Mariyit avoided saying "attacked."

His throat burned. He looked around to see if Haneri had left the water bottle—Mariyit produced a cup instead and carefully handed it to him.

Iata hated how his hands were trembling. He hadn't, for whatever reason, been as concerned about showing that with Haneri.

Mariyit was a friend, yes. But—

But.

"Not that I don't welcome the company," Iata started. He didn't feel the telltale ear pressure of a dampener in play. And he knew he was still Homaj.

Mariyit must have sensed the dilemma, because he smiled and said, "You've manifested Green Magics, Ser Seritarchus. I would be extremely remiss—in fact, it would be illegal—if I left you to your own devices just now."

Iata did not want to spar with Mariyit, not in any capacity, no matter if it wasn't real. He wanted to sleep again. No, he wanted to get up and see what mess had been made of his kingdom.

"Homaj," Mariyit said quietly. "I know this is hard. You have my full support. I must seal you, however. And the sooner that is done, the sooner the people will feel safer with where you stand."

It took Iata a moment to register what he meant, but—yes. Yes, and it was why Iata had never allowed himself to be sealed before, and why Onya Norren, and then Mariyit, had grudgingly agreed. He needed to be able to Change and needed to not be sporting a magicker's seal when he did so.

But now? It was bad enough with Imorie being a Rhialden

magicker, even if publicly they were only a contract Rhialden. But the people would be terrified of a Truthspoken ruler who was also a magicker. In their eyes, he could be anyone, anywhere, and also know every one of their innermost thoughts.

But then, he'd known he'd have to be sealed when he revealed his magics as himself. He'd known that.

His throat tightened. When he looked at Mariyit again, he knew there was a plea in his eyes and felt hot and sick with the shame of it, but he couldn't help it.

"I have to," Mariyit said, and that was the best apology he could give.

Iata nodded, and Mariyit picked up a shoulder bag he'd set on the floor and began removing supplies.

Iata didn't watch. He was not particularly willing to be a participant in this—and could he change this law now, even if he was the ruler, when he himself was sealed?

No. Because he would be back to the problem of the people being not just righteously cowed by their Truthspoken, but paranoid in a way that might push them over the edge. If he'd been able to do this his own way, spin it his own way, he might have softened those fears. But a ruler manifesting after being attacked?

And everyone would know now that he couldn't do violence. Couldn't defend himself. Well, or maybe now they knew that he could—it was possible for him to kill, even if it was absolutely not an option if he wanted to live himself. That Eti had survived didn't help things politically—which was a horrible thought, but now people would think that magickers could kill without consequences.

He'd seen a magicker dissipate after killing. He'd shared Eti's spiraling emotions, helped hold him back from that abyss, ground him in this world. Iata knew the truth of what happened to magickers who killed.

He hadn't planned any of this. He hadn't yet smoothed over the way for him to publicly be a magicker—but had he been fooling himself that he'd ever be accepted as a magicker? Here, in this kingdom? Anywhere?

He didn't look at the two boxes, the sealing instruments, in Mariyit's hand.

And he hadn't changed that law, nor had Maja, because he knew it would cost him public support.

Mariyit leaned forward. "Homaj. Will you let me steady you? You flickered there."

"I what?" he asked, as if he didn't know exactly what that meant, and the lie in that just now felt intensely wrong. He was a high-ranking magicker, and so was Mariyit—their magics were overlapping in a push for truth.

Mariyit squeezed his hand, lingering just a moment to give a calm that Iata was struggling to accept as a truth. Because it wasn't. He wasn't at all calm. He couldn't be.

Mariyit let go and gave a rambling explanation as he prepared his instruments.

"May I have your hand?" he asked, and Iata put it out, feeling the weight of the genetic recording crystal as Mariyit set it in his palm.

Mariyit lifted it again and continued his ramble.

"Where would you like the seal?"

Iata pointed to his left cheek, where Mariyit had his own seal. It was fairly standard, though not everyone chose there.

"This won't hurt," Mariyit said as he stood and crouched over Iata, aligning something cool against his face. "Not much, in any case. It may be uncomfortable for an hour or so after."

Mariyit's fingers brushed Iata's cheek as he fiddled with his tools, and Iata felt his intense distaste for what he was doing just now. And also, just a little, vindication. And shame at that vindication, as he knew Iata had felt that.

Iata didn't blame him for that. He knew what face was his

own just now. He knew what position he held. In Mariyit's place, he would feel the same.

He didn't flinch as the seal took hold. It did burn, just briefly, a nerve burn before the circuitry numbed his cheek to fully let itself integrate.

Mariyit pulled back, and Iata touched his cheek. He felt nothing different, but then, he knew he wouldn't.

"Do you wish to see?" Mariyit asked.

He thought about saying no, but found himself nodding.

Mariyit pulled out his comm, turned on the flat holo mirror, and held it out to Iata.

Iata took it, and let out a breath. Adeius, he looked awful. His usually tan and healthy skin—as Homaj—now sallow, brown eyes puffy and one bloodshot. His long black hair tied into a tail, but messy, unadorned. Someone had cleaned off all his cosmetics, and now he just felt bare. Hollow.

The coin-sized holographic seal, with a very dense fractal spiral pattern, glinted as he turned his head to examine it.

He made himself regard it dispassionately.

"This is my genetic rank?"

He hadn't been tested again since he'd first manifested. But this was a lot denser than his own very dense, removable seal.

Mariyit rocked on his heels. "Yes. Yes, it is. To your genetics now, of course."

But that wouldn't affect the rank.

"It's seventh," Mariyit said, and Iata heard trepidation in his voice.

He looked up. Examined Mariyit's own seventh rank seal. There was no higher rank than seventh.

Iata's seal was just as dense. Maybe...maybe a little denser.

He clicked Mariyit's comm off, handed it back.

Mariyit should have given him a false seal. Said his rank was lower. That would at least have made him less threatening. He wanted people to fear him as a Truthspoken, in the holy and Adeium-backed fear that gave him the power to rule this kingdom. He didn't want people to fear him as a magicker.

And maybe, truly, he didn't want anyone to fear him at all.

He rubbed his cheek again—it was sore, but that was a small pain compared to the others he was keeping at bay.

"I won't say thank you," he growled, absolutely Homaj.

Mariyit smiled. "I won't expect it. Welcome, Homaj Rhialden, to the ranks of Green Magickers."

Heat prickled all over him. And if he hadn't already over-taken Homaj's life, if Maja had only been away for a short time with the intent to return to it, what would have happened then?

And now? Now—if he wanted to rule this kingdom, he didn't have any other choice but to be Homaj.

But he wouldn't have to hold in his aura anymore. Oh, Adeius. He wouldn't have to.

"Are they calling for my abdication?" he asked, as Mariyit returned his tools to his bag.

"Mmm, some are. Some people are saying all of this is my fault, a conspiracy to infect the Rhialden rulers with unholy magics. Can you believe it?" He grinned, showing teeth. "You have allies, though. High House Xiao is publicly behind you, though that's not particularly surprising, given your parentage. Koldari has been outspoken in defense of both you and Imorie, too. I understand the Truthspeaker is hard-pressed not to appoint him the protector of all things Rhialden."

Koldari. Iata didn't have a solid read on Koldari. What trouble had Koldari managed to cause while he'd been stuck in the infirmary?

"And High House Javieri," Mariyit added, "is also showing their support. Lesander made a very pretty speech in the court-yard a few hours ago."

That took the wind from him.

He needed to see her. Needed to talk to Dressa, to Ceorre.

"Mariyit. Can you send—I don't have my rings, where is my ring comm? Or my hand comm, for that matter—"

"The Seritarchus Consort told me to tell you she didn't want you to do any work, and that she has all of your comms safe in her possession. If you were to ask."

Haneri. Maybe she thought she was protecting him, or maybe she had some other motive. Haneri was always full of motives.

"And where is the Seritarchus Consort?"

Mariyit shrugged. "In bed, I would imagine. She stayed with you a solid day until I relieved her around an hour ago."

Iata blinked to process that.

Then decided that his comm was not worth waking her just now. Not when he was feeling the need to close his eyes again.

But he said, "Please tell Ceorre I need to see her, and Ondressarie, and Lesander, as soon as they're able."

Mariyit considered him, as if to say that they'd come as soon as Iata was able, not the other way around, but he nodded.

"I will, of course." He bowed. "Rest well, Seritarchus."

3

VISITATION

Haneri ne Delor Rhialden is often seen as a political enigma. A force to be reckoned with in the early days of the rule of Homaj Rhialden, Seritarchus IX of the Twelfth Dynasty, Haneri mostly retreated from the public eye—only to burst out again into Valoran politics when she was needed most.

— FROM THE DOCUMENTARY *HANERI: A LIFE OF WOVEN SHADOWS*

It was nearing dawn.

Ceorre's apartment behind the Adeium smelled like tea and something sweet—maybe fruit, maybe a scent stick somewhere Lesander couldn't see.

She sat in a too-comfortable chair in the Truthspeaker's living room. Ceorre, who'd come in when one of Dressa's guards brought her here late that afternoon, had told her to wait. Ceorre had shown her a spare bedroom that she could sleep in if she wanted to, but she could hardly think about sleep.

Ceorre had told her not to leave, and said that if she did, there would be consequences. Lesander didn't know if the Adeium guards outside would let her go, but she didn't want to find out.

And this was all part of the test of her new and realigned loyalties. That much was obvious.

Ceorre had been gone for so long now, but Ceorre had a kingdom to hold together—which was Lesander's fault. Adeius, *her fault.* Lesander was hungry, but she hadn't yet dared to see if there was food in the apartment's small kitchen.

Dressa had spent all day doing—she didn't know. And that bothered Lesander intensely. She'd seen Dressa in only short moments all day, then been relegated here.

That afternoon, Lesander had gone out and pledged Javieri support and allegiance to the Rhialdens.

Her mother would be furious. Her mother would know Lesander had failed. And Lesander was torn between distress at that and emphatically *not caring.*

Finally, when she was working herself back up into a panic over just what Dressa and Ceorre were going to do with her, the entry door opened.

Lesander stood, breath catching, and turned to see who'd entered.

Dressa? She hoped it was Dressa. Or at least Ceorre—a break from this nothing, from not knowing what was going on or her own immediate fate.

But it was Haneri, Dressa's mother, who came into view.

And that...was unsettling. Lesander had observed the dynamic between Haneri and the Seritarchus, between— Adeius—*Iata,* and it wasn't the cold relationship Dressa ascribed to her parents. Not at all.

Lesander drew on her training, holding herself poised as Haneri approached, and Haneri seemed to be moving in a different world than everyone else. She wore a brilliant flowing gown tonight, hugging all her generous curves, a big puff of gauzy gold in her hair, her cosmetics impeccable. Absolutely gorgeous, and every inch the Seritarchus Consort. She made Lesander feel shabby in her day-rumpled teal suit and silk shirt, her makeup and hair which hadn't been refreshed since that morning.

Ceorre had been all glares since Dressa and Lesander had come to her the night before. Dressa had been...alternately open, supportive, and intense. Cold. So fucking cold.

But Haneri seemed exactly as Lesander had ever seen her: in possession of herself, taking no bull whatsoever, giving only the world as she saw it.

Lesander searched Haneri's face and body language for rage. For hatred. It had to be there, if what she'd seen flowing between Haneri and Iata was even remotely real.

"I just came from the Seritarchus's bedside," Haneri said.

Lesander barely kept herself from stiffening. She had decided, even with everything that had happened, that she would have just a little bit of dignity left. Just a small amount. And if they tried to take that from her—

She didn't know what she'd do. She hadn't thought past that night of the attack at all.

Adeius. That night.

She'd had all day and all night to think about a lot of things. That the man she'd stabbed was the Seritarchus, but not the one she'd actually been trying to kill. That her idea to use Iata to access Homaj had backfired because he *was* Iata. That he was, and had been for some time, a Green Magicker. And she'd just exposed that very vital secret. She might have caused the downfall of the kingdom after all, though Dressa and Ceorre were doing their utmost to stop that from happening.

Was that what she'd wanted? Had she wanted the kingdom to fall?

She'd pledged her loyalty to Dressa with all she had and all she was. Witnessed by a magicker and everything. Two magickers, truly.

But everything had seemed so desperate that night of the attack. And now...now, Lesander wondered if her mother would start plotting to assassinate her.

"Lesander," Haneri said.

Lesander jerked, flushing as she realized she'd drifted, and Haneri had said something more.

"Sit," Haneri commanded, and Lesander backed up into the chair she'd just left and sat again. Folding her hands tightly in her lap.

Haneri stood over her, arms crossed, brows raised. It reminded her, forcibly, of her mother doing the same. Or even her grandmother, the sour old dowager who her mother Yroikan had taken after. But even knowing Haneri's usual acidity, Haneri's posture still seemed softer. Haneri could be horrible, from all of Dressa's accounts and from what Lesander knew from her own research, but she wasn't a monster. She was *not* Prince Yroikan Javieri. And the base fact that Lesander had seen affection between Haneri and Iata was proof of that. Her own mother didn't care for anyone.

Haneri had once been the heir to a high house princedom, too. Haneri had also been betrothed to a Truthspoken. She'd renounced her former titles at her own wedding, but she hadn't completely foresworn her family like Lesander had just done— at least, she didn't think Haneri had.

With a sigh, Haneri sat down on a couch across from her.

"I understand your dilemma," she said. "I'm not trained in Change like you are, not more than the cosmetic kind, but I have evaku to rival a Truthspoken, and not the watered-down version most of the nobility use. But you have to understand— when you come to Valon, you are playing on an entirely different board. The Rhialden Court is not the Delor Court, not the Javieri Court, not any court but its own. It has very particular rules—all of those rules being that the Truthspoken know what you're doing. They are always, *always* ahead of where you are. And if you think you have outmatched them, they are in orbit, ready to blast you away if you so much as try."

Lesander studied her hands in her lap, though she was watching Haneri's body language out of the corners of her eyes, bracing against if Haneri would try to kill her to protect her daughter.

Or her...what? What was Iata to her?

"Dressa can't rule right now," Haneri said, "though the kingdom sorely needs her to. But she can't rule right now because of you. None of us trust you. You gave an oath, but then, you also gave an oath when you married her, and that you did not keep."

Lesander's gaze snapped up. "I did! I did keep it. I acted because if I hadn't, my family would have, and she might have been *dead,* and I couldn't—"

Her throat closed. Which was as well, because none of this was going anywhere good.

"Do you care about the good of this kingdom?" Haneri asked, relentless. The garnets in her earrings glittered with every move of her head, twins to her blazing eyes.

"Yes," Lesander hissed. Which was true.

"And do you care about it enough that if the way forward is for a Rhialden to rule, and always to rule, never a Javieri, would you still support your Rhialden wife?"

"That is my mother's goal, not mine."

Haneri pursed her lips, and a flicker of something Lesander couldn't name passed over her face. Something distant, maybe something old. And had Haneri's father, Prince Delor, sent her to the Rhialden Court all those years ago with a mission of her own?

Haneri inhaled sharply, some of her composure fraying.

"Then why, child? Why did you try to kill him? You've dealt this kingdom a blow to its core, at the moment it was most vulnerable. I am so glad that he lived, but it is even more complicated now that he did. Did you think you could step into that gap?"

"I—I don't—"

Her eyes were flooding. She rapidly smoothed the tears away, but more just came.

This was hell, wasn't it? One of them, anyway. This was reciprocity. This was punishment.

Haneri sat forward. Held out her hand. "Come with me."

Lesander drew back. "No. Ceorre said to stay—"

"And I, the Seritarchus Consort, am giving you my order. Also, my word—I'm not going to harm you. What happens to you belongs to my daughter. But you must come with me. Now."

Lesander swallowed, debated arguing.

Finally, she stood. She didn't take Haneri's hand, though. Not that Haneri seemed to think she would.

Haneri stood as if there was no care in the world. Haneri would be a match for Lesander's mother, she was fairly sure. Why had her mother told her that Haneri was almost a nonentity at court? That had been a gross miscalculation—one of many.

"Does Ceorre know you're taking me somewhere?" Lesander asked as Haneri led her out into the courtyard behind the Adeium, bordered on one side by the Adeium itself, and on the others by the housing for the speakers and Ceorre's own small residence. The sky shone with pale colors, but the sun wasn't up yet, the air damp and heavy and just faintly smelling of the river.

Lesander followed Haneri back into the Adeium proper. They passed Adeium guards, who didn't stop them, though Lesander was sure they had orders to guard her specifically.

The few speakers in the Adeium at this hour watched them pass, but also didn't stop them.

"She'll know now," Haneri said.

Lesander's stomach tightened.

One of Haneri's guards fell into step with them, the tall, pale Ina Vogret. Dressa had spoken fondly of Vogret before, but Vogret's look at her was hard. Lesander would find no love in this palace today.

They were halfway across the still-lit and mostly empty courtyard to the palace, where she'd made her speech pledging Javieri support the day before, when Lesander got up the nerve to ask where they were going.

But she knew. She knew in her bones where Haneri was taking her, and it was all she could do to keep putting one foot after another.

"We're going to see the Seritarchus," Haneri said.

4

THE OFFER

High House Javieri has always had a place among the highest of the fourteen high houses. As such, their rulers, like the other five high house princedoms, are ruled by hereditary princes, unlike the other seven lower high houses which are ruled by dukes. (For the purposes of this book, High House Rhialden is considered a royal house, not a princedom.) For a prince to give up their princedom is the greatest sacrifice they can make, even if it gains them a place in the Rhialden family.

— TOREN XELAÑI IN *HIGH HOUSE PRINCEDOMS AND THE POWER THEY WIELD*

No one was staring at Lesander as she followed Haneri into the palace infirmary. At least, not in the way Lesander kept thinking they should be.

Murderer. Assassin. Enemy.

The few people she passed bowed, both to Haneri and to her. The Seritarchus Consort and the soon-to-be Heir Consort.

The staff looked distraught, or harried, but nothing more than that.

By the time Haneri first knocked and then pushed open a heavily guarded door, Lesander's jaw was clenched so tightly that she was having to actively block the pain.

She expected the Seritarchus's guards to bar her way—but no, they didn't look at her any differently, either. Dressa had told her, between the meetings she'd held all day, that Iata was being blamed for this attack. That he was currently being searched for and would be arrested on sight.

Dressa had said this with a calm so deep she could see her own reflection in it, a horrible, surreal reflection.

Why had Dressa entrusted Lesander with the whole of it? That Iata wasn't a bloodservant at all but a full Rhialden, the older of the two remaining children of their parents. Couldn't Dressa see that Lesander was absolutely not to be trusted? Even if she had been verified by a magicker. Even if she'd made her oath. Haneri was right, she knew. She'd married into the Rhialdens, she had already given her oath, and she had betrayed that oath, too.

Lesander's thoughts stopped as she saw the person propped up on the bed, dark eyes darting from Haneri to her.

He was visibly Homaj Rhialden, if more disheveled than Lesander had ever seen him. No makeup, his long black hair pulled back loosely but bed-mussed. She couldn't see any difference in his body language, but then, according to Dressa, he'd been Homaj Rhialden almost the entire time Lesander had been at the palace. She wouldn't see a difference—he was the Homaj Rhialden that she knew.

His face was gaunt now, the shadows deep under his eyes. He had a blanket drawn up to his bare shoulders. A fluids line ran to a post beside him.

Forest green haloed him. And his cheek glinted with the circle of a holographic seal.

Lesander froze. She could not walk into that room. She could *not*.

Lesander caught her breath as she felt a hand on her back —Haneri's, pushing her forward with more care than Lesander would have thought. Much more than she deserved.

Haneri closed the door behind them. Locked it. She steered Lesander ever closer to the man on the bed, who hadn't taken his eyes off of her.

"Lesander," he said. "Daughter."

She coughed, choking on that. What the hell? Oh, Adeius, he had said that when he'd taken her into the city, and she had—

She dropped to her knees beside the bed.

Haneri swore, pulled her back up again. "Wait until I get the dampener on to have your breakdown."

Lesander just blinked at her, open-mouthed.

Haneri fumbled with a dampener, and Lesander's ears popped. Everything beyond a two-meter radius around her was a blur.

"Are you well enough to talk to her?" Haneri asked the person on the bed.

"Well enough," the Seritarchus said, though his voice sounded raspy, and not nearly as full or in control as it should be.

And now Lesander couldn't look away. She was close enough to touch him, and her gaze darted to his stomach, back up.

She didn't know what to say. He didn't look angry, just tired, and she didn't know how to respond to that at all.

Of course, as a Rhialden Truthspoken—and she had learned there was a *vast* difference between his training and hers—he could just be hiding his emotions well.

Haneri's hand pressed on her shoulder. "Tell him what you told me."

She spun to see Haneri's face. So she didn't have to look at him anymore. "What?"

"Tell him why."

She couldn't swallow. It took several tries. None of her training, none of the excruciating hours of maintaining her composure, no matter what her mother had thrown at her, had prepared her for this.

But Haneri's face was set. Lesander wasn't going to get around this. So she turned back around.

The Seritarchus's lips pulled tight, not quite a smile, not quite a frown.

He didn't look much older than she did most days, his mid-late twenties at most, which was from his Truthspoken Change training. His body defaulted to his prime. But just now...just now he seemed much older. Much closer to his actual age.

"I knew someone once," he said, then stopped, glancing at Hancri. He nodded. "My sister. Who decided it was better to do a terrible thing than face telling a terrible person no. She regretted that choice. But even though it was her choice, it was also a choice she was forced to make."

Lesander took a step back, shaking her head. "Don't."

She wasn't sure what she was saying. Only—Adeius, he should be furious with her. Not looking at her like he understood.

He should be ordering her death, by every law in this kingdom. Had he not, because he was a magicker? Would that count as violence to him?

But it was *justice*. Maybe it was a violence to let her live.

He'd taken her into the city, even knowing she was a fraud. Even knowing, and openly showing he knew, that she was illegally trained.

She should not be here.

He should not be telling her whatever family secrets he was sharing now—and they were family secrets, because she knew, and he knew she knew, that he was one of four full siblings, not the distant cousin to the royal Rhialdens that everyone thought. It wasn't her place to know these things. She shouldn't be in this same room with him.

He held out a hand, and she stared at it.

"Please," he said. "I won't force you. This is your choice. But I want to know what you're feeling. And I want you to know what I'm feeling."

She didn't want to know. But Haneri squeezed her shoulder, and she looked back to see Haneri's solemn nod. And maybe that was why Haneri had brought her here. For this, whatever this was.

She didn't see a way out.

And also…she did want to know. If she wasn't to be publicly blamed for this, she wanted to know how bad it would be to live under his rule from here on out. She knew what it was like to cross her own mother, let alone try to kill her.

She needed to know there was rage. There had to be rage.

Lesander gripped his hand, braced against what she was sure would be a gale force of unseen fury, amplified to her through touch by his magics.

But she was met with calm. She was met with fatigue, and frustration, and yes, there was also anger, but it wasn't directed at her so much as flowing around her. Well, maybe a little at her. He wasn't hiding that, either. But beyond all of that, she felt an overwhelming sense of his protection. Like he was placing himself between her and danger like a shield. Between her and her family.

Was she reading that right? She didn't have much experience with magickers. Hardly any at all.

But the sense of warmth, of protection, grew.

She couldn't help the sob. She was shaking her head again, trying to pull away, and he let her.

"You—" She pulled herself together enough to make her

voice steady. It was the only armor she had left. "You can't. You shouldn't—"

"I'm the Seritarchus," he said, and she had the impression he'd wanted that to sound steadying and firm, but it came out thready, with a cough.

She had done this to him. *She* had done this. No one else but her.

Lesander wet her lips. Shifted her weight. Tried a dozen different things to say, none of them passing her lips.

"I want to train you," he said.

And she took another step back.

"Why?" The word tore from her, but she'd just felt his emotions. Adeius, this was too much.

"Because I need another Truthspoken. And I want you to have another chance. A better life than you've had." He paused, licking his own lips, and Haneri handed him a cup from the bedside table.

Lesander watched him take a shaky sip. It was an ordinary thing, and vulnerable.

Adeius. She had done this to him.

"No," she said.

He handed the cup back to Haneri. "You don't think you deserve it?" His voice was growing stronger. "So earn it. You will absolutely earn it. But this isn't penance, and it isn't punishment. It's me using the resources I have at hand. And also, telling you that my offer still stands."

"I tried to fucking kill you!" she cried, and then pressed her hands over her mouth. Adeius, she hoped the dampener had been strong enough for that.

But neither he nor Haneri looked concerned.

"I know who you are," she said. "I—I figured out some of it, but Dressa told me the rest."

He nodded. "Then we are all on the same screen, aren't we? No more secrets. That is a good foundation to build from."

Would he please, *please* stop being so...so...not how he should be?

"I will need to rest for the next few days. But report to me when I summon you, and your training will begin." He paused, brow creasing. "If that is what you want?"

He was truly giving her a choice? She wanted to doubt that, but it was hard to doubt when she was this close to him, and he seemed to be radiating sincerity. It wasn't just his evaku projected through his body language, but it was in his very aura.

She glanced again at the holographic rank seal on his cheek, wanting to shrink back at that visible evidence of her immense stupidity.

His rank looked higher than Imorie's, and she was certain Imorie's was high, too.

She wished, she truly wished, he would shut her out. Tell her that this was all a cruelty. That he was showing her what she could never have, only to take it away again. Show her how worthless she truly was.

And maybe it would be a cruelty. Training with her mother had been nothing but torment, and her mother hadn't been Truthspoken, only determined that her daughter would be so. The trainer her mother had hired had also been a monster.

Iata's face shadowed, and Adeius, had he read her thoughts just now? Had he been trying to? Would he use his magics against her?

Lesander blinked hard, looked away, so at least he couldn't read her emotions through eye contact.

It was one of the most dangerous things she knew she'd ever say, but she said it: "Can I think about it?"

"Yes, of course. Tell Dressa what you decide."

He lay back again, his face looking grayer than when she'd come in.

Add that to her list of sins.

"Thank you for coming to see me. Haneri—" He nodded to —well, not his wife. Not actually his wife.

Haneri had a hand to Lesander's back again and was steering her out, but Lesander needed no prompting this time. It was all she could do not to run.

5

THE BANNER

> *We repeat: all violators of the Limited Advertising on Buildings Policy will be subject to steep fines and punitive community labor. This includes any message you wish to send to any other person, period. Please do not propose to your future spouse(s) on the walls of our city.*

> — PUBLIC ANNOUNCEMENT FROM THE VALON
> CITY MUNICIPAL GUARD

Not knowing most of what was happening outside the walls of Imorie's borrowed apartment was hell. Being useless to do anything about it was doubly so.

Imorie had already decided on leaving with Eti, and now they were pacing themself exhausted trying to decide if they should just go. They weren't a prisoner here. And their presence was actively harmful at court—now that Homaj Rhialden had publicly manifested Green Magics, he couldn't have Imorie and Eti around at court to remind people that magickers could kill. Or be exploited. Or that there were now two high-ranking Rhialden magickers—

never mind that Imorie wasn't supposed to be royal Rhialden. They knew that very few people would believe that now.

They had to go. And Eti was fairly vibrating with the need to go to his family, too, enough that Imorie was picking up on it and feeling that need, too.

But they couldn't even ask Iata just now. It had been a night and a day and most of another day, and all they knew was from a few dashed-out messages from Dressa, saying that Iata was doing a little better, mostly resting.

And what did that say about them that they were frustrated, and Iata was lying in the infirmary and might be there for days yet?

Would they be helping him if they left? Or abandoning him?

They couldn't abandon him just now. Or Dressa, if she was about to become the ruler, and Imorie didn't know if she was.

And a part of them, a part that they couldn't ignore or push aside as not them, damn their magics, wanted to claim this as their chance, too. If the Seritarchus had magics and it turned out to be okay, well, then the Heir—if they could ever be the Heir again—had magics, too.

They were not at all sure Dressa should rule, with Lesander by her side. Even having felt Lesander's intense, profound regret.

But Imorie was also not optimistic that they could, or Iata could, hold the rulership as magickers.

Eti, who'd dressed that day in the simplest of the clothes Zhang had brought for him, his dark brown hair hastily combed that morning and now mostly askew again, handed Imorie his comm. There were two holo windows up showing a city in chaos.

Word had spread quickly after it happened that the Seritarchus was a magicker. That Iata the bloodservant had betrayed and stabbed his Truthspoken—and Imorie could strangle Lesander for that necessary lie, magics or not.

There were riots. Of course there were riots, because it was bad enough learning that magickers could kill, but now the people had a ruler who was a magicker himself. Not just a Truthspoken who could read body language and intonation, but now also their innermost secrets. And the fear of the magickers, which always hovered in any conversation about magickers, had risen to a fever pitch.

There were harsh statements from every angle, so much vitriol against Green Magickers that the violence by proxy made Imorie's stomach ache.

They didn't want to see what Eti had pulled up, not truly. He'd been showing them headlines for most of the last two days, which was how he was coping with all of this, apparently. But he never showed them anything without reason.

So they zoomed the windows, skimmed the headlines, bracing themself for more crowdsourced violence—then paused.

And blinked. Because this was solidly not what they'd been expecting to see.

Oh, Adeius. Imorie zoomed in on one of the images accompanying an article and stared at it. They checked the timestamp —it had been posted fifteen minutes ago.

The image showed a building in Financial District with a huge holo banner projected onto its side—which was illegal except for special events. No one wanted ads everywhere.

Yet the holo glowed bright red, with yellow text:

Imorie, I'll take you offworld. Only ask. -K

Imorie let out a long hiss, biting their lip. Well that was absolutely unsubtle. They'd mostly forgotten about Koldari in the last few days, but apparently he hadn't forgotten about them. And of course he hadn't, with everything going on.

What the *hell* was Koldari thinking? Sending that sort of message publicly, and illegally, with everything else going on?

Well. And maybe this had been the only way to get through to them. Was Dressa screening Imorie's visitors?

Of course she was.

And if it had been reversed, Imorie wouldn't have let Koldari up to see their drastically reduced sibling, either.

Eti met their eyes.

There was growing hope. A hungry, eager need to look into this possibility.

"That's...a bad idea, Eti." They rubbed their hands over their face. *Was* Iata well enough to see them? They'd only been getting word through Dressa, and they hadn't wanted to ask. Hadn't wanted to disturb him if he needed the rest. Hadn't wanted to bring any extra attention to themself anywhere because they were a magicker just now in this palace, in this city, with everyone screaming for magickers to be gone.

Adeius, they *couldn't* go with Koldari. There were so many reasons why that was a bad idea.

"He's offering," Eti said. "And it isn't safe here." He was feeling that from them, too. Or maybe from the ambient mood of the palace, which Imorie swore they could feel through the walls. A silent and subtle contempt. And fear—a lot of fear.

Eti tapped at the other article, which detailed another violent anti-magicker riot. Anti-Truthspoken, too, and that was getting way out of hand.

Eti had chosen those articles and shown them with intent. Imorie almost laughed at that—he could play the court games, oh he could definitely play them. Anyone who'd successfully hidden himself as a magicker in plain sight for over a year—for all of his life—was not a stranger to manipulation, even if he obviously didn't like it.

But was it safe for them to travel? It certainly wouldn't be safe for them on Kalistré, Eti's homeworld, with the Javieris knowing that Eti might come for his family. They might be hoping Eti would come.

But here—Imorie, before they'd given up on watching the feeds the night before, had seen a rant from a prominent influencer about how Imorie and Eti must have infected the Seritarchus with their magics, and now people were talking about how Green Magics were contagious, even if that theory had been debunked centuries ago.

Adeius. Was it safe for them to travel at all? They couldn't hide their auras or their seals. Could Koldari provide any real protection, even being a duke and the head of a high house?

And why, truly, was he offering?

If Koldari wanted Imorie to come with him so badly that he publicly broke the law with that holo banner, and would have to pay a steep fine for it, then he'd have to agree to take Eti, too.

"This is not a good idea," Imorie said again.

But their eyes were still on Eti. And his need, his driving need, to go.

And they could almost feel with their magicker senses—and could they possibly feel the mood of a whole world?—that this world wanted them gone. Wanted them *out*. Maybe wanted them dead.

People wanting them dead wasn't a new sensation. But this…Imorie looked back at the articles again.

Their ears started ringing, a counterpoint to their racing heart. And they couldn't stop it. Because they couldn't Change to heal themself or hide, and they couldn't defend themself if attacked. Their only defense just now was to make themself invisible, and the very thought of that self-violence curdled their gut.

"But I'll ask the Seritarchus." At least, they'd try. Koldari… wasn't a good option. But he was *an* option.

And they also truly wanted to know what Koldari wanted with them. Imorie was much more important to him than they should be.

They leaned against the plush covers of Rhys's bed and pulled out their comm, which had been Iata's comm. He'd wiped it of anything related to his rulership, but he had let Imorie have a direct line to him—not that they'd dared to use it, dared to disturb him the last two days.

Should they dare now? Would he even be awake to get the alert? Would he have his own comm with him?

They bit their lip, hesitated, then tapped out a message anyway:

> Seritarchus. May I see you?

The reply came quickly:

> Hanerl tells me that's not a good idea. But I'll key you into the back corridors, if you wish to come. Or I can ask Bettea to get you.

They glanced up at Eti, who was close enough to be reading over their shoulder.

They'd only seen Bettea briefly since the night of the attack —Dressa and Ceorre had faer partially running the kingdom admin, as Iata had done for Maja as a bloodservant. Bettea had trained for it, certainly. Fae was meant to be Imorie's own support when Imorie would be the ruler. When Imorie had still been Arianna and the Heir.

Were they losing their bloodservant, too? Bettea wasn't just that, had never been just that. Bettea was their closest friend. Their sibling, now that Iata had adopted Imorie, cousin by blood. But the kingdom was meant to be run with at least two active Truthspoken and two active bloodservants. Right now, it had one Truthspoken in Dressa and one official bloodservant in Pria to try to cover the gap—and Iata himself had no blood-servant. The kingdom needed Bettea more just now than Imorie did.

And they knew Haneri was right that they shouldn't come —though the way Iata had phrased it made them think he wasn't happy that she was.

Imorie wasn't, either.

They typed again:

> I don't have to come. I want your permission to leave for Kalistré.

A pause.

Which turned into a longer pause.

> Koldari asked you to go. Do you wish to go with him?

Imorie looked to Eti and swallowed. They could both go on their own. And take Doryan, even, or take them either way as another buffer between Imorie and Koldari. But they were all still magickers. None of them could defend themselves. They could turn invisible if they absolutely had to, but Adeius, Imorie didn't ever want to repeat what had happened on Hestia. They had no desire at all to be hunted again.

They glanced at Eti's rank seal, glimmering in the overhead lights of Rhys's bedroom. Iata would surely be sealed by now, and did Imorie want to see that seal on their father's face? They'd seen Iata's aura before while he was Homaj, but it would be different, far different, to see the seal. To know that he, too, wouldn't be able to effectively Change, and not because his body was failing him.

Homaj Rhialden, publicly and visibly, was a sealed magicker.

As was Imorie.

Haneri was right, and there weren't a lot of times Imorie

could truly say that. They didn't trust Haneri's judgment at all, but they did trust Iata's. They shouldn't go to him right now.

They shouldn't, truly, be in this palace.

> Yes. I don't think Koldari will harm me. And I don't think he's working with the Javieris, like I first thought. I want to know what he wants from me.

> Then I'll send Bettea with you.

> No. You need faer more than I do.

Another pause.

> Then I'll send my guard, Farouk. He has my full trust and will bring one of my seals, perpetual, which you can use if you need it.

Imorie let out a shaky breath. Lt. Farouk had been their favorite among their father's personal guards since childhood —he had the Seritarchus's trust in large part because he wasn't afraid to stand up to him if he thought it was needed. And Imorie knew what kind of trust Iata was giving them with that seal, though with Farouk attached to it, they knew the guard wouldn't be afraid to stand up to them, either.

Ha. Iata knew their ambition wasn't small, or their hurt or their anger at being relegated to the sidelines, cut out of their birthright. Sending Farouk out of all of his guards was in part a safety valve in case Imorie decided to act above their current situation. Part guard, part babysitter.

And were they making the right choice here by leaving Iata to everything that was happening here? Iata needed all of his guards just now, and needed not to be distracted by Imorie's problems. Were they moving on emotions and not on facts? The Javieris hadn't made any further moves, but that didn't mean they wouldn't. And Iata would soon have to face the public as a magicker and deal with what came.

But Imorie knew in their core it was more dangerous for everyone for them to stay. They couldn't be here when Iata made his push to regain his power and command of the kingdom. To find some sort of balance and acceptance, any sort of acceptance, as a magicker ruler.

But they still asked:

> Is this a good idea? Truly? I can stay.

> I trust you, Imorie. If you feel you must go, then you must go. Take every care. Come back safely. Or if you judge it's not safe, or you don't wish to return for a time, I honor that, too.

A lump was swelling in their throat. They wanted badly just then to go and see him anyway, just to see he was okay, because —because that sounded a lot like a goodbye. And they weren't truly the sentimental type, but they didn't know how long they would be away, and while they knew he would recover, they should at least see him once before they left, right? There was a chance that they wouldn't come back, they knew that. They absolutely knew the risks of going to a Javieri vassal world to take back a family the Javieris had claimed.

Their comm chimed again.

> I love you, Imorie. Be well.

Imorie choked, their hand to their mouth. Maja had never sent them off on a mission that way. Maja had seldom—never? —shown anything like affection until possibly the last few days. It almost made them ask to see Iata after all and damn the consequences, but then another message came:

> I'm sending Farouk through the back corridors
> now. I've unlocked them for him. I'll unlock
> them for your biometrics as well. For when you
> return.

Eti exhaled a sigh, and Imorie almost startled. They'd still been aware he was there, yes, but they'd been fully focused on this conversation and everything it would mean for them.

But Eti's relief now was so intense it made Imorie shudder.

They turned, pressed a hand to his stubble-rough cheek, and he closed his eyes, tears starting to fall.

Adeius. Imorie pushed away from the bed and folded him in, let him cling to them. And he did, his whole body clenching with something that was deeper than sobs. His need, his crushing need to be on Kalistré right now took Imorie's breath away, because with him, it was their need, too.

Imorie's family was—for the moment—mostly safe. Which wasn't that safe. But safer by far than Eti's family.

"We'll get them," Imorie said. He nodded into their shoulder, fingers digging into their sleeves. And they both knew that wasn't anything Imorie could promise, but it helped all the same.

Imorie still had their comm in one hand, and they slowly typed out:

> Thank you.

They hesitated. Then, still awash in Eti's emotions,

> Be well, Father.

6

OUT THERE

> *She Who Wakes is most commonly characterized by rebirth, renewal, the season of spring, greetings, both new and continual relationships, and the start of a new cycle. She is usually associated with the pulse of life itself.*
>
> — R. TYTRI IN *SPIRIT ESSENCES OF THE GREEN MAGICKERS*

He hadn't yet Changed. His gender had slipped mostly back to male, but Shiera Keralan was a shield, a comfortable difference. Maja knew he was stalling, but—he didn't want to Change. Not yet. Not and have to move forward again.

It was the night shift of the second day traveling to Hestia. He was in the cockpit of the magicker ship—which was named the *Open Hand*, and he'd been trying to figure out if that was meant to be ironic. His feet were up on the dash while he watched the controls—but they hardly needed watching, so he was mostly staring at the grayed view outside on the screens. A slowly churning mass of...something. Below Space.

A lot of people thought that the gray streakiness was the blur of stars and void through the speed of travel. But that wasn't true. Below Space was different. Matter didn't behave the same outside the hull of this ship, and random eddies outside could crush them, if they were moving fast enough, if Onya wasn't currently reinforcing the hull even in her sleep.

Well, and that was a precaution, mostly. This Magicker ship was small enough that it could travel safely up to military speeds without a magicker on board. But they were pushing the limit of military speeds, so it was good to be safe, anyway.

Maja shifted in the co-pilot's seat and tried to refocus on the book he'd been trying and failing to read on his comm, in between looking at the board and staring outside. The book had won awards several years ago and was about the life of a fictional Melesorie who supposedly was based on one of his distant ancestors. He'd wanted to read it when it came out, but hadn't had the time.

It wasn't good enough to keep his attention from straying back to the slowly shifting swirls of Below Space outside.

And he didn't know what was up with him. He'd never been this unsettled by Below Space before. It was common, it was safe. It was weird, yes, but its weirdness had parameters. His growing unease the last two days had everything to do with the mess he'd left behind in the capital, and the mess that would meet him on Hestia.

So why, alone in the cockpit, with Onya asleep and Zhang asleep, with nothing but streaks on the screens outside, and the controls entirely quiet and ordinary, did he feel like he was being watched?

And the feeling was growing stronger.

Maja clicked off his comm—the book didn't at all live up to

the hype—and stood, stretched, flowed into a martial arts warmup. There wasn't much space in the cockpit—well, not any, really—but he could adapt to turn in place. It would be a challenge and get his mind out of whatever funk it was in.

Two minutes later, he'd had enough of the outside screens and turned them off. A few minutes after that, he checked again that the controls were on auto and fled to the common room to make himself tea.

His hands were, just slightly, shaking.

Adeius. There were no monsters outside the ship. There never had been, ever, in the hundreds of years Humans had been traveling through Below Space. Sure, there were ghost stories. Any weird environment bred ghost stories. There were superstitions, because there'd been superstitions as long as there'd been travel among the stars.

Adeius—Adeius himself was one of the greatest superstitions of all, the great god who was made of stars, or from the stars, or inhabited the spaces between the stars, depending on how you read the holy mandates.

Was he afraid that his *god* was watching him?

He abandoned his tea still steaming on the table, got up again to pace.

He'd abandoned his own holy mandate. He'd taken an oath to be the will of Adeius in his kingdom, and then he'd messed it all up. And then he'd abandoned his kingdom at its lowest.

Maja shook himself.

He hadn't abandoned everything. He was going to Hestia now to save Bettea if fae needed saving, and do his utmost to find out what had happened to Imorie and Eti, to contain any leaks, to generally clean it all up. Spin a new story if he had to.

He heavily sat back down, his legs feeling wooden from all the pacing.

He should be enraged. His child had been abducted,

tortured, forced to confess their identity. Pushed to such a brink that they'd manifested magics—and then chased like an animal until their capture.

To think about it *hurt*. It hurt with an ache so deep in his chest that he couldn't decide where it came from, and he knew every square millimeter of his body inside and out.

But the anger he'd felt when Imorie had told what happened had faded back into the all-pervasive, all-encompassing exhaustion.

He didn't know what he had left to give.

Maja took a breath, glanced again toward the cockpit.

Monsters. Nothing had ever been substantiated about anything actually living in Below Space—and he would know. He still had the highest security clearance it was possible to have.

He picked up his mug. And would tea possibly offer any kind of solace?

A hatch opened in the corridor, and he jumped, swearing as he sloshed hot tea on his hands.

His heart was pounding, and he bared his teeth, forcing his body to calm the hell down.

It only partially obeyed.

Onya Norren stepped into the common room in a purple robe, her gray hair frayed in its sleeping braid, squinting in the light. Oh Adeius, had he been making noise?

"Onya, I'm sorry—"

"Your thoughts are ridiculously loud," she said, and shuffled toward where he was standing by the beverage counter. "They intruded on my dreams, and I had nightmares. Monsters outside the ship, is it?"

She'd picked up on that? He'd known she was seventh rank, absolutely on par with or stronger than Mariyit Broden, who could command all the plants in a room to do his bidding. But he'd been in a different part of the ship, and she'd been asleep.

"Don't look spooked," she said as she dropped a cartridge into water and cupped her hands around the rapidly heating mug. "I've got my mind all through the hull, and anyone who's touching the hull—well, I can usually block that out, but I was sleeping. And like I said, your thoughts were loud."

He ran a hand through his blonde hair and waved to the seat across from him. She took it with a sigh.

"I'm sorry," he said again as he took his first actual sip.

She shrugged and glanced toward the cockpit. Her lined face had a few more lines than usual.

He spread his hands. "It's everything going on. And—Onya, I'm truly sorry, I never meant for everything to get so out of hand with the anti-magicker sentiments, with what happened at Imorie's engagement ball. That—that was entirely my idea for Iata to—don't blame him."

She took her own sip, grimaced. "Too hot. And we don't stock these ships with any of the good teas, do we? Maja—I don't see why you'd think I would blame Iata. Or you—you were protecting your child. I understand that one."

He cracked the knuckles of one hand, one of Shiera's habitual tics, and Onya laid a hand on his arm, just briefly, not enough to really feel anything from the touch.

"I don't blame you for that, either. I never have."

He closed his eyes, the pain he couldn't identify swirling back into his chest. She wasn't talking about his child anymore, but hers. Because she knew where his thoughts would go from there. To her daughter, who'd given her life to save his.

Her daughter, a magicker, had killed for him, and then dissipated.

It wasn't true that Onya had never blamed him. Her daughter's death in protecting him had been the first hurdle they'd had to cross when he was younger. He, the young Seritarchus, and she, already old then and deeply grieving. She'd had every right to resent him.

And now his own child had killed—before they were a magicker, yes—but killed all the same. He'd trained his children to kill if necessary, to defend themselves. The lives of Truthspoken were hardly safe. But he'd hoped they'd never, ever have to do it.

Maja shuddered and got up to refill his mug. Got out of touching distance of Onya—not that it really mattered if she could feel his emotions through her holding of the hull's strength.

"But you blame yourself," she went on. "For my child. For yours."

"I don't have a child," he snapped as he sat back down. "Not —not that one." Not after Imorie had asked Iata to adopt them. Mariyit had been right that he'd just lost a child. Technicalities or not, it was still there. And that hurt, too, a searing pain beneath all the other pains.

His brother had his kingdom now, and his child. One of those things he didn't want, the other —

"That's not true," Onya said softly, taking another sip.

And she would know. He sighed, tracing the faux-wood tabletop with his fingertips.

Imorie was changing as much as they could, inside and out, to get distance from the person they had been. Who they still should be, if he hadn't deeply screwed that all up. Or maybe they were becoming someone else altogether. Had he screwed up in wanting them to be so much like him that they'd never been able to expand into their own full self? Were they doing that now?

The irony, the absolutely bitter irony was that he'd never been himself, either. He didn't much like the person he'd been trying to mold them into.

Adeius.

But he hadn't given Imorie the Bruising Sleep. And he hadn't given them Green Magics. Those disasters weren't his.

He exploded out of his chair again. "Why? It makes no sense why they'd get the Bruising Sleep, and then become a magicker. Even the illness, and its timing, is suspicious when it shouldn't be, but the second? Right now, when things are already destabilizing, and there are the attacks with the Kidaa? Onya, I've been trying not to think about these things, because my mind is so worn out from trying to hold this kingdom together, and it's Iata's job now, but I can't stop. I can't *stop*. It makes no sense, unless there's someone behind all of this, and *that* makes absolutely no sense at all. No rational sense."

No more sense than his feeling of being watched—and maybe that had been a vague awareness of Onya actually in contact with his thoughts, but—

But he didn't think so.

He wanted something, needed *something* to blow this all open. Some breakthrough. A hint, a clue as to what was actually going on.

Would he find that on Hestia? He'd take even a scrap of a possibility of a clue at this point. A direction—any direction—to point himself in.

He ran his hands through his hair again, grabbed tight, stopped pacing long enough for his whole body to clench in the crawling feeling he was trying to fend off.

The feeling of being watched, and not just watched, but *seen*.

Onya tracked him, chin propped in one hand, her brow furrowed. She knew enough of evaku to hide her emotions from her face, though she seldom did that with him in private. What would be the point? He could read it anyway. As she could pick up on his emotions with a glance. Or, apparently, through the hull.

Which was irritating him now more than he liked.

He heard another hatch open in the corridor. Shit. He'd been louder than he'd thought.

Zhang stepped in, dressed in the blue knits she'd worn to bed, her bobbed hair looking hastily patted down. Her squint rapidly assessed the situation.

He held up his hands. "I'm fine, go back to bed. You need to sleep."

She ignored him and moved to get her own mug.

He sighed and rubbed his face in his hands. He could feel his own hair messed up from where he'd grabbed it, with different waves and coarser texture than his own, and tried to smooth it back down again.

He had a moment, just a moment, of feeling sharply out of place in Shiera's skin. But he took a breath, it passed. And he wrapped the difference around him tightly, fending off the unknown. He knew Shiera. He knew how she moved, he knew how to *be* Shiera. So he would be Shiera. It was something, at least, that he could control.

So he resettled himself into Shiera. Resettled his personality and his fears—the much more practical fears of an upcoming investigation.

Then he rejoined Onya, and now Zhang, at the table.

Zhang eyed him over the mug Onya had just given her. Her right brow twitched in that slight lift that always meant—always—are you okay?

Maja cradled his restless hands around his own mug, his twitchiness bleeding back through Shiera.

He ruthlessly reset himself again into Shiera.

He felt more than saw Zhang sigh.

"I agree with you," Onya said after a long moment. And he had to blink and run back through the conversation again. He'd been ranting before Zhang came in. "I agree that all of these events are more than they should be. When you live with feeling the interconnectedness of everything around you, as I do, you learn that coincidence is almost never just that."

Well. And he knew that, too. Green Magics were a very different thing than Truthspoken training, than evaku and social patterning.

But no, not quite so different.

Onya stilled again, and though he'd wanted to follow her thought, though his own thoughts were jostling to come out, he paused, hands tightening around his mug. She was tensing, her breaths a little faster than they should be.

"What?" he asked.

She hissed through her teeth. "Likely, shadows." She smiled, though it was an expertly forced smile. "But, I have been thinking lately, ever since the Kidaa attacks started. And I have little more to this than a weird feeling. But—"

She took a sip, long and contemplative, and he called on years and years of training to not try to shake it out of her.

Adeius. He was wound far too tight.

Maja's hand sought Zhang's beside him under the table, and she gripped his back. Steadying. There—always there.

"In magicker beliefs," Onya said slowly, "we revere the spirit essences of life around us. Essences like motion, or pivotal moments of change, or steadiness and solidity. She Who Wakes is the personification of renewal and life itself, because life is always waking."

He sat back. He'd studied magicker theology before, loose and rambling as it was, but he wasn't tracking. He had absolutely no idea where this was going, and he was exhausted, and now feeling much less interested in what Onya had to say than this conversation being over.

But Onya's eyes were bright.

"She Who Wakes," she said, fervor coming into her voice. "We don't know exactly where our beliefs come from, the magickers, I mean. They're more myths and allegory than a religion, really, passed down in conflicting and parallel stories through the centuries. Records have been corrupted and written over. And in some cases, we've only had an oral tradition, or songs and art, because that's more natural, that's a strength we can feel. But—Maja, I have been thinking about all of this. If our highest spirit essence is someone who wakes, that implies that, at some point, she sleeps."

He blinked slowly, his arms rippling in a chill as his hairs stood on end.

He still didn't know where she was going with this, but his ever-ready sense of patterns was kicking in. What if everything that was happening wasn't the design of one of the high houses —and how could it be? How could any of the high houses give someone Green Magics? How could they burn runes into the ground with absolutely no evidence of any equipment? How could they give his child a disease that no one understood, that itself defied thousands of years of medical logic?

"What if the Kidaa attacks are something waking up?" Onya asked.

His heart clenched, skipped, then escalated. Zhang made a noise, and Maja glanced down to see he was crushing her hand, and he didn't have nearly as much muscle strength as a mid-level palace bureaucrat as he did as an apex ruler, go figure. Zhang could easily best him in a fight just now. Which made him, of all things, grin.

Zhang was looking up, though, not at the ceiling, but past it. As if she felt what he'd been feeling, too. That overbearing sense of...something. Something out there.

Something watching.

Someone.

He sobered. It would be another half a day before they could land, and it couldn't come soon enough.

"Well," Onya said. "I haven't told about my latest godchildren, have I? It's been a while, Maja, since we last kept up, and that's entirely your fault, you know."

Onya was no doting godparent—not any more than he was a doting father.

But he followed her through a winding account of a myriad of magicker children's lives.

And it was soothing, for a time.

7

WHAT WE'RE DEALING WITH

If we truly understood the Kidaa, we might not have to watch their ships and activities so closely.

— HIGH GENERAL BANAMAR ABRET IN A
LETTER TO TRUTHSPEAKER ADUWEL SHIN
MERNA

Rhys stood beside their captain on the bridge of the border scout *V.N.S. Occam's Storm*, waiting. Hands clasped behind their back in the most composed stance they could manage. One hand nervously flicking behind them.

The Kidaa ship had never returned after the overlap, so on the morning of this, the third day, the captain had taken them into Below Space to continue on their patrol route. Rhys hadn't protested—not that they weren't feeling their nerve for protesting staying at the border at all—and they'd thought, maybe even hoped, that the Kidaa might not be back.

But now, out of Below Space again in the next uninhabited system, still trying to wake up from the alarms blaring a shipwide alert, Rhys stared at the viewscreen that wrapped around the front half of the bridge.

It currently showed an aft view of the three huge blunt Kidaa ships following the *Storm*.

Three of them. Adeius. And the number of Kidaa ships was a pattern that never held to the Kidaa's love of threes. They usually traveled alone, sometimes rarely in pairs, but never in anything Rhys had read did they come in threes.

One was Clan Starlight, the same ship that had overlapped with the *Storm* in the last system. But that had been the only ship present before, and now, not ten minutes after the *Storm* had exited Below Space on their next stop on the border patrol, these three ships had come in-system, exactly behind *Occam's Storm*, and just kept station behind them.

Just following the *Storm* for the last hour, not answering hails, both Human comm and maneuvering code, not doing anything but following them.

Rhys was about ready to strangle something. Or cry. They were likely to do either soon.

"Well," Commander Gian, the first officer said, rubbing his hands on the arms of his hover chair. "Well, we can't just stay here on alert forever. They're not doing anything."

Beside Rhys, Captain Nantrayan made a dissatisfied noise and frowned at Gian. It wasn't the sort of remark a first officer should make in front of the bridge crew, even Rhys knew that, and Commander Gian was usually a stickler for protocol.

The commander patted down his neatly combed black hair, lips pursed tight. As the officer on watch when the ship had exited Below Space, he looked a lot fresher than Rhys, the captain, or Misha, who was currently at the magicker's hull-bracing station.

The captain very pointedly did not look at Rhys, didn't ask them why the Kidaa were just now doing what they were doing. Rhys certainly didn't know.

There wasn't a person on this ship who hadn't hoped they'd left the Kidaa and their strangeness behind when they'd left the last system. Well, so apparently a few hours in Below Space wasn't remotely enough time to get away from the Kidaa.

Not that Rhys thought they should get away from the Kidaa. But now that the Kidaa were here, had followed them to the next system—and, Adeius, would have to have known they were coming here and planned ahead to arrive so soon after, and so close—what were they going to do about the Kidaa?

What were the Kidaa planning to do about them?

"Helm," the captain said, "try maneuvering code one again."

"Aye, sir."

Rhys heard the faintest change in the hum of the ship's engines as they surged, the ship weaving back and forth, before it straightened course again. That meant "talk" in the maneuvering code Humans had worked out with the Kidaa. At least, it did on the Human end of things.

They all waited a few minutes more, someone sniffling near the back of the bridge. Someone coughing on the upper level.

"No sign of response," the pilot said, and looked back toward the captain, a look that was almost pleading.

The captain chewed on her inner cheek. "All right, stand down from high alert, go to medium. Night crew, I know you were supposed to be off-shift a half hour ago—give me another hour more, please, and I'll reflect that in your pay. Magicker Moratu—please remain at your post, in case we have to leave. Pilot—take the conn until I return. Gian, Petrava, with me."

Rhys caught Misha's eye where she was slumped against her safety harness, one hand just barely touching the support post that gave her access to the greater structure of the ship. Her eyes were half-closed, and she gave Rhys a feeble smile.

Adeius, but Rhys was only awake by the grace of adrenaline, and the captain beside them didn't seem much better, though she was hiding it well enough.

It wasn't standard to exit Below Space in a system with the captain off the bridge, but then, little of what the *Storm* had been doing the last three days was standard. Rhys didn't doubt the captain had needed the sleep.

They all needed more sleep. There were few souls on the ship that had been sleeping well after that overlap with the Kidaa. They doubted there would be much sleep after whatever the Kidaa were doing now, either.

Rhys attempted a smile at Misha, and was warmed when she returned it. She swiped her fading green hair out of her eyes, her pale green aura faintly rippling. Her fingers gave a tiny wave, and she sent a grimace toward Commander Gian.

And no, Commander Gian had *not* in fact been kind to Rhys the last few days, and Rhys had to think it was because the captain had filled him in on exactly why the Kidaa might be interested in talking to Rhys.

And now the Kidaa were here again, with three times the number of ships, following the *Storm*. Were they here again to talk to Rhys? Would they try to overlap—and why hadn't they done so already? Why weren't they answering the maneuvering code? The Kidaa only answered that some of the time, yes, but...why just follow the *Storm*?

Rhys's nerves were too strained from the last few days to truly feel the panic they knew they should be feeling.

Okay, no, they were totally feeling the panic. It just hadn't gotten much better since the overlap.

"Petrava," the captain snapped, and Rhys startled. They followed quickly after her, doing their best to ignore Commander Gian's darkening scowl at them as he guided his chair out the double bridge hatch.

And now, Rhys had a different problem. Maybe a ridiculous problem, but it suddenly consumed their thoughts as they walked.

When the alarms had sounded, Rhys and Misha had both

tumbled out of their bunks and into uniforms. Rhys had been too preoccupied with figuring out the urgent puzzle of the Kidaa to remember to get their old uniforms laundered the last few days, so now they were wearing their crinkled and slightly smelly uniform from the day before.

The Kidaa were a much more alarming, much more urgent thing to panic about. But Rhys's overtaxed mind wasn't super interested in logic at the moment.

And they just really didn't want to embarrass themself in tighter, more smell-detectable quarters with the captain and Gian. They'd had enough of the sometimes deferential, sometimes hostile looks from the crew since the overlap, and didn't want them from the captain, too. Commander Gian…was probably a lost cause there.

The Kidaa had singled them out. The captain had singled them out. And whoever might have known about Rhys's identity before and was keeping quiet wasn't anymore. Everyone knew. And when they weren't thinking about the Kidaa, they were worrying over what everyone thought about it.

"Call up Hamid, too," the captain said to Gian as they exited the bridge into the corridor. "I want her in on this too."

Rhys got a sour taste in their mouth. *That* didn't bode well, none of this boded well, being called into a meeting of the senior officers. And Rhys absolutely did not know their place on this ship anymore. Not when everyone was treating them differently. Good or bad, it was all different.

Rhys had thought the deference would be familiar, but on Valon, everyone had already known who they were and adjusted accordingly. Here—here, Rhys had had something approaching normal, for a time.

The captain's office wasn't far from the bridge. Rhys waited for Commander Gian to enter behind her, then slipped in themself.

They told themself they'd been in far more terrifying

company—they'd grown up around Homaj Rhialden. Now that was someone who deliberately cultivated fear around himself. Rhys should be fairly immune to it by now.

But they quaked inside all the same. Because no, they weren't just Rhys Petrava here anymore. And they weren't sure at all what they actually *were* here. Or how they could influence this situation if it spiraled out of control.

Rhys could see that it was about to, in the twitchiness of Gian, in the too-rigid posture of the captain.

She stepped behind her desk and rubbed her hands together, but didn't sit.

As soon as Rhys shut the hatch behind them, Captain Nantrayan said, "We're going back to Valon. Everything I've been taught tells me that those ships out there aren't and can't be hostile, but my instincts are saying otherwise. Gian?"

Commander Gian stopped his chair by the captain's desk, eyeing Rhys. "I'm not sure why we didn't leave after the overlap. Sir."

Rhys's jaw tightened. Commander Gian shouldn't have said that in front of a junior officer, either. Either he was truly rattled, or good and truly pissed.

The captain's smile didn't reach her dark, slightly bloodshot eyes. She ran a hand across her close-cropped coiled hair before sighing. "Gian—"

"And respectfully, sir," Gian went on, "if you have any plans left to stay in this system, we should call for reinforcements. We should have called the first time. No word yet from Admiral Jaya?"

"There hasn't been enough time." Which, by the captain's tone, he already knew, and probably had asked before. "They'd be around four days' comm distance now."

"There needs to be more than one theater commander on this stretch of the border," Gian growled, and gave Rhys another look. As if the sparse command structure at the border was somehow Rhys's fault?

Their father might be a general, but Rhys had barely spoken to him in years, beyond a few terse communications sent every few months. And they might have grown up in the palace, but they had no military influence at all.

Gian had never been particularly friendly to Rhys, but he'd also never been outright hostile until after the overlap.

Rhys kept themself from fidgeting, barely.

Not many in the Navy, especially in the ships at the border, liked the nobility. Commander Gian seemed to have suddenly grown a particular hatred of them. It felt personal, though Rhys hardly knew why.

"I agree about the border command structure," Captain Nantrayan said, gripping and ungripping her hands, "but that's not my problem to solve, and it's not yours, either, Gian."

She turned to Rhys. "Your assessment, Petrava? What are the Kidaa doing here? Do they want to talk to you again, as you thought they would?"

Shit. She knew she was putting Rhys in the crosshairs, she had to know that. Commander Gian wasn't known for keeping his thoughts to himself, and he had to have expressed his distaste for who Rhys was to the captain already.

Rhys opened their mouth, but the hatch chimed, then let in Lt. Commander Friesa Hamid, Rhys's ops duty commander.

Short and solid and definitely not smiling, she glanced at Rhys, her expression tight. But maybe also a little concerned?

Did they have one ally in this room? Hamid, at least, would have had enough time to get used to the idea of who Rhys's family was—she'd already known.

Hamid turned, nodding to her seniors.

"Captain. Commander."

"Hamid—right, then, what is your assessment?" the captain

asked. "Have we ever seen three Kidaa ships at a time before? Does that mean anything?"

"It means we don't know what we're dealing with," Hamid said. "There have never been three, to my knowledge. I'll check again, but I'm very sure."

And she was right. Rhys knew that. They wanted to point out that maybe it had something to do with the Rings of Vietor song, "Cycle of Three," but they'd been churning over that the whole last hour of waiting on the bridge. They'd decided that if the song was related to what the Kidaa had to say, the three ships now held a different significance. It fit a different place in the pattern, at least, though Rhys couldn't say where or how.

"Petrava?" the captain said again.

And Rhys did some quick calculations to decide how to present themself just now. They were still, mostly, holding the pretense of Rhys the ordinary junior ops lieutenant. Friendly, affable, excitable. A last-ditch attempt at normality.

But they had a gut-feeling that continuing that here, right now, would only alienate their senior officers more. And they were a long, long way from home, with a desperate need for their seniors to listen to them when it came to the Kidaa.

Because those ships out there were here for a reason. The Kidaa had overlapped with the *Storm* a few days ago for a reason. And if that reason had been to talk to Rhys, terrifying as that was, then Rhys needed to have some say in what happened next.

They couldn't just go back to Valon. Not yet. Not especially now, with the Kidaa out there again.

They had a feeling deep in their gut, a thrumming sense that something was building, something really bad was coming. They didn't have more details than that, but that feeling...well, they'd had about an hour of sleep before the alarms blared, and it had been close to their wakeup time, anyway.

Rhys straightened, letting their bearing and body language

flow into how they might carry themself at the capital. Still mostly unassuming, but with the easy privilege they knew they wore like a second skin. No, a first skin. It *was* who they were. If still not entirely who they were.

Rhys marked Gian's curling lip.

"Sirs. I'm waiting on information from the Institute of Sullana. It's still my assessment, if the Kidaa have taken an interest in us and in this ship, that we should stay at the border—"

"They've taken an interest in you, Petrava," Commander Gian snapped. "And I'm not happy at all that the Seritarchus inserted one of his children—"

Rhys waved their hands in a sharp negative. "No, sir, I'm not—"

"You're *something,* Petrava," the captain sighed, leaning on her desk. "And I'm worried about what will happen when the Kidaa figure out that you aren't actually Truthspoken. The question now is, how important is this knowledge of the Kidaa you have in your head? And their interface with you? However you came about it, you do have insights that we don't, and I suspect other ships don't as well. We sent reports, but that's nothing like an actual asset. You're valuable, Petrava, and worth returning to Valon for to preserve and disseminate."

Rhys swallowed.

They'd sent a message back to Valon, to the Seritarchus, asking for help. Begging, really. But that message wouldn't have even reached Valon yet, with just over five comm days now between the *Storm* and the capital.

The captain tapped the surface of her desk with her knuckles and grimaced, waving the desk displays on. She eyed Rhys again, and Rhys didn't like that look at all. Had she decided to deal with them after all by not seeing them as the person they were but the symbol of their upbringing?

Adeius, and they didn't even have any of the benefits of that assumption. They weren't Truthspoken. They had no authority here at all but smoke and political threats. And Rhys wasn't about to threaten anyone.

Holos sprang up over the captain's desk, and she touched one. She expanded it to the width of the desk before she turned it so they all could read.

"This came in, priority drone already in-system, just before the alarms went off. Gian, thanks for the wakeup. I haven't yet decided what or how to tell the crew. I don't want a jumpy crew right now, not with those Kidaa ships right outside. Not when we don't know what they want with us."

"They want Petrava," Gian said.

And distantly, Rhys braced again for the onslaught. But most of them was focused entirely on the message over the captain's desk.

Their pulse jumped near lightspeed.

Adeius. *Adeius.*

The captain pointed to the holo window. "Read this."

They already were. And they went back to the top to start reading again.

This was from Admiral of the Fleet Dassan Laguaya. Priority One.

8

ARREST THEM

Of course I support the Truthspoken. It is my job to protect the kingdom, and protecting the kingdom means protecting the Truthspoken. I will protect the Truthspoken to my last breath.

— ADMIRAL OF THE FLEET DASSAN LAGUAYA,
WHEN AMBUSHED FOR AN IMPROMPTU VID
INTERVIEW

Rhys quickly reread the message hovering over Captain Nantrayan's desk:

From: Admiral of the Fleet Dassan Laguaya
To: All Valoran Navy officers ranked Commander and higher, in command of a ship, station, local headquarters, or outpost.

Priority One.

Seritarchus IX Homaj Rhialden has suffered an attack on his person and is in critical condition, though expected to fully

recover. Attacker is known to be Iata byr Rhialden, bloodser-
vant, who is currently at large. Homaj Rhialden manifested
Green Magics during the attack. All ships and stations are
advised:

Arrest Iata byr Rhialden on site, with deadly force if
necessary.

Watch for unrest and anti-magicker sentiments. Take all
precautions to protect magickers among crew and in civilian
ships and stations.

All space in Valon System is now under medium alert.

Standby for further instructions.

Rhys didn't breathe. Their gaze flicked up to the captain, who watched them with an alertness that made them want to shrink away.

They quickly returned to the message, rereading once more. Trying to make it all make sense.

They'd met Admiral of the Fleet Laguaya a few times, at social receptions or in passing. Laguaya had always been deferential, but never actually polite—they'd never been polite, as far as Rhys knew, to anyone.

Rhys had never particularly liked Laguaya, but Laguaya hadn't been overtly hostile, either, to them or anyone in the Rhialden family. Not that they knew of. Were there overtones of hostility in this message?

Was there something in how Laguaya called for the arrest of Iata?

Adeius, was that the sign of a coup on Laguaya's part? Had they or their people attacked the Seritarchus and then framed Iata for it?

No, no that didn't make enough sense.

Homaj was injured. Was Dressa okay? Was Ari? Would Dressa have to step up to rule now after all?

Iata had a kill order on him. Iata had always been intense, and he had always weirded Rhys out a little, but he and the Seritarchus were as tight as they came. There was no way Iata would try to kill Homaj, that screamed against every instinct Rhys had. So then something else must have happened, and this was the official story. Maybe a coup attempt, but not Laguaya's, Rhys was fairly sure.

Homaj was a magicker now. And that sat uneasy on more than one level. What were those odds, that both the Seritarchus and the former Heir had manifested within weeks of each other? That they'd both been attacked at the time of or not long before they'd manifested? Green Magics could run in families, yes, but not in that way.

Unless Rhys's very quiet, very dangerous hunch there had been right, too? That maybe there was something weird about the magicker attacking Ari, especially when Misha had reacted the way she had to the news of that attack. They'd thought, but they'd also been afraid to think, that the magicker might have —might just *possibly* have—been a Truthspoken, too. And if that was true, had Homaj been a magicker his entire rule? For Ari manifesting to make any kind of sense, he must have been.

But—but that also didn't make sense. He had no aura. The Seritarchus was a lot of things, but Rhys just didn't think he could conceal being a magicker for his entire rule. He was sympathetic to magickers, yes. But a magicker himself, all that time?

Rhys tapped the sides of their legs and focused, *focused* on the most immediately important information to them right now: no help would be coming from Valon. Not from Homaj, not from Dressa.

Would Homaj even be able to hold his kingdom if he was a

magicker? If Admiral Laguaya had warned specifically against anti-magicker sentiments? Was that a warning, or incitement? Rhys had heard some rumblings among the crew. They'd seen how some of the crewers and even officers were treating Misha after news of Imorie Rhialden méron Quevedo's involvement in several deaths.

Things were about to get a lot worse.

Commander Gian swore. "This was on that priority drone? It came in-system just before we arrived, I checked the timestamps."

Commander Hamid made a noise as she also stared at the message. "Fleet ops must have sent three or more drones to make sure it found us. Or maybe Laguaya sent to every system. Adeius."

Gian opened his hands to the captain. "I was going to ask after you had a chance to read it, Ira, but then the Kidaa showed up."

The captain nodded. "Which is unfortunate timing."

Rhys's thoughts raced ahead again. Comm lag. There was comm lag between the *Storm* and the capital—this had happened five days ago.

But if Rhys was reading the patterns right, the Kidaa had already shown they could act at a distance with their rune attacks. Could they gather information at a distance as well? Could they have already known Homaj was attacked, could they have known when it happened?

Was that why the Kidaa were here now, in response to this attack on the Seritarchus? They seemed interested in the Truthspoken, maybe it wasn't a stretch to think they would be interested in the fate of the kingdom's Truthspoken ruler.

But the Kidaa had never cared about Valoran internal politics before.

But why here? Why the *Storm*? Why...why Rhys?

The Kidaa had singled Rhys out, as Truthspoken, even if they hadn't been totally right about that.

We have spun. You have spun. Rhys still didn't know what the hell that meant, and why it was so important. Important enough for the Kidaa to actively follow the *Storm* to this new system.

If that was even their reason why. If whatever happening at the capital wasn't their reason.

And if the two things weren't also connected.

Rhys suppressed a shiver. Oh Adeius, how could they know what the Kidaa thought? They were just a junior ops lieutenant with some intensive pattern and logic training, which they were sure right now was currently glitching in their need to make sense of things—

"This," Captain Nantrayan said, "is also why I want to return to Valon. I know you're not Truthspoken, Petrava. And I'm not a politician and don't tend to mess with politics in general. It's why I'm out here, not trying to steer a capital ship. But you *do* have Truthspoken evaku training, that's what makes you good at deciphering the Kidaa patterns. And by my count, there's two Truthspoken left who are currently able, and one of them has also been embroiled in controversy."

Rhys swallowed. She meant Ari. Yes, the rumors around Imorie being Arianna were nerve-wracking. And they'd only grow stronger now.

"I'm not Truthspoken," Rhys said reflexively, but the captain had already said that. And she wasn't wrong that Rhys might be needed. They were trusted. They knew enough about the daily running of the palace to be summarily recalled to help—which they might be. Those orders might follow shortly.

But—

"The Kidaa certainly think you are," Commander Gian said, turning his chair to face Rhys. "Petrava—*Delor*—what are you actually doing on this ship? As a junior lieutenant—"

"I already explained to the captain, and I *am* a junior lieutenant," Rhys protested. "I went to the Academy, I earned—"

"Nothing at all in your life is earned," Gian spat. "You came here to take advantage of us for your own reasons, or maybe someone else's, and now, what, we're a part of your own coup? Are you in league with this Iata byr Rhialden? Get the Kidaa to legitimize your own bid to rule—"

Rhys gaped at him, incredulous. They took a sharp step back, ramming the back of their leg on a metal stand near the hatch. They hissed, shaking their smarting leg, but pulled themself together, glared Gian down.

"I'm a fucking junior ops lieutenant," Rhys growled. "That's all I am. That's all I want to be, I mean, maybe a captain someday—but, sir, I'm not a traitor. They're my family, I wouldn't—"

That he would even suggest—that he'd even make that leap—

But it might not be as far a leap as Rhys had thought. Not with enough pieces to draw conclusions. Not, even, when it had been Iata who had sent them to the border, not Homaj directly.

Adeius, no, but Commander Gian wouldn't know that. He was poking at the nearest available target.

"That's enough, Gian," the captain said. "And it's easy enough to verify, if any of us truly have suspicions, with our magicker. But I don't share your suspicions. Not on this one. Whatever the Kidaa want with Petrava, I don't believe it was invited by Petrava."

"But the timing," Gian barreled on. "Delor is here, and the Kidaa have been attacking, and Delor just *happens* to solve this big implausible mystery—"

"I haven't solved anything! Not yet—"

"—with a *rock song*, and then the Kidaa show up and want to talk to them, so maybe they're working with the Kidaa to become the hero, to overthrow—"

"No!" Rhys yelled. "What the hell, I wouldn't do that! And the Kidaa wouldn't even do that!"

Commander Hamid was beside them now, gripping their shoulder. "*Lieutenant,* calm down—"

They shook her off. Then paused, realized what they were doing, where they were—Adeius, they'd unbent too far. Farther, even, then they'd dare around the palace when it wasn't just their siblings.

They gulped for air.

Rhys didn't have their siblings' ability to calm their physical body, but they knew how to calm their mind and their nervous system through breath, through the unwinding of their thoughts.

And right now, it wasn't working.

They wanted to shake Gian, get him to understand that Rhys had nothing whatsoever to do with any of this other than being here.

But that wasn't true, was it? The Kidaa had singled them out.

The Kidaa had also used a song Rhys knew from a band whose lead singer they'd been low-key obsessed with for the last year. Rhys usually tried to play that down—they were supposed to be cooler than unabashedly crushing on the lead from one of the biggest bands of the moment.

Beyond the huge poster in their bedroom, which was acceptable enough because Jereth Tobrin was *hot*, they weren't sure even Dressa and Ari knew how much they liked the Rings of Vietor. They hadn't taken more than a long look of appreciation at Jereth Tobrin at Ari's engagement ball, though they'd wanted to. They hadn't squealed, or made like they knew all the words to most of the songs. Which they did, though Cycle of Three hadn't been one of their favorites.

Rhys needed their own secrets, too, in a palace full of secrets.

But why would the Kidaa choose that song? And how would the Kidaa have known Rhys was obsessed with Jereth Tobrin, if they'd worked to hide that themself?

Could Rhys possibly take the pattern that far? Had a connection with *Rhys* been the motive for the message in the attacks? Had the Kidaa actually been looking for them specifically, calling them specifically, and not just one of the Truthspoken?

They stood, frozen, their mind stuttering on that thought.

It didn't make sense. That couldn't make sense, could it?

No. No, The Rings of Vietor were just that popular right now. Their songs were everywhere—the Kidaa had just used the tools at hand.

"You should arrest Delor," Gian went on. "They're a threat to the ship—"

Rhys jolted their thoughts back to the present.

No.

They couldn't leave the border now. They couldn't be arrested. What was happening here, whatever the Kidaa wanted with them, with a Truthspoken—or maybe, just with them—no help would come from the capital. Rhys's plea wasn't going to be answered by Dressa coming, or Homaj, or anyone else with the authority to do something, who the Kidaa would actually speak to. They knew that. They *knew* that in their bones.

They were alone in this.

Rhys knew the Kidaa, maybe as well as it was possible for anyone to know the Kidaa. They knew the Kidaa's patterns, and the patterns here were all off center, and that was freaking them out in every way. That the Kidaa had followed them to this system was freaking them out. That there were three Kidaa ships now, when there were never three at one time, was freaking them out. And maybe the smartest thing to do would be to leave, to travel to Valon as quickly as possible.

But...

Leaving the border now would be the wrong move. It had been when the captain had thought they should before, it was doubly so now. They were almost certain the Kidaa, Clan Starlight, would try to overlap again, maybe soon.

What signal would that send to the Kidaa if they left? That they weren't listening, maybe. Or that they were abandoning ground, giving the Kidaa permission to move in themselves.

And if the Kidaa truly did have a way of doing things at a distance that Humans didn't know about, what would happen if the Kidaa felt slighted? Felt threatened? The attacks on other worlds had all happened without Kidaa ships in orbit. Without any ships in a position to carry out those attacks. So they'd had to be carried out from afar.

Somehow.

Could they threaten Valon? Was Valon already in danger?

If the *Storm* left now, and the Kidaa had followed them here, would the Kidaa just follow them there, too? Would Rhys bring the Kidaa straight into the kingdom's heart?

"We can't go," Rhys said. They glared back at Gian. "And I'm not a threat to the ship." They turned. "Captain, you can verify my truths. Misha—"

The captain looked grim. Like she hadn't wanted to call in a magicker, like this whole meeting had gone a different way than she'd expected.

But that, Rhys saw with a sinking feeling, was an act. They read the small signs of satisfaction in the captain's body language—she'd wanted this conversation to go the way it had. Whatever she was driving at, whatever she was trying to do here, she'd wanted this.

Rhys wanted to trust their captain, they truly did. But they also knew they couldn't—not with their own life, not with the kingdom. That was one lesson they wished they hadn't learned growing up around the Truthspoken—but they couldn't deny its need.

They were better trained for this situation than their captain. And could they honestly risk the kingdom to save an already burning career?

In their pocket, the Seritarchus's seal chip sat heavy, ready and waiting if they needed to use it. They hoped to Adeius that they wouldn't have to. But those three Kidaa ships out there told Rhys what stakes they were playing with.

The captain touched the comm controls on her desk. "Magicker Moratu to my office."

9

MY SHIP

Moral treason is such a fine line to walk. In one light, it's heroism. In another, an atrocity.

— T.M. NG IN *PRINCE VANA ONABRII: THE DYNASTIC SWORD*

Captain Natrayan clicked off the comm and gave an exasperated wave. "Petrava—this is my ship, not yours, no matter who your parents are. My decision. And unless you had a message that I haven't seen yet, which isn't possible because I've been watching, and unless you've received word back from Valon, which also isn't possible because there hasn't been enough time, you don't have any more authority to act here than you did the day before."

All of which was true. But it didn't stop Rhys from stiffening up. They knew they were right. They had to stay here and talk with the Kidaa, if the Kidaa wanted to talk again. But whatever the Kidaa were doing, Rhys had to stay. It was important.

But as much as Rhys couldn't trust the captain with the future of the kingdom, they knew the captain also couldn't trust them with the safety of her ship. Because those things might not go hand in hand.

Rhys wasn't sure just how much depended on this, but they couldn't afford—Valon and their family couldn't afford—to take this with less than the gravity it deserved.

Which could be everything.

"*Think,* Petrava," the captain said, "if we stay here, the Kidaa might bind themselves to policies that *you* make. What if they expect all of Valoris to act to *your* decisions? You're not Truth-spoken, no matter who you grew up with, and with the kingdom rulership in question, are you certain the new ruler will agree with your decisions?"

Rhys had to work not to glare at their captain. They had to remember that they *were* the junior lieutenant here.

But she was giving a whole lot of lie to her claim that she wasn't political. That was an entirely political speech.

Whatever was happening with the Kidaa was political, too, but not in a way that could wait for the trained diplomats. It just couldn't.

Rhys knew with a conviction they'd defend to their grave that the Kidaa, whatever they were here for now, wouldn't wait long to push for what they wanted, whatever that was. And Rhys needed to find out what that was. They all did.

Nothing back home would matter if the Kidaa suddenly decided to start a war and tore through systems in the wave of destruction they *could* be. If they wanted to be.

The hatch opened again, and Misha stepped in, her gaze flicking around them all before she settled on Rhys. Then looked back to the captain.

"Sir." She straightened. And there was the military bearing Rhys hadn't seen in her before, a discipline she'd been determined to ignore.

Rhys wasn't the only one trying to distance themselves from the necessity of their own persona.

"Ensign, please verify Petrava's truth," the captain said.

Misha's brows drew tight, looking a question at Rhys. And they were glad, so glad, she didn't just obey without thought—no matter that she was supposed to.

Of anyone on this ship, Misha, at least, was someone they could trust. Trust not to betray them, at least.

Rhys held out a hand, and she took it, her palm cool and clammy. Or maybe that was theirs.

Commander Gian barked, "Petrava, were you involved with attacking the Seritarchus in the capital?"

Misha jerked at that statement, almost whipped around to protest, but Rhys gripped her hand tightly with both of theirs, holding her steady.

She met their eyes. Her own were wide, her pale green aura pulsing as if with her heartbeat.

"No," Rhys said.

"Uh, that's true," Misha said, and coughed. Her brows rose incredulously at Rhys, and they could feel her urgent need to know what had happened. But they didn't dare shake their head to say they couldn't talk. That might look like they'd worked things out with her beforehand, and that would cast doubt on everything she verified.

Commander Gian shifted, looking annoyed that his accusation hadn't sunk home. "The magicker could be involved. They came in together, and the Seritarchus is now a magicker—"

"He's *what*?" Misha asked, whipping around again. "Gods, *what*?"

"Moratu—" the captain rubbed her hands together, her own nervous gesture.

"Misha," Rhys said, the word a snap, a command. Using—oh, Adeius—a tone the Seritarchus often used.

She refocused on them, her breaths coming harder. They could almost see the fear and confusion and—and, excitement?—roiling throughout her emotions.

"Misha," Rhys said calmly, "I'm not Truthspoken."

She blinked at them. "Well, I know that. True. Uh, mostly. You are a little."

Rhys grimaced. "I'm not an Adeium-sanctioned Truthspoken. I am trained in evaku, but I can't Change. So that means I'm not Truthspoken."

"Ah. True and true."

"That means nothing," Gian growled. "You're twisting words. Captain, you should detain—"

"Commander Gian," the captain snapped. "Let them finish."

And now it was a race to see if Rhys could figure out which answers would give them the best advantage before Gian asked the questions. They had no intentions, absolutely no intentions, of being arrested just now.

The Seritarchus's seal chip sat light but oh so heavy in their shirt pocket.

Commander Hamid stepped up beside Rhys. "Captain, I protest this treatment of my officer."

Captain Nantrayan held up her hands. "Yes. Yes—my apologies, Petrava. You should not have to have your truth verified. Not on this ship." Never mind that she'd asked that very thing a few days ago, before deciding to trust Rhys—well, trust them enough not to have them formally read. "I don't require this. Ensign Moratu—thank you. Please return to the bridge."

Misha gave Rhys a worried look before she stepped back. She eyed the captain, and Rhys knew she'd try to find a way to stay if they asked her too.

They widened their own eyes and gave their head a tiny shake. Rhys didn't like at all the way this conversation was going, and they didn't want her to get any more in the middle of this. They shouldn't have suggested she be brought in.

Misha stretched a not-quite-smile and slipped out again.

Commander Gian opened his mouth.

"Commander, get some rest," the captain said. "You have obviously had a long shift. I expect you to be refreshed on your next shift."

Gian hunched forward, poised for a fight.

But then he loosened his shoulders, touched the controls of his chair. "Yes, sir."

Rhys didn't think that fight was over, only delayed. But they breathed easier after he'd gone.

They heard Hamid let out a long sigh, too.

Treason. Adeius, the commander was accusing them of treason? How had that spiraled so far out of control?

Rhys's focus narrowed to keeping their breaths steady and even. Just breathing.

They'd been worried about their shipmates looking at them the wrong way, treating them differently, they'd been worried about—by all the stars and holy mandates—the stale smell of their uniform. But they hadn't thought they'd be accused of colluding against the Seritarchus. Of trying to overthrow him.

Except they had colluded against him in a way, with Dressa. Would that be used against them, too, if it was ever found out? That Rhys had helped push her to do what she'd done in becoming the Heir?

They had no idea what was going on back on Valon, if the Seritarchus was still alive, if Dressa had been forced to step up to take the rulership. And Iata *had* given them the Seritarchus's seal. What if—what *if* it had been Iata who'd attacked Homaj, and he'd given the seal to Rhys to pin some of the blame on them—

They closed their eyes, and Commander Hamid placed what she probably thought was a comforting hand on their back, but it felt like fire. They didn't want to be touched, it was hard to bear when every other sense was screaming, but they weren't about to shake her off again.

"Breathe, Petrava."

They did. It was the only thing they could think to do.

Rhys looked up at the captain, pleading. "He's my—Homaj is my—"

Not their father. Not that. But Homaj Rhialden had given them a home when they'd been dumped with Haneri. He'd given Rhys a family, let them grow up with their siblings. Let them learn. He was far, far from perfect. He could be an absolute bastard, and had been on many occasions. Too many to count. But Rhys had never wanted him to be attacked. Their insides clenched hard to think that there was even a chance, in the five days' comm lag, that Homaj might have died.

The captain looked unsettled. She smoothed her hands across the surface of her desk, waved off the holo window that was still hovering near the front. "Petrava—"

Adeius. Rhys looked away. They didn't want the captain to apologize to them.

They stood awkwardly as Hamid rubbed the center of their back.

One more breath, and they straightened, pulled all their training back in, got their emotions under control.

Iata had not attacked the Seritarchus. That wasn't at all right in the pattern. So then, the chips in Rhys's pocket were exactly what they were.

"The problem remains," Captain Nantrayan said, "that under standing protocol for dealings with the Kidaa, and following standing orders, we should go to Valon at military speeds. We should have from the start, with the overlap. Adeius, we should have left with your discovery about the runes, no matter how far-fetched."

Rhys opened their mouth to protest that would have been too soon, they wouldn't have had the proof they needed, but she held up a hand.

"Petrava, I don't even disagree with you that it would be diplomatically wise to stay. Strategically, even. The Kidaa want to speak with you. But I risk a court-martial if we stay here and you start dictating policy. Or—Adeius help me—treason charges. Because this all rides a dangerous line. Especially with what just happened at the capital. And especially with you being who you are. Gian won't be the only one making those connections, true or not."

Rhys's adrenaline was peaking, their legs starting to give.

"Rhys," Hamid said, "sit."

They didn't argue with that command, plopping into one of the chairs in front of the captain's desk.

The captain grunted and finally sat behind her desk, too, with Hamid taking the chair beside Rhys.

Rhys tasted a metallic tang, like iron, like bile. Because they knew what they had to do now. And they knew there would be no going back.

"Captain." Rhys reached an unsteady hand for the two chips in their inner shirt pocket, ignoring the small voice in their head screaming at them to *think* about what they were doing, just think. Please oh please don't make what Commander Gian had accused them of a reality. Think of the optics. Think what this would mean, for them, for their place in the Rhialden household.

But they couldn't see another way forward. If the captain wanted someone else to blame this on if it all went sideways, and if the Seritarchus disapproved, then they had to give it to her.

That's what the deal with Commander Gian had been, hadn't it? Meant to push Rhys into making a decision they shouldn't have to make, take authority they didn't really have. Meant to keep the captain from having to make a career-ending decision at all. Let the blame be on Rhys, or on Gian as the antagonist, if it went the other way around. Because they *had* to stay at the border.

The policy, those standing orders that they should return to

Valon, were wrong. They didn't take into account the Kidaa wanting to speak with anyone specific, because the Kidaa never had.

Rhys fingered the rounded edges of the chip that held the Seritarchus's seal. Then drew it out.

This wasn't treason. This was *for* the Seritarchus, not against him. This was for the kingdom. And Iata and the Seritarchus had given them this open-ended seal, knowing they might use it. Trusting Rhys's judgment—Rhys had to believe that.

"Rhys Petrava méron Delor," they said. The chip, which had lost its seal an hour after Iata had given it to them, as he'd said it would, now rippled across one surface. The seal of the Seritarchracy gleamed again, gold and intricate and obvious.

"Oh, shit," Hamid said. "Petrava—"

Rhys looked up. "This seal was *given* to me. For use in emergencies."

This seal wouldn't work without the Seritarchus's express wish and command that it did. Everyone knew that if someone held the Seritarchus's seal, they were meant to. And usually, those seals expired within two hours, the important task that was meant to be completed fully finished.

But Iata had said that this one was different. That if Rhys said their name, it would activate again, and it had.

And maybe that made sense—the chips that Rhys and Dressa and Ari had played with might have been meant for Valon, for the city, for temporary and immediate tasks. But Rhys had been going to the border, and it had taken weeks to get there. Of course there would be chips for situations where the Seritarchus needed a say but couldn't be there himself.

And the trust the Seritarchus had given them to entrust them with this—they hadn't really thought that through, or at least, hadn't let themself acknowledge it. They'd wanted to forget they had the seal at all.

Rhys set the seal chip down on the captain's desk, and an
array of holos popped up, with verifications, genetic acceptance
of the bearer's biometrics, every official credential. There was
even a vid message, set to silent at the moment, of Homaj
Rhialden speaking. Clearly on a several second loop. That
hadn't been a part of the seals that Rhys had used when playing
with their siblings.

Captain Nantrayan stared at it, her face going blank.

And Rhys had a sudden sharp panic that what if this had
been the setup? What if that recording would say the bearer
was a traitor?

Rhys reached to tap the holo's sound on before the captain
could, and the clip played, cycling through again:

"—Petrava méron Delor is the bearer of my seal with my
permission and my confidence. Their word is to be taken as
mine. Their commands as mine. Give them all of your cooperation and assistance. That is my command as Homaj Rhialden,
Seritarchus IX of the Kingdom of Valoris."

Rhys's teeth ground in their mouth, their fingers digging
into the hard arms of their chair.

They'd thought this seal was a mark of authority, yes. That
it would signal they were on the Seritarchus's business. It had
been a desperate move, hoping to get by on momentum and
bullshit, give them just enough authority to keep the ship at the
border, and likely be tried for it later. They'd known it was a
gamble.

They hadn't thought—Adeius, they hadn't thought that the
Seritarchus would personally endorse them. And to that extent.
A seal meant a bearer acted on the Seritarchus's will, but
this...this...

They didn't know all of Homaj's tells, but they knew
enough, and that had been Homaj Rhialden.

Rhys slowly unclenched their death grip on the arms of
their chair.

These chips were never given lightly, even the two-hour versions, and that Iata had given them one that hadn't had a time expiration on it, with this sort of endorsement meant...what?

"All the holy stars." Captain Nantrayan's expression was stone. "I hope you know what you're doing, Delor."

Rhys flinched at her using their mother's name. It had been less of a blow from Gian, who obviously didn't like them, than from the captain. Who, Rhys sensed, had been trying. Before she'd decided to put them out in front of herself as a noble shield.

The captain knew damn well what Rhys was doing. They were protecting her ass.

But maybe, just maybe, protecting them all.

If Homaj was alive, they had to do this. And if Dressa was the ruler now...they still had to do this. She would understand. She knew them better than anyone.

This chip, this seal, that endorsement—that was more authority than they'd thought they'd have. But it didn't mean they still weren't in trouble for activating that seal. Anything, absolutely anything, could be twisted, Rhys knew that well enough.

In any case, they'd just ended their career. Whatever they did from here, they would need Dressa's mercy, or Homaj's, on the other side of this. Not that their career would have gone much farther with everyone knowing who they were anyway.

"Petrava," Hamid said, and they could hug her for still using their preferred name here. "There's only three of us in this room. We don't have to have seen what you just did."

But they had seen. And the captain, Rhys was sure, wasn't about to back down from that.

Rhys held themself steady.

Steady. Emotions in check. Firmly set on the path through this maze.

This *wasn't* treason. They did have the Seritarchus's seal, and now his endorsement. But it wasn't a clear path of stated orders, either.

Impersonating a Truthspoken was a *capital* crime. Representing themself as Truthspoken was a capital crime, and showing this seal was, in a way, legitimizing that unspoken claim. At least, it could be interpreted that way. Commander Gian's assumptions could be solidified here.

Rhys knew that Homaj's tells were real, but who else here could verify that but Rhys? Videos could be faked. Gian could argue that had been Iata with a vid filter giving the endorsement, not Homaj, and that it was just another step in a much larger plot.

But Rhys wasn't claiming they were Truthspoken—they'd never said they were Truthspoken to the Kidaa, mostly, just tried to communicate in the way the Kidaa had presented.

They weren't denying the insinuation to the Kidaa, either, though. Or correcting the error. And it wasn't too far a step with this seal now active to go all the way. To actively act as a Truthspoken would in this situation, even if they weren't. Not fully.

And help would not be coming. At least, not soon enough to matter.

The feeling of danger with the Kidaa, of impending...something...was suddenly sharp enough to bring up bile. All the hairs on their arms stood up, their heart skipping a beat before it started hammering.

They'd made the right choice. Not a good one, but the right one. They knew they had.

"All right, Petrava," the captain said, and Rhys saw her shoulders relax, just a little. Taking Rhys's offered out. Letting Rhys take control of the situation.

But she'd used their ship name again, called them Petrava, not Delor. And that, weirdly, gave them more resolve than anything else.

"My responsibility," Rhys said. And felt the weight of that like a boulder pressing them down.

Was this what Dressa had felt like, taking over as Heir? Was that extreme hubris to even compare? Was Rhys way, way waaay overstepping any bounds they ever should have?

Yes. But did they see another choice?

"Are you commandeering this ship?" Hamid asked quietly.

Rhys blinked. "No! No, sir, just—we need to stay, to talk with the Kidaa."

Hamid smiled tightly. And Rhys got that. Their saying they should stay at the border, while having that seal, *was* making a claim over the ship.

They should absolutely back down right now, maybe even surrender themself to the arrest Gian wanted.

But every evaku and palace trained sense they had told them that if the Kidaa started a war, Adeius help them all.

They couldn't win. Humans could not win a war with the Kidaa. Not when the Kidaa could pick up and tow entire *planets* with their ships. Not when the Kidaa had technology Humans couldn't remotely understand, and could attack Human worlds from who knew how far away without having a ship in orbit.

Maybe the runes hadn't been attacks. Maybe they had been a warning, like the Kidaa had seemed to give Rhys in person. But Rhys still didn't know what the warning was for, or what danger was so great that the Kidaa would specifically request a Truthspoken to try to get their warning across.

Maybe it wasn't a warning but simply a threat. Though Rhys was still less sure of that.

And if it had been a warning, if the *Kidaa* were afraid of something and felt the need to warn the Humans about it, shouldn't Rhys be downright terrified? Shouldn't they all?

"My responsibility," Rhys said again, swallowing convulsively.

The captain, slowly, nodded. "This can't be done in the

shadows. So, Lt. Petrava méron Delor, you are off active duty, effective immediately."

Well. Well, they didn't like that, but it was fair. All things considered. They'd just stolen her ship.

"You are, however, granted field advisory status as a representative of the Seritarchus from Valon. You are not in my chain of command—however, you will not act without my permission on this ship, is that clear? If anything happens, and I'm not available, you seek the same from Commander Gian, or Commander Hamid. Clear?"

She didn't actually have the authority anymore to make that demand over them, and everyone in this room knew it.

Rhys squeezed their hands together in their lap, an anchor point. It did help.

They nodded.

"All right. I'll move you to guest quarters—"

"No! Please, Captain, I'm fine with Misha."

"I was under the impression that you didn't care to share your quarters."

So that had been a deliberate insult? Had she been trying to punish them after finding out who their family was? Had she been testing them to see if their supposed noble bearing would reassert itself, and they'd put up a fuss?

"I'm fine," Rhys said, and knew the tone they were using, were appalled that they were pulling from the acid tone Homaj used when he was truly angry. And that was twice, now, that they'd used the Seritarchus's own tactics.

The seal chip sat on the desk, glowing with the Seritarchus's personal seal, silent and condemning.

"I—I'm fine," they said again, softer, but the damage had been done. They didn't think the captain had missed that tone. Hamid, from the way her face had pinched, certainly hadn't.

And was this all worth it? Adeius, would it be worth it?

"Thank you, sir," Rhys said, standing before turning toward

the hatch. They paused, reached for the chip, and put it back in their shirt pocket. It was still faintly glowing, and Rhys had the strong suspicion that it wouldn't stop showing the seal after two hours this time.

They shouldn't have called the captain sir. They shouldn't even have thanked her—she'd done them no favors. They'd had to take this authority for themself.

But they weren't about to test that line right now.

Rhys fled as quickly as they could.

10

OPEN AIR

If you're going to Valon City on a day trip with friends, there are some sections of each district you definitely want to avoid. You should probably avoid Gold District altogether. Then again, the bigger monsters always did live in Financial District.

— POPULAR VID COMMENTATOR LAYIM VER CARO IN *A LOYAL ANARCHIST'S GUIDE TO VALORIS*

Imorie wrapped their knee-length coat around themself as they stepped out of the palace aircar onto the rain-soaked street. Iata's guard, Farouk, had insisted on using the car, conspicuous as it was—it might be obvious, but it was solid. And the riots in the city hadn't gotten better.

It was late Valon City evening, the air heavy with humidity, and cooler than it should have been in high summer. Imorie almost shivered.

But the *open air*. There was a freedom outside of the palace walls that Imorie hadn't felt within. The last city they'd been in hadn't been kind to them, but they knew these streets. They'd walked so many lives on these streets. And now they walked another.

"I don't feel any intention of violence around us," Doryan said, glancing around. They hefted their duffel on one shoulder —they'd insisted on carrying it, though Farouk had brought a hover cart.

"Other than," Doryan amended, "the usual sort of sleaziness you'd find in a financial district."

Farouk vented a soft "ha," but he was looking all around them, pistol still holstered but prominent on his hip.

Farouk towered over Imorie, taller even than Iata's guard Ehj, a muscled pillar of light brown skin and neatly tied back graying hair. He was younger than Maja, younger than Ehj and Zhang and the rest of the guards who'd been with the Seritarchus for over twenty years. He'd joined the Seritarchus's personal guards when Imorie was three and had swiftly become their favorite mountain to climb.

But Farouk looked older than his years, and the life of a personal guard to the Seritarchus wasn't an easy one.

Farouk wore civvies now, not the maroon and silver uniform of the Palace Guard, or the silver dagger pin of his place as a personal guard to the Seritarchus. He wore his tan civilian jacket and striped trousers with ease—he always wore whatever he wore with ease.

Farther down the alley they'd stopped in, another aircar descended. Sleek and dark blue in the ambient city lights, exactly the sort of understated sign of wealth that Koldari would use.

Imorie's shoulders tightened. This alley had been decided on as a random neutral meeting place instead of the palace— Koldari was keen to leave, and the palace was always full of fuss, especially in the evening. Farouk had vetoed meeting at the spaceport, as some of the worst riots the day before had happened near there, people asking for magickers to be put off-world.

But this alley wasn't convenient. And it wasn't really neutral, not to Imorie. It brought up too many memories of alleys on Hestia. Even though that had been day and this was night, and that had been on another world and this was their home, they were seeing another alley on Hestia just now. Buildings much lower, danger ahead of them. The gut-tearing feeling of being chased.

Beside them, Eti pulled closer. Was he remembering the same?

"Still no malice," Doryan said under their breath, though they were tensing now, too. "But I'm only fourth rank. I might be able to pick up if someone's really intent on harming someone from a short distance, but like I said, we can't rely on that."

Could Imorie sense more? They really hadn't had the chance to try, or do any methodical cataloging of their new abilities. They weren't going to get their training with the First Magicker, at least not for a while.

They drew a breath, centering in the same way they always had when playing a role, and became more aware of the minutiae of their surroundings. Would that work with magicker abilities, too?

Imorie felt Eti beside them as a blazing presence, a turbulent green. And Farouk as an alertness, an anxious reassurance. Doryan was also full of the life Imorie was calling *green*, but not as blazing as Eti, or as turbulent.

And ahead, they could sense lives in the aircar as it hovered closer into ground mode. Two lives, bright points of light in Imorie's awareness. But they had no idea how to tell what those people were feeling. Imorie was higher ranking than Doryan by raw strength, but Doryan had far more training and experience.

But Eti was looking, too. And Eti had both strength and experience.

"No malice," he said, his eyes narrowing, a faint breeze blowing at his hair. "Annoyance and impatience, though."

He was rooting himself into the earth, Imorie could feel it, readying his defiance. His body language was full of that belligerence he got around Koldari, and he moved himself in front of Imorie.

They tried not to be exasperated. All of them would have to live with Koldari for...however long this took. And this trip was for Eti. No, Imorie didn't trust the duke, but you didn't have to trust someone to have them work to your purpose.

The aircar settled, and the engine whined down to idle. The left door swiveled open, and Koldari stepped out, black hair pulled back in a tail but not otherwise fancy, his clothes well-cut but plain. His brown eyes quickly moved over their group.

Imorie glanced past him—they could see the outline of the other person in the car, but not their face. Iwan, his lover?

"I thought you'd come alone," he said.

Imorie narrowed their own eyes. Why in all the stars had he thought that? Or was he just making a jab at Eti?

"Eti Tanaka is with me. And the Seritarchus has assigned Magicker Azer to teach me. And Lt. Farouk to keep me safe."

Koldari's gaze lingered on the imposing wall that was Farouk. Then he shrugged.

"Well, then this is a more official exit? Good. I wasn't particularly wanting to get on the Seritarchus's bad side. Everyone should fit in the car, it expands—Iwan, be a dear and expand the back seat."

Then Iwan ko Antia was the other person in the car.

Imorie wasn't sure if that was good or not. They didn't know enough about Iwan yet to fully make a judgment of their character. But they would know in the next few days, wouldn't they?

Imorie ducked into the car, taking the passenger seat beside

Koldari. Iwan was already climbing into the back seat. Which... was odd, with them being Koldari's partner. Had that been an argument for Iwan to give up their more favored place in the car? But Iwan seemed unperturbed, giving Imorie a beaming smile in their handsome light brown face, the beads in their blue braids clinking softly together.

"Hello, Imorie," they said, and then yelped as Farouk ducked into the car to toss the bags past the expanding back seat. "Hello, giant of a man."

Farouk grinned, showing teeth, though he was too much of a professional to snap back. Iwan was being an ass.

"Please don't talk to him like that," Imorie said as Farouk ducked back out to get the other bags. "He's been nothing but respectful."

Because Imorie wasn't supposed to have known Farouk since childhood. Imorie wasn't supposed to remember bouncing around on his shoulders when they were with the Seritarchus but intent on running around, not letting the Seritarchus do his job. Farouk had been the *fun* guard.

Iwan shrugged. "But I'm not respectful. Never have been, sorry."

"Imorie," Koldari said, drawing their attention back to him in the driver's seat. He had a hand on the yoke. "We're going to the spaceport—don't worry, I've already made accommodations, and security will be there and discreet. I rented a private yacht."

And Imorie, with one last annoyed glance at Iwan, suppressed a smile at that. The Seritarcracy was the *only* renter of private yachts in Valon City, under legitimate and untraceable companies, of course. Working on the theory that anyone who didn't already have their own private yacht but could afford one in a hurry was someone who needed watching.

So there would be trackers hard-coded into the ship—good.

Imorie was sure Iata would be on that. Or at least, Dressa. Someone.

They swallowed, unsettled again at the shifting of their place within their reality.

Outwardly, Imorie nodded, still glancing back as Eti settled himself beside Iwan, and Doryan slid into the far back seat, with Farouk ducking after them, half bent over.

Koldari touched the controls, and the doors closed, the windows darkened, and the engine changed in pitch.

Imorie's stomach fluttered as the aircar lifted.

This wasn't a situation under their control. Under their guidance, maybe, but they would be largely dependent on Koldari's hospitality. And whims.

They looked back to Koldari.

"Kalistré," Imorie said.

He tilted his head. "Kalistré? That's where you want to go? What's on Kalistré? You don't have family there, do you?"

And oh, he would have researched every corner of their fabricated life. In between everything else, Imorie had been crash-reading up on the tangled existence Dressa and Lesander had fleshed out for them. It would hold up to most scrutiny, with all the inherent contradictions and idiosyncrasies that normal lives had.

"Eti's family," they said.

Koldari rolled his shoulders. "You want me to take a ridiculously expensive yacht to Kalistré to, what, drop the gardener off with his family? Couldn't he travel by freight?"

"To rescue his family," Imorie said, and didn't bother to hide the irritation in their voice this time. "Who are also unsealed magickers, being exploited by the Javieris—I thought you said you wanted to make right what you did at Windvale, not saying anything—"

He lifted a hand from the yoke as he set the autopilot. "Right, yes. Well, Kalistré it is." He paused, gave them a serious look. "But I won't let you go into danger. The gardener can rescue his family."

Imorie didn't point at Eti's aura as proof that he *couldn't* rescue his family, not with physical force, at least. And they couldn't do physical violence, either.

"That's why the Seritarchus sent Farouk, and he has contacts," Imorie said. "To help Eti, in thanks for helping me escape from Windvale."

Koldari's mouth tightened, and Imorie wasn't sure what that meant. Was that still anger, could it possibly be guilt? He was unusually opaque to them, much more than they liked, or maybe they were just too scattered to be reading him right just now.

Koldari banked over another street and sped up. Imorie could see the upthrust sinewy towers of the spaceport ahead, the tops and dorsal fins of the larger ships waiting on the pads.

Imorie had most of four days to work on Koldari, to get him to commit more than the ride to the planet. They'd seek out Iata's agents anyway, but Koldari's help on Kalistré would be useful.

Adeius help them. Koldari still wanted something from them—whatever it was, did he want it badly enough that he would help them rescue people he didn't know or care about for someone he actively despised?

Imorie was going to find out.

11

THE START

> *It is one of the Truthspoken Heir's most sacred duties to make sure their Truthspoken line continues.*
>
> — ARIANNA RHIALDEN, MELESORIE X IN *THE CHANGE DIALOGUES*

D ressa stared down at the softly humming incubator, not yet daring to touch it.

It had been one day since the lab tech had finished her work. The embryo that would become Dressa's first child was one day into an accelerated six-month gestation.

One day.

Easy enough to stop, to freeze, even, if she decided she'd just made one of the worst mistakes of her life.

Her child.

And not Lesander's.

The genetics lab was a heavily secured area of the palace infirmary—this room in particular most of all. In a few weeks, the incubator could be moved to her apartment—

Or maybe not. Did she think Lesander would kill a child?

But then, she hadn't thought Lesander would try to kill her father, either, or at least who Lesander thought was her father.

Now she touched the lid to the incubator, smooth gray metal and glossy white plastic. The readouts all showed good and normal, and it was possible yet for the embryo to have issues in the first few days, to not be viable. But that was rare, and almost vanishingly so in this particular lab run by this particular expert, the same woman who'd watched over Dressa's own incubator twenty years ago.

The lab was empty at the moment at Dressa's request. She'd wanted a moment with her future child. Her son or daughter or child, or all of the above, whatever they chose. Whoever they would be.

This child could be her own heir's bloodservant. But also, this child might yet be her heir. If Lesander…if Lesander proved to be less than Dressa hoped, though it cut to even think it.

Lesander's pledge to her had been sincere. Verified by a magicker—two magickers. Lesander loved her. And she loved Lesander. Those facts weren't in question.

But with the future of the kingdom riding on this, Dressa couldn't gamble. Not with this. She'd awakened the technician late that first night Iata had been attacked, leaving Lesander with Ceorre. The technician had taken her samples without question and led her on a no-nonsense tour of her options for an anonymous donor parent.

Dressa had wanted time to choose the attributes she wished in this child, because they would be her child, and care should absolutely be taken for such a precious thing as that.

But there hadn't been time. There'd hardly been time for this visit now, crammed as it was into the middle of a crisis. In the middle of lockdown.

She'd gone with her gut instincts and chosen some things on recommendation, some things at random.

She hoped to Adeius this child would forgive her for that.

"They must be able to Change," she'd told the technician. "Fully be trained as Truthspoken. And they must have at least a noble donor parent."

Donor parents weren't truly anonymous—genetics could be traced, to make sure that bloodlines weren't too over-crossed. But she didn't want to know. Politically, she needed not to know.

And so, her first child had been conceived, without her wife, and would come into the world fully alive in six months' time.

She hoped the kingdom would last that long.

Dressa slowly retreated out of the lab into the back corridors, leaving the incubator and its blinking lights in this too-sterile room. There was an entrance into the back corridors from this lab specifically—there needed to be, for discreet Truthspoken needs.

It took a considerable amount of concentration, walking back up to her own apartment, to keep her body's stress responses steady. Her mouth kept going dry, her hands kept wanting to come together, to twist around themselves in the knowledge of what she'd done. Of what she was still doing.

When she opened the panel door into her bedroom, Lesander was there, dressing for the Reception that Iata had called as his first public appearance after visibly gaining an aura and a magicker's seal. He wasn't truly ready for it—but, well, he had to be.

The restless kingdom couldn't bear any longer without word from their ruler, and Dressa hadn't been able to calm sentiments as much as she wished. She'd fielded more than a handful of questions in the last three days about her taking control of the kingdom immediately. No, not questions—thinly-veiled threats.

People didn't want a magicker for a ruler. They were afraid of a ruling magicker in ways that they'd never been when he was just a Truthspoken, even with a healthy fear of a Truthspoken's ability to be anyone around them.

It took Dressa a solid heartbeat to still herself and her roiling fear and nascent guilt and smile at her wife. Not too widely. She was still keeping some distance from Lesander, though it was killing her. And it was needed. She didn't have trust—she wouldn't have had to start a child without Lesander's knowledge if she had trust.

"You look lovely," she said.

And Lesander did. Her tired eyes hooding just a little at the compliment. The stray wispy red hairs around her temples, at the nape of her neck, more frayed than usual under her elegant twist.

It was late morning now. Dressa had been up all night—again—trying to deal with various crises, mostly handling things in the admin suites of the palace, as it was easier to direct the staff. And when she'd crashed back in her bedroom at dawn, she'd found Lesander sitting on her bed, knees drawn up, looking haunted and small.

"Your mother brought me here and told me to sleep," Lesander had said defensively. As if Dressa wouldn't want her here. "I wasn't sleeping well in her apartment."

Dressa had felt a stab of guilt, because yes, she had deposited Lesander with Ceorre again two days ago and then just been too busy to deal with Lesander and all the emotions that came with her. She'd been vaguely aware that Haneri had taken over Lesander's watching from Ceorre the last day, but had let it be as one less thing she had to handle right now.

Now, Dressa reached up, smoothing some of Lesander's hairs down. Neither of them had had much sleep after dawn, and not because they'd been spending that time together. They'd lay on their opposite sides of the bed, close to the edges, turned away. At least, until Dressa had fallen asleep, then she'd gotten tangled in the covers as usual.

Dressa had three hours of sleep, and she'd been smoothing away her exhaustion all day. Lesander had been awake when she awoke.

Should she ask Lesander to do a light touch-up Change? To better straighten her appearance, to look less exhausted?

But then, the Javieri prince looking distraught would play well to the court, wouldn't it?

And that observation, and the fact that Dressa was jaded enough to make it, cut to the core.

Still, Dressa slid her hands down Lesander's shoulders, catching her wife's hands as Lesander tentatively reached back for her.

Lesander's gaze dipped down to the floor, a trauma cringe that also cut to the core. Adeius. But she brought it back up again with the ferocity she'd gained in the last two days. The fear.

Dressa didn't have to be a magicker to know that Lesander was terrified Dressa would decide to dismiss her. To not trust her after all, despite Lesander foreswearing her Javieri name and titles and pledging herself to Dressa's and the kingdom's cause.

Oaths were binding.

But words were words. What good was a binding oath if you overthrew the government that made it official?

Dressa squeezed Lesander's hands and leaned in to kiss her.

Lesander froze, and Dressa pulled back.

"Not okay?" Dressa asked.

Lesander drew a shuddering breath, moved her hands, a fluttering motion, and Dressa let go.

"I want to," Lesander said. "I—sorry." Lesander gripped her arm, held both arms pressed tightly to herself, looked away.

Dressa, her throat burning, turned away too, felt at the edges of her own already styled curls. She'd decided to keep the curls, for now.

She sorted through options of what to say. She couldn't say she trusted Lesander, because that wasn't fully true, and Lesander knew her well enough now to read the lie. She couldn't say everything was fine, because it wasn't. She wasn't sure it ever would be, with a child, her child, now growing in the incubator on the floor below them. And still she knew she wasn't wrong to have done what she'd done. And maybe that hurt most of all.

When had she fucking become her father, making decisions at the expense of those she loved, for the good of the kingdom?

"I don't know what to say," Dressa said. "Can I just let my body say it?"

Lesander's smile was wry, a bitter twist to her red-glossed lips. "Maybe. That might be the truest way."

She stepped closer, and Dressa reached for her again.

"I'm sorry," Dressa said. "I didn't mean to sideline you with my mother, you are always welcome here, this is your home now."

But the apology was coming late. And it wasn't entirely true. Dressa was vacillating wildly between desire for her wife and repulsion of knowing Iata's blood had been on Lesander's hands.

The kiss was awkward, the most awkward they'd ever had, a fumble in the dark. Teeth and lips and tongues in slightly off places. A sour taste, and a desperate try again.

On the second time, Dressa closed her eyes and gave in to what she needed. And so, she thought, did Lesander. That kiss felt like a chance at redemption. And a prayer that would go unanswered.

She was crying, and it would mess up her makeup, but she cupped the back of Lesander's neck, and Lesander leaned into her, no intention of pulling away, either.

Until finally they broke for air.

And both stepped back, wide-eyed, Lesander first turning away to dab at her smudged lips, two colors mixing together.

"I'll fix it," Dressa said, and strode for the prep room. She didn't look back, but heard Lesander follow.

Lesander stood still, arms tight against herself again, as she let Dressa wipe off and reapply the smudged lip gloss.

Then Lesander held up a hand and carefully did the same for her.

The awkward glances were back. But it wasn't first love. It wasn't a crush, it wasn't bashful or adventurous.

Lesander set the lip gloss back down, and Dressa moved close again, haloing Lesander's waist with her arms, not quite touching. Just a closeness, for a little time.

Lesander closed her eyes, leaning her forehead briefly against Dressa's.

They were past the point of apologies having meaning, and in the part where it would just take time. If it would work again at all. Dressa wanted it to work with every fiber of her being.

But she didn't know. She didn't know.

Lesander nodded and stepped back. Her face composed and free of any signs of distress, as Dressa knew hers was, too. Not naturally, for either of them.

Her hand brushed Lesander's again, then she straightened. "We need to get to the Reception ahead of the crowd."

And Lesander nodded.

12

DUTY

The personal guards of the Truthspoken ruler are chosen by the ruler at the start of their rule, with the expectation that each guard will serve until their death or retirement, or the Truthspoken's death or abdication to their Heir. If a Truthspoken ruler dies on their watch, the ruler's personal guards will often flee, as all of them would be suspect to treachery. In a very few cases, they've been known to enact retaliation from the shadows. Regardless, these guards form a solid fortress around the ruler for the rest of the ruler's life.

— S.K. VARATAN IN "LIVES OF THE PERSONAL
GUARDS OF TRUTHSPOKEN"

Iata dressed slowly, Chadrikour helping him into a sky blue jacket, deliberately tight to show that he had little to hide and nothing to prove. He wasn't yet fully healed, but though his torso still had a patchwork of med patches, the bandages were gone.

The outfit had Homaj's usual flair, but it was understated, elegant today rather than flashy. His hair was loosely bound up —he'd fix that and his cosmetics later, also with Chadrikour's help. He was still having trouble with fatigue in his arms and upper body, though it was vastly better than it had been the day before.

He glanced around him and had the odd, uncomfortable feeling of not being able to fully place himself in his own surroundings, like he was timeless, but not a part of the flow of time itself.

That—that was from pulling strength from so much metal. He had yet another bar in his pocket just in case he'd need it today, though he was determined not to. The metal Mariyit had brought him when he was still unconscious had helped save his life, but his life wasn't in danger at the moment. The effects of so much metal would fade in another day or so, but for now, he anchored himself through his physical senses as much as he could.

He met Chadrikour's eyes in one of the closet mirrors. Her uniform and steel gray bob were impeccable, as always. But her brows were drawn, her lips tight and troubled. He hadn't told her yet who he was, and while his biggest secret was out, the other one still hung between them.

Did she know? Had she picked up on it after all these years?

But then, she wasn't Haneri. His personal guards had all had some training in evaku, official or not, and she was sure to have picked up more by proxy, but...she wasn't Haneri. She was trained to watch outwardly rather than in.

He turned, smiled tightly, and Chadrikour stepped back.

"Ser?" she asked, all business as usual, though he could hear the concern in her voice as well. "Are you in pain? Is there anything I can get you?"

"No, thank you." He took a breath. "Chadrikour—you have

been with me from the start. And I know you haven't been brought into as deep a confidence as Jalava or Zhang. And—I owe you an apology for that."

She shrugged uncomfortably. She never had been as willing to be personal with the Truthspoken as Zhang, preferring to keep her professional distance, even after all these years.

He and Maja had talked about this before, several times, over a span of years. Should they bring all of Homaj's guards in on these very potent secrets? But the less who knew, the less danger for everyone. He and Maja both knew how power could corrupt even those who were supposed to be unshakably trustworthy.

And, too, the less who knew, the less who were burdened with that knowing. Zhang's life had been deeply intertwined with his and Maja's, and she couldn't extricate herself. They hadn't even told Commander Jalava that he was a magicker, in large part trying to lessen the burden. Jalava had a family and enough on their mind.

Had that been a mistake? Jalava had been unprepared for his sudden flair of magics now, though with Imorie's manifestation, his own public manifestation at least had a security roadmap, if a hastily constructed one. Iata would have to have a conversation with Jalava, and he knew it would not be pleasant. Jalava had a right to be furious with him.

He ran a hand over his hair. "You're the captain of my guard —that's going to be permanent, unless you have a reason for it not to be?"

"No, ser. I would be honored."

But she didn't seem happy. She was still radiating concern. "And Captain Zhang, Ser Truthspoken?"

And therein was one of the problems. Everyone in the palace knew how attached Zhang was to Homaj, and he to her. Maybe not that they occasionally slept together, but, well— maybe so.

He debated whether he should hold out his hands, allow Chadrikour to read him through his magics. But she was loyal, she always had been. He owed her the courtesy of telling her the truth and trusting she would believe it.

"Zhang...will be going with my brother. Maja."

Chadrikour stiffened. She inhaled a sharp breath, surveyed him, his face, his body language. Oh she'd definitely picked up more than even a personal guard's share of evaku. But she hadn't seen this.

He held her gaze, pressed a hand to his chest. "I am Yan. Iata. The elder brother. Full brother. Maja has abdicated, in private. Right now, I am the Seritarchus. I have been for the last few weeks."

Another surveying look. And he waited, seeing how she would react. What she would do, especially with the public accusation and kill order over Iata byr Rhialden. None of the guards but Jalava knew Lesander was the attacker, not Iata.

He knew Chadrikour very well, but people could still surprise him.

Lesander had.

"At the beginning, you were switched," she finally said. "When the old Seritarchus and the Seritarchus Consort were killed. Your—ah, your parents. I remember the Truthspeaker calling Homaj out, and it wasn't who we'd thought. And then, that day with the Truthspeaker—though I know we don't talk about that. I can't deny, ser, that I haven't wondered if you didn't still switch sometimes. I have wondered at times."

He breathed a laugh, looked around for something to solidly lean on.

"Ser." Chadrikour helped him to one of the benches inside the closet.

And he wasn't smiling or laughing now. His breaths were coming short. His emotions just now taking too much of the energy he needed to maintain his body, to let it continue to heal.

"Ser," Chadrikour said again, "thank you for informing me. But this obviously distresses you—"

He did laugh now, and grinned up at her, all his own smile.

"Orilan," he said, and her brows rose. She wasn't as allergic to her given name as Zhang, but he had very seldom used it before. As either Iata or Homaj. "Thank you. We will talk more later. You need to know the whole of it, as the captain of my personal guard. But for now, know that the Truthspeaker knows, Jalava and Zhang know, as do the other Truthspoken and their bloodservants."

She nodded. "Okay. Yes, ser. And do you anticipate this being an immediate security concern? If people touch you, will they know you aren't Homaj?"

He held up his palms. "That's part of the issue. But—I am Homaj. Apparently will be for...however long is necessary. I'm just not Maja." He wondered if, with this latest development, he should legally change his name to Homaj, as he'd done for Imorie.

But his heart rebounded against that thought. He still had hope—maybe a slim hope now—that he might be able to rule this kingdom as himself one day. And despite what he'd just said...Homaj was not fully his own truth, at least not all of it. Homaj was a personality he'd helped to mold and had helped inhabit for years, yes. But it still wasn't himself. Any more than it had truly been Maja.

"For now," he said, pushing up off the bench, "I just need to hold the kingdom for the next few days. And the next days after that. And then...we'll see."

Chadrikour hesitated, then approached again to finish the buttons up the front of his jacket.

"And sorry for making you help me here," he said, waving

around him, "I know that's not your duty. I don't have a blood-servant."

She gave him a dry look. "Respectfully, ser, my duty is whatever you need it to be. Which I suspect is something you understand."

He did. Adeius, he did.

13

TURBULENCE

Do Truthspoken shine in a crisis? Or are all their flaws revealed, and we witness their masterful coverup?

— LORD DENOM XIAO IN AN ADDRESS TO THE
GENERAL ASSEMBLY

It was a moment Iata had dreamed about for years. Being able to step out into a room full of people, the highest courtiers and policy-makers, and not have to hide his aura. But in all his imaginings, he'd been himself. He'd been Iata, and he hadn't had a kill order out against him.

And he'd never, ever wanted the association of Green Magics to fall on his brother. That had been a fear for just as long—that he'd mess up one day, he'd slip, his aura would flare, or his touch might ignite a feeling that someone could identify.

He'd been meticulously careful for years.

But he hadn't anticipated being stabbed.

Iata, as Homaj Rhialden, Seritarchus IX, stepped out from the antechamber into the Reception Hall. Haneri followed behind him, but not beside him—he had to walk apart for this. He had to be a pillar of his own today.

Iata kept his chin level. He didn't scan the faces in the crowd until he'd stepped up onto the dais, taking his place beside Dressa to his left, and beside her, Lesander. Haneri might have settled beside him to his right, she had a right to that place, but she had argued for another to be in her place: Admiral of the Fleet Dassan Laguaya, grizzled and hard-eyed, their medal-laden uniform trim and short salt and pepper hair neatly combed, one of the very first people he'd ever pissed off as Homaj Rhialden. Laguaya had never been one of Homaj's staunch supporters—and that was the point. Laguaya would not calmly accept his bullshit, and everyone here knew it.

On the other side of Lesander sat Ceorre, wearing her red and violet Truthspeaker's robes, the golden pendant heavy around her neck. Hers was another carefully chosen place-ment. Ceorre was allowing Homaj and the Rhialdens to be centered here, consciously downplaying her power while lending her own weight to what would happen next. And to his right, beyond Laguaya and Haneri beside them, sat Jalava. Actually sitting this time, not hovering as a guard.

Commander Jalava's jaw was tight, face paler than usual, their eyes flinty. They met his gaze briefly.

He still hadn't had the chance to speak with them, beyond basic security dealings. And he owed them that. Oh Adeius, he owed them that and so much more.

And finally, beside Ceorre on his far left, sat Mariyit Broden. That had been a hot debate—would the First Magick-er's place at the table be seen as inflammatory, with the Seritarchus now being a high-ranking magicker himself? But Iata had won that argument with Haneri. Mariyit was the First Magicker, and this meeting involved magickers. Mariyit had a right to be here in his own position of authority.

Iata nodded to Laguaya, who nodded back, one brow slightly raised in question.

He ignored that question for now.

And only then, after he'd set himself in the center of all of these people who were a large part of his life in their own ways, did he dare to face the crowd.

Silence met him. He could hear the soft rushing of air through the vents, the nervous rustle of someone shifting in their seat. A sniffle. The collective scent of the nobility gathered here was expensive and intense. He wasn't sure he'd ever, *ever* seen a crowd of heads and representatives of high houses, high courtiers, and high-ranking members of the General Assembly so absolutely focused on a single goal: watching him.

With camera drones hovering above them all. This was going out on live, unfiltered broadcast. He couldn't afford to do this any other way.

"Thank you for coming," he said. Then pointed at the seal on his cheek. "I've manifested Green Magics, as you all can see. This was certainly not something I'd planned."

He didn't wait for a response, but hardened his voice. "I also did not expect to be betrayed by one who *never* should have sought me harm." He didn't look toward Lesander, and he hoped she would understand. The public would know he was talking about...well, himself, Iata, but he was sure Lesander wouldn't take it that way. He would have to talk with her later.

But there was no disturbance from that quarter, not even a twitch. She was too self-controlled for that.

"This is my promise to you, Kingdom of Valoris." He held out a hand to Laguaya, which they'd agreed to beforehand, and then reached past Dressa to also clasp Lesander's hand. Which she'd also, hesitantly, agreed to.

"With Prince Lesander Javieri and Admiral of the Fleet Dassan Laguaya as my witnesses, witness my truth. I will not use these magics against you, my people. I will not Change without the seal remaining visible. I will not touch you or meet your eyes without your giving permission. And if a task requires violence, that will be handled by one of my children. I promise you, I will give the same judgments I have always given, give this kingdom the same attention I always have.

"But I have been an advocate for magicker rights my whole rule, and I will not stop that advocacy now. That I now count myself as one of them is beyond the point. I wish prosperity and safety for all in this kingdom, no matter who wears a seal and who does not. No matter if they have an aura or not."

He looked between Lesander and Laguaya. One, a scion of a high house that had traditionally been an enemy to the Rhialdens. The other, a political opponent.

"I witness," Lesander said, her hand briefly spasming in his. She was doing her utmost, he sensed, to keep her emotions in check, and he was doing his utmost to keep what he still sensed from her from being picked up by Laguaya.

Laguaya nodded, their own emotions carefully neutral, but colored with distaste and the bitterness of a decades-long grudge. "As do I, Ser Seritarchus. You're clearly sincere."

And they intended, he sensed, to hold him to the letter of his promise of fairness for everyone, in their case in favor of non-magickers. Laguaya was not known for being overly tolerant of magickers. But Laguaya was excellent at their job, and well-respected.

He had what he needed. He withdrew his hands, folded them in front of him, his many rings subtly catching the light. His gold and ruby ruler's signet ring visible foremost among them.

"What I ask of you, my people, is to see the humanity of Green Magickers, too. I manifested because I was in shock and in pain. Any one of you in a similar situation might have manifested. Or might someday. That a contract member of my family also manifested is more testament to the danger my family routinely faces, not a matter of our genetics, not any moral faults, nor any outside means. As Rhialdens, there are many who seek to do us harm. Who will not heed the holy mandates of Adeius that Rhialdens who are Truthspoken are appointed to rule, under the will of Adeius."

He leaned forward, put more heat into his voice now. Anchored his feet firmly to the dais floor and projected his purpose outward from there.

"I am Human. I have skills that others do not, I have a mandate that others do not, but I feel, I breathe, I can die like anyone else. And the skills I do have are needed to uphold this kingdom so it may continue to thrive. To protect you and your children and their children against any threat, inside or out, to the safety and wellbeing of this kingdom. I intend to do the same with the new skills I've gained through my magics. I will not use these abilities against you, but for you. That is also my promise."

He sat back, and this was the point where Dressa was supposed to stand and make a brief speech in his support.

But someone in the audience stood instead.

Lord Denom Xiao, representing High House Xiao in this meeting. His second cousin. Denom was as tall as he was—as he was as himself—and as Homaj, he shared a light resemblance with Denom, in the broadest sense of also having some Xiao features. Which Denom had always flaunted. Denom was handsome, and he knew it.

Iata suppressed a flare of impatience. High House Xiao had been supporting him publicly in this crisis, as they always did, leveraging the fact that the ruler was half Xiao. But Denom was a prick of the highest order. Iata had never understood why the Prince Xiao left Denom to handle capital politics while they seldom ventured off the Xiao homeworld. Why Denom? Of all people, why?

"Yes, Lord Denom?" Iata asked.

Denom bowed a small measure, which was not enough by far. "Xiao supports the Rhialdens, as always—Seritarchus, will you please not meet my eyes, as you just promised?"

Iata drew a sharp breath, looking aside as he fought to clear his vision of sudden rage.

His thoughts sought the metal bar in his pocket, and he pulled, just a little, from its strength. Enough to steady himself and his hammering heart.

Adeius. He *had* just promised not to meet anyone's eyes, but Denom, whether he'd intended that as an insult or not, could bring everything down right here and now.

Dressa hissed beside him.

He shot her a glance, and her eyes burned back at him with everything she wanted to say about Denom, everything she wanted to do about it. Just asking for permission.

He gave the tiniest shake of his head and didn't *quite* smile. It would have been a rictus smile.

Iata made sure his gaze hovered just beside Denom's head and didn't meet anyone else's eyes in the crowd, either. Or the cameras. He didn't need anyone accusing him of reading them over the feeds, never mind that wasn't actually possible.

That promise not to meet anyone's eyes was going to be hard to keep. Necessary, but hard. And it was tearing at his insides that it was necessary at all.

"As I promised, Cousin," he said with acid, because though he wouldn't let Dressa go after Denom, Homaj wouldn't let an insult like that slip, either. "And what else can I help you with today?"

His obvious displeasure with Xiao's representative might drop Xiao's standing—well, maybe in some circles. In those that favored anti-magicker sentiments, Denom would be applauded.

Hell.

Had Xiao's position shifted? Was his being half Xiao, a half-Xiao *magicker*, a liability to their family?

Another person stood, Lord Qenna Kavan, one of the more staunch anti-magicker lords from the General Assembly. She gripped her hands tightly in front of her. As if she was braced against—what? His attack? His ability to rake through her thoughts?

"Ser Seritarchus, we in the General Assembly wish more assurances than you've given that you will not seek to disguise your seal and listen to our thoughts, attempting to influence members of the General Assembly to your bidding—"

Fucking hell.

"—so I propose, informally, and to be confirmed by a half session of the General Assembly later today, to implement scan checks for concealed magicker seals at the entrances to Assembly Hall, to be carried out at every session of the General Assembly—"

She didn't know how magicker seals worked. Adeius. They couldn't be concealed, that was the point. The seals were made to disrupt holo concealment, they wouldn't allow makeup to be smoothed over top of them. *That was the point.*

Dressa stood now. "You are out of line, Lord Kavan. Sit down."

Another stood, Duke Raharas of High House Raharas. "Of course you would support a magicker walking among us as one of our own," they shouted over the rising din. "You have everything to gain from—"

Lesander shot up. "Raharas, if you wish to keep those trade agreements with Javieri, you'll stop being a bigoted ass and—"

Iata pounded the table with both fists, rattling the scattering of comms and tablets and mugs on its surface. Beside him, Laguaya inhaled, a startled rush of air.

Some in the crowd quieted, but not enough.

So he did it again and roared, "Enough!"

14

ONE AMONG MANY

> *Control, momentum, and change. All three are facets a ruler must balance to adequately steer their kingdom.*
>
> — ANATHARIE RHIALDEN, SERITARCHUS VIII
> AS QUOTED IN *THE CHANGE DIALOGUES*

I ata stood, slowly and deliberately, and if his pounding the table hadn't caught the crowd's full attention, this now did. Then, when Laguaya stood with him, they quieted.

And that was dangerous. So, so dangerous, that these people—his people—revered the Admiral of the Fleet more than they feared him. He could almost feel the brewing coup.

His heart raced in his throat, a ringing in his ears, and he couldn't in that moment calm himself enough to stop it.

Should he abdicate? Was this the moment where he should publicly and formally abdicate to Dressa?

But the crowd hadn't calmed for her, either.

They were entirely losing their fear of the Rhialdens—no, that wasn't true.

They had the wrong kind of fear for the Rhialdens now.

Enough that they were doing everything they could to push the Rhialdens out.

He pointed to the seal on his cheek. "I can't remove this, not without intense pain and damage to my nerves, as well as a signal alerting both the First Magicker and any nearby guard authorities. It is the same for every magicker—I don't have a special seal. I have the seal every magicker wears—"

"With respect, Ser Seritarchus," Duke Raharas said, "you do not. The rank on your seal is higher than any magicker's I've seen. Certainly higher than the First Magicker's."

Iata glanced at Mariyit. Who just looked back, his mouth a grim line. As if he'd known this meeting would go so sour so quickly. He might have hoped otherwise, and Iata had foolishly —so foolishly—hoped, but Mariyit had known.

The camera drones whirred softly, moving closer, honing in on him. He couldn't cut the broadcast now, much as he deeply wished to.

"Yes," Iata said, "I manifested at a high rank. No one gets to choose what rank they—"

"Isn't it true that the highest-ranking magicker should also hold the position of First Magicker?" Raharas pushed.

Iata broke into a cold sweat, and there was no smoothing that now. Adeius, he *hadn't* seen that angle of attack. He hadn't. Either because he was still half-focused on repairing the remaining damage to his body, or because his reserves were strained, or because when his aura was out, he was filtering so much more sensory data, and he just wasn't used to that yet. Not in a setting like this.

But he hadn't seen this coming. And that failing—that utter *failing* when he always saw the tides around him, when he was so rarely caught off guard by political maneuvers, shook him from his center.

He wrenched his center back. It was the only thing holding

him together just now. Keeping him from bolting under the intense hatred rolling off so many in this crowd.

He could feel that, too, with his aura out and pulsing to the energies of everything around him. Was that hatred the normal animosity toward Rhialdens? Or hatred for him specifically, as a magicker? *Because* he was a magicker? Had all he and Maja done to lift magickers up to social parity done nothing?

He made his voice softer, forcing them all to quiet again to hear him. "The First Magicker is chosen by a combination of the Council of Magickers, the current ruler, and the current Truthspeaker. Mariyit Broden has been and remains the best possible choice to hold that position—"

"Ser Seritarchus," yet another member of the Assembly said, rising. Adeius, they were all interrupting him. They would never have done that even days before. "I support this claim that the highest-ranking magicker must represent all magickers."

This was calculated. Oh, this had been *planned*, and he and everyone else had been too distracted to gather that intelligence beforehand.

If they forced him into also taking the position of First Magicker, it would force him to divide his loyalties between the Green Magickers and the rest of the kingdom. It would make him accountable to no one as a magicker but himself—he would hold the keys to his own seal. He could have no defense but his own word and witness that he hadn't removed it to Change.

And that word wouldn't be good enough. He saw that clearly in their eyes, even those who hadn't been radiating hatred a moment before. They were now radiating fear. Not the fear a Truthspoken should rightly command, but the fear of a Truthspoken *magicker*.

And by this move they would take him down.

Was this where the Truthspoken ended, right here, on this dais?

Iata looked to Dressa, hating that he needed to look, knowing that this look right now might have just cost him the kingdom. He shouldn't be deferring to his Heir, not now, not in public. He was as much as admitting he no longer had the control to rule.

But Dressa glared back at him, giving her head one small shake. And that look seemed to say, "Don't you dare abdicate. Don't you *dare* let them win."

Adeius.

They'd pushed him. And all this world, and soon all the other worlds, were watching.

He was a Seritarchus—he ruled with strength and control. But he'd been around Maja enough to also know how to adapt like an Ialorius. To take the sour situation, turn it around, and make it his own. Rewrite the rules.

But this situation wasn't calling for an Ialorius, either.

He wanted to grin at Maja, to tell him he knew, he *knew* now what Maja had felt, shunting himself onto the path of a Seritarchus at the beginning of his rule, even though Maja's own natural instincts were Ialorius, adaptation and change. Because Iata was about to do it himself.

He tapped the table, shifting his thoughts, shifting his stance. Letting go of his roots, letting the situation carry him. He would be movement itself. He would be momentum.

He would have to do a lot of thinking later. A *lot* of rethinking everything on how he related to the court, to the kingdom, to everyone around him. Because if this was going to work, he had to carry it all the way.

"I'm formally changing my style of rule," Iata announced, and now the room fell dead silent again. No one had expected that.

"From this moment, I am Homaj Rhialden, Melesorie IX. Truthspeaker, do you witness?"

"I witness, Homaj Rhialden, Melesorie IX." Ceorre said, her voice carrying clear, and dousing the crowd like cold water.

He rapped the table again and stepped back, the room still mostly silent, everyone watching what he'd do next after *that* announcement.

Rulers so seldom changed their style mid-rule that he knew he'd just ticked a mark for history.

He held out a hand toward Mariyit Broden. "Mariyit. The people of this kingdom would like to see the voice of the magickers and the voice of everyone combined into one single, united front. One voice for everyone."

Mariyit stood. He bowed, deeply, and when he rose, his face was blotchy, his eyes shining with a fire Iata didn't have time to interpret. "I support unity in our people above everything else. Ser Melesorie, I concede my position, my title, and my responsibilities to you. Lead our people—all of our people—into greater peace."

Iata swallowed, he couldn't help that. And he gave the slightest bow in return.

"Thank you, Ser Broden," he said with all of his heart. "I accept your position, your title, and your responsibilities alongside my own."

He faced the crowd again, which had begun to murmur, and held up both hands. "I am Melesorie IX, the ninth ruler of the Twelfth Dynasty of the Kingdom of Valoris, and I am the First Magicker. A united voice for all of our people. No one, absolutely no one, has more voice than anyone else, including myself. The First Magicker is one among many—and so, now, is the Melesorie. I serve you, under the will of Adeius, for all of us."

Pandemonium erupted. Too many people shouting too

many things, and wondering, he rather thought, if he'd just undercut their own power, too.

Maybe he had. He hadn't had time to process what he'd just done, let alone for them to process it.

Time to make an exit.

Dressa's eyes weren't quite wide.

Laguaya's were, though. They leaned close as he made his way for the antechamber door.

"We need to talk. Ser Melesorie."

"Of course," he said. "Comm me. I'll reply directly."

And should he have agreed that readily? Should he be that open?

What was his place in any of this anymore, and was his pronouncement that no voice was heard more than any other going to be a stranglehold on him? Was that pronouncement going to break the kingdom? Or would it, in the end, be ignored as the kingdom carried on as it always had, the legal precedents superseding the heat of the moment?

He had momentum, he did. He wasn't yet sure what kind of momentum, but he had it.

And he had to keep moving.

15

THE MELESORIE

> *When you've been through a tremendous change, of course you'll see your surroundings with different eyes. You don't have to be Truthspoken to Change, to become a different person.*

— IATA RHIALDEN, AS QUOTED IN *THE CHANGE DIALOGUES*

They followed him through the back corridors, the whole parade of them—everyone but Laguaya, who'd stayed in the Reception Hall. No one said anything until they all spilled into his study, the panel door was closed, and he stood in the center of them all, his head spinning.

He glanced at the floor, which had the rugs pulled back, new floorboards covering the areas where the old floor had been ripped out. Mariyit had been back to the palace to transfer strength back into the room's support beams, but the floorboards around where he'd fallen had been a lost cause.

Those boards had saved his life.

Chadrikour had supervised the hasty reconstruction, which

had only finished that morning. The smell of freshly cut lumber and applied top coating was heavy in the air.

"Well?" Dressa asked. "Melesorie?"

He drew a breath and started to answer, but his attention was caught on Lesander, who was closing in on herself, moving closer to Dressa.

The last time he'd been in this room, he'd been attacked. And the last time Lesander had been in this room, she had attacked him.

Another breath to steady himself, to center. He might be in motion—he might be in constant motion now for the rest of his life—but position was relative. He would center the universe around himself just now and let *it* be in motion.

Or was that too Seritarchus of a thought? Adeius, it would take time to try to re-bend his outward personality, instincts, and actions to a pattern that wasn't natural to him. But he didn't have that time.

And he knew how to be a Melesorie, just as he knew how to inhabit the roles of any combination of personality types. He would just have to fake it until it became his reality.

"Do I have all of your permission to meet your eyes?" he asked. Because he had to ask now. Not that he thought any of them would have an issue with that—but it was a new part of the paradigms he'd set for himself.

It was Mariyit who shifted, grimacing. Mariyit, who was no longer the First Magicker, crossed his arms in disapproval.

"I don't like any of this. I don't like what they forced you to do. I don't like that you felt you had to pledge to not fucking *look* at them—because not even high-ranking magickers are required not to look at people, Iata, that just set a bad precedent—"

Iata held up his hands. "I'm sorry. I knew it was going to be an issue."

Mariyit closed his eyes, rubbed at his bearded cheek, visibly pulled himself back under control. "Not your fault that the city's full of bigots. The whole fucking *kingdom's* full of bigots."

Iata decided to ignore that for the moment, true as it was. The strength he'd gathered for that meeting in the Reception Hall was waning.

"There isn't enough of me to do your duties and mine, too, Mariyit," Iata said. "If they want me to hold the title, fine. *Fine.* But, can you please continue to function as you have? Be my— Adeius. I'm sorry. Be what you were to Onya before she gave up the position. You were running most of it then."

Mariyit nodded, shrugged, dropped his arms to his sides. "I can do that well enough, but you'll have to hold the seal and seal releases. And that will be problematic. Truthspoken."

A pain triggered in Iata's chest, a pull from self-protecting his still-healing abdomen. He stopped, pressed a hand to his chest.

He saw multiple people shift in discomfort, or protest, or concern.

But his eyes caught on Jalava, who was continuing to stiffen up to one side, another crisis waiting to happen. He needed to have a conversation with them in private, Adeius knew he did, but he needed to defuse some of Jalava's tension now, or the Commander of the Palace Guard wouldn't be thinking at their best. He *needed* them to be at their best right now.

Iata shunted off the pain and took two strides to stand in front of Jalava, holding out his hands.

Jalava only stiffened further, so he dropped his hands back to his sides. He knew Jalava didn't have a thing against Green Magickers—he knew that. But Jalava had a big thing about not being trusted. And they weren't wrong.

"I've been a magicker for nine years," he said quietly. "Maja and I made the decision to tell as few people as possible. Among the guards, only Zhang knew, because she had to personally guard me at times. Not even Dressa or Imorie knew until recently. We didn't want to complicate your life or your duties—"

Jalava looked up with novas in their eyes. "I've served you, and him, for twenty-three years, every moment of them loyal, every moment spent keeping you—both of you—safe. And you left out this detail, which I needed to protect you—"

"I know. I'm sorry. I trust you."

Jalava opened their mouth again, then visibly stopped themself from saying whatever they were going to say next. Their eyes were pooling, damn all the hells.

He wanted to grip their hands and show them the depth of his regret. The reasons...the reasons didn't seem to matter now.

"I should resign," Jalava said, rocking on their heels.

"No. Please, Jalava. I need my Guard Commander, and I need my friend. Whatever else—we will work it out."

Jalava looked away, smoothing down the front of their maroon and silver uniform, and Iata let them be, stepping back again. He was mostly sure Jalava wouldn't just slip into the back corridors and leave—they had the access, they could leave if they wanted. But Adeius, he had to let them be, whatever they chose. He couldn't dwell any longer on the hurt in their eyes.

Haneri drifted closer as he moved back to the center of the room and slipped her arm through his. He glanced at her, smiled, and also marked Dressa's frown.

"Everyone here knows who he is, right?" Dressa asked, more pointed remark than legitimate question. Mariyit had called him by name.

Dressa was getting that stubborn set to her jaw.

"He's Yan," Haneri said simply, glaring back at her daughter in challenge.

"Iata," Ceorre said, stepping closer, drawing attention to herself, trying to defuse as she always did. Or maybe she was forcing a different confrontation.

"I'm not entirely sure what just happened," she said. "You

changed your style of rule—that's a risk, but it did bend the situation, changed the energy. And having a few moments to think on it, I don't disagree with that decision. We will need momentum in the next days and weeks to pull through this. But your statement that no one's voice is above any other's—did you mean in the sense of demographics? Or did you mean—no, it doesn't matter, the nobility will have a fit over that either way. They'll say you're trying to take their power and give it to the magickers."

"And I will demonstrate otherwise," he said, dropping everything else in his thoughts to rapidly think through where she was going with that. He was already thinking behind the wave of his own velocity, and that wasn't good. He had to catch up.

"As soon as I'm recovered enough, I'll make myself visible," he said. "I'll be out in the city, helping with—with wherever help is needed. It's the only way through this, Ceorre, without abdicating, and I don't think that's an option right now."

"Because of me?" Lesander asked tightly. "Because I'm married to Dressa, and she'd be the ruler, and you can't trust me?"

Lesander and Dressa exchanged a tight glance, dismay and stubbornness rippling through both of them. And hurt.

"In part, yes," he said, and Lesander flinched. He held up his hands. "I'm not going to lie about that, not to you. No, I can't trust you that close to the center of the kingdom, Lesander, that trust must be earned. But also, if I'm forced to abdicate, that would greatly weaken the position of all Rhialdens, and the coup might happen anyway."

"It might still happen," Ceorre said. She glanced at Lesander, back to Iata. "We already had one attempt. Who will be next? High House Xiao? They haven't been as happy of late with the status the Rhialden ties give them—it's been a long time since your Xiao father held their voice in court, and you're thoroughly Rhialden. Denom seemed eager to cut you down, despite Xiao's official support, so I wouldn't be surprised if they turn against you officially." She gave a sour smile. "Blood ties mean little when power's up for grabs."

Ceorre waved toward Lesander. "Or will the Javieris make another attempt?"

"I won't—" Lesander said.

"We know you're loyal," Dressa said to Lesander, though Iata could sense plainly that wasn't true, "but you're certainly not the only person in your family. And hardly the most ambitious."

And Koldari had Imorie. Adeius, Iata was regretting that decision now, letting them go with him. Koldari had just been too adamant about it all, Koldari had to still suspect that Imorie was—or had been—Truthspoken. He'd sent word to his agents on Kalistré again to be on the watch and help Imorie as needed, but that help could come too little, too late, if Koldari was determined to make trouble.

Haneri squeezed his arm. He'd been tensing up, and that wouldn't help anyone here.

"This is new," he said, looking around him. "It was the path I saw to take, and I took it."

"It was the right path," Mariyit said with a sigh. He scratched the side of his beard again, which was in need of trimming. They were all a little ragged around the edges. "I should have sealed you at a lower rank, you were right."

Iata shrugged. That couldn't be changed now—the only way through was forward.

And would he have to learn to seal people now? He'd hold the tool that could release a magicker's seal. That tool was only to be held in the First Magicker's possession, locked to his biometrics, and never used except in dire emergencies...which mostly didn't happen. And every use of it was logged.

His skin wanted to crawl.

"None of us saw the First Magicker angle coming," Ceorre said, rubbing at the bridge of her nose. "And that is nothing we can change now. Iata—I know you can bend to a Melesorie for a time. But how long do you think you can sustain it? Maja didn't have magics trying to push him back into his own personality, and it was still a struggle."

Iata shrugged. "Maja was also learning how to rule a kingdom—I don't have that learning curve. And I have a lot more experience now than he did then. Than either of us did. But—I'll sustain it as long as I have to. Same as remaining Homaj. I will do what I must."

A nod from Ceorre.

"It isn't safe," Jalava said, still not quite looking his way, "for you to go out into the city just now. You'll have to do your 'helping' from the palace."

"Then keep me safe. Even if I have to have twenty guards around me at all times—"

"Then how will the people even see you?" Jalava asked, exasperation creeping into their voice. Their silver-blonde hair had slipped into their eyes, and they angrily shoved it back. "If you're so surrounded by guards, what's the point of being seen? Being seen to be paranoid? Being seen to not trust your people not to kill you?"

"That is a point," Dressa said. "And I don't like you going out there, either. You can't defend yourself. And people know that, and there's a lot of angry people out there making threats just now. Your whole 'voice for everyone' thing isn't making that better. Not yet, anyway. They'll think it's just for the magickers. Iata, you'll have to be harder on the magickers than you might normally be. No favoritism at all, and you might have to use negative favoritism, even."

But he was shaking his head. She was right, yes, but.

He wasn't going to take the title that had just been thrust on him less seriously than he should. Because the First Magicker was one among many, and with so much hate and fear flying around just now, every magicker out there would need more help and protection than ever.

He shuddered and leaned against Haneri, the room spinning.

"Take a step back, all of you," Haneri snapped. "He's still only three days out from a wound that would have killed *any* of you."

Another flinch from Lesander. Was he crazy to think he could still train her? That he could ever give her a life that was less dire than the one she'd grown up in?

"Yan," Haneri said, "sit *down*. You'll do none of us any good if you pass out."

He sat in his usual chair, Homaj's chair, his legs trembling, and he hated the weakness of it.

Then hated that he saw it as weakness. Hated the world that had pushed Imorie out to Hestia because of an illness that was no fault of their own, which had set off the rest of this disastrous chain of events leading to now. To right now, with him, now the Melesorie, with hardly a strategy ahead of him, with a kingdom in chaos, also now head of a group of people the rest of everyone else despised—

He stilled himself again.

No. The voices speaking of the magickers weren't all hate. He and Lesander had interviewed pro-magicker rioters a few nights before. He would do what he could, bolster support where he could. Do everything he knew how to change the narrative.

Because he was going to get through this. He would. He did have momentum. He had pieces in motion, and he would shape them as he went.

"I will need all of your help," he said. "You all either already have direct send privileges to my personal inbox, or will have it as soon as I can change that over." A quick glance at Lesander.

"Send me ideas. Tell me if I'm heading in the wrong direction. At least, until we have things stable again, but I want all of your opinions—I might not take them, but I'm asking, and I'm listening."

He'd undercut the strength of his rule, and his own reasoning, by changing his style of rule to something he wasn't at all used to. But still, looking back through that last meeting, he didn't think he would have changed that action. The next few days might be rough, as Homaj's first had been as a Seritarchus —oh Adeius, those early days had been rough.

But he did have help. And he wasn't starting from scratch, no.

He'd talk to Bettea and Pria as well, and Chadrikour. Bettea was already hard at work on the tasks he himself would have helped with for Maja.

Maybe it was a mistake for a ruler *not* to have a council of advisors around them. Other heads of other nations did, but the Truthspoken had always been expected to rely on themselves alone. And the Truthspeaker, as needed, but mostly themselves.

They were, after all, sanctioned to be the will of the god themself.

Iata sat back and closed his eyes, just for a moment, to assess where his body was right now. He was holding back the pain, and it wasn't truly as bad as it had been. Another day or two, and he should be almost fully healed. But he wasn't there yet. And his emotions and the strain of that last meeting hadn't helped his healing. His trying to power through all of this the last two days hadn't helped.

When he opened his eyes again, everyone but Haneri was gone.

16

MARRIAGE

I don't regret my marriage to Homaj Rhialden. I will never regret my marriage. It was a necessary political alliance, and it gave the kingdom two heirs, and I can't ever regret that. It gave me my children.

— HANERI NE DELOR RHIALDEN, AS QUOTED
IN *THE CHANGE DIALOGUES*

Iata started and sat up. Adeius, had he slept? In the middle of a meeting?

He must have. "How long—"

He was growing to hate that question.

"An hour, maybe a little more," Haneri said. She sat in the chair beside him, and now set down a tablet she'd been reading.

He hadn't had an hour. He needed to be up and visible, to keep his momentum going.

"Don't worry. Dressa's been busy, with Ceorre's help. They've been messaging you along the way—they said to check your inbox when you're able. I've been sorting out the current mess of Rhialden trade agreements with other high houses and commerce enterprises. The smart ones are staying on."

Her look did not bode well for whoever wasn't.

Iata wiped at his eyes and looked around for his comm. Haneri held it up, out of reach.

"Let yourself wake up first, Yan."

He raked back the loose hair that had fallen out of his braid earlier. "Haneri—"

She sighed and handed his comm over. He checked his personal inbox and skimmed enough to know that yes, Ceorre and Dressa did have it in hand, if a bit shakily after his shocker of a Reception. Had he truly done what he'd done at that Reception? It felt like a dream just now, a very vivid nightmare.

But Ceorre and Dressa were doing no worse than he would have done running on fumes.

He was still running on fumes.

"The economy is crashing after I changed my style of rule," he said. Not that it wasn't diving already.

"That," Haneri said, "or because of their bigotry."

"Or their fear."

"It's pretty much the same thing."

Iata set the comm down and sat back again, closing his eyes. He felt vaguely dizzy. His body, where parts of the wound and the surgery after were still healing, ached. Parts that hadn't been injured by the knife but damaged by the poison also ached. It had been too great an injury, with both the wound and the poison, to heal in one go. These kinds of injuries healed much better over time as his stamina recovered.

And still he was continually dipping into light trances to help ease it along, and that in itself was wearing him out. He just hadn't yet recovered the strength.

Haneri slipped her hand into his. Offering, again, her own strength for him to use.

His stomach soured, and he shook his head. "It's not an

ethical practice, Haneri, taking strength or life force from another person. In dire emergencies, maybe, but not a regular thing."

She didn't withdraw her hand. "Then, comfort. You don't need to magically draw on comfort to have it."

He grunted and felt Haneri's mood turning pensive, holding back something she wanted to say. He tried to ignore it, to let her be and focus on the roil of his own thoughts, but the feeling in her was only growing stronger.

"What?" he growled.

She swore. "I forget that you can read my thoughts, and I really don't like that."

"I'd be worried if you did. And I'm not reading your thoughts. Not trying to, anyway. Your emotions. I'm extrapolating the rest, because my damned mind won't stop."

He was falling back into his own speech cadences, and that was a balm. He needed that, after he'd stretched himself into so many unfamiliar places today.

"I'm feeling yours, too," Haneri said, voice softer.

He opened his eyes. He'd expected her to be defensive. He'd rarely, if ever, known Haneri to be soft. But he'd seen an entirely different Haneri in the last few days. Last weeks, really.

He met her gaze, his sense of her emotions intensifying, and knew her sense of him would be clearer with both touch and visual contact, too.

Tired as he was, he couldn't quite hide the jolt of desire that wrenched through him.

He blinked. Or was that from *her*?

She leaned across the chair arms between them, and he leaned toward her, too.

But that would be awkward—and now he had a decision to make.

So he pushed up, still a little shaky, and flopped down again on the couch, the synth-leather creaking. Without a word, she followed, until they were sitting knee to knee, shoulder to shoulder.

She smelled faintly like the perfume she usually favored, a spicy musky blend, but she hadn't worn it the last few days, he thought. Or at least, not much of it.

That small gesture, that small kindness when all his senses were overloaded, when he hadn't had to ask for it, suddenly tightened his chest.

They stared into each other's eyes, too close, but both afraid to break the connection of whatever was happening just now.

She reached for his cheek, a tentative, bracing touch.

She leaned toward him again, her braids brushing his sleeve.

He drew a shuddering breath and held up his hand.

"No. You're my brother's—"

"I'm married to Homaj Rhialden. And right now, you are the only Homaj Rhialden I see. And you told me I'm not even married right now, if Maja abdicated. So I can do what I want."

He was still shaking his head, but it was slowing as he saw the look in her eyes. Had anyone ever looked at him like that before?

He'd seen lust in people's eyes, strangers who he'd met and seduced, or they'd seduced him. People he met in the city and then never saw again, because that was his life. People of all genders—mostly femme, because his attraction was mostly to femme people—but he'd explored every avenue of himself thoroughly. And been any number of people in return, trying to carve out small places for himself in a life that mostly wasn't his own.

Bloodservants couldn't form romantic attachments, not anything serious—and where would be the time, anyway? He'd mostly crashed into the city after an extended time of being Homaj, when that reality crashed back into his reality of being

Iata, and he needed to ground himself in something that was his own.

But he hadn't been able to have even that release, those feeble connections, the last nine years since he'd been a magicker. He couldn't suddenly spring an aura during the unguarded moments of sex. He couldn't hide his aura while he slept.

Haneri's look now was something between concerned and ravenous. She cared. More than lust—this was much, much more than that. And that thought tightened his chest further with a growing fear.

He wasn't himself. Adeius—not even this moment was his own. If she was desiring him, she was desiring Homaj, not Iata—

And did that matter, especially now? When he knew that this was his body from here on out? This body had been his for so much of his life that it was his own. He was exactly as at home in this body than his as Iata. And he knew, no matter what shape his body took, it always was his own. Maja's twin just now in many ways, but not Maja.

It wasn't as if he *wasn't* Homaj, the public persona, too. This persona had also become his own, and he'd shaped it just as much as Maja.

Did any of that matter if right now he was feeling horny as hell, frustrated and confused, and just wanted...well, her?

He had so much to do. He had a kingdom to wrench up, by any means he could, from a spiral into the void. He had a new style of rulership to think through as thoroughly as he was able and adjust his strategies accordingly. Adjust his own personality, the order of his thoughts. No, not the order, the *momentum*.

And all of that, in this moment, was not as important as the person who sat next to him. Femme with an aggression that bordered on performance. Less graceful than forceful. Round edges and unnaturally vibrant beauty.

He'd wanted her for a lot longer than these few minutes. He wanted her, as much as he could get of her, for as long as he could have her. Adeius, but he did. And he didn't have enough defenses up to push that longing away.

"I never consummated my marriage," she said. "Not that it was ever anything other than a political marriage, and consummation is relegated to the historical vids. But I never did. We never did."

That confession, which he'd already suspected, wasn't helping things.

And he was also having trouble, knowing she'd never been attracted to Homaj before, with thinking she was now. Even though he could feel it, and feel it was still building.

"Haneri—"

"I don't care what you look like," she said. "I've never cared if you were Iata or Homaj, and I have always known. And I've never wanted Maja when he was Homaj. But I have, when it's you."

She let out an explosive breath. "And I knew you'd *never* cross that line. Never. Because you—you're *yourself,* aren't you? But I'm not married to him now. And he's not Homaj now, either. He has exactly no claim over me. So I want you to—"

He kissed her. And she tasted like she had that day she'd kissed him a few weeks ago, sweet and just a touch bitter, and years worth of feelings he'd shoved down as unhelpful and nothing he could pursue rioted back up again. Became a raging, uncontrollable fire.

He'd been trying these last weeks to keep them contained, but Haneri kept *being there,* close and constant. And she was saying now she didn't want him to push these feelings back down. With their hands linked and his magics amplifying their emotions between them, it was clear to both of them what they both wanted.

"I don't think," he said between kisses, "that it's a good idea...to do this right...now..."

She made a low noise that pulsed straight through his nervous system, but pushed him away with the tips of her fingers on his chest, like pinpoints of fire.

Adeius.

He hadn't wanted her to agree with him.

Haneri smiled ruefully. "No, you're right, I don't want you to damage anything you've just healed. Not that I don't want to do this."

She leaned in for one more kiss, then moved herself back on the couch. Which was torment, though he knew it was for the best.

For now.

But she still kept a hold of his hand.

And then didn't, because they were only building each other up again.

He had to catch his breath.

"What I wanted to ask you," she finally said, "and knew the time wasn't appropriate, was to transfer my marriage contract to you. I am still, publicly, married to Homaj Rhialden, if not to Maja. Never to Maja again. So I want that transferred to you. Have Ceorre do whatever she needs for it to happen. I know that won't be public, publicly nothing will have changed. But I want that. And I think you need that support, too."

His brow furrowed. "Haneri, please don't do this out of some sense of duty—"

"Why not?" she asked, squaring her shoulders. "I was never allowed that choice with Maja. I want the choice for this to *be* my choice, and I'm choosing you. I want more than a loveless life in this palace. When Chelsa died—" She choked, fingers digging into her thighs, cutting small trails in the fine fabric of her gown.

Her lover, Lord Chelsa Fadira, had died in an aircar accident five years ago, shortly before Haneri had gone into her seclusion. He'd always suspected it was part of why she'd sheltered herself away from the rest of the court.

She'd never talked about it. Not, he thought, to anyone outside her own staff.

Haneri had loved Chelsa. Truly loved her, and the grief he felt from her now, even not touching her, stole his breath again.

And there had been Maja, as Homaj, cold and openly hostile to Haneri. Spurning her, dismissing her. And Iata hadn't been present for her, of course, because he'd had to keep his distance, even when he was Homaj. Most *especially* when he was Homaj. She was his brother's wife, not his. Though he'd suspected she'd been hurting, and almost certain of it when she'd gone into her seclusion.

But it hadn't been his place to pull her out of that seclusion. And then...she just hadn't come out, not until a few weeks ago.

She reached again and squeezed his hand, her face hard but her emotions showing a different picture. "Don't apologize. You weren't the one who hurt me. And I'm well aware I helped make that bed, too. I'm not the easiest person to be around. If you haven't noticed." She grinned with all her teeth.

"Yes," he said. "Yes, I'll ask Ceorre."

She bit her lip and looked, for the first time since he'd known her, a little unsure.

His wife. She would be his wife shortly.

There was a joy, an unsquashable joy rising up past all the other fears.

And maybe—maybe he hadn't let himself connect to anyone, maybe Maja would have been fine if he had, but he hadn't let himself because he'd known his heart was already given to someone who could never return that same regard.

But she could now. She was asking him, telling him she cared in the same way.

Would Maja be upset about that?

Maja had never done anything but cast Haneri aside. And Maja wasn't the ruler anymore.

Haneri would soon be his—well, his own Melesorie Consort. But the title mattered much, much less to him than Haneri.

Than knowing he could give her more than coldness and hostility. Knowing that he might—he might actually be able to give her love.

He leaned back across the distance and slowly, with much more attention and tenderness this time, kissed her again.

17

THE TEST

I wish so much that you could be, just for a moment, not my prince but my love.

— OLUN SHIRALL IN THE VID DRAMA *NOVA HEARTS*, SEASON 9, EPISODE 12, "GENTLENESS"

It was the evening of the day after the Seritarchus had become the Melesorie. Lesander had spent this day and most of the day before in an absolute whirlwind of a social campaign, deflecting questions about where Imorie had gone, along with did she think the Melesorie should actually *be* the Melesorie, and wouldn't it be better if the Heir stepped up now instead? Because how could a magicker fairly rule the kingdom?

The questions weren't quite treason. But then, who was Lesander to judge what was treason?

The people had, at least, stopped judging Dressa's competency to rule—and she'd mostly abandoned the airy socialite aspects of who she had been at court. Which Lesander kind of missed, though Dressa in power mode was also extremely hot.

And Dressa had stopped shoving Lesander at Ceorre or
Haneri or whoever would have her. Dressa had kissed her
again, nuzzled her neck, they'd had a decent cuddle the night
before. They hadn't done more, not yet, and maybe they were
both too fragile for that yet.

But now, Lesander had been summoned. A single, short
message on her comm:

Tonight, my study. Use the back corridors.

She'd been dreading this ever since she'd sent a yes to Iata's
question about training her. She'd weighed all her options, had
weighed what she herself wanted, because she was being given
a choice, and that was such a new experience that it should be
treasured.

Unless this was all leading up to an immaculate and thorough revenge, which she also couldn't discount. Though
watching how Dressa responded to Iata—with a respect that
actually seemed deserved—Lesander didn't think it was
revenge.

And him telling her to use the back corridors? She
shouldn't have access at all.

Adeius. But she could Change her palm to Iata's own DNA.
Or Arianna's, if she wanted to admit that she'd studied stolen
DNA before she'd even arrived. Imorie's, she assumed, would
not work.

She didn't dare attempt Dressa's biometrics.

In the prep room, Lesander handed her comm to Dressa,
who was sitting at her vanity. Pria, dressed immaculately in a
brocade coat and trousers Lesander knew was equal to the cost
of a small—and maybe slightly older—interstellar ship,
worked through Dressa's hair with a dry conditioner. It smelled
like plums.

And here was another reminder that bloodservants were

hardly servants. Dressa had said Pria wasn't as fully trained as Iata, but she was still Change-trained. She was still royalty, still blood. And she was still in training to be Dressa's shadow co-ruler, if not quite in the way that Iata had been with Homaj.

So Dressa said.

Today, Pria's short black hair was artfully messy. She eyed Lesander through a spike of bangs with open hostility. Pria had never been particularly friendly to Lesander, but just now her glare could chisel through stone.

After Dressa had explained who Pria's father was... Lesander didn't really blame her.

Dressa took Lesander's comm and read the screen with Iata's message on it, her sculpted brows climbing. She handed the comm back.

"That's a test," she said. "Which of us you choose to use for the biometrics."

"Yes. I thought as much." Lesander eyed Pria. She didn't want to be as open around the bloodservant as she was when she was alone with Dressa, even though Dressa didn't seem to get that. To Dressa, Pria was just family.

And would Lesander ever have that status in Dressa's eyes? To actually and truly be family? Would she ever deserve it?

Dressa loved her, yes, but love didn't always mean family.

But then, family didn't always mean love, either.

"Any advice?" Lesander asked.

"Don't try to kill him," Pria said under her breath.

Dressa sat up straight, her feet thumping hard on the carpeted floor. "Adeius—Pri, give me the bottle, I'll take it from here."

Pria's glare transferred to Dressa, turned admonishing.

"I've slept in the same bed as my wife the last two nights and I'm still alive, if you haven't noticed," Dressa snapped, getting just a little of her father's sharp tone. Which she seemed to notice and checked herself, sitting back again. "Well, I'm not going to start worrying now."

"I'm worried about him," Pria said. "He shouldn't be alone with—"

"Pri!"

Pria opened her hands, let the comb she'd been using drop to the floor, and marched out.

Dressa pressed both her hands to her cheeks.

"She's...not taking this well."

Lesander said nothing. What in the worlds could she say to that, that she'd now come between Dressa and her bloodservant, who were supposed to be closer than siblings?

Dressa swiveled in her chair and looked up at Lesander with narrowed eyes. "Don't you blame yourself, not for her. We've never gotten on as well as we should, Pri and I. We're just...very different people."

Dressa sighed and bent to pick up the comb, flicking shut the bottle of conditioner. "Our parents did their best to make sure our personalities would be compatible." She shrugged. "There's only so much you can guess beforehand, though."

Dressa grimaced, a weird lopsided frown which was a new tic that had started just after...well. And Lesander could hardly blame Dressa for being upset about all of this, too. About her.

Lesander had given up her family for her wife. She had done that. That should count for something—that should count for a lot.

But she had a large debt to pay before she could come even close to forgiveness, or trust.

She had a summons, though. While the Melesorie hadn't specified a time, "as soon as possible" was implied.

She held up her palm. "The test?"

He would know which person's genetics she used to gain access to the back corridors. And maybe it wasn't even safe to use Iata's own biometrics, with the kill order out on him.

That thought sent another spike worming through her gut.

She'd been trained for how to kill a Truthspoken, but she'd never been trained to handle the guilt of it after. In her mother's eyes, there should have been no guilt.

And the guilt of, in the end, betraying her family. Betraying both of her families, not truly belonging to either. Despised by both.

Dressa leveled a look at her. One of those too-seeing looks Lesander was coming to seriously dislike.

Lesander squirmed. And was not proud of it, before she regained her composure. But she knew Dressa still saw.

Did she revel in it?

No. No, that wasn't Dressa. Dressa wasn't even close, not even a little, to the sadist that was Lesander's mother. And her mama, too, if she was honest. No one could be in tandem with Yroikan Javieri and keep their morals intact.

"It's your test," Dressa said. "I won't help you cheat." Then her face softened. A little. "At least it's Iata teaching you. My father...hmm. Yeah, I would have helped you cheat with my father."

And with those ominous words, Lesander made her way into the bedroom. On the way, she concentrated and Changed the DNA in her palm to...okay, Arianna's. The genetics that Imorie had to leave behind. Cards on the table—she wasn't going to hide from Iata exactly what she'd been trained to do. Even if she'd talked her mother out of marrying Imorie and then replacing them.

Killing them. Then replacing them.

Lesander shuddered again before she brought herself back under control.

She hadn't been alone with Iata since that night. He'd known who she was, he'd known she was illegally trained—and that much had been glaringly obvious—but he'd still taken her with him into the city. And when she'd been in distress, he'd embraced her.

And she'd stabbed him. She'd been facing him. She'd watched the moment that realization hit his eyes, the slightest flicker of surprise, the universe of hurt.

She would relive that moment in her dreams every day of her life, she was sure of it.

The panel door, which she'd watched Dressa open before, clicked open, and she slipped into the back corridors.

18

TOO MUCH TRUTH

> *Change is so much of who we are that when you try to view a Truthspoken away from Change, there is no context. If there's no Change, there's no Truthspoken. But I wonder sometimes who I would have been without it. Who you would have been, Uncle. Who my children would have been, and my parents, and my siblings. Would we all have been better without it? Or just have different problems?*

— HOMAJ RHIALDEN, SERITARCHUS IX IN A
PRIVATE LETTER, NEVER SENT; PUBLISHED IN
THE CHANGE DIALOGUES

Lesander tried to push in the panel door to the Seritarchus's study, but it wouldn't open for her, not even with Arianna's DNA in her palm. It would have for Iata's, though, she was fairly sure of that. Was that also a part of the test?

The door clicked and swung inward. Iata stood there, a silhouette in the light behind him. His posture was rigid, though she couldn't see his face well enough to read more. A long weave of three large, loose braids hung over one shoulder, glossy enough to see in the light, glinting with red nova hearts woven into them. His shoulders puffed with gauzy pastel taffeta.

Lesander had never seen any signs in anything she'd seen or read of Iata to indicate he was other than firmly masc. But as Homaj, he wove through expressions of gender fluidity like he'd been born to them.

And maybe it was more complicated than that. Lesander was finding that everything at Palace Rhialden was more complicated than that. For her to have thought she could play on the same level as the Rhialden Truthspoken was...appalling. And appallingly naïve.

Iata was a man who'd performed before an entire kingdom for half of his life. Or maybe all of it? Which was the real Iata, the intense and rigid bloodservant, or...whoever this was before her now?

Every nuance of this man was exactly what he wanted it to be—except, maybe, the glint of the seal on his cheek. And the flare of deep forest green around him.

Iata stepped to one side, and she slipped past him into the study.

He shut the door quietly behind her.

"Thank you for coming. What I would like to do tonight is mostly talk through what you already know. Then we will begin to assess the limits of your education and what you still need to learn."

Bile rose up, and she pushed it back down. She still couldn't quite believe he was willing to train her as a Truthspoken. What they were doing now was so illegal—but then, he was the ruler. And his rulership itself wasn't exactly legal, or at least, not all above board. He wasn't above the law, but he was still at its pinnacle.

A ghastly part of her whispered, what if she could finish the job she'd started right now, kill him and then rise to power with Dressa?

Or—or—what her mother had wanted, kill him and then kill and replace...well, it wouldn't be Arianna now, it would be Dressa. She could replace Dressa, she passably could—maybe not in the Truthspeaker's eyes, she'd have to find a way to kill Ceorre, too. And Haneri.

And Imorie and Rhys while she was at it, wouldn't she?

But she knew Dressa's every tic and nuance. Everything that Dressa had shared with her, and Dressa had bared her soul.

At least, she'd thought.

A vicious part of Lesander was proud she'd gotten this far into Palace Rhialden politics. She'd made the mistake about not knowing who Iata really was, but that was hardly a mistake she could be blamed for.

It might even help the kingdom to have the ruling magicker gone. And the bulk of the Rhialdens. The Rhialdens were on a fast slide downward, and she could save them—their family name at least—from the fall.

Lesander could win back her family. And she wouldn't be a failure. She wouldn't have to be estranged from them, as she knew she would be now. Then *she* could sit at the pinnacle. She could hold the power. For once in her life, for fucking *once* not be beholden to everyone else's whims, and their cruelties.

She'd only have to kill everyone around her.

She'd only have to kill the woman she loved.

And this man, right here, who'd refused to die the last time. Who was still, *still* offering to teach her.

Lesander shivered. She wasn't aware that she was crying until the room around her blurred.

And Iata was there, nearby but not touching, the aura around him radiating his concern—she could feel that, palpably feel that from him. Adeius, he should not be concerned for *her*. He shouldn't.

Her chest constricted.

"I'm a horrible person," she choked. "You shouldn't train me."

"No, you're not," he said, with such definitive finality that any thoughts to the contrary shied away from her. "And that is the truth."

It rang in his voice, was searing in his dark eyes when she met them.

"Come on," he said, and led her to the powder blue couch in the center, taking a seat in the wingback chair across from her.

He eased down with less grace than he should have had, his mouth tight. Was he still in pain? And that was her fault. How could he say she wasn't horrible—how could she have felt that truth from him—

But magickers would reflect a person's truth, not necessarily *the* truth. If Iata had decided not to believe that she was horrible, it still didn't mean it wasn't true. Just that he was delusional.

"Lesander," he said, and there was enough ache in his voice it made her look up again. "I'm sorry."

She gaped at him, shocked into asking, "What the hell did *you* do to make you apologize to me?"

He'd done nothing. Absolutely nothing to deserve what she'd done to him.

He grimaced. "I didn't see. I let my own opinions of your family inform my opinion of you."

She wrapped her arms around her stomach, leaned forward on the couch. "When Imorie first came back, when you—Iata —brought them back in the corridor—that was you, wasn't it?"

He might not be angry with her now, but he had been then. His rage had been nearly solar.

He let out a long breath, exhaustion pinching around his eyes. "Yes. I was angry—not at you, specifically, but the Javieris. But at the time I'd equated them with you. The Javieris coerced Eti into using his magics illegally. It's how Imorie was caught."

Lesander froze. She hadn't known that. And she still had the nagging sense that Eti was familiar—had she seen him before? On her homeworld, had they—whichever Javieri had been using him—brought him to her mother's palace?

No, no she didn't think that was it. She was sure she hadn't met Eti until the palace here. Until a few days ago.

But she absolutely believed her mother was capable of using Green Magickers in that way. Her mother had never liked magickers, with an intensity that felt like a grudge.

"I didn't know," she said carefully, attentive to every nuance of his reaction.

He nodded, accepting her statement as if it was truth—and he would be able to tell that, wouldn't he? His aura flared denser around him than any other magicker's she'd seen. Bright enough that he'd been forced into taking the position of the First Magicker. She *was* talking to the First Magicker.

Lesander halted her blanch, and knew, for a moment, the fear that all the other nobles must be feeling. That this person could both read her body language and peer into her soul with a glance. What secrets could she ever hide from him? What part of her soul could she hold separate enough that he'd never see?

She swallowed, forced herself to meet his eyes again. "You asked me what I thought about magickers, when we went into the city."

"And did you give me truthful answers?"

"Yes." She had. She hadn't known he was a magicker then, and she'd known what was at the end of that excursion, what she'd planned to do. But she'd let herself pretend, just for a moment, that her life was different. That he really was the person who'd trained her, who asked her opinions and truly seemed to listen. Who walked her through the why of things and didn't scream at her when she didn't understand.

She'd almost dared to hope that she could have that life. He had offered to train her, and she knew now he'd really meant it. But she'd known it had to be a lie. She'd thought she had no other choice but to carry out what she'd come to do.

"Good," he said, and smiled, leaned back. "It's a foundation from which to start."

And his face was so earnest. She was off-kilter, too open with him just now, partly because he was not holding his own guard up. She could very clearly see that he was not Homaj Rhialden, though his likeness was perfect, and he was still using most of Homaj's mannerisms and cadences. His hands glittered with Homaj's rings, his elaborate hairstyle a marker of Homaj's tastes, his puffy designer blouse with all the fashion-setting extravagance Homaj was known for. His eyes were sharply lined, his lips a deep violet. A contrast of pastels and rich darks.

But there were a dozen little things that were off from the man Lesander had been made to obsessively study. The way he was sitting, the projection of power, the...empathy. Adeius, this man wasn't at all how Dressa had described Homaj Rhialden, because he *wasn't*. He might project that personality if he wanted to, but he wasn't the tyrant Lesander had been sent to overthrow, through death or through her slower victory of time.

And if he could see through her soul, he was allowing her to see his as well. She could feel in her gut, clear as a gong, that he was being sincere, no intention whatsoever to mislead her. He wasn't trying to mislead her in his role as Homaj, either, it was simply where he was mostly settled just now.

He still wasn't mad at her. Not in any way that mattered. He should be, by every right in the universe, he should be.

But he wasn't.

19

WORTH SAVING

Void is a color for when the world
hasn't seen the blaze
of who you are.

— OWAM, EXCERPT FROM THEIR POEM
"BECOMING FIRE"

Iata frowned slightly, and Lesander almost crumpled—
what had he seen or felt, what had she done wrong? Had
he found a layer of her soul that was not worth saving?
She wouldn't be surprised.

He sat up again, sat forward, some of the strength coming
back into his expression, some of the fatigue leaving.

"We don't have to do this," he said. "I'm not forcing you to
train. This will always and only be your choice."

She swallowed and grabbed for the nearest excuse.
Anything to get out of his unasked for pity.

"You're busy. I know you're busy, you certainly don't have
the time to—"

"This is a break," he said, his frown deepening. "This is rest, and how I keep my sanity in the maelstrom. Adeius, Lesander, give me the benefit of knowing my own choices."

She recoiled, and she watched him recoil, too, then hold up his hands, his eyes a little too wide.

"Forgive me. Adeius, forgive me. I am—I'm not used to moving in a Melesorie personality, and I'm misfiring at the wrong moments. That was not called for."

He wouldn't be in this position at all without her. He wouldn't publicly be a magicker, and he wouldn't be in the pain that he *was* trying to hide, his only insincerity.

And of course he was still in pain. She'd rammed a poisoned knife into his stomach, after he'd given her a hug.

She stood, her throat burning. "I'll go."

"You can," he said. "You absolutely can, with no consequences. I mean it, I don't have to train you. I want to. You have so much potential, Lesander—no, you are already there. Your performance as Iata, as me, was excellent, you were an attentive student throughout the tunnels. You were a help to me in a politically difficult situation with the Municipal Guard, and if you wish to help me at all, and help this kingdom, I could truly use the help of someone else who's Truthspoken-trained. I am desperately short on those just now."

Slowly, slowly, Lesander smoothed out her dark blue linen tunic. She tucked her hair behind her ear, her eyes on the floor, and sat back down.

And Iata's very open posture eased, as if she was doing him a favor.

He'd just said that she was. She'd heard the ring of truth in those words. It was edging her near panic.

"Lesander," he said, spreading his hands wide. "I'm not Prince Yroikan. I'm not your mothers. I'm not the person who trained you—I have my suspicions on who that was, and if they're correct, I am deeply, deeply sorry for what you had to endure."

She swallowed hard, an audible squelch. And her flooding eyes were betraying her. She pushed hard into a light trance to keep them from betraying her further.

Her training had been torture, in every sense of the word. Lesander had thought that was just how it was. Teaching her to forcibly rewrite her genetic code, to siphon away the pain of it in her mind when it was immediate and demanding. And then all the training in quicker and quicker Changes, forced to go again and again until she was so drained she could hardly stand—

She stared at her hands, tightly knotted together in her lap. How long had she been quiet? How long had she been tangled in her thoughts?

The holographic hearth gave a crack. The faintest simulated scent of woodsmoke hung in the air.

"It should never have been like that," Iata said, and she heard the anger in his voice now. Saw the echo of his face in the corridor when he'd glared at her. All of his anger, then, focused on her.

"There were parts of my own training that weren't pleasant," he said, "but steps were always taken to teach in a logical order. I knew how to block pain by the time I had to use that skill to progress."

Lesander's trainer had screamed at her while she'd been crying, protesting the need to—

Well. Something had to be broken in order for her to learn how to heal.

The room tilted now, and she broke out in a cold sweat.

She was going to be sick.

No. No, she knew how to handle this. She was calm and in control. She could smooth away the nausea, and wrap up those memories in a tight bundle and shove them aside.

"I know trust has to be earned," Iata said, "and that means I have to earn it, too. Truly, the greater burden is on me—"

She jolted up straight. "No! No—" She'd known what she was doing. She'd absolutely known when she'd plunged in the knife.

Lesander gripped her legs so tightly she was sure she'd have bruises.

He twitched forward, as if he wanted to come toward her. To comfort her, even. But he didn't, and for that, she was intensely grateful.

"I know," he said in a near-whisper. "I *know* what it's like to have parents who raised you to a singular purpose. Who never once let you see love, not the kind of love you needed. I might not have your past, Lesander. But I have my own. And I do know that."

He stopped and looked toward the hearth, the intensity of his attention easing like the passing of a spotlight.

He frowned and—and his aura flickered once, then went out.

Lesander let out her breath, her whole body easing. It had been too much, there had been *too much* truth in this room. Sometimes some of the lies were necessary.

He gave a wan smile. "Forgive me. Again. I'm not used to having my aura out, and it seems to be strengthening the more that I do." He shrugged. "When I'm around Maja, he knows me so well that—well. I'm not particularly used to the effect it can have on people."

He clasped his hands together on his knees. "Lesander, I truly mean my offer to teach you. But this might not be the right time. The wounds—no, forgive me, that's not the right word—the trauma is too fresh. And too old, I think. We can resume this later if you wish. Or, again, not at all. You don't have to be Truthspoken."

Her heart kicked into a staccato rhythm. Adeius, no, what if he decided for himself that now was not a good time?

She'd thought—well, she'd been afraid to train with him

because of what he might do or say to her, not actually because she didn't want to train. She did want that.

"It's already what I am," she said. "Change-trained, I mean. I want—"

She hesitated, but he waved for her to continue. And she did, slowly, feeling the ideas out. Knowing, for a dizzying moment, that he would listen to them. That he actually *wanted* to hear them. Things she'd hardly dared to think about.

"I want to know what it's like, when it's not broken. I mean, is this a bad life, when it's not all...pain?"

She did know how to block pain. Oh, she knew how to block pain.

Remembering the pain of Dressa forcing her to Change quickly made her breath catch. That had bothered her more than she'd let herself admit. It had been too close to her own training. Far too raw.

"What?" he asked. More a prompt, she sensed, than a demand. She could read him now with her own trained senses, not having to see the full blaze of his open soul.

And he truly couldn't sense the depth of hers just now, could he? His attention was focused on her, reading her, but it wasn't the same as when his aura flowed around him.

Lesander's shoulders eased in her relief. And whatever he read in that...was what he read.

She couldn't tell him how Dressa had handled that forced Change the night of her attack—and Dressa hadn't been wrong. Dressa had had every right.

Or had she?

Lesander shook her head and saw Iata relax. Nod. His posture still open, his sincerity telegraphed. He was being deliberately careful, like she was fragile. And maybe that wasn't wrong, too, as much as it galled her.

But she didn't want to stay wounded. She didn't want to let her family win.

Adeius, she wanted a life where she could look at her wife and just love her. No pretenses, no secrets between them but the ordinary small things partners always kept to themselves in the fluffiest vid dramas, her very secret guilty pleasure. Just the small things. She wanted trust. She wanted to know what it was like to trust. And be trusted.

The hearth crackled again, and she flinched.

Iata glanced at the hearth, twisted one of his rings, and the flames banked to embers.

"No, it's not a bad life," he said, answering her earlier question. "It's hard. It's intense. It can be filled with a hell of a lot of anguish, but it's rewarding, deeply rewarding. Change is a part of who I am, and if you were raised to it, however you came about it, it's a part of you, too. If you want to know what a life of Change is like lived to its fullest, with support around you and others who can Change, I would love to help with that. And if you wish to learn what a life is like without Change, too, or those obligations to tie you down, I can help with that, too. You do not need to be anything other than what you wish."

Lesander nodded. She did know the lie in that—neither of them would ever fully have control over their own lives. His belonged to the kingdom. Right now, his life wasn't even his own.

But she wanted a chance to make hers her own, because it never had been before.

She nodded again. Took a breath. She did want this.

"Okay," she said. "Here's what I've been taught."

20

WEDDING PLANS

I met Homaj Rhialden three times before I promised my life to him, and he to me. Once, when we were children, and my parent presented me to the Seritarchus and his family as the heir to a high house princedom, and therefore a rival. Once, when I was twenty-two and he was eighteen, and he barely gave me a look before sliding his eyes away again. And once, the day before we married, when he met me on the landing pad behind the palace. And that time, he smiled at me, and took my hands, and led me inside. But that wasn't the man I married.

— HANERI NE DELOR RHIALDEN, AS QUOTED IN *THE CHANGE DIALOGUES*

"Mother," Dressa said, bearing down on Haneri in the corridor. It was early enough in the morning, and her mother was, again, heading toward Iata's apartment. Which seemed to be an utterly common thing these days. Which on the surface might even be normal—she was, after all, married to Homaj Rhialden.

But Iata wasn't the person her mother was married to. And Dressa, who'd managed to set this whole new wrinkle aside the last few days, needed answers.

Dressa waved toward her own apartment, and Haneri, arching one immaculately sculpted brow, inclined her head and followed. Dressa still outranked her mother, but she had no illusions whatsoever that her mother cared anything about that.

Dressa didn't quite storm into her prep room, startling Lesander, who covered it with a graceful rise from her desk.

"Talking with my mother," Dressa said, "you're fine."

Lesander hesitated, giving Dressa a look that Dressa chose not to interpret, then sank back down again. Lesander's gaze slipped to Haneri, but quickly away again.

Her wife had been subdued since her meeting with Iata the night before, but Dressa hadn't pried open more than Lesander was willing to give.

And then Dressa held the door open for her mother to step into the bedroom, shutting it a little harder than necessary behind her.

"In a temper, are we?" Haneri said. She looked around, and...and Dressa had to cover her flusterment at the unmade bed, despite Lesander and her only sleeping next to each other just now. Nothing more. Not anything more, though Dressa's veins were burning for that *more* again, for both her and Lesander to get past what was between them—and *Adeius* she could not think those thoughts in front of her mother.

Haneri smirked. Turned back to her.

So Dressa went on the attack.

"What are your intentions with my—"

"With your father? He's not. He's the better person by far."

Dressa blinked rapidly. Was this thing between them new? Was it old?

"How long have you—have you two—"

"Dear daughter." Haneri clasped her hands, looked around, and slid back into her default mode, the cold and critical authority figure, aloof and never really a parent.

Which was an act. Dressa *knew* it was an act. She'd seen her mother around Iata, knew that Haneri was capable of feeling things other than spite.

"Don't you do that, Mother. Not to me. Not now."

Haneri only smiled.

Dressa stepped closer. "I need to know. You owe me that much—both of you—all of you think that you can keep me out of the loop when I'm one of the only reasons the kingdom is still holding on just now. You have to tell me what's going on!"

Haneri's face shifted. Just a subtle changing of tension in her facial muscles. But the spite was gone. And Dressa was talking to her mother. Actually her mother.

Her eyes stung and she let them. Because why did all of this have to be so hard? Everything was so hard just now.

"I love him," Haneri said. "That is the truth of it. He loves me. What we've done about that is not particularly your business, Dressa, any more than you'd like to tell me what you do in that bed over there—"

Adeius. She was burning again.

"—but Iata and I are going to make our marriage legal. To Homaj, of course. But, to him."

Dressa took that in.

And the way Haneri put just that tiny amount of tenderness in his name, on "him"—that tiny bit spoke volumes for her mother.

Haneri had hardly left his side since the attack. And Dressa had seen the way Iata looked at her mother. Her own father had never looked at her mother that way. There'd been nothing between them but the spite Haneri was so fond of.

And then there was that kiss, a lifetime ago. When Haneri had kissed Iata in the Reception Hall antechamber, and he'd kissed her back.

"Did you know it was him when you kissed him? That first time?"

"I always know when it's him. And that wasn't the first time."

Dressa bunched her hands into the sides of her skirt, slowly released them again. Steadied herself.

She looked at her mother, wanted to say...something. Something that would turn everything that was upside-down back right again.

She wanted...she wanted, what, affection? Like parents actually gave their children in the vid dramas? She didn't know if Haneri was capable of that. Or at least, not to her.

But who else could she talk to? Ceorre was busy keeping the kingdom from crumbling, and Ceorre was more practical, more pragmatic than Dressa would like. Pria had been giving Dressa meaningful glares that all amounted to *get rid of Lesander already*, and Dressa was very much over that. Lesander...well, Lesander was the problem, wasn't she? Dressa didn't have Rhys, and she desperately, desperately wished she did right now. But Rhys was two weeks away at the very best speeds.

Dressa briefly toyed with the notion of ordering Rhys home, she could do that. Iata might not even object. But—no. No, better Rhys not be here tangled in this mess if it all crumbled.

"You're doing your best," Haneri said.

Dressa refocused on her. Was her mother actually trying to give her a pep talk?

It broke the dam. Dressa shuddered, and oh no, she did *not* want to cry in front of her mother. Not the wrenching sobs that she felt trying to rise up. That she'd been smoothing away and shutting down for days now. This was not the right time. She didn't have the time for this at all.

Her mother froze. Went colder again, but Dressa knew it as a defense mechanism, not what was actually happening.

"I—" Dressa looked toward the closed door leading back to the prep room.

She strode toward Pria's room—empty at the moment—and her mother followed.

Dressa closed that door behind them, too.

She felt vaguely trapped in her own apartment, living with a woman who had tried to kill—and what was Iata to her, even? Her uncle, yes, but she'd started to think of him as a better version of her father. The father she'd never had a chance to have, because he'd been a controlling bastard—

"I started my first child," Dressa choked out.

Iata would know. He hadn't said anything, but he'd know.

Had he told Haneri?

But her mother often knew things, too. Far too much.

Her mother just nodded—then yes, she did know.

"Mine," Dressa said. "Not Lesander's."

Another nod.

Haneri stepped closer. Pressed a hesitant hand to Dressa's wet cheek.

The touch sent a jolt through Dressa, it was too much. Too different, too unexpected, too unknown.

She bit her lip to keep from screaming as she turned away.

And then stared at the wall for several minutes, trying to get herself back under control.

"You actually love your wife," her mother finally said. "This child—that's practical. And with the way a Javieri would be trained, Lesander might understand that. She knows what she did. She knows—Dressa, turn around. I'm not interested in talking to your back, and this is important."

Dressa sobbed a laugh, because yes, that was also her mother. No sugar-coating, not ever.

Her mother's eyes were burning. "There are two good things in this palace right now. You, and *him*. And now, there will be three. This child. It is a rotten, rotten world to bring a child into. But it's the world you have to give them, and you can only give them what you have. And you must do what you must do to keep them safe, to keep them from being swallowed up in this hell of a palace."

Dressa was shaking her head, hand to her mouth. "I shouldn't have even started, it was a moment of weakness—"

"No," Haneri said, with enough force to make her pause. "Do you know why I had five contract children started before I married Homaj? Every one of them but Rhys was to fend off an enemy of Delor before they could chip away at my family's power. And Rhys was to secure military favor and gain preference for a base on the Delor homeworld. It was my duty, Dressa, to protect my family. To help my family prosper. It is your duty now to protect yours. This system is rotten to its core, but it's still holding these worlds together. And you can't afford to let it fall. You can't afford to not have an heir that is yours and yours alone."

Dressa closed her eyes. That wasn't the answer she'd been looking for. She wasn't even sure if it helped. She didn't want it to be true.

And if it was true, if she accepted it as truth, would she end up like her mother? Bitter and with very little love left to give anyone?

She didn't want that with all her heart.

Dressa pursed her lips, studying her mother. Haneri was poised as always, her long braids wrapped up in an iridescent webbing, stabbed through with diamond combs, looking vaguely like one of Haneri's sculptures. And beneath it all, although there was fire in her eyes, Haneri looked...exhausted.

But then, they all were. It had been a very not-fun few days.

"Do you want me to be there? When you marry Iata?" Dressa asked.

It was her mother's turn to blink. And it took a moment, and Dressa saw the surprise on Haneri's immaculately composed face before she could stash it away.

"If you want."

Dressa nodded. "Okay. Let me know."

"And we should move up your wedding," Haneri said. "Official wedding. Within two weeks, I think, that might be the soonest possible for a public event. We do still need it to be a public event, even if a smaller and more manageable event. More secure. Still, it might be an excellent distraction for the people to latch on to."

"They'll think I'm preparing to take over the rulership," Dressa said, her insides going cold.

Her mother pressed her full lips tight. "It might be that, yes."

Haneri knew what the people thought of their ruler being a Green Magicker. Dressa knew. And Dressa couldn't lie to herself about how bad it was indefinitely, even if she needed to right now.

She nodded. Because what else could she do?

"Now let me into the back corridors," Haneri said, "I have to talk with Yan."

21

THE INVESTIGATION

*We pride ourselves that there is little crime on Hestia.
There is no need. Our cities and towns are filled with
ample resources for whoever would need them. People
come to our world to relax, and there's recreation in
abundance.*

— NIMARAN VER CINCRIN, ATTORNEY
GENERAL OF HESTIA, AS QUOTED IN AN
EDITORIAL PIECE FOR *HESTIAN HERITAGE*

He still hadn't Changed. It had been a brief and terse
fight with Zhang, who'd said he needed to be at his
clearest, and if he was uncomfortable, he wouldn't
be. But he'd tried to explain that he *needed* that discomfort right
now. Because it was something he could focus on that wasn't
everything else.

So they landed at the Windvale Estate landing pads—
which was a mostly empty field in desperate need of a mow—
with him trimly dressed as Shiera Keralan, mid-level administrator from Palace Rhialden, second to Captain Zhang of the

Seritarchus's personal guard. Zhang was the one who was actually in charge of this investigation, though he was in charge of sorting out the political angles.

This hierarchy would, he suspected, have the desired effect on Windvale's staff. Shiera, as a palace administrator, wasn't nearly as intimidating as Captain Vi Zhang in full and stoic captain-of-the-ruler's-personal-guard mode. And she hadn't spared any polish on her boots and uniform, either. All her abbreviated medals were on full display on her chest, her silver buttons shiny, black boots glossy.

Count Alix Badem, the newly minted Count of Windvale Estate, had landed the day before, and now greeted them at the landing field.

Badem was young, mid-twenties, with electric green hair that was plastered down in the stifling humidity on her light-brown face, her lips curved down in an irrepressible frown. She had a tattoo of a rose on her neck—a static ink tattoo, not holo.

Badem seemed more belligerent than cowed by the Valongrade officials who'd just landed on her doorstep. She even went so far as to help Onya, whose back was acting up again, into the hovercar, despite Onya's vivid and obvious aura. Which made her rise quite a few points in Maja's calculations.

"I've begun my own investigation, of course," Badem said, as the driver took them at a sedate pace in the—thank Adeius—air-conditioned car toward the estate house. "I found the staff in considerable disarray, although I've heard I have Duke Koldari to thank that they were not left in complete chaos. He left a report on my aunt's—well, my—desk, before he left, which I heard was also in some hurry. The Racha Guard impounded Imorie Rhialden méron Quevedo's ship, by the way, for their investigation. I can give you that paperwork as well."

Which was one of the loose ends he'd need to wrap up, yes. He'd sell the ship and arrange for the funds to be returned to the original owner, with extra for their silence—

No. No, Imorie's DNA would be all over it, wouldn't it, and they'd Changed on the ship, their Truthspoken DNA as Arianna would be there as well.

And he also didn't want the ship to become some vid feed billionaire's content focus for a month. Knowing the vid feed undermarket, that's probably who a ship associated with such a high-profile scandal would sell to.

He'd arrange for the *Jade Crescent* to be flown back to Valon, where it would be stripped, refit, cleaned of *all* DNA, and added to the palace's small reserve fleet.

In the hovercar, the new count fiddled with a nova heart ring on one finger. She sat across from him and Onya, with Zhang beside her, Zhang and her facing toward the back. Her entire posture was defensive.

Maja made his own posture attentive, non-judgmental. He usually was a bit more opinionated as Shiera, but this wasn't the right time. He had no intention of being sidelined here, but Zhang was playing her role well. He'd continue to be her second, not point on this mission.

Alix Badem looked up at Zhang. "Whatever my aunt did here, Captain, whatever horrible things she's done, and I'm trying to find it all out—I had no part in it. My family—we weren't close. My aunt had no children, I was her only heir." She smiled tightly, her fuchsia lipstick puckering around the edges. "I think she thought she'd just live forever." Alix shrugged.

Zhang asked, "Were there any cameras inside the interrogation room? This is something I particularly wish to know. Both of the victims were unable to complete their debriefings without significant trauma, and so we don't yet know what happened in its entirety."

Alix visibly swallowed. And Maja almost felt sorry for her, because he knew what it was like to be dropped into a tumultuous situation, having to clean up the messes of his elders, who were supposed to know better.

He leaned forward, took a gamble, and gently touched Alix's hand where she was gripping her knee. The count stiffened, but met his eyes.

He read the open fear there, at what he and Zhang represented, maybe, as those the Seritarchus had personally sent to investigate. Fear of what they might find, certainly. Fear of a permanently tarnished reputation and political disfavor before she even fully inhabited her new position. Maybe fear of criminal charges brought upon herself.

He drew back. He shouldn't have touched her.

He met Zhang's eyes, and hers widened slightly.

Beside him, Onya shifted. And did she sense what he was about to do?

He needed answers and needed them fast. He needed to know what had happened to Bettea, needed to know what these people knew. What the old Count Badem's lot had done to his child. He needed Alix's absolute cooperation. Could he get those things as Shiera Keralan? Could even Zhang get them, with all her weight as captain of the Seritarchus's personal guard?

Maybe.

But if he said he was Iata byr Rhialden, bloodservant to the Truthspoken?

Zhang caught his eyes again, gave a tiny shake of her head.

He drew in a long breath.

And if he said that, he might have his answers faster, but he'd also have to explain that bloodservants could Change. He'd only have to give up a secret that had been closely guarded for centuries.

That ominous feeling he'd had on the ship in Below Space hadn't lessened, and it was itching at him now, a thrumming drumbeat in his head pushing him to get in here, find what he needed, rescue Bettea if fae needed rescued, and leave. Go back to the capital as fast as he could, or...no. Go...where?

This wasn't him. Whatever this was, it was messing with his head.

Or, had he finally started to crack completely?

Rattled, he sat back, pulled his hands into his lap, and locked them tightly together.

"So," Zhang said, pulling Alix's frowning attention back to herself. "So Duke Koldari left. Do you know where he was headed?"

Maja shook himself, wrenched his thoughts back onto a more productive path. Was it what he knew was ahead of him that was throwing him off so completely? He needed to know what had happened at Windvale, but he also didn't want to know.

"Koldari said he was going to Valon," Alix said. "He also took his partner with him, Iwan ko Antia, if that's relevant, and Imorie's servant."

Adeius. Neither of them had asked about Bettea yet. He'd known Zhang would work the question in when the timing was right.

"The servant, Jis Ameer, went willingly with Koldari?" Zhang asked, without any particular emphasis. Just a part of the line of questioning. Even while his hairs stood on end.

And if Bettea was with Koldari, they might all be landing on Valon now. They could have crossed paths in Below Space. Damn the communications lag—though he'd still needed to come here.

"I suppose so, and I don't know why they wouldn't have gone with Koldari willingly, unless you have a reason?" Alix was looking less sure again.

Maja unlocked his hands to turn his palms up, sliding again into the role of comforter to Zhang's provoker, though it wasn't exactly in Shiera's nature.

"The captain is merely covering all angles, Ser Count, I'm sure you can understand. It's—" He glanced to Zhang. "This situation is tricky politically. With the ties to the Javieris, and the involvement of an unsealed magicker being coerced into—"

Alix lifted her chin. "Whatever ties my aunt had, I don't have them, I assure you. I have had no dealings at all with Green Magickers, and I don't intend to." Her gaze flicked to Onya Norren, who'd been mostly staring out the window. Not quite invisible, but not asserting her energy into the conversation, either. "Uh, with your forgiveness, Ser Magicker."

Onya shrugged. "No offense taken, Count Badem. I am here to replace the magicker who left their post in Racha. I'm not a part of this investigation."

Alix looked dubious, but nodded. Did she recognize Onya as the former First Magicker? Maja couldn't see anything more than ordinary suspicion around Green Magickers. He decided to count that as a no.

The car sighed to a stop on a circle of gravel outside the main house, and his stomach turned. Because here—here was where he'd sent Imorie, and here was where they'd been harmed.

22

THE GARAGE

"With enough rain, even flowers rot beneath their roots."

— UNKNOWN, COLLOQUIAL SAYING FROM THE
RACHA REGION ON HESTIA

Maja squinted up at the stone and steel monstrosity that was the Windvale estate house. All peaks and edges, razored in the sunlight. Modern fifty years ago, hardly fashionable even then. This was where sick people came to get well?

Well, he already knew this estate had claws.

He narrowed his eyes as he stepped out of the car.

"I will have my people see you to your rooms," Alix said, clasping her hands together through a now-forced hospitality.

"I would like to see the interrogation room first," Zhang said.

Maja's nails dug into his palms, but he didn't contradict Zhang. It would be better to have that part over with.

Alix went back to trying to hide being flustered, and now Onya came alongside her.

"I'll go into the house, dear, thank you. I'll be staying the night until I can catch a ride into the city tomorrow. It's too late in the afternoon otherwise."

Onya was hardly the gentle aging magicker she was presenting herself as. But the act effectively diverted Alix from her rising tension.

"Oh—yes. Yes, that's fine." Alix flagged down a porter who'd just stepped out and pointed toward the car's trunk. "Take care of the bags and see the magicker inside, I'm going with—I'm taking our other guests to the garage."

The porter visibly tensed, eyeing first Zhang, then Maja.

"Yes, Count Badem," they said, and quickly began to unload.

Was this person here before the old Count Badem's death? By the efficiency with which they pulled out the bags, setting them in a neat row on the ground, yes.

"Are you sure I can't persuade you to rest, first?" Alix asked Zhang. Pleaded, almost. "Have a meal? I'm sure it's much better to—"

"No, we're fine," Zhang said with a small smile.

Alix swallowed. But she nodded and began to lead the way on the path that wound around the main house toward the large garage on the right.

Maja took in everything, more surreptitiously than Zhang— it was supposed to be her job, not his, to find the hidden dangers. Shiera, as an administrator, wouldn't have that same training.

But the landscaping of the estate was well-kept, tropical foliage mixing with some more temperate foliage, all of it lush and competently trimmed. Vibrant flowers clustered around the walls of the house in strategic places, and a stone bench sat under a tree. Farther on, near a distant patio, he could hear either a stream or a fountain. Ryam the gardener had done good work—or had this been Eti's influence?

When they rounded the side of the house, he tried to see where Eti might have been caught and Bettea stunned. He marked the door to the kitchen, and the door which led to the hallway with Badem's office, where Imorie would have been dragged out. He thought he had them right.

But seeing these places, seeing Imorie's descriptions made real, only made the nausea rise.

They'd done those things to his *child*. And to Iata's child. And to a magicker they'd forced to illegally gather secrets for them. Eti had almost died to protect Imorie—for that, and because he and Imorie had attached themselves to each other, Maja would protect them both however he could. He'd help them get closure if he could.

The criminals here had also forced Imorie to give up who they were, an act of ultimate defeat for a Truthspoken, and that burned with a rage he didn't know how to quench.

Here. This had happened *here*.

The late Count Badem wasn't *this* Count Badem he was following now, he knew that. But knowing she was still a Badem, carried the same name and some resemblance to the images he'd seen of the Badem Eti had killed, was doing unwanted things to his head. To his rising, oncoming fury.

He flexed his hands.

Zhang glanced back at him, slowed her steps so she was beside him. She leaned close. "You don't have to see the inter-rogation—"

"I do," he hissed. His ears rang, drowning out the various bird calls around them. "Don't try to protect me."

"I'm concerned for our count's safety as well."

She pulled away again, and he swallowed.

He wasn't in charge here, and she wasn't his guard. Yes, if it came to it, he knew she'd protect him, but his dynamic with

Zhang was still changing. He had no rank here at all, no power except from genetics and long habit.

Maja set his mind to patterned breathing until his hands began to unclench.

Alix led the way into the large garage full of the estate's various cars, and his relief at being out of the heat again felt like a betrayal. She took them all the way past the cars to the back, to a hidden chamber, and then down a set of stairs. As Imorie had described.

Maja's dread grew with every step down. He didn't want to be here. He wanted to be *anywhere* but here.

Alix paused at the dim landing at the bottom of the stairs to unlock the door. Then they all stepped into a medium-sized room, which lit up with cool overhead lights as they entered.

He almost expected blood on the floor, but there was none.

He had the story, mostly, up until this point. He'd heard enough to want to murder everyone who'd held his child here himself. But they were all dead already, and that seemed intensely unjust. He wanted to resurrect them just so he could murder them again.

Which...was a ridiculous thought. Adeius.

He couldn't have stopped this, because he hadn't known it was happening.

But he could have stopped this. He could have not sent Imorie away. He could have not been a fucking insensitive *ass* and not let his child's illness be the reason he cast them aside.

No matter the consequences, no matter the shift in public perception that would have happened if the public learned the Heir had the Bruising Sleep. They could have weathered that, much better than they were weathering all the disasters that had followed his decision.

He was having to work hard to keep his eyes dry, his pulse steady, his breathing even.

Zhang's boot scuffed the floor, a deliberate redirection of his attention back to her. She met his eyes, a passing glance.

Steady. Adeius, steady.

There was a metal chair bolted to the concrete floor in the center of the room, with the crumbled remains of what had been shackles scattered around it.

Bile rose.

Zhang was looking up, looking all around. She'd pulled out a scanner and was searching for any signs of surveillance equipment, concealed or otherwise.

But after a moment, she shook her head.

"No surveillance."

So Badem hadn't wanted records of what had happened here—unless she or her people had carried recorders or cameras on their own persons.

Zhang asked, "Where are the bodies, and the personal items each had on them when they died? Were there any electronics found on their persons—"

"Racha's Municipal Guard came," Alix said. "Koldari called them, and they took the bodies and processed them. I did request the reports from them, but haven't received them yet. Koldari—Duke Koldari said in his note that he searched the bodies himself. He left the contents in my office, and he didn't allow the Guard to take those things, only catalog them. I can show you."

Zhang nodded, still scanning, while Maja tried both to take in everything and see nothing.

His child had sat there, in that chair, and been forced to give up their identity. Had known they would likely die. If Eti hadn't used his magics to kill, they might have.

No, would have.

He couldn't stop the nausea this time. He banged out the door, up the stairs, and sprinted to get out of the garage. Outside, in the too-bright sunlight, he bent over, hands on his knees, panting. Bile rose in his throat, but the retching wouldn't come.

He choked around a sob and almost wished it would. Because that would hurt less than the searing pain tearing through his heart just now.

He stood, hunched over, still shuddering. Just fucking retch already. Expel all the horror, the anger, the *guilt* that was wrenching him apart.

He'd let that one sob get past him, but he really just wanted to cry. That would be an entirely inappropriate reaction as Shiera, though. It hadn't been Shiera's child who'd been restrained to that chair. It hadn't been Shiera's child who'd been forced to give themselves up, who'd feared for their life.

It hadn't been Shiera's fault.

Vomiting, though, would be understandable for anyone who knew the particulars.

Maja heard a noise behind him and jerked around to see Zhang jogging toward him from the garage, looking disheveled. Had she run, too?

He didn't see Alix yet, though he doubted she'd be far behind.

Zhang stepped close. She wasn't supposed to be as publicly familiar with Shiera as he knew she'd want to be with him just now.

Maja blinked and felt his sense of gender shifting, and closed her eyes in exasperation. Well, at least she was already Shiera. She sighed, her perceptions realigning with her body.

Zhang paused, her eyes flicking between Maja's. Zhang knew her too well and gave the smallest nod of understanding.

"It's not your fault."

Maja closed her eyes against a growing flood.

Then she smoothed the tears away. Did her best to dip into enough of a trance to smooth away the nausea. And it left her, left her feeling numb in its absence. It felt almost like a betrayal.

But at least Bettea was gone and out of danger from those on the estate. Though she wasn't sure being in Kyran Koldari's hands was a great improvement.

Bettea had been alive when fae'd left, though. That was something.

That was a lot.

"Thank you, Captain," Maja said, straightening into a semblance of Shiera's usual confidence. "I'm...just not used to seeing a place of torture. We don't keep dungeons in Palace Rhialden." She smiled tightly. And it was a poor joke.

Zhang couldn't hide her own gray complexion. "It's not something I'd ever want to get used to." She placed a bracing hand on Maja's shoulder, a gesture between colleagues, and Maja had a moment's disorientation, wondering if Zhang was comforting her or trying to comfort herself.

Maja covered her hand, just briefly, shared a look.

Alix jogged up, her mouth a tight, distressed line.

"Forgive me," Alix said. "I read Koldari's report, I know what happened was horrific. We should go inside, I'll call for dinner—"

Maja pressed her hand to her stomach at the thought of dinner.

"Uh, or not." And then Alix just stood there, at a loss.

Zhang turned up her hand. "Not quite yet, I think, Ser Count. Thank you. Though if you could prepare it for an hour from now, that would suit. I will stay with Keralan. She will be fine shortly."

Maja just breathed. And she would be fine. She had to be.

23

IMPOSSIBLE

> *We have exhaustively researched all possible connections between the disease known as the Bruising Sleep and the physiological and religious condition known as Green Magics. Both conditions have evaded our attempts to research them, which is one of their similarities. We have been unable to make connections, however, beyond the superficial, and must therefore conclude that the few similarities are coincidence.*

> — S.D. PALLICA AND Q.M. VER KEITA IN
> "ASSUMPTIONS IN THE COMPARISON OF
> GREEN MAGICS AND THE BRUISING SLEEP"

The day after the Kidaa followed *Occam's Storm* into the border system it now patrolled, the captain collapsed on the bridge.

Rhys was there. They were still wearing their uniform, that hadn't changed, but the captain had insisted they pin the off-duty tag to their shirt front, as well as the collar tab that was reserved for government advisors. It was...well, embarrassing wasn't the right word. And everyone already knew who they were now. Maybe everyone expected this of someone of Rhys's rarified company.

They hated that so much it burned, but they were already well versed in ignoring the stares, the looks of resentment, as much as they still cut.

Captain Nantrayan was standing behind her chair, both arms braced on her chair back, glaring pensively at the three Kidaa ships centered on the viewscreen. Still following the *Storm* and correcting their heading to any turn the *Storm* made.

The silence from the Kidaa was growing deafening. It was, Rhys was beginning to suspect, an answer in itself.

The *Storm* was supposed to leave this star system at the end of the second watch today to go to the next system in the route, and normally, that would be routine. But the captain hadn't given any orders to prepare to move on.

And that was actually Rhys's decision, wasn't it? They hadn't talked to the captain about it yet. Rhys was pretty sure they were both stalling on that one.

Rhys had taken the station designed for political or military observers, to the captain's right. Which had been mostly vacant until this point.

And that was definitely not helping the stares. From people they knew, people they'd played games with and eaten meals with and joked with for months. People who looked at them now like they were a stranger.

And weren't they?

Rhys was also lost in thought, staring at the Kidaa ships, trying for the hundredth time to find something new to add to the unfinished pattern, when they heard a soft exhale. A minuscule rush of air. And then the muffled thump of someone hitting the deck.

Rhys was up, spinning around, dashing in the direction of the sound.

Growing up around Truthspoken, they'd been ever wary of an attack on their siblings, and had been trained by the Seritarchus's personal guards along with the Truthspoken and bloodservants on how to handle such situations. It was just part of living with Truthspoken.

They'd been through even more scenarios in their mind, thinking through what they would do if anything ever happened to Dressa, or Ari, or the Seritarchus, or their mother. How they would help and shield and protect.

There had been a few assassination attempts—mostly centered on the Seritarchus, and nothing that had come close to Rhys. Nothing that had been more than mildly dangerous.

But Rhys had always known the worst was a possibility. And they'd been thinking about it between bursts of thinking about the Kidaa—what might have happened to Homaj, and what they might have done if they'd been there. If they would have been able to help, to stop it.

Their danger reflexes kicked in now.

Rhys skidded onto their knees on the deck before they fully realized it was the captain who had fallen.

They caught their breath. Oh Adeius. The captain had collapsed.

They looked up—the bridge hadn't fully realized anything was wrong, though Rhys saw a comm tech at one of the rear stations rise.

"Captain—" the man said.

"Call the infirmary," Rhys barked. "Get a medical team up. She's collapsed."

And that did cause pandemonium. Not chaos—the crew was too well-trained for that—but a controlled and furious motion.

A weapons tech got down to cradle the captain's head with their hands, as Rhys felt her neck for her pulse. There, thank Adeius. She had a pulse.

They checked her breath, visually checked to make sure she hadn't broken anything obvious when she'd fallen.

She was breathing fine. Her pulse was a little fast, though.

Adeius, what had happened?

They looked up as medics flooded the bridge. Rhys jumped back when the medics shooed them off.

They swallowed. They weren't in the chain of command anymore—and their actual status hadn't been entirely communicated to the crew, just...observed. Rhys wasn't even sure where they fit in all of this themself. Except as the one who had the final say in anything regarding the situation with the Kidaa.

That chip in their pocket still showed a seal, though they hadn't shown it to anyone but the captain and Hamid. And Misha, late the night before, who'd stared at it with a sort of grim dread and asked, "Well, are you screwed? Are we screwed?"

Rhys seriously didn't know.

They glanced at the Kidaa ships on the viewscreen—no change. And why would there be?

"Sir," one of the bridge ensigns said. Rhys looked around them. They weren't the ranking officer here, there was an ops lieutenant who had always been off-shift from Rhys who was just now staring them down. But the lieutenant wasn't taking command. She was looking to Rhys.

They were all looking to Rhys, because Rhys had been sitting next to the captain. Because Rhys was known, now, as someone who stood in the corridors of power. Who might actually know what to do—never mind that a few days ago most of these people wouldn't have trusted Rhys to do their laundry if asked.

Rhys swallowed.

Should they accept that assumption of command?

But someone had to, even if only until this was sorted out.

"Call Commander Gian to the bridge," Rhys said. "I—"

They watched the medics pushing the captain out on a hover gurney. "I'm going with the captain."

But that solution, they found when they reached the infirmary, wasn't as simple as they'd hoped. Because Commander Gian was already there, his chair beside a medical bed in an open cubicle, trying frantically to wipe off the glow of green around him.

Rhys stopped short just inside the hatch, gaping before they caught themself and snapped their mouth shut.

What the *hell?*

Every hair they had made itself known. Their gut churned with a deep and building foreboding.

"You have to be able to do something!" Gian was shouting to two medics hovering over him.

Commander Gian had manifested Green Magics? Adeius, what? That had to be—no, that shouldn't be—

Gian's eyes locked on theirs. "Petrava! What happened with the captain?"

"I—"

Rhys took a breath, centered. Pretended they were in the middle of an imaginary crisis with their siblings, and everything they said mattered. Every nuance of posture, every twitch, every syllable. This was a game.

It was easier if they could pretend this was a game. Just for a little. To let their screaming mind catch up.

"She collapsed," Rhys said, a little breathless. Because that's what they should be. "It happened seven or eight minutes ago."

"I know that," Gian snapped. "The bridge called down." His eyes were glassy, and he looked perilously close to a panic attack.

No, no, he was already having a panic attack.

Rhys stepped closer. "Commander, what—"

"Stay *back* Petrava! Nothing like this happened before you came on board!"

That wasn't fair, Rhys had been on the ship for six months before they'd gone back to Valon. That all of this had started when they'd returned had to be coincidence.

The fact that it wasn't coincidence, and that Rhys felt the pattern of that fact to their core, was something they couldn't deal with yet.

Because no one could give anyone Green Magics.

No one.

They turned as the medics transferred the captain to a bed on the other side of the room from Gian, then pulled the curtain mostly closed around her.

Rhys moved toward the opening to the captain's cubicle. There was something they needed to know. Very much needed to know, because there was another impossible piece fitting into their pattern.

"Do you know what's wrong?" Rhys asked as the ship's doctor breezed past them into the cubicle.

"Lieutenant," the doctor said, without looking back, "I haven't looked at her yet. And you need to be gone." He pulled the curtain tight.

Rhys touched their shirt pocket, thought about bringing out the Seritarchus's seal. It would, at least, get them answers, if there were any answers to give.

But that would be overkill. That was the wrong move, a very wrong move.

"Check for the Bruising Sleep," Rhys said through the curtain, their throat tightening around the words.

The doctor poked out of the cubicle again, gave them a sharp look, then snapped his finger and pointed emphatically *away* from the cubicle.

Rhys backed up, stood in the center of the infirmary, thoughts whirling. Their gaze fell back on Commander Gian, who was hunching in on himself, breaths heavy. His newly acquired aura still flaring in jagged spikes of jade green.

Gian was watching Rhys with teeth bared. Was he in pain? Rhys had no idea if manifestation was painful. They'd never thought to ask the few magickers they knew—and it hadn't felt like a decent question to ask Misha. Not when she hadn't even shared anything about her own family.

Rhys crossed to the wall comm. They flicked to shipwide, emergency channel. "Magicker Moratu to the infirmary."

"Don't—" Gian growled, but he was shivering now, arms wrapped around himself. Rhys didn't like him, not especially after this last week, but it made them sick to see him so vulnerable. His chair rattled softly with the movements.

Rhys thought about pulling the curtain to Gian's cubicle closed, but Gian kept looking to Rhys as if Rhys might be able to do something. Adeius—what?

How were they supposed to know what to do? Adeius, what should they do? The captain and first officer had been incapacitated in, what, minutes?

They thought of the three Kidaa ships still behind the *Storm,* steadily maintaining their stations.

Rhys swallowed.

With the captain and the first officer out of play, Lt. Commander Hamid would be in command.

Okay, and so Rhys could do something about that. Hamid wouldn't know what had happened, or she'd already be here.

They went back to the comm. "Commander Hamid to the infirmary."

And then, they waited. Because they were absolutely sure that Gian wouldn't let them try to do anything to comfort him, if Rhys even could. Maybe Rhys being here was enough—Gian still kept looking their way, and it seemed to steady him. Even if Rhys was currently who he was trying to blame.

The medical sounds from the captain's cubicle continued, but didn't really change. Low chatter, the clicks and beeps and whirs of instruments and sensors.

A medic came back to Gian and tried to give him a sedative, but he smacked their hand away—and then cried out as he bent over, both hands pressed to his stomach.

Violence. Shit. Magickers couldn't do violence.

Misha arrived first, panting, her cheeks flushed. She took one look at Commander Gian, gaped at Rhys for a solid three seconds, then rushed forward.

"Commander, Commander, I'm here. I'm here. Let me take your hand, okay? Please, sir? I can help with this. I can help you through it. I've done this before, with myself, and one of my fathers is a magicker, and my younger brother. We've all done this before. It's scary at first, but that will fade—"

"Don't patronize me, Ensign," Gian growled. But he did take her hand. "I just need you to make it go away."

Rhys turned away at the helpless break in Gian's voice. Adeius, they didn't want to witness this.

The smell of fear, of panic, in this room was making them nauseous.

Misha tugged Gian's curtain halfway closed, but Rhys could still see them both, and maybe Misha was keeping that avenue open if she needed help. Commander Gian was difficult on a good day.

Misha didn't answer Gian's demand to make it go away. There was no answer to that demand. Because if no one could give anyone Green Magics, no one could take them away again, either.

Except.

Except the captain and the first officer.

At the same time.

Just now.

Rhys moved to the captain's cubicle again.

"Doctor—"

The doctor pushed aside the curtain, thick brows pinched. "How did you know?"

Rhys blinked, took in a breath. "Is it the Bruising Sleep?"

"Lieutenant, you don't have a right to know that—but, yes. It is. Now I'm asking you, how did you know? I make a habit of checking up on the captain's health every week, and she's shown no signs of any illness."

The Bruising Sleep, though, could onset itself at any time, at any strength. And it also couldn't be given or taken away by any means that medical science knew—it was the only disease that had ever so thoroughly evaded Human understanding. The only one.

And *Human* understanding.

Rhys took a step back. "I—someone in my family has it. I watched them collapse before, I've seen this before—"

They'd realized that, thinking through everything that had happened with Ari. They had seen that, though hadn't been overly willing to tease it all the way out in their mind—the Bruising Sleep was supposed to be a common illness, but of course that was bullshit. But Rhys had still been hoping another answer would present itself.

But now...it fit the pattern. And what had happened with the captain fit the pattern. Rhys still wasn't entirely sure what that pattern was or what it meant, but it was coming together.

"Well," the doctor said, wiping at his forehead, "thank you, that saved me a few hours of preliminary tests before treatment, though I should run them anyway. It's a raw deal, I'm sure you know, but I do have the means for treatment here, if keeping it from worsening, at least. We'll need better facilities for her to truly make progress. They don't generally give the expensive drugs to the Navy." A grimace.

And Rhys understood. The captain's career in the Navy was effectively over, or at least, would be significantly paused. Would be different on the other side of this.

Rhys had a moment to wonder why the doctor would give

them that much information, before Commander Hamid
breezed into the infirmary.

She looked around—and froze when she saw Gian leaning
close to Misha, which she could better see at her vantage. Did
she see his aura?

Oh. Yes, she definitely saw it. She whirled and found Rhys,
and was already striding toward them as they hurried over to
her. The storm in her eyes a shield for her fear.

"Lieutenant, what the *fuck* is going on?" Her voice was low,
jagged. "I heard the captain collapsed. And Gian?"

"Commander Hamid." Rhys fought the urge to bow instead
of salute. Their capital training, which was holding back the
tide of their own panic, warred with their military training.
"Captain Nantrayan collapsed on the bridge, yes—the doctor
said she has the Bruising Sleep. Commander Gian just, uh,
manifested. I don't know the details there."

Hamid pressed a fist to her mouth, took a second to
breathe, focused more sharply on Rhys's face.

"Both of them?"

"Yes."

"At the same time?"

"As close to it. Maybe exactly."

Hamid's face contorted, and Rhys nodded.

"That doesn't feel like the random chance it should be," she
managed. And Rhys nodded again.

There. Now that someone else had said it, they couldn't
pretend it wasn't real any longer.

Hamid might not have Rhys's training in evaku and social
patterns, but she was ops through and through, she made it a
point to know every detail of what was going on around her.
And she knew how to draw conclusions from that data, too, and
apply them to the day-to-day running of the ship.

"No, sir," Rhys said. "It doesn't feel like coincidence."

They stared at each other.

Occam's Storm was being followed by three Kidaa ships, one of which had contacted them before. And the Kidaa had followed them here, to this system—Rhys didn't think the system was as important to the Kidaa as the *Storm* itself. And the people on it.

Rhys.

Their two commanding officers had just, suddenly, and at the same time, been beset with the two conditions that had foiled any attempt to explain them for decades or centuries. Green Magics, especially, had been around before the Humans had even met the Kidaa, the Bruising Sleep something that had started to become a rising epidemic twenty or thirty years ago, though it had been identified as a disease for much longer. Rhys would need to look into that more.

Ari had the Bruising Sleep. Ari had manifested Green Magics, too. Ari had been on a path to becoming the most powerful person in the kingdom.

And Kidaa always knew the leaders of a ship. Always, unerringly, overlapped to the leaders.

Rhys remembered from studies growing up that there wasn't supposed to be a link between magics and the Bruising Sleep disease, despite a few similarities in how they both randomly manifested and had no known antidotes—but that didn't mean there weren't links.

Kidaa weren't supposed to follow border ships and identify people who'd grown up around Truthspoken, either.

And now?

Was this possibly an attack by the Kidaa? Had the Kidaa figured out a way to give someone Green Magics, or give them the Bruising Sleep?

And *why?* Green Magics weren't a disease, though they'd affect social standing, and certainly would change someone's life.

They could also effectively keep someone from doing

violence. If every Valoran became a magicker, none of them could fight.

Was this, then, a painfully slow and centuries' long invasion? Did that make sense?

No. Maybe—well, no. It didn't fit anything Rhys knew about the Kidaa, and even if humanity's base assumptions about the Kidaa were deeply, fatally flawed, they couldn't have gotten every detail wrong.

So could the Kidaa trigger whatever happened to make someone a magicker?

Or...and Rhys had to clamp down hard on their emotions to keep from shaking themself. Was it possible that Green Magics was a thing that had originated with the Kidaa, even?

Misha had said she'd felt the Kidaa's minds when their ships had overlapped. And that they might have felt her mind back.

Hamid snapped her fingers in front of Rhys, and Rhys jumped.

"Petrava. What are you thinking?"

They swallowed. "Why not—if the Kidaa can give people Green Magics, and give people the Bruising Sleep, and they gave both to the ship's commanders—why not instead give them to me?"

They shuddered as the thought fully formed. Because it was built on impossible premises, and their whole paradigm of everything they knew was shifting in that moment.

Hamid blinked. Hesitated. She was struggling with these conclusions, too.

"Because not everything revolves around you, Petrava," she said. Though there was no heat to it.

And Rhys wasn't sure it was true.

"Go back to the bridge," Hamid said. "If the Kidaa twitch—use your discretion. And tell me immediately. I need to talk to Gian and the doctor, then I'll be up."

Rhys nodded, because that was the only response. There was no "yes, sir," because they weren't in her chain of command anymore. And that she was giving them the bridge drove that home. Their calling her "sir" earlier had been a mistake in the moment.

"I'll keep you informed," Rhys said.

24

STATUS CHANGE

Every contact we have ever had with the Kidaa has been peaceful.

— ADMIRAL BRYNC QUACH IN HER REPORT
"THE STATE OF AFFAIRS WITH THE KIDAA"

R hys sat rigidly on the alert in the bridge observer's seat for an hour. They couldn't bring themself to sit in the command chair, even if Hamid had given them the watch.

And then when Hamid came to the bridge, looking grim, they waited another hour with her. And then another more. The entire bridge crew of the *Storm* humming with the sort of tension that cracked the soul.

No alert lights were on. No visible signs that they were all in imminent danger. No real understanding of what that danger was, or could be.

And nothing happened. The bulky, blocky Kidaa ships didn't move from their stations. They didn't try to overlap, or signal. There was no attack—and Rhys didn't know what a

Kidaa attack in space would look like, anyway.

Unless it had already happened.

In those three hours, Rhys silently ran through hundreds of scenarios, of reasons, of possibilities, trying to find the edges of the pattern. The attacks carving runes to the lyrics of a rock song. The overlap with *Occam's Storm* and trying to —what—warn Rhys? Warn Valoris? Warn Humans in general? About what? And now what had happened to the captain and commander, the Bruising Sleep and Green Magics.

None of it was coincidence. Rhys knew that with the same growing certainty that Ari having both the Bruising Sleep and now Green Magics, and Homaj now manifesting Green Magics, couldn't be coincidence.

Their family. This had hit their family. The Kidaa had... what...attacked their family?

And what if the Kidaa *had* been attacking Valoris for centuries, and the Humans hadn't known enough to call it a war? Context was everything.

Were the Kidaa trying to talk to Rhys to negotiate a cease fire? *We have spun, you have spun.* Adeius, if they only knew what those untranslatable parts were.

Or was that the wrong context, too, was all of this just a precursor of something much more ominous to come?

The pattern in their mind still fit the idea that the Kidaa were trying to warn them of something. And Rhys wasn't sure that was the less terrifying of possibilities.

Rhys quietly tapped on the arm of their chair and stared at the viewscreen. The Kidaa ships in this aft view were so unmoved in their course they could have been a painting.

And all of this, the not knowing, the lack of definable actions to take, the impossibilities, was keeping them so tense their neck ached just sitting there.

And it was their call. What they did from here, whether the

Storm should run now or stay and deal with whatever else the Kidaa dealt to them, was Rhys's call.

It was Rhys's decision.

And even if the captain hadn't been in the infirmary, and Commander Gian had still been fit for duty, it would still be Rhys's call.

They hadn't sent word back to Valon yet, and they didn't think Hamid had, either. They'd watched her, and she hadn't done anything like touch the comm controls. From the way she'd come in earlier, all disheveled and her short hair mussed and uniform slightly askew, Rhys was almost certain she'd come straight from the infirmary. Escaped from the chaos of the infirmary, more like.

And when they sent back to Valon, what could they say? That the Kidaa had attacked the ship by giving the captain the Bruising Sleep, and making the first officer a magicker? It was even more ludicrous than the Kidaa using a rock song to communicate. If anyone believed them—and just now, after the attack on the Seritarchus they might—it could cause utter chaos.

But if the Kidaa could influence things from a distance, the minimum six days of travel back to Valon, even at the highest possible military speeds, might still not be fast enough to warn Valon of what might be coming.

What was possibly already here.

Commander Hamid's looks in their direction were growing less surreptitious and more frequent. Less patient.

This was Rhys's call, and they had to make it soon. Either the *Storm* ran to Valon to give their world-shattering but extremely vague and circumstantial information, keeping the crew theoretically safer than they were now, or they stayed. And waited to see what the Kidaa would do next, Adeius help them all.

Rhys slowly stood. These last three hours, the bridge had

mostly worked in silent efficiency. The only sounds the clip of reports and orders. The hum of the ship's systems and all the things no one was willing to say out loud.

Rhys didn't want to break that fragile calm. Didn't, Adeius, want to order Hamid to do anything. They wanted to go climb in bed, pull the covers up, and pretend that none of this was happening at all.

Hamid watched them stand, hesitated only a moment, maybe warring with the broken chain of command, then set her jaw and rose, too.

She handed command of the bridge off, gave Rhys a hard look on the way out, and then pulled ahead to lead them toward the senior officer's quarters. Her own quarters.

Neither of them spoke on the way. What they needed to say was much, much too volatile for that.

Hamid slapped open her hatch and waved Rhys inside, then stood rigid, gripping both arms. Looking younger than she was, and scared.

Rhys swallowed—Hamid had always been unshakable. And just now—just now she was looking to them. As if they might possibly have the answers.

Rhys glanced around, stalling, their fingers drumming a tight pattern on their pants leg.

They'd never been in Hamid's quarters, they'd never had a need to. The space wasn't much larger than the space they shared with Misha—it wasn't a large ship. But like Rhys, Hamid's private spaces were full of the personality she didn't share in public, like the holo tattoo that she kept mostly hidden beneath her collar. Her quarters overflowed with colorful prints and rugs, a deep blue bedspread on the double-wide bunk, a striped orange towel by the extended sink drawer. She had a private washroom, and of that, Rhys was envious.

When Hamid didn't say anything, Rhys took a breath.

"Commander—"

"Drop the junior officer act, Petrava, I am in no mood."

They stiffened, but nodded. They hadn't, really, been trying that hard to maintain that personality. Habit, mostly.

"Commander," they said, with an entirely different inflection, and Hamid's mouth pulled tight.

How the hell did she want them to relate to her?

They forged on.

"I've been thinking through everything, and what information we have—"

"And?"

Rhys swallowed. "Either they've been attacking us with Green Magics and the Bruising Sleep for a long time, or both of these things are something our species share that they also know how to trigger at will though we still don't, or they're using these things as a means to try to wake us up to whatever they're trying to warn us about. Or, as a means to communicate —Misha said she could feel Kidaa minds, and there might be something in that, too. Maybe giving Commander Gian Green Magics was an attempt to bridge our communication gap."

"But then the captain?" Hamid asked. "What possible use could they have for giving her a debilitating illness?"

"I—" Rhys spread their hands. And Ari, too. Why give Ari both? "I'm only telling you what might be possible." They saw more possibilities than that, but these were the most prominent in their mind. The ones that made any kind of sense in the pattern.

Hamid passed an unsteady hand across her eyes. Muttered, "Fucking stars and all their hells."

Rhys shrugged their helpless agreement.

"So we don't even know if it's an attack, I mean something done with malicious intent," Hamid said. "We still don't fucking know what the Kidaa are intending with all of this, and we don't have enough information to make a solid plan, but we can't just keep waiting, Petrava. We can't not send to Valon, and we can't keep the crew in danger. I don't want anyone else to manifest, or get sick—"

"I know," Rhys said, fighting to keep their calm. "And agreed. If I send under the seal, it will give us better encryption and higher message priority, reach the Seritarchus the fastest." They paused. "But a message coming from the border under that seal could cause its own panic." And further implicate them in all the wrong kinds of plots from the capital just now. Commander Gian hadn't been wrong that all of this looked bad.

They could try to use Truthspoken inference code so no one could actually read the message if it was intercepted, as no interstellar comms were completely unhackable. They'd played enough games with Dressa that they were pretty sure they could get the context right so she'd understand. But how did you convey that the Kidaa had given two people conditions that were absolutely impossible to give? How could you say that through context, or convey the intense dread of what was going on without being able to say just what you were afraid of?

"So do we skip sending the message and carry it ourselves?" Hamid asked, watching them closely. Deferring to them, yes, but she was bracing for Rhys's no, and preparing to argue.

It was the argument Rhys had been having with themself.

This information was hot, so hot that Rhys felt like they were standing in the center of a volcano about to erupt. If they sent it or took it back with them with the ship and all its crew, either way it had to go to Valon as soon as possible. Rhys couldn't justify delaying any longer.

But the Kidaa were here. And Rhys was here. That argument hadn't changed. Those reasons for staying hadn't changed.

And whatever else was happening, the Kidaa were trying to communicate...something.

So Rhys was back to the same problem as before, if amplified a hundred-fold. Go back to Valon, or stay at the border and try to find out what the Kidaa were actually after?

Commander Hamid shifted, her eyes narrowing. "Petrava, our commander—both of our commanders—have just been taken out. Off the effective board. I spoke to the doctor, and Captain Nantrayan will need to remain resting as much as possible because stress will trigger and exacerbate the illness. And Commander Gian can't command a military ship, especially in this kind of situation that might require violence, Adeius help us all. He can't. So that leaves me, and you. And the other hundred and eight people on this ship. Against three Kidaa ships, who've already demonstrated they can attack us without firing a shot—"

"We don't know it's an attack—"

Hamid's face screwed up. "Petrava! Two people's lives were just destroyed—they are my commanders, Rhys, and my colleagues, and they're yours, too—"

Did she think they were being unfeeling, weighing all the possible outcomes before they made their decision? Or was she assuming that because Rhys was who they were, growing up the way they had, that they'd been taught not to care? That everyone to Rhys was just a piece on a board to move at will? Was that how she saw them?

That shouldn't have hurt just now, of all times, as much as it did.

Of course Rhys cared. They cared so much they'd barely been sleeping this whole last week trying to connect the pieces, trying to understand. Knowing that so much might hinge on it.

They kept checking the people around them to make sure no one had spontaneously manifested an aura, or come down sick with the Bruising Sleep. They'd checked their own hands more than a few times themself, half expecting to see green at some point.

But it was their decision to leave or stay, and they hadn't yet made that call. They knew the responsibility here, and they knew some of the possible costs. Just because they needed to make a decision on which terror to run with, which risk to embrace, didn't mean they didn't care about the people behind the variables. Adeius, they cared.

But they couldn't give in to their emotions. They couldn't. They couldn't crumble.

Rhys knew Homaj Rhialden was a bastard. And just now... they were feeling, just a bit, the other side of having that kind of authority. Of everyone looking to them to have some kind of answers.

And maybe they weren't showing it, but they were *scared*. Adeius, oh Adeius they were scared.

Hamid held up her hands again. "Okay. Okay, I get that this is a lot. So, you think they're still trying to warn us, or get us to do whatever they wanted us to do before. So how in the worlds does that help their cause to turn around and attack our ship's commanders?"

"I don't know—"

"You *have* to know, Petrava, we're—"

"I don't know!"

They flinched, because that was a loss of control, and they desperately needed control right now. Rhys flexed their hands at their sides and glanced around, but there was no real space in the furniture-cramped cabin to move about. No good excuse to. So instead they crossed their arms, pressed tightly against themself, as Hamid had earlier, and wished...wished they'd never shown that damned seal.

No, that wasn't true. They wished they didn't know what they knew, wished they weren't a semi-royal masquerading as a semi-competent lieutenant, wished that they weren't the person the Kidaa had singled out for whatever they wanted.

And...no. None of that was really true, either.

They wished that a part of them didn't thrill a bit to be

standing in the center. To having, for once in their life, a responsibility that was actually important. Something more than just being a semi-royal sibling to Truthspoken.

Rhys drew a long, long breath.

Hamid recrossed her arms, too, her brows up.

And she was right, what the Kidaa had done to the captain and commander didn't make sense in the context of everything else. Why go through all of the *strenuous* trouble to carve out lyrics to a Rings of Vietor song on half a dozen worlds and then just...attack the people they were trying to reach? Rhys didn't have the context yet, but that context did exist. They knew it had to.

"I don't know," Rhys said again, more quietly this time. "No one knows. And that's why we have to stay, just a little longer, and try to understand—"

Hamid opened her hands, turning a tight circle. "Adeius, Petrava! I won't risk any more of this crew, not a single one—"

"Then why are you even asking me—"

"Because you hold our lives in your hands—"

"And I won't risk the worlds!" Rhys roared back. "They're all at risk! Commander—" They paused, licked their lips, tried to tamp down their terrified fury. "It's my family, too. It's all of their lives, all of the kingdom's. The Kidaa can already do this from a distance, they did it to my sibling, gave Ari the Bruising Sleep and Green Magics both."

Hamid reared back, shock registering. The rumors had been floating, yes, that Imorie Rhialden méron Quevedo was in fact Arianna Rhialden. There had been a few lesser, more malicious rumors about Ari also having the Bruising Sleep, someone on the crew knowing someone's uncle that had gone to Hestia to be treated. Those rumors had felt gleeful that a Rhialden, even a minor Rhialden, might have contracted an illness usually reserved for the lower classes.

"And the Seritarchus?" Hamid finally asked.

"It can't be a coincidence, either. There's just...no way his manifesting now is a coincidence. Even if he was attacked."

Hamid's face pinched. For all her usual presence, she looked like she wanted to cry. And Rhys understood. Oh Adeius, they understood.

But they held themself together. They kept their face as clear of their own fears again as they could. And they didn't particularly care that they were pulling from both Homaj's and Ari's gestural playbooks now, it was steadying them in the moment. Giving them just enough courage to do what they needed to do.

Hamid rubbed her neck, rippling her holo tattoo from the pale lines Rhys usually saw through deep red and orange. Was it a dragon? Even with her collar pushed down a bit, Rhys still couldn't see much.

It was an anchoring detail. A strange and comforting counterpoint of normalcy to the hurricane going on in their head.

"Is it a dragon?" Rhys asked.

Hamid froze, staring at them like they were crazy. Then she looked down, as if she could see her neck. She pulled down her collar. "It's my fucking cat. That I had to leave with my partner, and I miss."

And Rhys didn't know why that, of all things, made the tears sting.

Hamid let go of her collar, looked away. Cleared her throat.

"Look, Petrava. I know my work, and I know when I'm outclassed. I know you're not Truthspoken. I get that. But your training, whatever it is, lets you see patterns that I just can't pull together yet. You knew this was coming before it did—all of this with the Kidaa. So—if you say we need to stay, then we'll stay. I will trust you in this. I am with you in this."

Rhys gave a tight nod, their throat swelling again now for a different reason.

And maybe they weren't looking at the Human picture as

much as they should be, too. Hamid had a partner. She had a pet tattooed on her neck. She was a person, and so were the rest of the people on this ship. And all of those people, any of them, could be given the Bruising Sleep, or Green Magics. Their lives pushed into directions beyond their control.

Or worse. Just because the Kidaa had never been known to kill didn't mean they never would. Rhys was sure of that now, too.

Their heart was pounding again. And they might be using their evaku training to hold themself together, but no amount of evaku training without Change could help calm their screaming body. Their body that wished so hard right now to run away.

Staying kept the crew in danger. And getting this information back to Valon was as absolutely essential as anything Rhys had ever done in their life. But a message sent through interstellar comms wasn't enough—not enough context, not enough information without the risk of causing kingdom-wide panic. Yes, staying could also mean more information. But...but.

Rhys cleared their throat. Coughed, and pressed a palm to their chest to hold themself together. "We'll stay until the end of the third watch. If nothing happens with the Kidaa by then—"

"We send back to Valon either way," Hamid said.

"Yes. I'll go work on the inference code now."

Hamid breathed out an exasperated sigh. "Of course you'd know how to do that."

"My siblings," they said. "Did you play games with your siblings? Do you have siblings?" They hoped that wasn't a sore subject like the cat.

"I have three. And not those sorts of games, Petrava. We actually played sensible games for growing children."

They shared a tight smile, an understanding, even. It was a

weird moment. And Rhys wanted more than ever to melt away into the background, to hide.

They were not normal. They were not and never would be, and they'd been such a fool to try.

Trying to be normal had brought them here. And they were holding themself together with every trick they knew, but beneath it all, not far beneath it all, twelve-year-old Rhys was suddenly, again, having to confront the reality that they were alone. So very much alone in a world that didn't want them.

They touched the chip in their pocket and didn't bother to be subtle about it.

Hamid noticed, but she didn't say anything. She just waited, while Rhys remembered what the Seritarchus had said. Homaj Rhialden had said he trusted them.

Homaj did nothing without purpose. Nothing at all. Rhys had replayed that short recording in their thoughts between everything else, in between other much more urgent thoughts. That recording, too, was keeping them together. And freaking them the hell out.

Because Homaj Rhialden would never have let Rhys into his household, would never have allowed them to train alongside their siblings, if he hadn't had a purpose in that, too.

"Petrava, we'll do our jobs. Do them well. We'll get this crew safely home, and get the information safely home."

And though they knew she was still deferring to them, with that seal in their pocket, with who they were and what they knew, Rhys was glad, so glad, that she wasn't laying this entirely on them. *We'll* get this crew home. *We.*

"Well," Hamid said, "and if anyone else manifests magics or gets sick before then, I want to leave right away. It's an enormous risk as it is." She kneaded her hands together, then seemed to realized she was doing it and dropped them to her sides. "And if not even the Seritarchus is safe from the Kidaa, if this is really happening, then Adeius help us all."

Rhys wholeheartedly agreed with that sentiment.

And if they'd given themself the deadline of the end of third watch, and it was mid-second watch now, Rhys wished they had some way—any way—to clearly to convey to the Kidaa their dismay. Their confusion. Their fear, even. To try to understand exactly what the Kidaa were thinking. What this was about, what any of it was about.

They could try the maneuvering code again, but that hadn't worked when the Kidaa had followed the *Storm* in-system. Could Rhys possibly think it would work now? No one had tried after the captain and Gian had gone down. And there was the risk it might provoke the Kidaa further, because they were way off any known precedents and procedures now.

But Rhys had to try. They had to know more, if they could. Try one last time to talk to the Kidaa before they left.

Rhys straightened, and Hamid raised her brows.

"I'm not going to like what you just decided, am I?"

Rhys coughed. "I want to go signal that we want to talk. Just one more time. A few more times."

Hamid considered a long moment. Rhys wasn't making it an order. Adeius. They wouldn't do that.

But they wouldn't back down on this one. Not before they took the *Storm* back into Below Space and completely left behind their chance for answers that might be vital, absolutely vital, for protecting the kingdom.

Hamid waved toward the hatch. "All right. Ship is yours."

25

THE CRASH

So maybe you should just lean into the wind, remember who you are.

— OLUN SHIRALL IN THE VID DRAMA *NOVA HEARTS*, SEASON 3, EPISODE 4, "HIGH PLACES, LOW PLACES"

They'd been through the Windvale records, and the records weren't as thorough as Maja would have liked, but there were encrypted sections they'd take back to Valon for the forensic experts.

They'd been to Racha. They'd talked to the Racha Guard and retraced the steps of the chase, so now Maja had a picture of his child being hunted in public. But he also, finally, had a better picture of what had happened in the city.

He was somewhat male again—his gender had tilted back a few hours after his freakout outside the garage, and then taken its usual sliding course through somewhat male to a little more male to mostly male to just a tiny bit male and around again.

His presentation had stayed firmly femme as Shiera Keralan, but that was a choice, and it grounded him.

And today, he'd interviewed a good portion of the Windvale staff, those who hadn't left. He'd heard a lot about how they'd thought something was a little off, but they hadn't known what, and hadn't thought to ask. Or maybe had been afraid to ask. Those who were truly guilty had fled.

And the Javieri involvement? The estate's comm logs were part of the encrypted data, and some communication might have been done from Badem's personal comm, which conveniently hadn't been tied into the estate's network. And which hadn't been in the small pile of personal effects found on the bodies. Anything relevant to the Javieris had probably been taken by the fleeing staff. Those who'd chased Imorie and Eti into Racha had also fled.

Maja could read when someone was lying, and he hadn't at all felt the need to bring Onya into these interviews. These people were obviously not the enemies he was after.

He had found a scalpel. And he'd stared at that scalpel a long, long time.

He did have names, though, of the staff that were missing. That was something.

And Adeius, Maja wanted to be off this world, wanted to be back on Valon, wanted to be near his child so that they didn't have to feel alone through this. He shouldn't have left, he knew that now. He'd had to leave, yes, someone had to come here. But maybe it shouldn't have been him.

He'd been running. Again.

"Hey." Zhang squeezed his shoulder where he sat on the made bed in his room at Windvale. Her room was beside his, but not adjoining. But they'd come to his room to lay out what information they had and figure out what to do next.

"You need a break," Zhang said. And it was more order than observation.

He snorted, fell backward on the bed to stare up at the ceiling. "Maybe."

Did he? Where could he go on the estate, or even in the city, that wouldn't remind him of what had happened here? His total and immense failure?

"Really," Zhang said. "The estate has trails—there are hoverbikes in the shed. We can take two, go out for a few hours."

He stared up at her incredulously. "Am I supposed to have *fun*?" There was no way. Absolutely no way.

"You're supposed to get out of your head for a few hours. I don't care if you have fun. But we're here, it's a resort world. Or we can go to another estate. I don't care."

He sat up again, tugging on the thin chain of the necklace he wore, one of Shiera's lockets. Her only bend to sentimentality.

Maja caught the tightness around Zhang's eyes, the tension in her own neck.

He *did* need to get out of his own head if he was forgetting how much this affected Zhang, too. Zhang had watched Imorie grow up right alongside him. She wasn't their parent, but she'd been there all the same.

And would a few hours make the difference? He had leads to check out yet, and he wanted to track down the truly guilty employees of Windvale, the co-conspirators. He needed to know what they knew.

That Zhang was suggesting this at all meant either he was near his breaking point, or she was.

The time truly could make the difference. They had leads, and they had to follow them. But it had been over six days now since the event had happened. Anyone who'd been determined to get off Hestia would be away by now.

He closed his eyes. Tugged on his locket, and tucked it back inside his shirt. "Two hours. Then we go chase our leads."

She nodded, her shoulders relaxing, just a little.

He smiled at her briefly, the only true affection he could show in this role, then followed her down the stairs. They tracked down one of the staff and marched out to the large shed at the beginning of the gardens, back behind the main garage.

"The bikes are here," the grounds worker said, "and all the safety gear is on this wall. The helmets have built-in comms. Just be careful around the turns, we've had a few people lay their bikes down on the trails and get hurt. First-aid kit is in the side pouch."

Maja eyed the bikes and shared a look with Zhang. They weren't like the electric bikes he used to ride into the city on Valon, but full sport hoverbikes with much heavier engines. They could keep pace with regular traffic.

He might be worried about sabotage by the staff if they hadn't only just decided to ride them.

They chose their bikes, grabbed helmets that mostly fit, and set out on a trail that wound around the gardens and toward the open fields.

Zhang, ahead of him, opened the throttle. So he did, too.

And the speed was good. Adeius, good to focus only on the path ahead of him. On keeping his balance, on the grass and trees zipping by and the wind tugging its resistance.

He wanted to cry at the sheer sensory release of it all.

Maja tapped his helmet comm. "Zhang?"

"I hear you, Shiera."

"Good."

Zhang pulled out into another field, then took a turn to the left, following the treeline.

"Is there a map?" he asked. "Or are you just following—"

Ahead, his world turned into blazing white fire.

"Fuck!" he yelled, and threw his bike to the side, skidding to bleed off speed. He was still moving too close to the fire.

Adeius, *fire?*

He abandoned the bike and dove off of it, rolling until he stopped a few meters away.

"Fuck." He hurt. He'd banged his shoulder, certainly.

Panic set in, and he pushed up. Zhang had been just ahead of him, the treeline still to his left. Had she veered into the field, as he had?

"Zhang!"

He hadn't hit his comm—he hit it now.

"Zhang! Zhang, where are you—"

"To your left."

He whipped around, looked past the flaming ground ahead and saw she'd also laid her bike to ground right under the trees. She was tangled with her bike in the underbrush and struggling to get up.

He ran out of the field and over the sloped, grassy trail.

"Zhang, are you hurt!"

He was limping, but a quick, erratic delve didn't find anything broken. But then, he wasn't concentrating too hard. His eyes were only on Zhang.

He skidded down beside her, pushed branches out of the way so he could better get to her, then tore off his helmet.

"Zhang!"

She was struggling with hers, and he pulled it off, too.

"Think my ankle's broken," she said. She was breathing heavily, still trying to push up.

He glanced at the bike, but it was beside her, not on her, further into the underbrush.

The engine had cut off, and he saw one of the hover bars at the bottom was bent. The bike's controls were flashing a red warning light. Shit, and it wouldn't be safe to ride like that, might veer heavily in one direction if it even worked at all.

He snapped some of the branches off and helped Zhang up to stand, and she leaned heavily on him, keeping weight off one foot.

He stumbled, and fuck, as an overworked palace administrator, Shiera wasn't exactly in shape. Well, he'd manage.

He turned them around again, where was his bike—there.
And they should be able to both get on, if she held tightly
behind him.

His eyes strayed back to the fire. Which he was having
trouble registering as something that had just *happened*.

Shock. Was he going into shock? Was he already in shock?

Probably.

The fire was only a smolder now, small trails of orange and
smoke. Not the blinding white of before.

What had that fire been? Adeius, had that been a missile?
But there'd been no force of impact, so it couldn't have been.
Did someone know he was here? Was someone trying to stop
the investigation?

But he couldn't wrap his head around there being no explosion. Unless the fire *had* been the explosion?

New panic tore through him. They had to get away, go as
quickly as possible, before another strike could happen.

Zhang was taller than him at the moment. They struggled,
one step in front of another, across the trail and back into the
field to his bike. The field wasn't planted, the ground rocky and
uneven.

He prayed the bike would work. Prayed they had the time to
get on and get away.

"Comm," Zhang said. "I don't have my helmet, it's back
there. Where's your—"

He set Zhang down and ran back to get his helmet. He
darted back and scooped her up again, handing the helmet
over.

She put it on. Her voice was muffled, but he heard, "This is
Captain Vi Zhang of the Palace Rhialden Guard to Racha
Guard, with Shiera Keralan, envoy from the Seritarchus, at

Windvale Estate. We've been attacked by what might have been an orbital weapon, possibly a laser."

A laser. Maybe. But ships weren't typically equipped with laser weapons, they just weren't as effective as energy pulses or missiles—

"Please send emergency vehicles. Repeat, we've been attacked—"

He noticed she hadn't called Windvale Estate. And she did invoke the Seritarchus.

But was it orbital fire? Maybe it didn't matter if it made sense or not—they had to get out of here.

He set Zhang down near his bike and strained to pull the heavy bike back up to vertical, squinting up in the bright blue sky. His bike's engines had cut off, too, as a safety function, but he didn't see any damage on the bike itself beyond some dirt on the hover bars.

And dammit, it wasn't even in storage mode, which would have it hovering close to the ground. The hover function wasn't on at all, so it just sat on the ground, awkward and heavy.

But he managed to get it upright, then pressed and swore at the controls until the hover came back on and it balanced.

Maja looked back, again, at the fire. It was mostly clearing, smoke hovering in the air, leaving only a few orange patches that were still burning. It had hit the edge of the trail, he thought, partly in the field, and there might be some danger of the nearby trees burning. But that particular spot was more sparse, the air was humid enough, the ground wet enough, that he didn't think that would happen.

Was this sort of fire consistent with orbital bombardment?

Maybe. A pinpointed burn? A mining laser, maybe? Fine-tuned? Was he a target right now, standing in the open?

But his gut was telling him something different. His panic wasn't quite in the right direction—he didn't urgently feel the need to flee. Something was wrong here. Something was very wrong here.

The feeling of being watched that he'd felt in Below Space, which had lessened after a few hours on Hestia and been nearly absent when he was just focusing on riding, came back as strongly as he'd ever felt it.

He started toward the burn site. Or crater. Or whatever it would be—he couldn't see yet, it was just over a slight rise in the field.

"Maja!" Zhang yelled in alarm. "Maja, we have to go! Get back to the bike!" And that was just how rattled she was, that she'd used his name.

And it was how rattled he was that he didn't correct her.

He neared the rise, close enough to see through the smoke, and he could finally see what had been burned—no, etched—into the ground.

Not very large. Maybe three meters across.

A Kidaa rune.

26

THE RUNE

Do the Kidaa have a rune for 'fear'? Or 'hope' or 'love'? Are we the only beings in this universe that feel any of these things?

— DR. BLINN MENDOZA IN THE DOCUVID SERIES *WHO ELSE IS OUT THERE? (AND ARE THEY FRIENDLY?)*

Maja stared down at the rune. Did he know what it meant?

No. How could he? He'd never had time to study the runes.

Rhys would know.

"Maja!"

He drew a sharp breath, turned around to see Zhang with her teeth bared, walking on her bad ankle toward him.

Oh, no.

He ran back to her, and she fell into his support, wobbling them both before they steadied.

He heard the sound of engines now and looked up to see

aircars, or maybe a large airvan and a shuttle, hurtling toward them. From the direction of Racha? Yes, he thought.

The shuttle slowed and made a vertical landing nearby in the field, not over the rune. The airvan circled uncertainly, and the terrain wasn't the best for landing a city vehicle, but it settled down a little crookedly beside the shuttle.

The shuttle's hatch opened, disgorging Racha Guard in combat armor and people in medic's blues.

"Captain Zhang? Ser Keralan?"

A person ran over to them, fit and femme, and from the tabs on her collar, she was a major and used she/her pronouns. No, not Racha Guard. This was a response from Hestia's scant military reserves.

"Are you hurt?" the major asked.

"Her ankle is broken," Maja said. "I don't know my own injuries. I don't think anything's broken."

But he still hadn't had time to thoroughly check. And his eyes kept straying back to the rune.

A *rune.*

How? How had there been a Kidaa attack here, the farthest they'd ever come into Valoran space? Hestia was even farther from the border than Valon. And *here*, right here, mere meters from where he'd been?

How was that even possible?

It wasn't a coincidence. A large and very loud part of his mind was screaming that this *wasn't* a coincidence.

"Ser Keralan, please, come to the shuttle. We're evac'ing you to Sinnat Atran base. You'll be safe there."

Maja blinked, disoriented. What?

He'd zoned out.

They'd removed Zhang to a hover stretcher, and a medic was checking her while another pushed the stretcher toward the shuttle.

He blinked again at the major. "It was a Kidaa attack."

From the tightening around her mouth, she knew that. Of course they would have checked the satellite feeds.

"Ser, my job is to get you to safety—"

"I need to talk to the admiral of the system—"

"Ser, please. Please come with me to the shuttle—"

She reached for him, and he stepped back out of reach. "No, I need to talk to—I'm—I'm—"

He couldn't say he was the Seritarchus, because he wasn't. Or that he was Maja. That would be the greatest disaster, with Iata holding the rulership as Homaj on Valon. He couldn't say he was Iata, either, because he'd still have to explain his not *being* Iata. He'd have to tell her that bloodservants could Change, and he knew nothing about her.

So. He'd have to go with her to the base and find a way there to speak to the general in command.

Maja refocused on the shuttle and nodded. The major, looking relieved, led him in, and moments later, they were in the air.

HE ZONED out again for a short time. The shock, maybe. Then one of the medics gave him a quick heal patch, with its self-calculating mix of nutrients and drugs, and his thoughts began to clear.

Zhang, across the aisle in the bare-bones military transport shuttle, was lying on the bench with her leg propped up, her face tight as a medic set her ankle. Then she'd refused painkillers.

"Captain Zhang," he said.

Zhang started to look his way, then flinched and made a small sound that ate at his heart.

"That's it," the medic said, "that's the last. Patching up. I can give you a—"

"No," Zhang said. "I need to think."

Yes. They both needed to think.

Another medic near him finished his scan. "You have some whiplash and some bruising, Ser Keralan. You should rest for the next few days."

"I'm fine," he said, and crossed the aisle to sit beside Zhang where she lay. She reached over and gripped his hand tightly.

"You'll be fine," he said. "You'll be fine."

"Ser Keralan." The major had been beside him before he went to Zhang, and now sat across the aisle. "We've prepared rooms for you both at the base, you can stay there as long as you need. We can guarantee your safety on the base—"

"Can you?" he snapped. "We were attacked in an open field —did you see a Kidaa ship in orbit? Did you—"

"Ser!" The major's lips pulled tight. She wiped back a loose braid that had come out of her bun. "Ser, this incident is classified, and if you must speak to someone about it, please wait until you can speak with General Kim at the base."

He started to argue that they might not have time—that crawling feeling of being watched was suddenly overwhelming.

Watched.

By the Kidaa? Had the Kidaa tracked him here? Did they know—oh Adeius—did they know who he was? Even here, as Shiera Keralan?

Zhang squeezed his hand again, hard. He didn't know if that was reassurance or her trying to bear her own pain.

"What did it say?" he asked the major. "Tell me that, please. What did the rune say? The kingdom could balance on this one."

The major just stared at him.

"Please! Please, you have to have—"

"Ser, I'm not privy to that information. You'll have to wait—"

He buried his face in his inner arm and waited out the rest of the flight trying not to scream.

"Administrator Keralan. I'm sorry, I am truly sorry for the attack, but you have no military authority on Hestia, and this is a military operation."

"It's not an operation at all, it's a fucking—"

Maja stopped, drew a long, long breath.

General Kim was an older person, maybe twice his age, who'd semi-retired on Hestia in one of the quietest posts in the kingdom. Medium brown skin, curly salt and pepper hair, Army uniform trim if a little age-worn, firmly androgynous.

Maja had met the general once before at a function in Valon City. They'd not been memorable in any sense. And his memory was excellent.

He stepped closer. Debating, again, his crisis of authority here. He needed information. And he needed not to be seen as anyone other than Shiera Keralan. Who couldn't get information. Dammit.

Zhang wasn't in the room, she'd been taken to the base infirmary for more treatment.

He was alone with the general in the general's office, but he didn't know the security here, didn't know the surveillance, didn't know anything other than what information he needed to acquire.

"General, what's your clearance?"

The general gave him a look that was clearly annoyed.

"Standard gold, fleet-wide. Which is higher than yours, I checked. Now, you're welcome to send to Valon for an increase in clearance—"

"Give me a tablet with a scan pad. Access to the interplanetary network."

Maybe he didn't have to say who he was. Maybe he could just prove that he had access and let the general decide who he was.

General Kim reared back, eyes narrowing. "I don't think that's a good idea. Ser Keralan, this interview, which is a *courtesy,* is over—"

"A scan pad. Please. This is not going to go well for you at all if you don't."

He shouldn't have threatened, he knew that the moment it was out, and he saw the tightening of rage around the general's thin lips.

But General Kim might have seen enough of Maja's own rage to give them pause.

They eyed him again, then went behind their desk and brought back a tablet. They handed it curtly over to him, and didn't make more fuss than that. At least they'd never been memorable in that way, either.

Maja focused inward, shifting his palmprint, for a moment, to—to, Adeius, he still couldn't use his own. To Iata's. It took a moment, still rattled as he was, and the general was growing impatient again.

But he pressed his palm to the tablet, then tapped a sequence that would get him into the emergency planetary systems. Iata had as much practical clearance as Homaj had.

From there, he wove into the personnel records of Palace Rhialden—which would only be updated there two and a half days from now when the comm drones relayed the changes—and gave Shiera Keralan full military clearance.

Zhang already had it. And maybe this had been petty, and reckless, and he would regret it later—he could have just waited for Zhang. But her playing her clearance card wouldn't have gone over well, either.

It was understood and respected that Palace Guard and general military were their own separate entities. If she decided to pull her political weight, it could mean trouble. General Kim didn't have to obey any of her orders, and she had no rank over them—not even an equivalent rank in the Guard, important as she was to the daily life of the ruler.

General Kim had unbent as Maja worked, trying to see what he was doing, their frown only growing deeper. And then their whole body stiffening as they started to realize who they might be dealing with.

They opened their mouth, and he saw the shape of the word forming: Truthspoken.

"Don't say it," Maja snapped. "I'm not."

And let them decipher that.

Done with the problem of clearances, he backed out of the systems, sealing them all back up again, and retreated completely from the tablet, giving an erasure of signature command at the last.

He handed the tablet back over.

"Check my clearance now."

The general eyed him warily, then did. Their frown deepened.

"What was the rune?" Maja asked. "Was it one you could easily decipher, or do you need to have the experts—"

"'Storm,'" the general said. "The rune means, as far as my people can tell, 'storm.'"

Maja went still.

The attack had not been a coincidence.

The message had not been a coincidence.

Storm.

His mind leapt immediately to the closest and strongest association: *Occam's Storm*, near the border with the Kidaa. Rhys's ship.

"Does that mean something to you?" the general asked. "Something I should know?"

"Yes," he breathed.

He briefly considered what he should tell the general—but he shouldn't hold relevant details back. There wasn't, he sensed, time to spare in relaying information through interstellar comm channels later. Hestia had been attacked, and its defensive force needed to know what was happening and how to defend.

Not that he truly knew either of those things.

He tucked his still-wind-tousled hair behind his ear, held out his hand for the tablet again, and the general, reluctantly, handed it back.

He hadn't let his palm Change itself back yet, just in case he'd need that access again. He input Iata's codes again, got back into the system, this time opening the secured comm protocols installed into every official government and military system. He tapped out a quick message:

Going to the storm. Was meters from a Kidaa attack on Hestia. Am fine. Rune was "storm." IbR

That last—he had to do that last, and hope Iata forgave him. He truly couldn't leave the general not knowing where the lines of authority were here, not in a crisis.

The comm line was secure as they came—which was not nearly enough—but it would be encrypted end to end and only openable quickly by the Seritarchus's hand, or the Heir's.

His rage earlier, his petty revenge on the general just doing their job, had drained away.

He showed the tablet to General Kim.

"This," he said, "will be sent with the highest security encryption in the kingdom. This *is* above your clearance, General. And you won't breathe a word of it. We are investigating this. I'm going to go take it straight to the source the Kidaa seem to be indicating."

He didn't know if that was wise. He still didn't—entirely— know these attacks were from the Kidaa. But—but, he did. He knew this was something more than the squabbles of high houses.

The rune had been carved *meters* from where he rode with Zhang. There might be some plausible explanations for that, but the chain of coincidences in all directions was too much. Far too much for the situation to bear.

General Kim met his eyes. Searched a hesitant moment. And whatever they saw in him, he wasn't sure, he wasn't at all in control of himself just now. But there was only one person with those initials he'd signed who might have the sort of pull Maja was claiming just now.

The general finally nodded. "Thank you. Sir."

Maja let out a breath, pulled back the tablet, and spent a few minutes rewriting the message in Truthspoken inference code. But he left the word "storm," and emphasized around it. And he left the signature. He needed that part of it to be clear, too, that he'd used Iata's identity on Hestia.

Maja sent the message.

He wasn't sure the general actually believed he *was* Iata, or just that he had authority and access the general didn't. But they had said "sir." And he'd demonstrated enough access to the interplanetary system that he should have given Kim pause, at least.

And if General Kim demanded he demonstrate Change, it could cost them their career. A fine and dangerous line to walk.

He handed back the tablet again. "I'm Shiera Keralan. *Only* Shiera Keralan. Understood?" And there, he was confirming that part, at least that he could Change. Dangerous as that also was.

But his read of the general as unremarkable also extended to their vices—they had none that he knew of. This wasn't a person who would be easily blackmailed, or would have motive to sell this sort of information.

"Yes, sir." The general frowned down at the blanked screen

of the tablet. "Do you have any more information on this attack that I need to know?"

And how the tables had turned.

He took no pleasure in it. Not this time.

"I'm going to *Occam's Storm*, the border scout ship, which may have more answers. I know one of the officers onboard personally. But we're flying in the dark on this one, General, though I hope I can help with that soon. Please tell the system admiral that you spoke with a representative of the Seritarcracy. You may mention my name—Shiera Keralan. Or Captain Zhang's, if that's easier to swallow." A small smile, and he couldn't help that. "Say that the Seritarcracy already has agents investigating this new attack. For orders—I won't presume to give them, and I don't believe your system is in any further danger, based on all previous attacks."

"There was no ship," General Kim said, and past their annoyance, Maja now saw the fear in the general's eyes, the set of their jaw. "I've read about the other attacks in inter-system reports. There has never been a ship—not Kidaa, or Human—in any position to make this kind of attack on the ground. What happened—it shouldn't be possible."

Maja nodded. "General, can you please, when Captain Zhang is finished in the infirmary, have us lifted back to Windvale Estate? We have a colleague there I need to pick up, and then we will be leaving in our ship. I don't believe this attack originated at Windvale, and we must leave quickly, so I don't require an armed escort beyond the lift in. Please clear us all the way through to take off, no obstructions."

The general's lips pulled tight, still not liking this, but they nodded.

"Yes, sir. That is reasonable."

27

THE CHALLENGE

> *Pettiness is bred just as surely as cruelty. But it doesn't have to be.*
>
> — T.C.O. DENOVALO, POLITICAL INFLUENCER,
> IN A POST ON THEIR FEED

Iata breezed into the private meeting room, Haneri a few steps behind him, as she had been all morning. They'd been playing it off as her helping him recover from his injury, and he'd been playing up the pain that had mostly subsided. But that explanation was a shield, and so was she. A shield when everyone was determined to exploit his weaknesses as a magicker. Which truly pissed him off.

Haneri had needed to physically block at least four people so far today from touching him. And those were only the ones who'd managed to slip through his guards.

The person he was scheduled to meet was already in the room, and seeing that person did not enhance his mood. At all.

"Lord Xiao," he said, smiling tightly as he waited for Denom

Xiao to make his bow. Which he did, in as exacting a fashion as Koldari had a few days before.

Actually, Iata was growing to appreciate Koldari's tact. He'd had a mountain of thinly-veiled insults thrown at him these last two days, an entire *mountain*.

Denom's bow was so shallow, so quick, as to make Iata think his cousin thought the requirement to bow an insult to himself.

"Melesorie," Denom said, and smiled. The word was like venom in his mouth.

Iata made the mistake of meeting Denom's eyes. It was habit, and his thoughts were very much on controlling the urge to reprimand Denom—subtly, of course, and with the right amount of insult. But...but he couldn't do that. Not when everything was so volatile. And not while his aura was out and pulsing like a beacon around him. Anything even hinting of violence was catching him in the gut today.

When his eyes met his cousin's, Denom jerked back as if struck and threw up his hand. "Cousin, I did not give you permission to look at me—"

Oh hell and all the holy mandates.

Iata strode toward him in the center of the room. "I didn't say I wouldn't look at you, Cousin. I said I wouldn't look into your eyes. But you, Denom, are family. I meet the eyes of my family."

There, have that conundrum. Denom couldn't both play on his ties to the Rhialden line and deny the familiarities of family.

Denom's lips twitched, his face twisting, just briefly, into something ugly before he regained control. He might be a fool, but he was still High House Xiao through and through. And Iata didn't at all like that Denom had chosen to wear his long hair in a style similar to one Iata often favored as Homaj, his eyes shadowed with far more makeup than usual. Again, in a style similar to Homaj's. Was he trying to set himself up as an opposing and equal force to the Rhialden rulership? On what actual grounds?

Iata felt a dissonant pang, a truth surfacing with his magics that he didn't have time to look at just now. The long and familiar pain of never having known Jamir ne Xiao Rhialden as his father when his father was alive. Never having known his Xiao family except from a distance, and through the persona and lens of Homaj. They had no idea whatsoever that he—Iata —was one of theirs. Outside of Homaj, that was.

Those sorts of unwanted insights had been frequent of late. He'd never lived with his aura out all of the time, and it was wrecking havoc with all the wounds he'd decided to set aside in favor of getting on with his life.

He drew a steadying breath, but Denom spoke before he could.

"First Magicker—"

Iata stiffened. Very few people had yet dared to use that title to his face, and none of those conversations had been pleasant.

"I'm here on behalf of the General Assembly," Denom went on, not meeting Iata's eyes.

And Iata's foreboding grew. He'd wondered, when he saw Lord Xiao on his tight schedule. He'd seriously doubted the meeting request was anything so benign as a familial visit— though he'd been dreading that, too, if Denom had come with a formal reprimand from Prince Xiao, or broken trade agreements with Xiao worlds. Things were just fragmented enough right now that both were possible.

But the General Assembly? Denom was a member. The Assembly had little power to effect change at the level of the rulership, that task was reserved for Truthspoken and the Truthspeaker, occasionally with weight from the high houses. But the Assembly could, by law, open investigations into both Truthspeaker and Truthspoken, or call for a re-evaluation of a ruler's rule if they thought the ruler posed a serious threat to the kingdom.

In all of Valoris's long history, a vote of no confidence had only been cast once, during the last Onabrii-Kast war, and that was a time of utter chaos. Situations were almost always resolved another way. The proposed vote had to have a seventy percent majority backing to even bring it to a reigning ruler.

As Denom was doing now? And why else would the General Assembly send him?

Which meant that Denom had that seventy percent behind him.

Beside Iata, Haneri, who was currently glaring plasma cannons at Denom, folded her arms to present a wall against whatever else Denom was about to throw at him. Haneri had been doing her best all day to reign in her usual bent toward casual and scathing insults. And she'd been mostly successful, but whatever she was trying to accomplish, it was making him jumpy. It just wasn't who she was. And when he was unstable in who *he* needed to be as a Melesorie, it was throwing him way off balance.

Iata wished fervently right now that Haneri would rip Denom a new one.

Denom shot a look at Haneri, but she just glared back at him. And Iata watched the slight subservient signs in Denom's body language, the signs of wanting to back down from Haneri's silent onslaught, and that at least was satisfying.

Denom refocused on Iata as the easier of his two targets, and *that* was alarming. Iata knew exactly how intimidating he was as Homaj Rhialden.

"First Magicker, it's my solemn duty to inform you that the General Assembly has called a session for three days from now to vote on no confidence. Many members are in agreement that your manifestation as a magicker has put the kingdom in danger and compromised your judgment. We wish for you to step down in favor of the Truthspoken Heir, Ondressarie."

Iata kept his breaths even, but he let his anger show. And that aspect of being a Melesorie, not so tightly controlled as a Seritarchus, was liberating.

"Denom Xiao," Haneri said, advancing, "you are a fucking ass."

Denom took a step back. "I didn't ask for the Melesorie Consort to be present at this meeting—"

"I didn't ask for your permission to come," Haneri shot back. "Now tell me, please, why you think this *stupidity* is a good idea right now when the kingdom is struggling to stabilize? I'd really like to know, Denom, because I thought Xiao was smarter than that, I really did."

Iata fought the urge to smile.

"Haneri," he said mildly, "we must at least hear my cousin out. This wasn't his idea, but the General Assembly's. He is only the one to bring it to my attention."

Haneri paused, but not before she had Denom's back to a sidetable, rattling the tea service on top.

And as much as he was enjoying the show, and weathering the pain from that small and petty and entirely deserved violence, this wasn't good politics.

Iata pulled himself back to center, or at least what was functioning as his center right now. He approached calmly, posture open and neutral. He would not tell Haneri to back down, but she glanced at him, and stepped back anyway.

Denom still cringed as he approached. Adeius.

He stopped, held up his hands. "I'm a magicker, Cousin. I can't do violence—"

Denom caught himself, held his ground. "That's not true. It was proved not true by the two criminals you pardoned—"

Iata's rage ignited again, and he advanced again, coming to stand beside Haneri.

"Haneri isn't wrong," he said. "If you want to put the kingdom in danger just now, yes, let this vote go through. Further destabilize and erode the foundation I am rebuilding. Do that, and the Assembly won't have a kingdom to safeguard. I would happily hand over this rulership to my daughter, who is deeply capable, but I know that will only hurt the kingdom just now. So go ahead, Cousin, let the Assembly destabilize everything we've all worked for, what I have literally *bled* for—"

Denom threw up a hand to block Iata's view of him. Shit, he'd looked Denom in the eyes again.

But though he'd been the one to promise that publicly, everything in him, everything in him *boiled* at that promise's necessity. And Denom's handling of it.

Was Denom Xiao actually scared of him, or playing this for all its political worth?

Both, he thought. Absolutely both.

Iata started to step forward again, then paused, ran through his thoughts, assessing where he was going.

And this—this wasn't him. He didn't have this kind of temper, this was part of trying to shift himself into the more volatile bounds of a Melesorie personality.

Bile stung the back of his throat and he stepped back again. He couldn't hold out his hands, couldn't concede, couldn't show weakness. But he was damned if he was going to take from his dead older sibling's playbook. He would not be *that* kind of Melesorie.

He glanced at Haneri—she'd been helping him find the bounds of his new Melesorie personality, and had, ironically, tamped him down at least twice today, but right now he only saw her own fury.

And it was deserved, it really was deserved. His cousin was being horrible, and Iata didn't think for a minute that this proposal of Denom's wasn't politically calculated to propel Denom personally as high as he could manage.

The snake.

"You are a blight on this kingdom," Denom growled, bracing against the table behind him. "Both of you. All of you are. That the Rhialdens have manifested magics twice now makes me think we should vote to bar the Rhialdens from the rulership altogether—"

"That," Iata said, "is the purview of the Truthspeaker, and hers alone." He sighed and rocked back on his heels, finally looking away from Denom's general vicinity. It wrenched him when he saw Denom's relief at that.

Did his cousin have teeth? Did the Assembly? They might not be able to depose him even with a vote of no confidence, but that wasn't the point. The General Assembly was literally the court of public opinion. If he lost there, he might as well abdicate, because he'd have lost the ability to control the kingdom's respect. And fear. And that respect and fear was the only weapon a Truthspoken truly had.

And had he lost those abilities in his own person, with trying to shift himself into a Melesorie rule? How he'd acted in this meeting wasn't entirely out of character for Homaj, but it wasn't how he should have handled it at all.

"Three days," Denom said. "This was a courtesy to inform you. It doesn't change the vote, or its outcome."

And without even a bow, he strode out.

28

AN ERRANT IDENTITY

> *I fear for my sibling sometimes. And I'm not willing to commit more than that to even these letters, which I will never send.*
>
> — HOMAJ RHIALDEN, SERITARCHUS IX IN A
> PRIVATE LETTER, NEVER SENT; PUBLISHED IN
> *THE CHANGE DIALOGUES*

The door slammed behind Denom, another insult in a string of insults.

Iata looked to Haneri, and for a moment, just stood there. Feeling entirely unmoored in what had just happened, and no less angry for it.

Then the door opened again and Chadrikour stepped inside, her face stoic as usual, but Iata read her own anger. Even not knowing what had been said inside, Denom slamming the door was enough for her to be angry on Iata's behalf.

He waved her off. "I'm fine. We're fine. My cousin is in a bit of a temper. He is not worth our rage."

Chadrikour looked unmoved by that and pointedly raised

her brows at him—he knew he was still showing his own temper—but she ducked back out and more quietly shut the door.

And then Iata stood there, not taking his own advice, breathing through his own rage.

Haneri didn't move.

"I am right," she said. "Denom is a fucking ass."

He barked a laugh, Homaj's dry laugh. And put a hand over his eyes and choked on a sob, that one burst of emotion before he bared his teeth, a much less restrained gesture than he'd normally ever use, and pulled his aura back in. He needed not to feel so much right now, not to feel so entirely much.

Ironic, wasn't it, that the very thing he'd been wanting for years was his now—the freedom to be a magicker and have his aura in the open. And now here he was, sucking it away again.

Pulling his aura back in wasn't as easy as it should have been, even with a few days of not doing it at all. He'd never had a few days before, he'd been concealing his aura ever since those first frantic few days after he'd manifested. Then, he'd spent every waking moment—and most of those he should have spent sleeping—trying to follow Mariyit's directions on how to conceal his aura at all. He'd had to turn himself inside out to grasp how.

Iata slowly massaged his forehead.

And Haneri breathed out, moving in front of him, her light-woven holographic headband rippling through deep violets. Glaring the full weight of her soul into his eyes.

"Denom Xiao is an ass," she said again, slowly, and with great emphasis on each word. "The General Assembly are fools."

"And they'll drive us all into the ground," he said, and let Haneri help him to the uncomfortable couch in one corner of the meeting room. He didn't truly need the help, though he felt the fatigue in his bones that hadn't left him since the...incident. Yes, he was calling it that.

He opened his mouth, but Haneri held up a hand, pulled a dampener from her pocket.

And he sighed at the necessity and pulled out his comm, checked the time. They had eight minutes until his next meeting. Not enough time to go up to his study for any kind of true privacy. There were privacy systems here, yes, but he trusted little, ever.

Haneri clicked the dampener on and waited for it to fully activate. The room blurred slightly around them.

"What might be justice," she said in a low voice, sitting down beside him, "is to have Lesander impersonate you again —you as Iata—and then go out and catch *Iata* publicly and with spectacle. Then draw out a long trial for everyone to actually focus on instead of trying to tear down their ruler. Give them an enemy to unite behind."

He made a face. "That isn't funny. Not even a little, Haneri."

"I'm not joking."

He turned to study her. Considered her gorgeous, flawless face, all the nuances, all the hardened edges. And even now, even in this moment, he wanted to touch her lips. He wanted to cup the back of her neck and draw her to him. He wanted to taste her, to drown in her.

But she was serious.

And who were they, who were they at all, that Haneri could suggest such a thing?

"I'd never do that to Lesander after the hell her family put her through. But even if it was an option, it would be my own death, wouldn't it? I'd never be able to be myself, be Iata, again."

"With me, you could," she said. Still deadly earnest. "And anyhow, you've been Homaj long enough and often enough that it's as much you as it ever was Maja."

He opened his hands in partial agreement. "But it's not all of me. And not—not who I want to be, without cease, forever. I'd be shedding one life in the shadows for another."

Though with the seal on his cheek, he didn't have much choice, did he? And yet his stomach turned at the thought of firmly and fully closing that door. Haneri's idea wasn't even a bad one, politically—he wouldn't do that to Lesander, no, but Bettea would impersonate him if he asked. He knew that. Or Maja, even, when Maja returned.

Though the spectacle Haneri was describing, for that to work, would be damaging to anyone who had to live through it. Deeply damaging.

Adeius, no. It was a horrible idea. And he was feeling desperate if he'd even for a moment entertained it.

"What am I even doing?" he asked. "How I handled Denom—"

"You were attacked by someone you would have somewhat counted on to support you five days ago. Less than a week. You're mostly healed, yes, but those wounds aren't all physical, are they? You know they're not. And what did you do to your attacker? You decided to call her your daughter. Yan—that anger has to go somewhere."

"I'm not angry at Lesander. Her family—"

"Yan. The anger has to go somewhere."

He met her eyes, looked away.

"It's trying to fit my personality into that of a Melesorie. It's throwing everything off."

"That too. But that wasn't the wrong move in the moment, you know that."

He opened his hands, conceding the point.

Conceding...defeat?

He hadn't thought that after he'd been revealed as a magicker his life would be easy, not at all, but he'd hoped... Adeius, he'd hoped he'd be less tired. But now, he was under constant assault. Almost every person he saw—every noble, at least—hostile.

Haneri sat back hard, sighing the couch cushions behind her, a low and lingering gust. Iata spared a small grin, remembering pranks with gusty chairs and couches when he was a child.

Haneri turned to give the cushions a glare. "This couch needs replaced. Wasn't this here when I first came to the palace? I remember having an argument with—well, *you*—on this couch. Adeius."

Maja, she meant. And Iata, despite having grown up in this palace, around Truthspoken, despite having made secrets his entire life, was thoroughly sick of dancing around them. It had been so much harder, too, with his aura out these last days. He could feel every untruth like a needle in his soul.

They shouldn't be talking this freely here, even with the room's privacy systems still on, even with the dampener/scrambler on. But he needed to right now. He just needed to talk it through, because his head was too crammed to make sense of it from the inside anymore.

"But this system, Yan," Haneri went on. "And why don't we let them tear it all down, if that's what they want? Wash our hands of them all. Go live somewhere else—anywhere outside Valoris. I'm done with them all."

But her words held no fire anymore.

And he was losing it too, wasn't he? Losing hope that he could ever fix this kingdom on his own. Rule it on his own.

Should he abdicate?

The thought was increasingly omnipresent.

There had to be another way out of this. Had to be. Some strategy he hadn't tried. He wasn't letting himself think as a Seritarchus, and that was also throwing him off intensely. But it was yielding new ideas, too.

His comm beeped.

Iata's stomach tightened, because with all the ongoing crises that were threatening to overwhelm his inboxes, he'd set both staffed and automatic message filters so tight that very little could get through to his comm's alert system.

If a family member was attacked, or a mass act of violence happened on Valon or another Valoran world. A declaration of war. A Kidaa attack.

Or word from either Maja or Imorie—and it was possible for word from either of them to have come his way at this time. Just possible.

He pulled out his comm, and the message notification popped up.

His breath caught when he saw the sender initials, and the private ident code. Both were his own, as Iata.

"What?" Haneri asked.

"Maja. He's using my identity."

Haneri swore, voicing what Iata was feeling.

Maja couldn't yet know Iata had been attacked—or at least, hadn't known when this was sent. Couldn't know that there was an arrest or kill order on Iata's own head. If he was using Iata's name, or much worse his appearance even, he was in trouble. The news would have come in by now, and Maja would be—

Not killed, he hoped with all he was. Taken. He could only hope taken into custody. And, he thought with growing horror, would Haneri then have her trial after all? His brother playing the part of Iata, the villain? Maja's final performance.

Iata shook himself and refocused on the message, tapping it open. His thoughts were fraying in this rewriting of his personality.

Then, he stilled.

Haneri, who couldn't see the text at this angle, his comm automatically shielding it, gripped his arm. She'd felt his shock.

"What? You just went from afraid to terrified."

Iata felt blood draining from his face, his limbs, and he

thought, and thought again, and thought *again*, of what the hell this could mean.

"He's been attacked. By the Kidaa. On Hestia."

He reread the message, retranslating quickly from the inference code, checking to make sure he hadn't made a mistake. It meant that Maja was going to *Occam's Storm*. He'd been very close to a Kidaa attack on Hestia, within meters of it. He was currently fine. The rune the Kidaa had carved on Hestia was "storm." And he'd signed this message with Iata's initials.

So then, he'd shown the original message to someone on Hestia before coding it, someone those initials would mean something to, more than one of Homaj's other random identities.

Who? Iata thought quickly through possibilities, settled on the most likely being either Racha's head of the city guards or the commander of the military reserves on Hestia. Possibly the system admiral, though that position was less strenuous than General Kim's as the planetary commander—probably, most likely, General Kim.

"Storm," he said. "That can't be a—"

"Let me see the comm," Haneri said.

"It's in inference code. You won't be able to—"

"So translate it," she said. "And I probably have more context than you think."

He tapped the screen and quickly entered his translation, then widened the security viewing allowance. He held it out to her, and she leaned close.

Haneri coughed. "Rhys."

Iata nodded.

"Yan, there is no way that attack on Maja was random."

"No," he agreed, still staring at the shallow holo text—both the original message and the translation—on the comm's screen. He checked his translation again from all angles that he could see, and, no, he hadn't gotten anything wrong. The code wasn't as embedded as it might be, Maja had meant for this to be absolutely understood.

Iata looked up at Haneri. Just stared, for an indefinable moment, into her golden-brown eyes. He could feel her fear rising with his own.

Fear about what this meant for the kingdom, for this feeling that there was a much, much bigger orchestrator of everything happening than what he could see. Than what he could plan for.

And Maja might be walking into all of this as Iata, with a kill order on his head.

There was nothing Iata could do about that. The border with Kidaa space was too far away—*Occam's Storm* was a minimum five days' comm distance away. Minimum. Maja's own travel time to the *Storm* would be at least a week from Hestia if he still had Onya with him, and Iata would bet he did.

And when Maja got to the *Storm*, if he had fully embraced being Iata, and there was a good chance of that if he'd let General Kim think he was—what choice would he have but to either out himself as Maja or carry on being Iata, no matter what came? He might have had little choice on Hestia, too. Iata knew his brother too well to think Maja would assume his identity flippantly.

Zhang—maybe Zhang had enough pull on her own to stop whatever the captain of the *Storm* might do to Maja, but Iata didn't know. He'd studied Captain Ira Nantrayan of *Occam's Storm* to decide if she was safe to place Rhys under, and she had been, for the most part, an ordinary border captain. A little strict, a little wild around the edges as most border captains tended to be. But how would she react to—well, to whoever Maja was when he showed up?

Iata had given Rhys his seal.

And he knew Rhys knew that seal was only to be used in emergencies, and *absolutely* to be used if it was needed. He hoped Rhys understood just what he'd given them, a slice of immutable power in a place he himself couldn't reach in time. He'd recorded an endorsement that would make that power absolute.

"I gave Rhys my seal," Iata said. "Indefinitely."

Haneri's face went tight with displeasure, but she nodded.

"I always knew that was inevitable, them being drawn into all of this. I don't like it, Yan."

She sighed. Waved at the comm. "But I don't like that, either. And for all of Maja's faults, I am glad Rhys will have someone on hand."

"I'm rather thinking it might be the other way around, if he's still me. If he's as rattled as I think he'll be."

He hoped, Adeius he hoped, that Maja could hold on through the strain just a little while longer. And whatever strain this Kidaa attack had added to it all. But then, Maja had always done better on missions than in the midst of the capital's crushing responsibilities.

And should he send word to *Occam's Storm* that the person with Captain Zhang was to be trusted? Even if it got there late?

Not if Maja might have to publicly out himself as Homaj, and what a disaster that would be.

Iata exhaled slowly, did some quick comm math, and set an alert for when he might expect word from Maja when he arrived at the *Storm*. Ten days, minimum.

And it was best time he had that promised talk with Admiral of the Fleet Laguaya.

29

THE STRENGTH OF THE SHIP

> *It's like you're in the bones of the ship. You feel yourself in its skin, repelling unwanted pokes from Below Space outside. It's not that different than swatting at flies.*

— FIRST MAGICKER MARIYIT BRODEN,
INTERVIEWED IN THE POPULAR VID ZINE
VALON CITY SUNSHINE

I morie slept most of the first two and a half days to Kalistré, and that galled them. They hadn't intended to, and they'd thought, with the treatment patches for the Bruising Sleep, that they'd have more control of their body than that.

But maybe it wasn't about control. And maybe they would, some day, have to face that they'd never have full control of their body again. There was treatment, yes, but there was no cure for the Bruising Sleep.

But they weren't willing to deal with that today, and so they applied their cosmetics with fervor, copying what Dressa had done at the palace. Pushing it all that bit further masc, the angles of their face contoured sharper, their brows and upper lip darker, and yes, that was a place they could land for a while.

They synced the holo tattoo beside their eye to their comm and highlighted it in silver, the swallow's wings now fluttering iridescent green. If they had a glaring green new aura, might as well run with it. They eyed their piercings, their gel-spiked indigo hair, and nodded. Maybe they'd get another tattoo. Or another few.

Imorie stepped out of the small washroom in the cabin they shared with Eti, finding him on the bed propped against the pillows, scrolling through his comm.

Kyran hadn't looked happy when Imorie had said they and Eti would be sharing a cabin, and, what, had he expected Imorie to share with him? He had his own partner, Iwan.

But, no, that wasn't the impression Imorie had gotten, or what little impression they'd been given before the Bruising Sleep had pushed them under for most of two days. Kyran just didn't like Eti. And Imorie couldn't say it was entirely unwarranted, given that Eti had been an unwilling spy, but it wasn't deserved now.

Imorie climbed onto the bed, which was smaller than Rhys's enormous Truthspoken-sized bed had been, Eti now closer beside them. Which...was a little weird, because Imorie had still only known him for weeks, but Imorie wasn't yet willing to give up sharing the bed. And neither, it seemed, was Eti.

There was comfort in closeness. And in knowing that the person next to you absolutely, completely, knew you—where it mattered, at least.

He looked up and showed Imorie his comm—a strategy game. "It's old, but it was already on the comm, and I always get stuck at the one level."

Imorie peered at it. "Ah. This one." It was a level with Kidaa blocking shipping lanes, where you had to decide how to communicate with them to move forward. A completely unrealistic scenario, as Kidaa had never done that, but the game had solid strategy bones.

Imorie shrugged. They'd never gotten stuck at this level. They'd finished the entire game in two days when they were thirteen, and their father had picked apart their entire performance, citing diplomatic weaknesses, strategic missteps, and the body count they'd wracked up by the end of it. They were sure they'd played the game well, or at least, played it as well as the game's makers had allowed them to.

Eti held the comm out to them. "Can you get me past this, without violence—"

Ah. Without violence. It was possible to play and beat the game without violence, as their father had very emphatically pointed out, and did Imorie remember how he'd said to do it?

This wasn't a Truthspoken lesson. Eti wasn't in training. It didn't matter if he passed this level or not, or how he passed it, it truly didn't—except that he wanted to. And that he was a magicker. And that made everything so much harder.

So Imorie took the comm, stared at his stats and options for a few seconds, and then set the next decision tree in motion.

They flicked through the next screen, made sure it would work, then handed it back. "This will get you past in five more screens. Choose the orange options. Not diplomacy there, but stealth."

Eti blinked at them, then focused back on his comm, his lips moving silently as he read and touched the screen. A few moments later, he grinned. "I'm through."

He looked up, and that moment of joy, just that small moment, faded. Faded back into the worry that Imorie had seen every muzzy time they'd gotten up to stumble to the washroom or tried to force down a light meal, which Eti had brought.

They couldn't tell him it would all be okay. They weren't that cruel.

"I'm going out," Imorie said. "To eat." It was late, ship's time. And they were truly feeling hungry for the first time in days, though their stomach was still sour.

They pressed a hand to their growling stomach, and Eti looked up, pocketed his comm, and came with them.

Imorie didn't tell him he didn't have to. They knew he didn't want to go out of the cabin but would anyway, to be near them. His aura was growing clearer still, the murky notes nearly gone. And it was better, they knew, when he was near them.

The yacht Kyran had rented was larger than the magicker ship they'd brought to Valon, with the central corridor on the upper deck holding eight cabins—six passenger, two crew— leading to a cockpit that was almost big enough to be called a bridge. The lower deck held a mess and rec area, a small gym, and a holo theater. Aft of it all, the engine and mechanical compartments kept the ship running. The ship had come with both a pilot and an engineer, both of whom Imorie had briefly met before the haze of sleep had overcome them.

Imorie slipped into the lift with Eti. The walls were paneled in luxurious synthwood, though Imorie could still see the seems. A plush yacht, but not the Truthspoken standard of luxury. Not really Koldari's either, they suspected.

It was a few heartbeats before they stopped on the mess deck. Imorie scrunched their nose up at the smell of strong coffee, not what their stomach needed just now, but followed the smell anyway through the mess/rec room and into the small galley.

Where Doryan was perched on a stool at the pass-through counter nursing a steaming mug, an array of holo windows around them.

Doryan looked up, waving the windows to private, and smiled as they stood.

"It's late," Imorie said.

Doryan carried their mug back out to the mess, blowing on the steam before they set it down on one of the tables. "Yes, and it also takes a fair bit of concentration to keep the ship's hull strengthened through the flows and eddies of Below Space. Looking up facts about ecosystems on various worlds helps me concentrate."

"Have we had trouble in Below Space?" Imorie asked, feeling a chill. They glanced to the single window in the mess hall, which was just now showing a holographic forest at night, not the gray-ish streaks that were actually what was outside. Which was...jarring.

They'd seen their share of weird reports about ghosts in Below Space, or the weird pressures on the hull of a ship as it traveled at faster speeds. Most of the reports they'd put down to superstitions.

"Oh, nothing major," Doryan said, "but I've had to shift the points of strength on the hull from fore to aft to upper port in the last few hours."

Imorie caught their breath. "You've been awake this whole time. It's almost four days travel to Kalistré at military speeds—"

"Just over three. I'm pushing it, so the ship can go faster." They smiled wanly, then settled down to nurse their mug. "Hence, the coffee. Iwan also gave me a mild stimulant, so I'm a bit twitchy. They are actually a trained medic, did you know that?"

Imorie hadn't, but they certainly filed that away.

"Thank you," Eti said, almost a whisper. Because Doryan was doing this for him. For his family.

Doryan gave a tired nod. Then straightened again. "Oh, what can I get for you? I made more coffee, that's fresh, I certainly need it, but I know there are leftovers from the dinner Koldari made the night before, uh, and dessert if you want it—"

Imorie waved Doryan down. "I'm fine, I want to look myself."

But Doryan followed them back to the galley anyway, still nursing their mug.

Doryan paused, leaning on the counter, and gave an enormous yawn, and then a second yawn. Finally, they made a defeated sort of wave.

"Eti, do you have any training at all in shifting the strength around a ship's hull?"

Eti shuffled into the galley behind Imorie. "No, but I can sort of feel Below Space outside the ship."

"Well, that's a start. I'm not sure I can hold out the full three and a half days. Even drawing a little extra strength." Doryan nodded at the sagging pocket of their overshirt. Which was distinctly metal bar-shaped. And if they'd brought metal to draw strength from, could Imorie get some from them? They would have to ask later, when the time was more opportune.

Doryan rubbed at their face. Their eyes were vaguely bloodshot. "And if I can't last that long, we'll need to drop to commercial speeds for a bit for me to catch some sleep."

"Teach me how," Eti said. "I'll do it, shift the strength of the ship, while you're sleeping."

And of course he wouldn't want to lose any time.

Imorie opened the well-stocked cooler, pushed aside various containers on shelves, some labeled with a stylus, some auto-labeled—and Imorie was pretty sure that synthesized fermented milfish eggs were *not* one of the container's contents, so the labels weren't likely all that accurate. Adeius, and they couldn't even think about eating that if it was true, or their stomach would go straight to sour again.

Doryan nodded to Eti. "Well, it's not hard, but there is a trick to it. I wouldn't normally trust someone so new at this with a ship at this speed, never having done it before, but you're strong enough, and meticulous enough, I think, that you can do it." They yawned again. "Just hope I'm coherent enough to show you." Doryan took a long swig of their coffee.

Imorie decided to ignore the containers and poked at two wraps in sealed foil. Was this the leftover dinner? They didn't know.

Imorie brought the wraps back to the square table Doryan had chosen before, one of three scattered among the various lounge chairs and two overstuffed couches. The tables had holo controls in the center, which looked to favor gaming interfaces, but they weren't on at the moment.

Imorie took a seat, Doryan reclaiming the seat they'd chosen before across from them, and Eti sitting on the side to Imorie's right, between them both.

Imorie carefully undid the foil on the wrap, smoothing it down. And thankfully, what was inside smelled hearty, not spicy. Was that thoughtfulness from Koldari? He'd certainly eaten enough of the spicy color-coded food on Hestia, and he'd seen that Imorie couldn't.

Imorie mulled on Koldari—*Koldari*—being thoughtful as Doryan explained how the structure of the ship was designed to let magickers easily move strength around within it. Or, as Doryan put it, move a solidity of mass and intensity of the residual presence of life, which Imorie's tired mind didn't fully grasp. But the aim was to push and pull this strength from one area of the ship to another, shoring up the hull, running strength through the magic-conductive alloy beams and supports that ran throughout the ship.

Imorie did know about that part, they'd studied how travel at military speeds worked before. That was only prudent for a Truthspoken who would travel at those speeds at some point in their life. And their life might depend on knowing how it all worked so they could push a ship to the limits of safety without a magicker, if needed. Commercial safety standards were far from the same as Truthspoken emergency standards, if it came to it.

"So with this support structure within the ship, you'll always have a tap into the structure of the ship as a whole," Doryan went on, "which in turn will help you feel the strength of the hull. Navy ships leave some of the magic-conductive beams exposed for the highest amount of physical contact possible in a battle, but the concealed structure in civilian ships is fine—there are a few points of direct touch access if needed."

Doryan pointed at the comm panel beside the hatch. There was a hand-wide section of bare darker metal beside the controls.

Imorie's attention focused. So that was where they could interface with the ship directly? The magic-conductive skeleton of the ship?

"There, you can touch the metal and be in immediate contact with the structure of the ship," Doryan said, and Imorie nodded.

And resolved to get good at this. Because if they were a magicker now, and as high-ranking as they were, they would absolutely use those skills to all advantage.

Eti glanced at Imorie, then got up and went to press his hand to the panel.

Imorie, around a bite, asked, "What does it feel like?"

But Imorie was already sensing for the magic-conductive metal within the ship, and they felt it—once they focused on it, they could easily feel the skeleton of the ship, the condensed strength of the ship as a whole running through the conductive beams.

Adeius, the ease with which they felt the strength of those beams, now that they knew what to look for, made pulling strength from metal bars feel like walking underwater. They would have to be careful not to pull strength from the ship by accident, or pull it at all—a magicker was only meant to redistribute a ship's strength, not steal it.

Imorie stopped chewing as they focused on feeling where the strength was most concentrated—just now, that seemed to be a point fore, ventral, starboard, and that point was shifting along the hull. They felt the touch of Doryan's thoughts, but not like when they were touching someone directly. More like an awareness that Doryan was concentrating on this same structure of the ship, too. That Doryan's will was consciously shifting the flow of strength around the inner structure to the outer hull.

This was wild.

And how did Doryan know where to shift the strength?

Imorie felt Eti's awareness of the structure now, too. And followed his thoughts along the structure to where the hull felt...oppressed.

"Ah, you feel that, both of you?" Doryan asked, draining the last of their mug across from Imorie. They'd grabbed a pastry from the cooler, too, and started pulling the doughy pieces apart. "Good. Watch, then."

And Imorie watched in their mind, with their still-untrained magicker senses, as the feel of the ship's structure subtly shifted, with Doryan slowly drawing more strength from all around the ship toward the area of the hull that was—not in distress, really, but—well, "oppressed" still felt like the right word. Like pressures from without were trying to push in. Not in a way that would immediately buckle the ship, but in a way that might, over time, cause long-term structural damage, or overall weakening of the hull.

And Imorie knew that part of it, too—a medium-sized ship could travel through Below Space at military speeds, but risked light damage that might, several trips later, cause an actual concerning buckle in transit.

Or, there were times when that hull distress could suddenly

be more extreme, and a ship would be in trouble, regardless. Larger ships always had these difficulties and sometimes needed more than one magicker monitoring the hull in transit, or else needed to stick to commercial speeds, taking around twice the time as military speeds.

Imorie watched as Doryan continued to shift strength along a slow path, following the line of hull oppression.

"Can I try?" they asked.

Doryan hesitated. "Carefully. It's similar to drawing strength from an object, but you don't pull it into yourself, you push it along the path you wish it to go. Some magickers view the structure as a whole, too, and merely nudge the strength of that whole in a given direction."

That was how Imorie had seen it. They set down their half-finished wrap, wiped their hands, and stared at the far wall as they focused fully on the inner structure of the ship.

Doryan was withdrawing their attention from the oppression of the hull, allowing Imorie to fully examine it and... slowly...measure the strength of the structure of the ship. They continued, as Doryan had done, to concentrate that strength along the path Doryan had started.

It wasn't a large difference of strength from the rest of the structure, they weren't pulling strength in a large amount, not anything that would damage the rest of the ship. More like tipping a glass so that the water flowed just a little more to one side. And then back again, and Imorie felt a new, smaller oppression forming on the other side of the ship.

"There's two, and one hasn't finished," Imorie said.

"Then ease a bit more strength toward both. You only need enough strength to give the stress point a light resistance, enough to cancel out the force on the other side."

Imorie nodded, then winced as their head twinged with a headache.

"Let me take it back for now," Doryan said. "We're traveling as fast as it's possible to go in this yacht, which is faster than I'd normally take a ship of any size. It takes more concentration than usual. And maybe we should slow to typical magicker speeds—"

"No," Eti said. "Let me try."

He sat down again beside Imorie, his sleeve brushing theirs. Imorie felt him touch their own strength, briefly, reassuring himself that Imorie was okay, then shift his attention back to the ship.

They smiled at him, a small smile, though he didn't see it. His concentration was now fully on the ship.

Imorie withdrew from holding the structure, taking a deep breath, blinking to clear their head, focusing back on the room around them. The coolness of the synthwood table. The solidity of the deck beneath their slippered feet. The light tang of their wrap, cheese with white tomatoes and golden pinor relish.

How was Doryan doing all of this and also talking to them? Eating? Doing anything at all?

Imorie hadn't given much thought to how difficult it might be for a magicker to sustain a ship at military speeds. They'd never had to before.

Then Imorie felt a prickle on the back of their neck and looked up to see Kyran Koldari in the open hatchway to the corridor, watching them.

30

DATA TRANSFER

Everyone in the Kingdom of Valoris has an identity in the Valoran system, whether they were born there or not. But because both cosmetic and medical genetic therapies are so common, and cosmetic and medical surgeries, identity is factored from multiple points. You will have multiple back-pings on your records when you enter Valoran space.

— ANONYMOUS, IN *VALORAN SPACE, I AM IN YOU*, A POPULAR CROWDSOURCED TRAVEL GUIDE

Kyran Koldari smiled as Imorie looked his way. A genuine smile? It seemed so, reaching his eyes in his ruggedly handsome tan face, his dark hair loose around his shoulders tonight.

"It's good to see you up," he said, "and I see you've found dinner. Or is it breakfast?"

Eti glanced warily at Koldari, then focused back on the ship.

Imorie stood, carrying their wrap to a different table. Just because Kyran was giving them the means to help Eti's family didn't mean Eti trusted or liked him any more than he had before. Imorie wished Eti wouldn't be so obvious about that mistrust, though. Playing Kyran was a delicate game.

Kyran followed Imorie, settling across from them. Closer now, Imorie saw his hair was a little damp, like he'd just taken a shower. He smelled like hotel soap. Yeah, this yacht definitely wasn't high on luxury.

"Did we wake you?" Imorie asked.

"No, I was up." He frowned at Eti, then pulled out his comm, waggling it in the air in front of Imorie. "I have data for you. Everything on the current state of Kalistré I was able to pull from the nets before we went into Below Space. And on Rivan Tanaka, Eti's mother. Who, curiously, has a very blurry ident image. I wouldn't recognize her on the street except by the broadest of features."

There was sharpened interest in his eyes, a calculation that Imorie wasn't sure they liked. And they understood—no one should have a blurry ident image. Even if an image was captured blurry, systems extrapolated and would rebuild the lossy features. Her ident image would have to be blurry on purpose—on a governmental level.

Imorie pulled out their comm and tapped it into receive mode. They didn't like receiving data directly from Kyran Koldari, but the security protocols on their comm were the tightest possible in the kingdom. This comm had been Iata's, after all.

Kyran touched his comm to theirs, and they drew it back, pulling up holo windows.

"I gave a copy to Magicker Azer as well, and your guard, Farouk, while you were asleep. If you're determined to see this through, best to be prepared."

Imorie met his eyes, tried to gauge what his motives were in helping them with this. He hadn't at all been happy that Imorie's choice of destination from Valon had been Eti's home-world, to rescue his family. But he was taking them there all the same.

Imorie thought about making a jab about him suddenly being willing to help, but—no. He was doing what they wanted him to do.

So Imorie flicked through the holo windows, taking another absent bite of their wrap. The data was system traffic reports, military status reports, police reports. Current maps, housing records—oh Adeius, and that would be a large file—and a hundred other folders with similar bits of information. Some of it public, some of it...less so. Gained with Kyran's ducal clearance, or from a hasty favor from the Javieris, who owned Kalistré? Or...some other means?

Could Imorie count on this information being accurate? It would, at very least, be more than five days out of date.

Imorie swiveled around. "Eti, where is your family located? What address?"

Eti turned, not at all startled by the question. He'd been listening, of course, not that they'd been trying to be private. And he might have gleaned some of it directly from Imorie, too. They could still sense him clearly, even across the room, his emotions knotted together with his concentration on the ship.

Could Imorie afford to distract him?

Eti rattled off an address, and Imorie queried the database. Okay, a residential neighborhood in Gayatl Dri, a mid-size city on the southern continent. It was autumn there now, cold, a rainy season. Residents would speak Valoran, but there was a strong presence of Iére, a local dialect that was fast becoming a language of its own. That was not a dialect Imorie was trained in, though if there were audio files, they could mimic the accent—

They swallowed, glanced up again to Kyran studiously *not* watching them. Which meant that of course he was.

Was he seeing how Imorie, someone who was definitely not supposed to be trained in the Truthspoken arts of royal-grade evaku and Change, as well as impersonation, infiltration, improvisation...well, how *would* Imorie Rhialden méron Quevedo handle a rescue operation? Possibly—and Adeius, they hoped not—a pursuit. Or, worst of all, a post action clean-up.

Imorie felt Eti stiffen and did their best to send what calm they could his way.

They waved the global map around to Kyran. "Have you been to Kalistré?"

He raised his brows as he glanced at the map. "A few times. On business—never to this city." Dismissing it as if it was beneath his attention. It wasn't any kind of capital or major commerce center, not even of its own district.

"How would you recommend approaching Eti's family?"

His lips tightened with displeasure, but he sighed, leaning forward to study the map. Kyran zoomed in, panned around a minute, then pointed at a marker in the city proper. "City guard station. That's where I'd start—the Seritarchus already sent word ahead of us to extract Eti's family? The guards might have already done so. Or if not, if there's a complication, they'd know that, too."

Except, the Seritarchus's agents didn't always work with local guards, but they'd likely have the guard headquarters under surveillance, to know what was going on in the city.

Imorie knew the name and location of one of the agents on Kalistré, but that woman had been stationed on a different continent. Farouk would know how to contact her, though, or signal her to contact. Farouk probably had a lot more contacts than Imorie knew of—they'd memorized a lot and kept that list in their head current, but they couldn't memorize the status and details of more than a few hundred agents at a time. Not with every other detail they had to track in the running of the kingdom.

This was, Imorie knew, part of why Iata had sent Farouk, because knowing those contacts was a part of his job. And Farouk would be able to make contact much more discreetly than Imorie, especially with them being a magicker—and a currently infamous magicker at that.

Imorie could make the agent contact, too, with codes in the planetary system. But that...that was a card they wanted to hold in reserve. Because only Truthspoken should have that sort of access.

Kyran tapped the table with one manicured, clear-lacquered nail. "I don't want you to go rushing off to Rivan Tanaka's residence, I want you to do this smartly. You're under my protection now, and I intend to protect you, whether it's from street criminals or Javieri agents."

"They'll be watching Rivan's residence, won't they?"

Imorie knew they would be, of course they would be, if the Javieris hadn't removed Eti's family already. But Imorie was still supposed to be a minor contract noble caught up in the over-whelming politics of their royal bloodline, not a Truthspoken with trained knowledge of hostage situations. Not enough trained knowledge, but enough to know this might be dangerous.

"Likely," Kyran said, with a dark look again toward Eti.

Imorie scowled and leaned forward. "Will you get over hating him? It's not his fault that the Javieris coerced his family—they threatened his mother and his sibling—"

Kyran held up his hands. "I get it, but that doesn't make me trust him."

"I know what he's thinking," Imorie said, "and no, he doesn't like you, but he has good reason, because you gave him good reason. Doesn't mean he's out to get you."

They'd pushed Kyran, speaking as familiarly as that. Calling him out on this. And how would he respond? What would that show them of his agenda and what he really felt about Imorie and his relationship to them?

Kyran shrugged and stretched. "You don't maintain your position as the lowest of the high houses by trusting every random person who comes along."

"So why do you trust me?" Imorie shot back.

"Ha. I don't. Doesn't mean I also won't protect you, or that I don't like you. I have learned it's wise not to trust anyone. I suggest you learn the same."

"Even your partner?" Imorie pressed. "You even don't trust Iwan?"

Kyran smiled. But he didn't answer that one.

31

RECOGNITION

It was raining today in Gayatl Dri as Lord Arda Javieri visited the Adeium for the Celestial Celebration with his second husband, both of them wearing Halcyon's fall collection.

— FROM THE KALISTRÉEN LIFESTYLE FEED
ELEGANT INFINITY

When they landed at the port in Gayatl Dri, Imorie knew Eti was jittering to get out and get to his family, but Farouk had them waiting by the boarding hatch instead. Which was probably wise.

Imorie stood in the short corridor between the mess and gym with a steadying hand on Eti's shoulder, trying to keep Eti's intensity from overwhelming them. Trying not to be as impatient as Eti felt, because they knew security had to follow procedures, especially on this Javieri world.

Near the hatch, Farouk frowned at the security screen with his own trained intensity. The hatch itself was still firmly closed.

"Any enemies out there?" Imorie asked, unable to keep some of Eti's impatience from leaking into their voice.

The guard huffed a laugh. "It's raining, if you count the weather as an enemy."

Imorie scowled. "So we take a car. We weren't going to walk."

Farouk looked up, straightened, bracing for a confrontation. "I should go out and make contact with the Seritarchus's agent first. That's the safest way."

"You," Kyran said, crowding into the corridor with Iwan, "should stay on the ship. You're far too *guardly*."

"We're also taking three magickers," Farouk rumbled. He pulled out his comm and brought up what looked like a surveillance net, tapped a few commands. "We're not going to be utilizing stealth here."

"I'm coming with you," Kyran said. Imorie had thought he might—every cue he'd been giving the last day was of someone who didn't want to let Imorie out of his sight. He'd been hovering, far too much in their personal space again, but they hadn't thought of a good way to tell him to back off. "Iwan will stay on the ship, though. As will the crew, to be ready to lift quickly if we need to."

Beside Imorie, Eti held his arms tightly around himself. He shrugged his shoulders, and Imorie let go, giving him space as his fear continued to rise. But they'd stopped needing touch to sense each other's moods.

Eti looked up, straight at Kyran. "Thank you."

And the sincerity Imorie felt from him was a surprise, because Eti certainly hadn't been going out of his way to show Kyran he was grateful, despite them being here for Eti's family.

Kyran just gave a nod. Bent to kiss Iwan, gently caress their cheek, before Iwan slipped away again.

Then Doryan bustled up, their black sealing case shouldered over one arm.

Eti stiffened, and Imorie felt their own hackles rising.

"Can't you leave that here?" Imorie asked. "I doubt we'll have the time to stop and seal a magicker."

"It's protection," Doryan said, rubbing at their thin beard. "It's the means by which I—which we all—can help them."

Eti touched the seal on his own cheek, his mouth tight. But he nodded.

And Imorie sighed. They hated the seal on their cheek. Hated that it was permanent, that it hadn't been their choice. But Doryan wasn't wrong that it was protection. No one would be able to force Imorie to use their magics in the same way that Eti had been forced. And no one would be able to force Eti again.

Farouk clicked off his comm. "All right, we'll go. It looks clear, but be on the watch."

Eti tensed, glancing to Imorie, then was first out the opening hatch behind Farouk.

Outside the yacht, the sky was heavy with clouds, and in the crowded spaceport, the air thick with the smells of industrial lubricant and rain pinging on hot metal hulls. They took a ground shuttle to a disbursement area, getting some looks with their cluster of three magickers, but Imorie sensed no more than ordinary prejudice around them. Which was ugly enough on its own. Imorie found they had to keep their eyes from meeting other people's, lest they accidentally catch those ugly emotions.

Adeius. And would they ever get used to that?

A few people looked like they recognized Imorie and Eti—or maybe Kyran, even. Imorie was deeply glad for the aircar Kyran called when it came, and they all bundled into the hushed, luxurious interior.

Farouk navigated from the dash, while Doryan spoke softly to Eti in the backseat. Somehow, by Kyran's design, Imorie had ended up sitting next to him in the second row of seats.

Kyran leaned back in his seat, arm over the back of theirs next to him. Imorie had decided that Kyran really wasn't interested in them sexually, so there was at least that. But why was he so possessive of them? Why was he so intent on helping them? It was absolutely not out of the goodness of his heart.

"My family almost won this world," Kyran said into a beat of silence in Doryan's and Eti's conversation. "The Koldaris had bought mining rights to this system before it was settled, but the Javieris overbid that company's shares and bought it out." His smile was tight. "It's not a great world. Rains far too much in just about every climate. Too much ocean, too much humidity, too many storms."

Eti shifted in the back seat, but didn't contradict Kyran.

"The air is good, though," Doryan said. "Or at least, I'd imagine it is, outside the city. Fresher than Valon's."

Kyran shrugged. "I prefer the air on Sangor Brec. It's fresh and generally a lot drier." His homeworld, which had much cooler climates overall than Kalistré.

The cab banked, following Farouk's directions, and set them down outside a three-story office building with a flat, monochrome facade.

"Looks friendly," Doryan muttered, peering up.

This would be where Farouk was checking on his contact, then. Imorie said nothing, and Farouk didn't offer information—they were still in a public cab.

"Wait here," Farouk said. He touched a control on the dash, and the tint on the windows darkened. "Don't remove the privacy screens." He glanced at Kyran, said a grudging and pointed, "Ser."

Imorie hid a smile. Farouk had always projected outward politeness, a necessary skill in one of the Seritarchus's personal guards, but they knew his wilder streak. He'd more than once encouraged Imorie and their siblings in their own mayhem, once stubbornly facing down the Seritarchus when Homaj was working himself up into a rage. Farouk had said it was his idea to turn the terrace garden into a re-creation of an infamous ball that had taken place at Palace Rhialden eighty years ago, resulting in three public poisonings and many more injuries in the panic that had ensued. And it had been his idea, after Rhys had asked a question about a vid drama they'd watched portraying that event.

That had ballooned into an elaborate play-by-play re-enactment, complete with vid-worthy drama and Truthspoken-trained immersion, but Farouk had been teaching along the way on how to avoid such poisonings and public disasters in the future. Imorie still remembered his steady insistence on, "If there's a panic in the crowd, use all of your skills to redirect their attention. And if you can't do that, get away as quickly as you can. No amount of social standing is worth your life."

Farouk glanced back at Imorie as he left the car, just a look, but that look said everything. Stay, be safe, I'll be back shortly. I'm helping in every way I can.

Imorie tapped the arm of their chair while they waited for him to speak with his contact inside. No one was talking now.

But Farouk was back quickly—too quickly—sliding back into the dash seat and calling up the maps again. He stabbed at the waypoint he'd set for Rivan Tanaka's residence, and the cab lifted.

"What did you find?" Kyran asked, before Imorie could.

"An empty office," Farouk said. He watched the map. "Which shouldn't have been empty. It will take me time to try to locate who we're looking for again, or find out what spooked them. Do we have that time?" He looked to Imorie, not Kyran. "It might be best to leave now." Because if it was the Javieris who'd evicted the agents, or killed them, then Farouk was right, they had no time left.

"We're not leaving without his family," Imorie said, meeting the guard's eyes.

Farouk nodded. He'd known they'd say that, but he'd had to try.

Farouk punched a security override into the cab's system—which was a risk, and the parallels to their desperate flight on Hestia weren't lost on Imorie. But, the override let him take manual control, and he circled the area around the building where Eti's family lived.

Behind Imorie, Eti sat forward, tense, his hand now gripping Imorie's shoulder. They reached up and squeezed it. They did their best, their absolute best, to steady him.

Farouk hadn't said anything about calling for backup, and Imorie understood—if the Javieris owned this world, they would own the guards in every city, too. Any attempt to get help from the city guards could put them, or Eti's family, in more danger.

Finally, they banked down, joined the traffic on street level, and turned right into the temporary visitor pads outside the apartment building.

"I have the code to get in," Eti said, already moving for the cab door.

"If it hasn't been changed," Farouk said. "Eti—wait. Wait for me."

Eti froze in the small aisle by the side door, every line of his body tense, but he did wait. And Imorie slipped past Kyran to crouch beside him, their breaths coming shorter than they should, the excitement draining them. They took Eti's hand and slid their other hand into a pocket where Doryan had given them two metal bars earlier. For use in emergencies, but—Imorie had to function.

They slowly pulled strength from one of the bars. Eti tried to give them strength, too, but they refused the help.

"You need your strength, too," they said into his ear, and he nodded.

Kyran sat forward and touched a pistol concealed in his

sleeve that Imorie had marked earlier, but he didn't draw it. And of course, Imorie, Eti, and Doryan couldn't go armed.

But they were obvious enough as hell. When they stepped outside, any people nearby shied away from their car.

Farouk, tall and imposing as he could be, shifted his stance and opened his posture to have more civilian and approachable body language, and that did help, despite what Kyran had said before.

Would the Javieris know they were coming here? The passenger manifest on the yacht had been privated, thanks to Kyran's clearances—which would only show that whoever was on the yacht was wealthy enough to have prepaid government approval clearances. The manifest was only openable by direct query with sufficient planetary-government-level clearance, and that would always alert the ship. As far as Imorie knew, that hadn't happened yet. And it likely wouldn't, because few people wanted to ruffle the tempers of the wealthy and powerful—even *other* wealthy and powerful.

But the city would have surveillance, of course. Had Imorie and Eti—and for that matter, Kyran—been identified by city systems? Most likely. And that information passed to the Javieris.

Farouk's guard's glare, softer-focused and casual now, still scanned everything—he was just more circumspect about it.

He came up behind Imorie, guiding them with his hand light on their back, a fatherly sort of role. Imorie shifted their own body language to match, glancing up and giving him a warm smile.

And together, they all trudged into the building's sparse lobby.

There was no door guard—it wasn't that kind of building.

Eti let go of Imorie's hand to approach the security kiosk and pressed his palm to the scan plate.

And if every other surveillance measure hadn't alerted the Javieris to their presence here, this certainly would now.

A loading holo popped up, and Imorie held their breath.

Behind Imorie, Farouk shifted, a warning to be on their guard. Not that they needed the warning—they were tense as hell and ready to try to make themself invisible if they needed to.

The kiosk chimed, and the glass door into the building corridor clicked open.

Eti nearly ran for it.

"Steady," Doryan said softly, and Eti glanced back, slowing his steps to a brisk walk.

In the corridor, they all crammed into the lift, and though Imorie was looking everywhere, they saw no signs of obvious human surveillance. But then, the Javieris would certainly have the whole building under watch. They might already be on their way now.

The lift doors opened again on the third floor, and Eti did run now.

"Eti, no, wait—"

Imorie lurched after him, aware, all too aware that this could be a trap, there could be danger, there might be Javieris waiting inside the apartment to take Eti out. To take Imorie. To do whatever they wanted to do on their own world.

But they wouldn't harm Kyran Koldari. They couldn't touch a high house duke without consequences.

Eti reached a door, pressed his palm to the scanpad, and then rushed inside as soon as the door opened, Farouk growling a curse as he whipped around Imorie to follow Eti inside.

Inside, the apartment was dim, the window tints near opaque. Imorie had the impression of a cramped sprawl, not tidy but not unclean. Small kitchen and dining room, overstuffed living room. A messy desk in one corner near an opaqued window. Plants...everywhere.

"Mom!" Eti shouted, weaving through the living room and into a hallway on the far side.

"Eti," Farouk hissed, but Eti didn't stop.

Shit. Imorie charged after them both, crumbling the rest of the metal bar they'd been tapping.

"Mom!"

A higher-pitched voice called back, "Eti?" Then, "Stand back!"

A crash.

Imorie skidded to a stop around the corner, hand braced to catch themself on the wall before they collided with Farouk, who'd drawn up, hands raised.

A woman around Eti's height had pulled Eti to her and was glaring up at the guard. She wasn't armed, and she didn't show an aura, but the air seemed to warp around her all the same, crackling with a promise of violence. Imorie could almost feel it thrumming in the plants around the apartment.

Eti pulled back. "Mom, no, they're with me!"

The woman looked past the bulk of Farouk to Imorie.

And Imorie shuddered. Because they recognized her.

Adeius, they *recognized* her.

Her image had been obscured in the database, and that made sense now. Because she was supposed to be dead.

32

THE JAVIERIS

> *The Javieris own or control as vassal worlds more worlds than any other high house, even the Rhialdens.*

— EMRE PATEL IN *DECONSTRUCTING OUR TIMES: A PEOPLE'S PERSPECTIVE ON NOBILITY AND THE HIGH HOUSES*

Imorie braced on the wall and stared at Rivan Tanaka. Because the woman was obviously Eti's mother. She had the same angular face shape, the same nose, same demeanor as Eti.

They knew her. They hadn't met her, but they'd seen pictures of her.

Because they'd studied all of the high houses, especially the Javieris.

A report of a tragedy. Semlin ne Krata Javieri. Wife of Niom Javieri, the younger half brother of Prince Yroikan Javieri and a prince in his own right, though not *the* prince. Semlin hadn't been married to Niom Javieri for six months before she was killed in a tragic aircar accident—and this had happened before Imorie was born.

Except here she was. And though she was older than the images Imorie had studied, and though her hair was different in cut and color, her cosmetics were different, and even, Imorie saw in the dim light, her eye color, they knew it was Semlin ne Krata Javieri. Imorie did not forget faces. Not ever. The body language matched, too. They'd seen vids of Semlin before the crash.

Imorie glanced to Eti, who, once he'd assured himself his mother wasn't going to harm his friends, had embraced his mother with a fervor Imorie hadn't seen since they'd known him. His face was currently buried in his mother's shoulder, but Imorie *never* forgot a face, or its details. And they thought over Eti's face again now, and picked out—Adeius. Picked out what should have been obvious to them, the small similarities to Lesander's features—the much, much stronger similarities to Niom Javieri. In the placement of Eti's cheekbones. The shape of his chin. His build, even. Adeius.

Adeius.

Eti didn't know. Imorie was absolutely certain he didn't know who his father was.

They met his mother's eyes while she held Eti tight.

Rivan Tanaka. Semlin ne Krata Javieri. A tragedy indeed. The tragedy, Imorie was sure, was that Rivan had manifested Green Magics.

She was still suppressing her aura, and she was unsealed. So the rest of that tragedy was what the family she'd married into had done about her being a magicker. And what they were still doing now.

Imorie's anger rose like a wall of flame, and with it, the nausea, because they absolutely wanted to do violence to the Javieris. To any Javieri that would cross their path today—if any dared.

But they choked on bile, bent over their stomach, forced breath into their lungs again, tried to get themself to calm the fuck down.

Rivan's lips drew tight as she watched Imorie. She'd be able to see Imorie's many-layered soul, see they were, at very least, heavily trained in evaku. But Imorie knew, from seeing Dressa and Iata, and then Lesander, that the difference between even Rhialden trained Truthspoken and Truthspoken trained by anyone else was large.

Rivan would know what Imorie was. If not who.

"Eti," Rivan said, stroking his hair before pushing him gently back. "Eti, you brought guests."

Such innocuous words.

Farouk flexed his shoulders and shifted, moving to one side to let Imorie better see. Not quite a measure of trust, but a concession that this was necessary, and that Imorie could better handle this situation than him. And that nothing would be accomplished if he was positioned to guard Imorie against Rivan just now.

Imorie glanced back to see Kyran right behind them, Doryan behind him in the narrow hallway.

"They're with me," Eti said, which wasn't particularly helpful, then asked, "Where's Geyl?"

He looked around and started to pull back from his mother, muscles tensing to go dash around the rest of the apartment, but his mother gripped his arm with a fast grip that belied her calm, holding him back.

And then—then Eti stilled. Because he'd be feeling what his mother was feeling, wouldn't he? And he had to be feeling some of Imorie's rage, because Imorie was sensing his own growing, numbing fear.

Imorie didn't think they felt anyone else in the apartment. Not Geyl, Eti's sibling, who would also be a magicker and should be bright in their senses.

Kyran Koldari stepped into the space between Imorie and their guard and bowed, and Imorie was sure that Rivan had recognized him.

"Ser Tanaka. I am Duke Koldari—your son is under my protection. I'm here to take you offworld, at the order of the Seritarchus."

Not...exactly. But Imorie didn't contradict the stretched truths. Not that Rivan wouldn't hear the stretched truths, too. If Eti was as high-ranking as he was, Rivan was almost certainly high-ranking, too.

And here, again, was a member of a high house, a ruling family, with drastically high magicker strength. But Rivan had married into the Javieris—her own family, Krata, was only mid-nobility. If there was a pattern here—well, and Imorie still didn't understand how there could be. It wasn't possible to give someone Green Magics. But even if there was a pattern, it didn't make sense.

Imorie swallowed. Eti was Lesander's cousin. He was Lesander's *cousin.*

Did Kyran know? Was there any recognition in Kyran's eyes? Kyran had remarked on Rivan's blurry ident image on the ship, he would certainly be alert to nuances now. But Imorie had been too busy being shocked by Rivan to pay attention to Kyran, and that was a mistake, because they were learning that Kyran covered his reactions quickly and well.

Rivan nodded to this introduction, still keeping Eti close.

"Ser Duke." She looked to Imorie. "And I have watched the news, painful as it's been. You are Imorie Rhialden méron Quevedo."

Imorie nodded. What Rivan didn't say was there was certainly speculation about Imorie's actual identity, and more so now that the news of the attack on the Seritarchus had spread.

Rivan stepped closer to Imorie, reaching out a hand.

Kyran jerked as if to stop her, which was interesting, because Farouk only twitched.

Rivan paused, palms up, her lips twisting. And maybe the irony wasn't lost on her that she'd been the one on the defensive a minute ago. That all of them were mistrustful of each other.

"May I?" she asked Imorie, and Imorie alone.

Imorie held out their hand, because they knew there would be little they could keep from this woman. And because Eti was clinging to Rivan hard enough that he'd be able to sense any danger from her, though Imorie didn't know if Eti, in that moment, would move to help them or his mother.

But Imorie needed Rivan to trust them. This woman—this discarded Javieri—was suddenly very, *very* essential to what was going on. The Javieris exploiting an unknown magicker family was one thing, and bad enough; the Javieris using magickers from their own family was entirely another.

Rivan's touch was cool, her palm calloused. Eti had said she was also a gardener, and that he'd learned most of what he knew from her.

Eti met Imorie's eyes, nodded firmly, because he'd feel Imorie's own suspicions and fears, though Imorie didn't know if he could tell the context. He'd absolutely know something more was going on, though.

Yes, he trusted his mother. Imorie hoped to Adeius that trust wasn't misplaced, because Eti didn't know the whole of it.

Rivan's wariness was like a metallic tang in Imorie's awareness. And Rivan wasn't going to be subtle about this, either, because Imorie felt a pressing urgency from her to know who Imorie was. Really was. Just who it was who'd been tangled up with her son, and if Imorie had harmed him, or...the other way around.

Rivan would have seen Eti's murky aura on the news, and she had to have known what that meant as well.

I am, Imorie thought, forming each distinct word in their thoughts, *Imorie Rhialden, officially the adopted child of the Seritarchus. But I was born Arianna Rhialden.*

A name that, even as they were settling into being Imorie, they ached to reclaim as their own. And it hurt, it physically hurt to say it, even if in their mind.

Could Rivan hear those thoughts directly? Imorie was able to direct thoughts at Eti when they were touching and the other way around, though what they'd shared so far was mostly impressions and emotions. And thoughts didn't always translate to words.

Imorie got back from Rivan, like an echo of words from a distance: *Born Semlin Krata. But you know that.*

And then Rivan let go.

"Mom," Eti said, "Imorie's with me. They're helping me. It's okay. But where is Geyl—"

Rivan turned to him, pressed both hands to his cheeks, looked between his eyes. The moment felt intensely private, and Imorie and the rest of them intruders.

Eti's eyes filled. He reached out beside him, and Imorie shifted to take his hand again, gripping tightly.

Something which Rivan noticed even through her own tearing eyes.

"They took Geyl," Eti said. He choked on the words, but said them again, with more force. "They took Geyl!"

"Yes. And, Eti—you shouldn't have come back. Because you're their price to get Geyl back."

Eti shuddered, his aura flickering, and Rivan gripped him tighter.

"No, Eti, no. This wasn't you. This isn't your fault—"

"If I'd—"

"This," Imorie hissed, "is Yroikan." Because they'd studied Prince Yroikan as a rival to the Rhialden line, and this entire thing had Lesander's mother's hands all over it.

And what did Yroikan Javieri want with Eti? Other than to shut him up after what had happened at Hestia? Would she, in fact, harm him? Her nephew?

Yes. Of course she would. Lesander had spilled a whole lot of damning garbage about the Javieris that Imorie wouldn't soon forget. All of it too twisted and tangled in other political strings and personal stakes to actually do anything about it.

"We'll get them back," Imorie said to Eti, and he turned, his eyes locking on theirs. "We will go and get your sibling back, and you're not going to stay with Yroikan, or be used by her, or whatever else she wants."

"Forgive me," Rivan said, "but whatever this conversation is, my apartment is bugged. And if we're going to be leaving, we'd best leave now. My handlers will be here soon."

Beside Imorie, Farouk shifted, pulling out his comm. "I'm calling the city guard. We do need backup. I'm using a royal code—this will take first priority."

Imorie didn't like that, it wouldn't go well with their denying that they were, in fact, Truthspoken, but Farouk had their immediate safety foremost in mind.

"I'm not taking you to Yroikan," Kyran said, crossing his arms. "Any of you. I'm happy to take you all off this world, but I will not take you to Ynassi III. I have more regard for your safety than that."

Imorie glared back at him, but didn't contradict him— they'd have that conversation on the yacht. And maybe he wasn't as closely allied to the Javieris as Imorie had thought. From his body language now, would he even be welcome on the Javieri homeworld? The high houses couldn't directly go to war with each other, under Valoran law, but they could certainly employ assassinations and other means of sabotage. Wars weren't always fought in the open.

But what could Imorie say, when they still didn't know why he'd helped them this far? And he couldn't know, not for sure, that they'd once been Arianna Rhialden. They'd once been the Truthspoken Heir. Imorie had no great protection to offer on their own.

"Ser Tanaka," Doryan said, stepping out from where they'd been waiting in the background. They held out their open hand, the other hand carrying the case. "We must seal you first. I must. Before anything else. So you are not able to be misused again."

Rivan's eyes hardened. "I would agree with you, Ser Magicker, but my child, my *other* child, is in Javieri custody. And one of the conditions of their safety is that I not seek any help from the local magickers."

"I'm not local," Doryan said calmly, brushing past Koldari and Farouk. Imorie pulled Eti aside to let them approach Rivan, too.

Imorie hated the idea of sealing Rivan, hated it to their guts and to their marrow, but Doryan wasn't wrong. And now, knowing who she was, Imorie knew the sealing had to happen. Just as their own had needed to happen.

Doryan snapped open their sealing case and quickly brought out a blank seal disk and the genetic scanning crystal. "This won't take but a minute."

Rivan stepped back, hands up. "Truly, if you're all here—I've seen the rumors on the feeds about Javieri involvement in what happened on Hestia. You were there, so you know, you all do know what they're capable of. You know what they did to Eti. They will harm Geyl if—"

Her voice broke. Panic was growing in Rivan's eyes, the air taking on that warped quality around her again. And she had no idea of what the Javieris had just tried to do in the capital, of how high the stakes had become.

Imorie looked to Eti, and he touched his mother's arm.

"Mom. The Javieris want me, right? They won't harm Geyl until they have me."

"They're also using Geyl to control me," Rivan spat. "They'll use any excuse to do their harm—"

Behind Imorie, Kyran let out a low hiss. He'd already said he wouldn't go to the Javieri homeworld on Ynassi III, but his face was twisted now with more emotion than Imorie usually saw in him. And it looked, like every expression he wore, genuine.

Imorie couldn't play his games right now. But they couldn't call him on them, either.

"What," they growled.

He met their eyes. "I have a thing against people who kidnap children. No, this isn't my business. Going up against Yroikan is definitely not what I wanted to do."

And what did that mean, that he had a thing against kidnappers? Imorie wracked their memory but couldn't think of anything they'd read that indicated kidnapping featured anywhere in Kyran's past. And he'd said children—he didn't have children. And he'd been an only child.

"We'll politic our way out of this," he said. "It will cost the Koldaris dearly, but, we will." He narrowed his eyes, and that shrewd anger might have been the truest thing they'd seen from him all day. If only they knew exactly what it meant.

"Geyl has even less protection than Eti," Rivan said, meeting Imorie's eyes. She followed that with, "Because they're not as fully trained a magicker as he is. But, the Javieris will of course train them. They'll use my child, another of my children, as a weapon."

Imorie swallowed, catching her first point. They'd been assuming that Geyl and Eti were full siblings, but no, that couldn't be true. Eti had said Geyl was nine years younger than him, just barely a teenager—Geyl's birth would have been long, long after Rivan had broken from the Javieris. Or been forced to hide.

Geyl wouldn't be Javieri. And that meant they were even more expendable than one of the Javieri bloodline.

Imorie made their posture as non-threatening as possible and held out a hand, palm up. "Please, Rivan. Let Doryan seal you." They touched their own cheek. "Even the Seritarchus is now sealed."

Rivan trembled. She closed her eyes, her lips parting to bare her teeth.

But, she nodded.

"I'll be quick," Doryan said, hurrying forward. They looked back to Farouk, who'd put his comm away and was moving now to stand guard at the end of the hall, watching the apartment door. His pistol was out, and Imorie's insides crawled at even the thought of the weapon.

And what would Imorie be able to do if the Javieris did burst in here?

Nothing. They could do nothing but become invisible and ultimately harm themself. They couldn't protect anyone else.

"The city guard is also on their way," Farouk said. "That might be enough to deter any Javieris aware of guard movements."

Imorie doubted it. This was a Javieri world.

Rivan held still, her jaw tight, as Doryan pressed the crystal to her cheek, and then the blank seal. The sealing was over in less than a minute. Rivan winced as it took hold, but said nothing.

Rivan's image had been obscured in her ident documents, which wasn't an accident. That should have been corrected, but it hadn't been. And Rivan was still recognizably herself enough, once you looked close enough, that she wouldn't have completely fooled the planetary surveillance networks on her own.

Or else she would have been found out as Semlin ne Krata

Javieri much sooner, wouldn't she? This wasn't just a coverup, it was a global conspiracy.

Rivan touched her newly sealed cheek, glanced at the seal on her son's face, and squared her shoulders.

Doryan packed their instruments quickly, snapping the case shut. "Do you need to pack clothes, any personal items?"

"No time, I think," Kyran said, pulling up his sleeve to reach his own concealed pistol.

And Imorie heard the soft thunk of the apartment door unlocking from the outside. Because of course the Javieris would have access.

"Let me out first, when it comes time," Kyran said to Farouk. "They can't kill me. Not without a shitload of consequences."

Farouk grunted, but nodded, pressing himself just around the corner and aiming at the door.

Rivan pulled Eti and Imorie back farther down the hallway, against the wall.

"Don't kill," she said, her eyes glinting. "Whatever you do, whatever you're tempted to do, don't kill with your magics."

Imorie chilled all over. And they felt Eti shudder, his aura going a little more murky again.

Imorie tightened their grip on Eti's hand.

"We're unarmed!" a voice called. "Escort only!"

Imorie glanced at Rivan, who'd tensed.

"Know them?" they whispered.

"Yes. He doesn't usually come himself, that's far too obvious. But he's Lord Arda Javieri. One of Yroikan's minor cousins."

Imorie didn't have to ask if she trusted this person. That answer was obvious.

"You are trespassing on private property," Farouk boomed out. "You were not granted entry."

"I own the building," the baritone voice called again. "I know Etienne Tanaka is with you—I only need him to come with me, I don't want any other trouble, no trouble at all. It's pertaining to a previous arrangement, Etienne knows his legal responsibilities, all is good—"

Rivan bared her teeth. "*Legal* responsibilities. They're hardly trying to be subtle. They don't even care if anyone makes the associations—"

"The city guards are coming," Farouk said to the Javieri lord. "I suggest you back off, go back outside, and we'll work this out when they arrive."

A pause. "You're one of the Seritarchus's personal guards," Arda said, "escorting two known criminals—"

"I am escorting two people who were exonerated of all blame in an unfortunate situation." A dangerous edge was creeping past Farouk's professional tone.

"All the same, I'm here to make sure they cause no trouble—"

"They are under my protection, and so under the Seritarchus's protection. They will not cause any trouble. You have the Seritarchus's personal guarantee."

Imorie swallowed. Iata had given Farouk one of his seals to use in case of an emergency. For Imorie's own use, if needed, but Imorie didn't doubt Farouk would be keyed to use it, too. Would he pull that out now?

Into that silence, Kyran stepped out, despite Farouk's twitch to bar his way. Whatever they'd agreed beforehand, the situation had gotten tenser.

"Lord Javieri, everyone here is under my protection as well," Kyran said. "If you know they're here, you also know I'm here. And you don't, right now, particularly want to cross the head of another high house. *Lord* Javieri."

Imorie held their breath, holding tight to Eti, and Eti to his mother. They could still see Kyran where he stood facing the door.

Tall and proud and looking in every measure the head of a high house dukedom. Imorie didn't trust him, not a bit, but whatever he was doing now certainly wasn't cowardice.

Unless he'd been working with the Javieris and was still working with the Javieris. Unless all of this was a sham, and... Imorie still didn't know why. *Why?* Why step out like this and put himself into danger for them otherwise?

"Ser Duke," Lord Arda finally said. Tightly. And with prejudice.

"Let us pass," Kyran commanded. "Everyone with me is returning to my yacht. My yacht will lift and break orbit and leave the system, unchallenged and unmolested."

"Ser Duke, you might be the head of a high house, but this is a Javieri world, I'll need to submit to Javieri authority—"

"I am in a hurry," Kyran said. "If you would like to start an inter-house war, right now, you can detain me as you will."

Another pause. Then, "You may go, Ser Duke."

"And all those under my protection, which is everyone else in this apartment."

Pause.

"Yes, they may go, too."

And Kyran marched forward.

"Go," Farouk said tightly, waving for the rest of them. "Right behind me."

The hairs on Imorie's neck prickled as they stepped out, hand in hand with Eti, and met the glaring blue eyes of a pinch-faced man in what looked to be his late middle age. There was little resemblance to Lesander, or Eti, in the Javieri lord's features, but the sneer was very Javieri. Imorie had never met this lord, and Imorie had memorized the higher-ranking members of all of the high houses. Even minor lords could be dangerous, though—as they'd experienced at Windvale Estate.

Arda Javieri glared at first Eti, then Imorie, then Rivan as they all passed. Lord Arda said nothing more, only holding the door open as they filed through.

And Imorie was braced for the betrayal, for the shots to ring out, every step.

But no shots came.

They met the city guards in the building's lobby, spent precious minutes as Farouk explained that he was acting on the Seritarchus's orders—without bringing out the seal, but with verifying his identity on a scanpad. Kyran explained that if the guards didn't personally guarantee all of their safety and escort them to the port right now, there would be hell to pay.

They all piled into a city guard deployment van, and every minute, Imorie's hand tight in Eti's, they braced for the shot that would take the van down.

But it never came.

They reached their yacht, which Kyran had called ahead to power up, the docking clearances already in place.

They boarded, and were lifted within minutes.

And then they were in space.

And finally, Below Space.

They were safe. Safe.

So why did Imorie feel like they'd lost that battle? Like the danger they were heading into was the greatest of all? But then, they were about to go to the world of their family's greatest enemy. Facing someone who wouldn't hesitate to kill any Rhialden for kicks, if there was even the slightest chance of getting away with it.

No, they were not safe at all.

33

PIVOT

> *Truthspoken are unique in that they're trained to fully assume personality traits if they're required for the successful ruling of the kingdom. There have been more Seritarchus rulers than any other style of rule, and a Seritarchus can make the kingdom flourish through steadier times, or bring steadiness out of chaos. But sometimes a Melesorie's force of momentum is needed to carry us through difficulties.*
>
> — DR. KIRAN STRIGEN IN "THOUGHTS ON THE NATURE OF TRUTHSPOKEN PSYCHOLOGY"

Iata calmed his center, checked his thoughts in the patterns they were running—increasingly and chaotically Melesorie—and waved to Bettea from where he sat in his usual chair in the sitting area of his study. Bettea had been working at a desk brought in from another room, placed not far from his own desk. And now fae stood, moving swiftly and silently toward the door. Moving entirely differently than fae would have as faerself.

Fae had Changed, and while fae would always first and foremost be Imorie's bloodservant, Bettea was trained in how to run the day-to-day of a kingdom. He'd asked and fae had agreed to take over the administrative running of the kingdom that he himself had done for Homaj, when Maja was Homaj. He simply couldn't keep up with it all on his own. Especially not when the kingdom was working through the current crises.

And—and he couldn't say it wasn't in his thoughts—he also wanted Bettea to know how to actively rule the kingdom, know all the nuances and political details. Just in case he was forced out of the rulership and Dressa couldn't rule, for whatever reason. Up to and including impending Javieri influence. He was so short on active heirs just now that he was pulling on every string he had.

Bettea opened the door and stepped back as Admiral of the Fleet Dassan Laguaya entered. First giving Bettea a hard look before they shuffled toward where Iata sat in the center of the study.

And that was part of the plan, too. Bettea looked visibly Rhialden, much more than fae had as faer preferred appearance. Bettea's hair was darker and long, bound up in a masc style, skin tone more tan, overall appearance having a very Rhialden cast. The face shape, the cheekbones. Let people speculate about another Rhialden on the scene and how they got there, a diversion from their panic over Iata's aura. He wasn't offering a name, and no one yet had dared to ask.

And let them, too, get used to the idea that there might be another Rhialden heir, if it came to it. Not Truthspoken, but. Maybe give them some ease when they saw Bettea didn't have an aura, too.

He had instructed Bettea to push far away from any of his own mannerisms as Iata, because people would be speculating on that, too, that fae was actually Iata. And that was a danger, yes—though it wasn't publicly known that bloodservants could

Change, enough of the small Changes bloodservants were capable of had leaked out over the years that there were always rumors.

Bettea was obviously a few decades younger than Iata would be, but it *was* public knowledge that Truthspoken could appear younger if they wished. It took much more active work to appear older, as Iata well knew.

He and Dressa were working on leaking the story that Bettea was a child of a Truthspoken who'd sworn off Change. The former Truthspoken would not be mentioned in court, and let the court run circles over that, but the Truthspoken's child was here now and should be treated with the respect due to a member of the royal Rhialden line.

Laguaya pursed their lips as they continued to watch Bettea, and Iata waved faer off with a small annoyed flick of his fingers.

Bettea gave a masterful look of disdain, unartfully hidden in a bow, and stalked out.

And let Laguaya chew on that dynamic.

"Who is that young person?" Laguaya asked when the door had shut behind Bettea.

Okay, so no one had yet dared to ask until Laguaya. But then, Iata had known Laguaya for years. He had dressed them down the very first day he'd been in charge of the kingdom as Homaj—the first day of Homaj's rule—and that was nothing either of them would ever forget.

Laguaya settled themself on the couch across from Iata in his wingback.

Iata studied Laguaya, his longtime opponent. Their neat salt and pepper hair, trimmed short. Their impeccable uniform with its rows and rows of abbreviated medals. Maybe the most dangerous person in the kingdom just now as far as someone who could actually pull off a stable coup if they thought it would be good for the kingdom.

And that was the thing with Laguaya—they'd always been

ambitious, yes. But they always, *always* put the good of the kingdom before their own needs. He hadn't understood that at the start of Homaj's and his combined rule. But he understood it now.

His thoughts tripped and went...sideways.

Melesorie. A rule by momentum, unpredictable and dangerous for it.

He took a breath, and between heartbeats rearranged everything he'd had planned for this meeting.

He'd been dreading it, and the Kidaa attack on Hestia had pushed up its necessity, but no, *no* this was an opportunity.

"Dassan. I apologize for not having this meeting sooner."

Laguaya's eyes strayed from the door Bettea had exited back to him. "Apologizing, Homaj? Is this aura doing you good?"

They smoothed out their uniform trousers, a nervous gesture. Laguaya had never tried to hide their body language, but they'd rarely shown nerves around him before.

But then, everything had changed when Homaj Rhialden had manifested Green Magics in the public eye. And at the Reception, Laguaya had witnessed his tumult of emotions.

Everything was about to change again.

He held out his hand, very carefully keeping his body's responses in check. Terror. He was suppressing terror just now, because if he'd just wagered wrong, if he'd read Laguaya wrong all of these years, he was handing over the kingdom.

Laguaya frowned, but reached across the low coffee table between them and took his hand. "Is this going to become a habit? Do I need to prepare myself for my thoughts to be read—"

As soon as Laguaya's hand was clasped in his, he said, "I am Iata Rhialden."

He was ready for them to jerk back, and kept their hand held tightly when they did so. He said, before they could say anything, "And I'm the Adeium-sanctioned ruler of this kingdom."

Laguaya stared at him, breathing heavily, for several heartbeats. He locked eyes with them and didn't look away. He didn't drop any of his mannerisms as Homaj, but he couldn't veil his own truth in his eyes, in his touch. Not when Laguaya was looking for it.

"Both of these things," Laguaya finally said, "they feel partly true. Explain. Please. Because I have a kill order out for you, for —Adeius. For attacking *you* apparently, because that seal and aura don't lie. This"—they nodded at their hand in his— "doesn't lie. You're definitely a magicker."

"Do you want to keep verifying—"

"No, truly," Laguaya said, and he let go. They took their hand back, rubbing it slowly. He hadn't thought he'd gripped their hand that hard.

"Okay," they said, *"Iata."*

"It was me, way back, who tore you and Abret down on my first day as the interim ruler."

Laguaya sucked in a sharp breath.

"Okay, so you've been Homaj all this time? I knew bloodservants could Change—"

"I'm the elder full sibling, ahead of Maja."

Another moment to digest that. Laguaya swallowed.

And he knew where that was going—to him being behind their fathers' assassinations, and his sibling Vatrin's disappearance. He quickly said, "Maja is fine. We have been sharing the ruling of this kingdom for twenty-three years. I am happy to verify this truth again—"

Laguaya held up their hands. "All right. These are all massive fucking secrets you're handing to me, Hom—Iata."

"You can call me Homaj," he said. "It's my name as much as his, after all these years. You are talking to Homaj Rhialden."

Laguaya muttered something that sounded distinctly like

"fucking Truthspoken" and shifted in their seat. "Okay—okay. So why tell me this now? You and I have never been friends. You don't trust me, and I don't particularly trust you, especially with this new shift to a Melesorie style of rule—you're erratic. I think what you just told me is a part of that, you wouldn't have done that as a Seritarchus. And your rule is falling apart. And none of this is why I came here—I came because of the news from Hestia that there's been another Kidaa attack—"

"I know," he said, and pulled out his comm, calling up the message from Maja. He turned off the privacy on the holo window and spun it around, zooming it so Laguaya could see his translation beneath the inference code.

Laguaya read quickly, leaning forward. "I haven't seen that."

"Because it was sent to me."

"IbR. Iata byr Rhialden? Then—"

"That's Maja. I sent him to Hestia to figure out what exactly happened with Imorie and Eti—"

Laguaya stabbed a finger at him. "Is Imorie Arianna?"

"No. And yes."

Laguaya wiped their mouth. "Who the hell attacked you, Homaj, in your own study? If—if—Maja sent this from Hestia—"

"Lesander. Who is, incidentally, illegally trained in Change."

Laguaya licked their lips, their eyes a little wide as they looked at him, then went back to reading the message again, chewing on the side of their cheek. They'd grown less stoic over the years, easier to read. Hardly easier to deal with, though. They'd always been like trying to lead a bucking stallion.

"Yeah," they finally said, waving a finger at the message. "This is a mess. But that doesn't answer why you're telling me—"

"So that someone who I know has the best interest of this

kingdom at heart can witness what is actually going on, if no one else can."

They stilled, met his eyes again.

And he wasn't about to ask them permission to hold their gaze, despite the game he was playing with everyone else.

They didn't look away, and he respected that to his core.

"Do you expect another attack on your person?" Laguaya asked.

He spread his hands, laughing without humor. "Of course I do. I'm a magicker. I'm the *First* fucking Magicker."

"From Lesander?"

"No—from her family, though, I'm not sure. I've considered that you're in an excellent position to run your own coup, but I don't think you'll do that unless you see it's best for the kingdom, in which case, I might welcome you to it, Dassan.

"And on top of all of this"—he waved at the message—"I gave Rhys Delor my seal before they left to return to the border on *Occam's Storm*. Because I don't know what's going on with the Kidaa, and I need to."

Laguaya started. "Oh you should have led with that. The *Storm*. The rune, the Kidaa—" They stood, so used to their own place of command that they were ready to pace here. They seemed to catch themself, but he waved them on.

"Do what you need to think. I just let go of all pretense here."

They made a helpless gesture, starting a circuit around the room, rubbing at the back of their neck. They'd already pushed their neatly styled hair askew.

"This is a pattern," they said. "I haven't been able to find the pattern in the Kidaa attacks, but you can see it?"

"I'm seeing more of it," he said, and rose to come around the wingback he'd been sitting in. He leaned against its back as Laguaya circled behind him. "Dressa sees the same. The Kidaa attacks, the Bruising Sleep. The fact that Imorie and I are *both*

drastically high-ranking magickers. I didn't, by the way, manifest a few days ago, I've been a magicker for nine years."

Laguaya stopped, gave him a dark look, before resuming
their circuit.

"So it shouldn't be possible for someone to give someone
the Bruising Sleep," they said. "I assume that is why Arianna
was sent to Hestia, to treat the disease? Yes, that makes sense.
You, of course, were the magicker that took her down at her—
ah, they're using neutral pronouns, forgive me, I'm still piecing
this together. So you didn't give them the Bruising Sleep."

"No. And that public display was my excuse for an inspec-
tion of them to see if they did have the Bruising Sleep, as
magickers can sometimes see. Their passing out...was not the
intended result."

"Hindsight is a bitch."

Iata barked a laugh.

"So they got the Bruising Sleep," Laguaya said. "And ended
up at a treatment center on Hestia that was a front for information snatching. With a magicker who's a Javieri cousin—"

Iata jerked around, with them moving behind him again.
"What?"

Laguaya stopped. "You didn't know? I of course looked into
Etienne Tanaka, and it turns out that his mother—who by the
way barely exists in any records and has no clear images in her
ident docs, which in itself is suspicious as hell, I had to order
fleet surveillance from orbit—she's the wife of Niom Javieri.
The *dead* wife, do you remember when that happened, what a
horrible tragedy that was? It wasn't true. The report only came
back a few days ago."

Iata straightened the front of his blouse in annoyance.
Laguaya had known he hadn't known. Of course he hadn't
known, and Laguaya would have known if he'd given the order
to dig into Eti's family himself, military comm networks being
what they were, and Laguaya being who they were.

Instead, he'd pawned it all off on his agents on Kalistré while he'd been too busy trying to keep the kingdom from crumbling around him. And he'd known, he'd *known* Eti had been important, if only to Imorie, which should have been enough. He'd done what he thought he could, but...Dassan had done more.

Dassan gave a small smile, their pettiness satisfied, before it faded again, and they sighed. "Forgive me. You handed me an enormous amount of hot leads just now, and I should have handed this right back. It was, truly, one of the things I wished to discuss today. Though I did half suspect you would already know."

34

EVERYTHING

I never used to think confession was a virtue. Now, I sometimes wish it wasn't.

— HOMAJ RHIALDEN, SERITARCHUS IX IN A
PRIVATE LETTER, NEVER SENT; PUBLISHED IN
THE CHANGE DIALOGUES

Iata opened his hands, waved back to the couch, and they both returned to their seats.

"So," Laguaya said, settling in again. "Imorie is with Koldari, who was involved with the Javieris on Hestia—"

"That hasn't been proven. But I don't trust him at all."

"And you let your child—forgive me, your brother's child, do I have that right? Yes."

"Actually, my child. Imorie is Maja's by birth, but I did adopt them, legally."

"Of course you did," Laguaya said with an exasperated wave. "So they are with Koldari, he has ties, some sort of ties, to the Javieris. The Javieris and Koldaris both had Kidaa attacks on their worlds. Among others. But notably, them. Koldari was in a place that treated the Bruising Sleep, that also was the place where Imorie was sent—yes?"

"Yes, though neither Maja nor I knew anything about the racket going on there."

"No, of course not." And that was said without sarcasm, thank Adeius.

Laguaya went on, "And now Imorie has manifested Green Magics, and you already had Green Magics—both of you, if you're telling me right, the ranking members of your royal generations. Publicly remaining members, anyway. Yes?"

A chill passed over him, because he had missed that detail. He'd been thinking about it in terms of just being in his family, and he was used to being a magicker by now. And he hadn't, when he'd manifested, been as actively ruling the kingdom as he was now. But he was still the eldest of the Rhialden siblings of his generation still in power. His oldest sibling, Vatrin's bloodservant, Eyras, was still out there, but—

"Yes," he said.

"And now Maja, who is on Hestia, has been attacked by the Kidaa, with a rune that was plain enough he recognized it as a clue for him specifically. So we can only assume that the Kidaa —or whoever is carving these runes—knew both who he was, as I'm assuming he wasn't Homaj if you're Homaj here, and wanted him at the border, on *Occam's Storm*."

They pursed their lips. "There is nothing unusual going on with the *Storm*, that I know of. But there's a five to six day comm lag, depending on the relay drones and information priority, and a lot can happen in five days."

Another chill, a different type of fear.

"Rhys was researching the Kidaa," Iata said. "I gave them my seal to be able to send messages back without fear of repercussions. Rhys—Dassan, Rhys is nearly as trained in evaku as Dressa or Imorie. If they're at the forefront of information coming in about the Kidaa, they might be piecing things together that the experts won't see."

"And they're a steady officer, if mediocre in performance," Laguaya said. Then smiled, the irony plain. "Which, I now gather, was intentional."

Iata shrugged. He'd seen Rhys meld seamlessly into the friendly, slightly clumsy, average-ability officer. Not forgettable by any means—Rhys was Rhys—but not someone you'd call for your first pick in a crisis. Not unless you knew who they really were beneath the act.

"You are right, though," he said, "we can't know what happened—or is happening—on *Occam's Storm*. And if these attacks are actually from the Kidaa—because there still have been no signs of any ship in orbit, anything actually carving these runes into the ground, correct?"

"As far as I'm informed, correct."

He nodded. "Then they might be carried out from a distance. Impossible as that seems—we still don't understand the Kidaa's drive systems, and how sometimes they seem to be following the rules of Below Space, and sometimes their ships appear faster than they should be. The Kidaa might be reacting to events we don't know about yet."

Laguaya shifted. "There have been scattered reports in recent days of ships' magickers saying they feel disturbed when entering Below Space. Not all of them, and I thought it was maybe all the trouble with magickers of late"—a tight smile in his direction—"but maybe that's not something to dismiss."

This was new. And not at all something he liked.

"You should have brought that to me, as the First Magicker," he said.

"The reports were copied to Green Hall, as is anything to do with ships' magickers."

Iata gave a frustrated nod. Which Mariyit would be handling, because he himself didn't have the time.

"This wasn't a position I asked for, but yes, point," he said.

He wanted to pace as Laguaya had, which wasn't usual for him. It was this damned Melesorie energy, and he found his knee bobbing.

Dassan frowned at that, but didn't comment.

"So, all of this—*all* of this together," he said. "If Maja was Changed on Hestia, there is an extremely low chance that anyone could have guessed his identity. And I'm here, so there's no reason they should think he's Homaj."

"He signed the message as Iata, could someone have suspected his identity as Iata? Or could he be plainly using that identity?"

"Yes, but—I think he both used that to move someone to his needs on Hestia, and sent that to me as a signal. It's the way the original message was worded, we have more than one layer of code in the message itself."

"That I'm well aware of," Laguaya said, and it was his turn to give that smallest of petty grins.

He held up his hands in concession. "So, Maja wasn't himself and wasn't me—me as Iata, I mean. He would have been keeping as low a profile as possible on Hestia, with Zhang."

"I did know Captain Zhang went, and Shiera Keralan, and Captain Temir—ah, is he Temir? That would make sense to have a persona among his guards." They sat back, brows up. "Or is he Keralan? Damn, I've worked with Keralan for years."

Iata just smiled. He had to hold something back, because even while this conversation was moving at the speed of light, and he knew things now that he hadn't before, he was still deeply, deeply galled that he'd told Laguaya anything of what he had. He was feeling more than a little dazed.

"All right, regardless," Laguaya said, accepting his deflection, though he knew they were still churning on the problem. "It's not likely a Human could have known who he was. Possible, but not likely, unless you have a massive leak in your intelligence network, and I haven't seen explicit signs of that. Or unless perhaps there were magickers involved, and that's an angle I don't like at all—have you considered these Kidaa attacks were made by magickers? No one has been deliberately hurt, though there was that one death on Sangor Brec."

"No," Iata said flatly. "Because I know what happens when magickers do violence, and this is definitely violence. And that's not how Green Magics work."

Laguaya nodded. "So another rune was carved out near Maja, giving directions to the—fucking hell. He *is* Keralan, too, isn't he? And Temir? He's both of them, personas for different circumstances. In the report—it was right in front of Shiera Keralan." Laguaya wiped a hand across their eyes, sighed.

Iata laughed, because it was ridiculous. All of it ridiculous, this dancing around each other, keeping all the information they had separate. And he was still doing it now.

Laguaya smiled in sour appreciation. And he noted the hints of betrayal in their posture. They had worked with Shiera Keralan before—mostly everyone who'd been in and around the palace had worked with Shiera at some point, she was one of the personas Maja had used more steadily over the years.

But that was how Truthspoken worked. Everyone knew it—they could be anyone.

And no, he didn't like Laguaya, but maybe they had deserved better than to be deceived by the people around them, the people they served. No matter that Iata had been taught the necessity of deception, no matter that his role as Homaj ran so deep that it had become a large part of his reality, with his aura out around him now, he felt the subtle violence of it. The destructive force behind those lies.

"I'm sorry," he said.

Laguaya held up their hands, fending off the apology. "You're Truthspoken. Adeius, it's your holy mandate."

He nodded. Maybe it wasn't an excuse he should lean on, but it was true.

But he respected Laguaya. And he respected their tactical mind. Laguaya had held the position of Admiral of the Fleet for almost three decades, maintaining a razored edge over everyone around them, including the kingdom's enemies.

"Last thing," he said, shifting in his chair, pulling attention back to less unsteady things, "is that Denom Xiao told me the Assembly is planning to give me a vote of no confidence."

"I did know that, and if you will believe me, I'd been coming to warn you about that, too. And is it related? The timing, at least, is opportune."

Iata stopped his bobbing knee with an effort. Crossed his legs, placed his hands on either chair arm, the gauzy sky blue of his sleeves sighing around them.

Laguaya watched his movements but still didn't comment.

"So," he said. "All of it. What do you make of it?"

Laguaya sat back, chewing again on the inside of their cheek. Eyeing him again, and he knew they wanted to say something they weren't saying. "I do think this is orchestrated. Whatever is happening, it has a definite origin point."

"Yes," Iata said fervently, and with no pleasure.

Laguaya nodded. "It's been bothering me, all the disparate pieces. Bothering me intensely. And—Homaj, I'm not going to be able to rescind my kill order on you—on Iata—before your brother gets to the *Storm*. If he's being Iata in any way, he is in danger."

"I know. Rhys has my seal—a perpetual seal, and they know that. I can only hope people have cool enough heads to know what to do with all of this."

Laguaya swore softly. "You said you're ruling the kingdom—you're the Adeium-sanctioned ruler, you said—do you mean alongside him? Maja, I mean?"

"Maja has already legally abdicated. And I was planning to

step up in my own right, as Iata, before Imorie came back as a magicker. That would have been after Dressa's wedding."

"Ah. For what it's worth, I'm sorry about that."

He shrugged. And best answer that very first question Laguaya had asked, too, while he was at it. Because his reasons for why he was telling Laguaya all of this were catching up with his actually doing so, and he saw that one question as absolutely vital.

"The young person, who saw you in, is my eldest child. Bettea."

Laguaya blinked. "Your eldest—not Maja's? Not like your own parentage?"

"No, Bettea's not Maja's or Haneri's. Fae's mine. And trained enough that, if it comes to it, fae could rule. With as much bloodline claim as Dressa or Imorie."

"And the other bloodservant, Pria?"

"Also mine. Trained, but not, I think, of the right temperament. But also, if it came to it, an option."

Laguaya looked down.

And Iata stilled, because yes, there it was, all of it in the open.

And he knew what he was thinking, but he wanted, truly wanted to know what Laguaya was thinking.

He waited. He waited while Laguaya was silent, churning on all of it.

They made a humming noise. Nodded again, and looked up. "If I had to make a guess on my gut, it's the high houses—Javieri, certainly, and possibly also Koldari. As much as Denom Xiao is an ass, I don't think the Xiaos are involved. But not just the high houses. I truly think the attacks are from the Kidaa, and I'll tell you, Homaj, that chills me to my bones. Every last one of them."

He carefully eased his fingers from where they'd begun to

clench the arms of his chair. It was where his thoughts had been going as well.

"The high houses are after your rulership," Laguaya went on, "but the Kidaa are after...what?"

"I don't know. And I'm not afraid to say that it terrifies me."

"And me."

Laguaya rose again. He rose with them, because he felt the urgency now. He'd been distracted by his incident, his injury, but the message from Maja had brought it all back. He wasn't ruling this kingdom so much as reacting to someone else's machinations. And he did not like that at all. Time to turn the tables, if he could. Adeius, he hoped he could.

"If we send more ships to the border," he said, "we risk signaling war."

"And if we don't, we risk losing a war."

He wanted to say the Kidaa had only ever been peaceful, but he'd heard Rhys's concerns when they'd been talking with Dressa in the terrace garden. And he trusted Rhys's gut almost as much as his own. As any Truthspoken's. They were just too well-trained not to see the patterns and react, even before they knew what it was all about.

"You can't abdicate," Laguaya said. "And you can't be anyone but Homaj."

"Agreed, on both counts."

"And you picked a hell of a time to change your style of rule, I can see it has you off balance."

"It was that or lose the rulership right there."

Laguaya nodded. They'd been there.

They sighed, turned toward the door. "The fleet's already on medium alert because of the Kidaa attacks, and then the attack on you—"

They stopped, turned around again. "Forgive me, I'm already in action mode, you didn't dismiss me. And despite everything you've told me—Adeius, because of everything you've entrusted me with today, and I am deeply, deeply grateful, Iata—you are still my ruler. You are still the person Adeius has placed over this kingdom, whatever that means for the rest of us. Thank you for trusting me."

And they bowed. Deeper than they had ever bowed to him before.

He swallowed and came around the couch to give his own deep nod back, a little lower than was justifiable from his pinnacle to theirs. His own respect, deepest respect.

"If you and I can keep our heads, we might weather this," he said.

Laguaya nodded, smoothing back their hair. "And the Truthspeaker, I presume. I'm not going to presume more of my own power than I've been given."

"And you have my deepest gratitude for that as well. You were saying—"

"Yes. The fleet is already on alert. I'd like to step up the alert, under the pretense of increased tensions and the kingdom's security. As much as I'd like to rescind the kill order, it is useful—"

"Yes. I don't like it, but agreed. If it's going to affect Maja, we can't help that now."

"And I would like to converge some of the border ships on *Occam's Storm*. Just a few. Captain Nantrayan has a steady head, but she's never actually seen action. Not many of us have, if I'm honest. It will take long—long for the order to get there, longer for the ships to converge. If Maja is there, and Rhys is there, and you trust Rhys enough to give them your seal—well, that is a level-headed presence at the border. Level-headed enough. Do you wish to send anyone else? Anyone specific?"

But there was no one else just now that he trusted to send, that he didn't also need.

No, he trusted both Rhys and Maja implicitly.

And he had a feeling that Rhys was about to step into the thick of it—if they hadn't already.

"No. They will be enough. When we have reports from the border—then we will decide what to do. If it hasn't already been decided, and Rhys will have that authority if it comes to it."

"All the same, I'd like to send in one of my more experienced tacticians with a small battle group to the border. We'll call it exercises."

"Yes. Agreed. Thank you, Dassan."

He turned to head to his desk, head as stuffed as it could get. This was almost, *almost* worse than trying to suppress his aura, bending his personality into a shape that wasn't natural to him.

He turned back a step later, as Laguaya was reaching for the door.

"If something happens to me, or if I'm forced out, or—"

Laguaya held up their hands. And he saw it again now, that look they'd given him before. It was...foreboding. Maybe, maybe more certainty than he liked. Dassan saw the patterns, too, brilliant fleet administrator that they were.

Iata was holding onto the rulership by a thread, and that thread was likely to snap.

"Then I will do my utmost," Laguaya said, "with what you've given me, to support Dressa, to maintain the Rhialden line. And failing that, to maintain the kingdom."

"And Lesander," he said. "And Haneri. Their family loyalties have both been in question at times, but they are loyal. Both of them are loyal. Protect them, Dassan."

Laguaya gave him a long, level glare. Then bowed again and retreated. They shut the door quietly behind them.

And he stood, his heart hammering, silence ringing in his ears.

He'd just given them everything, his longtime political rival.

Laguaya could have him imprisoned, have him dead within the hour. They truly could. There was a kill order on him that Laguaya had initiated, and he'd just confessed his identity.

But they wouldn't do that. He knew that as surely as he trusted Maja and Rhys to handle the border.

Laguaya had been headed toward a coup because of the mistrust, because of the rift between the military and the ruler-ship—a rift he'd helped cause.

And now?

Now, he could only hope they'd sail course with him for a while. See the kingdom to better shores.

35

WAITING

Duty on the edge.

— SHIP'S MOTTO FOR THE BORDER SCOUT
SHIP *V.N.S. OCCAM'S STORM*

"Sir. The Kidaa are moving."

Rhys, who'd scattered an array of open holo windows around them while they sat bridge watch, looked up. The viewscreen at the front showed the tagged Kidaa ships, as it had since the Kidaa had arrived, but now the distance between the center ship, Clan Starlight, and the *Storm* was shrinking.

Oh, Adeius. Were the Kidaa going to overlap? Would they finally get some answers?

Rhys had, under Hamid's guidance, directed the *Storm* in the subtle maneuvering code hours ago, trying to get the Kidaa's attention. And...nothing had happened. Again. Nothing, for hours.

They were still trying the maneuvering code every half hour, but it was nearing the end of the third watch, and they'd been dreading—and, if they were honest, hoping for—turning to head back to Valon.

Rhys, in the observer's chair, had a moment, a single moment, to freeze.

Commander Hamid had gone to bed after a long day. The captain was still in the infirmary. Commander Gian had—so Hamid had said—finally let one of the medics sedate him enough to sleep. Misha was still with Gian in the infirmary, and she'd been with him all day.

And Rhys—Hamid had left them the bridge. Left them in command of the whole ship. Had put them back on active duty, in their nebulous provisional status. Had said, "Wake me if anything so much as twitches, Lieutenant."

"Call Commander Hamid to the bridge," Rhys said to the comm tech, standing and clearing their holo windows to move toward the ops station behind them. Ensign Neri Wawuda was on watch there, and when she looked up, Rhys swallowed at the fear in her eyes. At the way she looked at Rhys—not as a friend anymore, but as someone who had the power to make this situation different than it was. Better, maybe. Or worse.

Neri moved aside as Rhys leaned over the displays, taking in all the information they could at a glance. Rearranging two of the holo windows to better see the data.

The Kidaa ship was coming up from behind on a steady acceleration. They were not angling to go beside the *Storm,* but coming straight on. They were almost certainly trying to overlap.

And should Rhys move the ship away? Was there danger?

But that was why they were still here. To talk. That was why Rhys had been signaling them. Rhys didn't understand the delay—had the Kidaa been debating among themselves on what they should do and only just now reached a decision?

Rhys didn't know the minds of the Kidaa, as much as they'd studied. And they desperately needed to understand what the

Kidaa wanted. For everyone. And what had happened with the captain and Gian had only opened a gulf of more terrifying questions.

At least—at least no one else had manifested Green Magics, or come down with the Bruising Sleep. Rhys was still most of the way braced to get either of those things themself, as someone the Kidaa saw as a person of power. Well, and that was truer now than it had been the first time the Kidaa had overlapped.

Rhys stood back from Neri's station and returned to the center of the bridge, but didn't sit. They watched the front screen, now showing a zoomed panoramic view as the Kidaa ship approached from behind. The blocky ship was getting larger at an alarming rate.

"Comm, shipwide," they said, and took a breath. "All hands to stations. Kidaa ship on aft approach for overlap. Commander Hamid to the bridge. Ensign Moratu to the bridge."

The comm chimed off as the sirens started to blare.

Rhys swallowed. Adeius, but they hadn't thought they'd have to issue orders like that. They'd thought the captain would, or Gian, or Hamid. Someone other than them.

Then Rhys forced themself to sit again in the observer's chair. Then, eyeing the captain's chair with its much, much better systems controls and displays, Rhys held their breath and transferred their butt to there.

They braced as they sat, half expecting another alarm to go off. Or someone to jump up and say they shouldn't be sitting in the captain's chair. But no one did. Rhys didn't catch fire.

Hamid would be here shortly, and Rhys needed the better data displays in the meantime. Until Hamid got to the bridge, Rhys was in command.

And maybe they should have been sitting in the captain's chair all along.

Rhys glanced up over their shoulder at the ops stations on

the bridge's upper level. "Ops, I want all the data as you're pulling it, anything relevant, sent to me. Don't filter it."

They waved up the displays on the arms of the captain's chair, and the immediate world around them flooded with dozens of windows of raw data, auto-filtered system reports, charts, math, with inset views from every camera angle that could see the Kidaa ship.

The ship had halved the distance between them in the time it had taken Rhys to sit in the captain's chair.

Shit, shit it was accelerating, coming in faster than Rhys had thought. The Kidaa didn't usually come in this fast for an overlap.

Rhys, noticing their leg bobbing rapidly, their shoulders tensed from the noise, made a face and pressed a control to stop the sirens. But they kept the alert status holos on—those would show pulsing red orbs near the ceiling of every corridor, and show a red pulsing icon on every comm panel not in use. No one would miss that the ship was still under alert.

But their tension relaxed, just a little, when the sirens stopped.

Were they trained for this? They'd trained for eventual command in Academy, sure. Though Rhys had never been the leader of any given squad of cadets. Were their games with their siblings any help to them here? Other than pretending mightily that they knew what they were doing?

"Sir," the pilot said, and they were a full lieutenant, outranking Rhys. In military ranks at least. Short, thin, coiled black hair buzzed tight. Rhys had never been close with them, but had met them often enough in the corridors, in the gym. "We should go. We should get into Below Space before that ship reaches us."

Rhys took a breath. "No, we need to—"

"Sir! Seriously, we should go! We're not a warship, we can't deal with those Kidaa ships on our own—"

"They have no weapons," Rhys said, keeping their voice calm. And that training, right there, was useful.

They straightened subtly. Pulled, again, from what they'd observed in Homaj. And maybe some of Ari's presence, too. Drew the center of authority to themself as inherent.

"They attacked the captain and commander!" the pilot was rising from their seat now, eyes and attention off their controls.

"Resume your station," Rhys said. And added, "Please." They inwardly cringed at that—that was a mistake. And the pilot seized on it.

"Rhys, I don't know what you're playing at, but these are our *lives*—"

Rhys eyed the Kidaa ship rapidly approaching the aft hull. They checked the graphs—the Kidaa ship had slowed, at least, for the actual overlap, but was still coming in fast.

Rhys added snap to their voice this time. "Lieutenant, resume your station. Comm, shipwide: aft overlap in one minute."

The pilot stormed toward them. "Get out of the fucking chair, I don't care if you're a capital favorite, I outrank you—"

Rhys stood. Planted themself to the deck, borrowed their body language wholesale from Homaj Rhialden when he was at his most incandescent.

"Stop," they said. One clipped word.

And the pilot stopped. Mouth opening, brows furrowing.

"This is my decision," Rhys said. "And I'm playing for the lives of the kingdom."

The pilot's throat bobbed as they swallowed.

"Thirty seconds to overlap," an ops tech called.

"Resume your station," Rhys snapped to the pilot, who finally held up their hands, walked quickly back to their seat. Sat with hunched concentration.

Rhys's own loud swallow, they feared, betrayed them. But no one else protested. And glancing around the bridge, it looked just that little more cohesive, everyone sitting a little taller and with more purpose than before.

Because Rhys had, fully and publicly, just taken control. And because they'd stated the purpose in all of this.

The fate of the kingdom.

Adeius help them all.

The bridge hatch opened and Hamid charged through, still buttoning up her uniform jacket, her hair hastily wet and combed.

"Give me a report, Petrava."

The dissonance of that order with the moment before, with its tone from a commander to a junior, rocked Rhys on their heels. They did a quick assessment—Hamid's presence was tensing the crew back up again. That shouldn't have happened, and they didn't want to lose the cohesion they'd had a moment before. Not now.

So they kept their bearing. Still, gallingly, owed to the Seritarchus.

"Commander," they said, with respect but not deference, "we have fifteen seconds to aft overlap. Approaching fast. We should probably face behind."

Hamid surveyed them as she approached the captain's chair but leaned against its back, not yet coming around to sit in it. She noted, of course, Rhys's open spread of holo windows around the chair. And even though she didn't have evaku, she'd absolutely note Rhys's bearing. Rhys was broadcasting control like a loudspeaker.

"You know what this is about?" she asked, brows raised.

"Not yet," Rhys said, and moved back to the chair to check the time.

"Kidaa overlap on the aft hull," an ops tech announced.

Rhys suppressed a shiver, but stepped back again into the open space in front of the command stations. Opened a hand for Hamid to join them.

And that was pretentious, but Hamid strode to their side without question.

They both positioned themselves facing the back of the bridge to await the inevitable.

The ghostly outline of the Kidaa ship's nose formed so quickly this time it expanded to span the bridge before Rhys could blink. The outline of the other ship passed in a blur, ghostly Kidaa rushing past them, until it slowed, slowed, came to a stop.

Rhys could just barely make out the outline of what they thought was the same room the Kidaa leaders had been in when they'd overlapped with the bridge of the *Occam's Storm* before. But facing the other way around now, and Rhys was trying not to be so disoriented by that.

There was a single Kidaa, already facing them. Were they one of the ones Rhys had spoken with before? They were tall, their gray-gold skin darker with more gray than gold, their tough skin carved with runes. They looked down at Rhys with their oval eyes on their wedge-shaped head, hands clasped in front of them, four legs restless.

Yes, it was the Kidaa who'd been in the center before. Rhys thought they recognized the pattern of runes, and they definitely recognized the sense of authority that this Kidaa carried. They weren't quite as tangible as they had been before, though, and what did that mean?

The Kidaa rumbled, and the *Storm's* systems attempted to translate.

"Human one, you have spun, we have spun. Comes from the perimeter. We are."

Rhys tried to puzzle that out and blinked. Oh, sometimes the Kidaa used "I am" statements in a way that meant remaining, being here in a specific place. "We are here continually," not just "we are." Or rather, in context with "comes from the perimeter," maybe "we are here waiting?" Waiting for someone from a perimeter somewhere?

"You're waiting for someone?" Rhys asked. "You're waiting for another Kidaa ship?"

"Human one."

The Kidaa hadn't started with the same preamble they had before. There felt like an urgency to this conversation. And it was without the usual ceremony, without the three Kidaa—there were *always* three Kidaa, just like there were *never* three ships. And a Kidaa ship had never, to Rhys's knowledge, over-lapped from behind. What did that mean? Was it a social power play? Did it hold some other significance, maybe a signal of casual conversation rather than formal conversation?

"Who are we waiting for?"

Music blared from the bridge speakers, and Rhys cringed their hands up, stopping short of covering their ears.

We surf on the plains
while we run
while we drive.

Not the Rings of Vietor this time, but one of their predecessors, the older multi-platinum Anti-spin Connection. That was from their song "Drive." Not their best song by a long shot.

The music abruptly stopped in the middle of the chorus.

And what did *that* song mean? That didn't fit any pattern Rhys knew of—though, if the Kidaa were waiting for someone, maybe it meant that someone was coming quickly. Running.

Rhys looked up into the Kidaa's oval eyes, high on the wedge of their head. The Kidaa blinked their eyes, a thick membrane visible as their lids retracted again.

It almost looked like a deliberate expression, and the body language seemed tense, but Rhys couldn't trust that assessment if it was based on their understanding of Human cues.

Adeius, they didn't know enough. *They didn't know enough.*

"We are," Rhys said, echoing the Kidaa's words.

The Kidaa made a swooping gesture with two fingers.

Then the Kidaa became intangible again, like the rest of the Kidaa ship, and then...just stayed where they were. Rhys waited, expecting the Kidaa ship to back off again, because that's what usually happened when the Kidaa went intangible again, but it didn't. Nothing happened.

Absolutely nothing was happening as it should be just now.

The Kidaa they'd spoken to just stood there, a ghostly outline. If Rhys watched closely, they could see the gentle movements of the Kidaa's breathing.

And the Kidaa could see theirs. They were still studying Rhys back.

Rhys's heart stuttered. And what was this now? If the Kidaa were waiting for someone, if Rhys possibly had that right, were they just going to...stay here? Just stand here, half on the bridge of the Kidaa ship, half on the bridge of the *Storm?*

The bridge hatch opened, and Rhys jumped.

Captain Nantrayan stepped through, leaning heavily on Misha with one arm, a cane with the other. Oh. And that was why Misha hadn't come yet.

The captain looked at the Kidaa, still a ghostly outline in the center of the bridge. She didn't say anything, though, as she made her slow way across the bridge to stand on Rhys's other side, opposite of Hamid. Hamid, for her part, had been very still. Exquisitely silent. Rhys read the panic and didn't blame her one bit.

The captain stopped, fighting to catch her breath, then took a long inhale and bowed stiffly to the Kidaa.

The Kidaa turned to look at her. But they didn't become more tangible, just stayed a translucent outline.

Rhys felt a sudden and intense spike of anger. Was the Kidaa studying their victim? Had Clan Starlight given the

Bruising Sleep to the captain, or one of the other clans? Someone on the Kidaa ships had. Of that Rhys was almost certain.

And Rhys saw, too, the simmering rage just behind the captain's eyes. Etched into every line of her posture. She wanted to challenge the Kidaa. She wanted to demand answers for why a day ago she'd been healthy, and today she was not.

Rhys shunted their own rage aside. They had to. It would do absolutely no good, and they had to steady the captain before she started an interstellar incident.

"I think," Rhys said in a low voice, "that they're waiting for someone. And that they're going to wait right here."

The captain hissed through her teeth. Then made a small noise of pain and maneuvered, with Misha's help, around the Kidaa to sit in her command chair. She glanced at Rhys's still open windows, then brushed most of them aside.

"Do we know how long this is going to take?" Captain Nantrayan asked.

Adeius, she looked worn. The lines on her face furrowed much deeper than they should be. Her mouth pinched. Hands slightly trembling.

Rhys stepped closer to the single Kidaa and gave the smallest bow. "Human one wishes to speak with Kidaa one. Comes from the center, breathes from the center."

But the Kidaa only looked at them, then looked away again.

"Well, then," the captain said with a sigh. "I guess we wait."

36

CHANGE AND CHANGE

> A Truthspoken's personas aren't just tools used to gather or insert information—my personas were always a part of me, different facets and ways to experience the world. If we're the eyes and ears of Adeius, then we must see from all points of view, even those we find less than satisfactory.
>
> — ARIANNA RHIALDEN, MELESORIE X IN *THE CHANGE DIALOGUES*

Dressa's public wedding was set for two weeks out. She had no mental space to think about it, to gather all the details, certainly not after Iata had briefed her on what was happening with her father. And Rhys. That Rhys had Iata's seal and might be in the center of whatever was happening with the Kidaa sat like a gnawing claw in her gut—and there was nothing she could do to help. Even if she wanted to go to the border, she couldn't.

She had a wedding in two weeks.

And with the state of the kingdom, possibly a bid to rule.

So Haneri had taken over wedding plans, also scheduling in a much smaller, private ceremony with her and Iata in three days, to be officiated by Ceorre. Dressa would be there. And so, apparently, would Lesander, who Iata had asked, too.

Neither Dressa nor Lesander really knew what to do with that.

But this thing with the Assembly and the upcoming vote of no confidence—the vote would happen in two days. That was something that needed handled, and Iata couldn't. And he couldn't ask Dressa to handle it, either, he couldn't ask anyone—if he was ever questioned on his influence over the Assembly, and he might be, he couldn't lie about that.

Dressa was absolutely sure the Assembly would have someone read Iata with any kind of testimony. The Assembly might not fully have the teeth to make binding policies in the kingdom, but they certainly could cause trouble—even and up to forcing the ruler to testify before them in a hearing for a vote of no confidence.

The timing was horrible, and that was planned, Dressa was sure.

Dressa leaned on Lesander's desk in her prep room, making Lesander look up and arch her brows. Which, for a stuttering moment, had Dressa tracing the elegance of those brows with her eyes and wanting to reach out, follow the curve of Lesander's cheek to her lips—

"I thought you had another meeting?" Lesander asked.

Dressa drew in a breath. "It was with Laguaya—I canceled. You and I need to do something."

Lesander sat back, waving away the holo windows where she'd been—at a glance—studying the system economic trends since Iata's attack. Since her attack on Iata.

Dressa had seen the projections, and they weren't good.

"Do what?" Lesander asked, and though she hid it well,

Dressa didn't miss the wariness that had suddenly underwritten everything about her wife.

Dressa grinned, and not a particularly nice grin, she knew. But it was hiding her own unease about what she wanted to do.

"My sibling, Imorie, has a persona in the General Assembly that they use to occasionally sway opinions. A smarmy, sycophantic lord who has ties to most major members. I accompanied Imorie a few times, when I was still being sent on missions. I'm going to go Change into this person now, and you're going to Change to come with me as my aide."

Lesander looked between her eyes. "Does the Melesorie know—" She shook her head. "No, he wouldn't. This isn't by his command, he can't command you to do this."

"Exactly."

Lesander stood, following Dressa into the bedroom. "What about Pria? Shouldn't she be the one to accompany you on a mission like this, as your bloodservant?"

But Pria, again, wasn't there. Dressa had gotten tired of Pria's constant attitude about Lesander and tasked her with helping Bettea with the kingdom's administration.

She understood Pria's anger, she really did. But it was interfering with her own duties, and Dressa couldn't have that.

"Pria doesn't Change easily," Dressa said. She pulled back the covers on the bed, waved her wife to the side where Lesander typically slept.

"You want me to Change now?" Lesander asked. Not, probably, because she was surprised. Dressa read the tightening of her posture, the closing of her expression. Even more than the wariness now was Lesander's fear.

"You've Changed in front of me before," Dressa said.

"Yes, but—"

But that had been *that night.* Dressa knew. And she'd ill-used Lesander that night, too, forcing her into a fast and dangerous Change.

"We're not going to Change that quickly," Dressa said. "Not a long Change, but—"

Lesander nodded, climbing into bed. "Who do you want me to be? Do you have a genetic profile, can I see a scanner?"

Dressa did have a profile in mind. She had thought, briefly, about having Lesander use the identity she'd used when going with Imorie—but that would be too weird.

So she'd settled, instead, on borrowing the identity of a lower palace administrator, someone who wouldn't be implausibly corralled into a minor lord's orbit for a few days. The administrator herself had been given a large stipend in untraceable cash and sent on a quiet vacation that morning in one of the Melesorie's private shuttles. If any of this damaged the administrator's career, Dressa would make sure she was well-compensated.

Dressa pulled out a genetic scanner built specifically to aid in Change, which she'd programmed that morning. She handed it to Lesander.

Lesander flicked it on, studying the screen. "Administrator Zara. I've met her. Worked with her briefly when I was hunting down Koldari."

Lesander swallowed. She didn't ask if it was okay if she impersonated this administrator. The administrator, having worked in the palace this long around Truthspoken, would almost certainly know what it meant to be whisked away like this, and had agreed to the stipend. Dressa hadn't had to take that step, but—she'd wanted to do this right. Her father and Imorie hadn't been afraid to skate past ethics, but Dressa didn't want to be that kind of Truthspoken.

"And who will you be?" Lesander asked. "You said it was a lord?"

Dressa pulled out her own genetic scanner—she'd given Lesander Pria's. On her screen was the genetic characteristics, in Truthspoken syntax, of one Lord Mynin Jadiar, a second child of a minor noble house, more self-important by far than actually important. It was a persona Imorie had been cultivating since their mid-teens, pushing the bounds of how old they could appear at the time with Change, and a persona that was now fairly well-established.

Lord Jadiar, of course, wouldn't have been seen at the Assembly recently with Imorie offworld and unable to Change, but there were automations in place with all established Truthspoken personas to keep up correspondence, accounts, travel, everything needed for a healthy public and private persona. Lord Jadiar had been ill the last few weeks and would be returning to the Assembly Hall today.

"Lord Mynin Jadiar," Dressa said.

Lesander's brows twitched before she smoothed out her expression. So the name was familiar. But of course Lesander would have studied everything about Valon politics with the job she'd been sent to pull off.

Lesander nodded and settled back. "I can do this."

Dressa smiled, climbing in and settling down herself. "I know."

She reached and squeezed Lesander's hand under the covers. Lesander's look was tentative, more nakedly hopeful than Dressa had seen in days.

They still hadn't slept more than beside each other. They hadn't been together.

Dressa stretched and kissed Lesander, gently, on the lips. She felt Lesander shudder.

Then she pulled back, let go. Even though a very large and very loud part of her wanted to linger. To *deepen.*

"Can you take less than an hour and a half for this Change?" she asked.

Lesander considered. "I think so. This person isn't so terribly far from my own height, and there are some similarities in facial structure."

"Can you do it," Dressa asked more quietly, "without pain?"

Lesander met her eyes.

It was as much apology as Dressa could give right now. With everything still raw beneath the surface.

Lesander nodded, then closed her eyes.

Dressa resettled and closed hers, too. It was a measure of immense trust to begin a Change in anyone's presence, knowing how vulnerable she would be.

But she heard Lesander's breaths deepen as Lesander slipped into her own Change trance. Dressa, after a few breaths, went under, too.

37

TRUTHSPOKEN MISSION

You all know it's statistically impossible for the Truth-spoken to have slept with all ten thousand or so of you in the last year, right? Like, there's no way. There's three of them. And I'm pretty sure they're very busy ruling the kingdom. So give it up and own up that maybe some of your conquests were just kind of ordinary.

— ANONYMOUS26671-L2 IN THE CHATSPHERE *I THINK I SLEPT WITH A TRUTHSPOKEN*

When Dressa woke, they were both different people. Lesander was still in trance, though her features looked about where they needed to be. She'd be done soon.

Dressa let herself ease out of her trance slowly, stretching out her toes, scrunching her shoulders. Breathing through different lungs.

Different body, different bounds. Still her own, though it would take her time, as it always did, to inhabit it. And she wasn't keen on this taking any longer than was necessary—Iata needed her here.

She had cleared the rest of her schedule for the day, citing internal meetings, but that wouldn't last more than a day. If her mission to the Assembly needed more time than that, she'd have to Change back to herself, then Change to Lord Jadiar again.

Well. She always had been fast at Changing to someone else if she needed to be. She just didn't like it.

Dressa reached for the water bottle she always left beside her bed—just in case—and propped up enough to drink it. She rooted in her bedside cabinet for an energy bar and found one, quietly peeling back the wrapper. She'd brought a cooler of food with her when she'd come in earlier, leaving it in the prep room. They'd both need to replenish reserves before they went out.

The rhythm of Lesander's breathing changed, and Dressa looked over.

Lesander's eyes fluttered, her breath caught, and she jerked upright, eyes wide.

"Whoa," Dressa said, holding up a hand. She winced at her different voice, a little smoother around different edges, and ruthlessly incorporated it into her image of herself. "Lesander, you're fine, you're with me—"

Lesander focused on her, her panicked expression not changing.

Then—then she relaxed.

"Dressa."

Lesander lay back with a thump. Pressed both palms over her eyes. "I thought—"

Well. Dressa didn't have to think far to wonder why Lesander would panic. Lesander wasn't supposed to Change. Lesander wasn't supposed to know how to—and then she'd come out of her trance, in a body that wasn't her own, to a stranger beside her.

Dressa rummaged for another energy bar, grabbed another water bottle from the cabinet, too, and handed both over.

Lesander sat up, raking a hand through her hair.

It was black. Dressa would need to cut it—Lesander hadn't shed and regrown it in the style she'd needed, that would have taken more time, and been a mess, the cut would be faster.

Lesander surveyed Dressa with an odd look.

Dressa, feeling more self-conscious than she should have been, looked down at herself.

She knew exactly what she looked like. A little paler, deep maroon cosmetically altered hair in loose waves around her shoulders. The same length as hers had been, though Lord Mynin Jadiar's hair tended to be shoulder length or longer, so that was fine.

Lord Mynin Jadiar was also one of the only personas Imorie had that was much physically larger than Imorie typically preferred. Mynin was just a centimeter shorter than Dressa, close enough that the height part of the Change hadn't been drastic. Solid, stocky frame, small breasts, muscular. They obviously worked out.

Dressa thought Imorie had been going for size presence in the Assembly, not just sheer personality, and some people would certainly react to that and give Mynin more time, and more space. Mynin wasn't so much attractive as...solid.

And an absolute ass wipe. Dressa was not particularly looking forward to that part, but it was a necessary part of the persona.

Lesander finally tore her eyes from Dressa, inspecting herself. Tan skin, much more freckled, hands thinner and fingers slim. A little larger in the bust, a little wider in the hips, a little more round all around. Pretty, but not stunning.

She pushed out of bed, rolling her shoulders, stretching.

Dressa watched her, looking for any more signs of distress. They were there, but not so much as before.

"I have food in the prep room," she said.

"Yes, I saw the cooler." Lesander paused. Adjusted her accent and diction and tried again. "The cooler's in the prep room."

Dressa nodded, in both confirmation and approval. "Eat, then shower, then dress. I'll cut your hair while we eat."

As they ate and she worked around Lesander, deftly cutting her hair into an asymmetrical bob, Dressa slowly eased herself into the accent, diction, and mannerisms of Lord Mynin Jadiar.

Her body was becoming a little less foreign. It always took time—for her, at least.

By the time she got to the shower, she was mostly settled.

Clothes—well, she'd kept some of Imorie's varied Truth-spoken wardrobe that had been in the closet when she'd moved to Imorie's apartment, the pieces she'd thought might be useful. Some of them had been among Mynin's preferred style, in their fit. She chose a blue tailored suit with silvery piping that was meant to mimic a Navy uniform without being offensively obvious about it.

Lesander sifted the racks and came back with something plainer. Professional, yes, and styled enough for the palace, but bland.

"Yes," Dressa said. "And this—" she grabbed a red silk scarf from a hanging rack. "Just a little bit of flare."

Lesander smiled, nodded.

And it wasn't long, then, before they were moving through the back corridors, Dressa mentally running through scenarios of how the day ahead might go. She had a plan in mind, but of course that would need to be highly adaptable. She had people she wished to see, to talk to. But they might be busy, or not wish to see Lord Mynin Jadiar. She certainly wouldn't have welcomed a visit from this lord if she was in the Assembly.

Dressa wasn't planning to waste her time trying to convince the known detractors to back Iata as a magicker ruler. She would focus her efforts on those who might swing their votes—which would be interesting, since Lord Mynin Jadiar wasn't a fan of magickers themself—but she had some ideas.

She would do her damnedest all around. Her life, her future, was also at stake. And she didn't want, with all her heart, to see Iata fall under this bigotry. The Assembly's challenge of his rulership was pure bigotry masquerading as politics.

Dressa led them to a small private aircar garage beneath the palace, and after lifting, set the aircar on a circuitous route around the city. After a reasonable time, they ended up in front of the large stone and steel edifice of Assembly Hall, smack in the middle of the busy Financial District, with its glittering skyscrapers and multi-tier traffic.

The aircar had chameleon systems and had subtly changed itself along the way. Its ident and broadcast signals had changed, too. It could avoid the city's systems entirely, but that would have been far too obvious to pick out for anyone watching. And everyone was always watching.

Dressa transferred Lord Jadiar's ident codes to the Assembly security systems and set down on a timed pad in front of the Assembly. She told the aircar to park itself and wait for retrieval.

She clicked off her comm, a subtly modified civilian model, and stowed it in her jacket pocket. She'd use it to recall the aircar when she was done.

"Ser Jadiar?" Lesander asked, when Dressa paused a beat too long looking up at the abstract slant of the Assembly's roof, squinting through her sunglasses at the glare. It had been a while since she'd been on an active Truthspoken mission, at least one this important—barring what she'd done impersonating Imorie a few weeks ago. But that had been drastically different.

No one had sent her on this mission. She'd sent herself. Which did, she found, actually make a difference.

"Yes," she said absently, now fully centering in Lord Jadiar's personality. She glanced aside at Lesander, just a glance. "Follow me, Administrator. And don't bother me unless I ask you to."

Inwardly, Dressa sighed. This was going to be a long day.

38

ASSEMBLY HALL

Our kingdom's values are our most important asset. We must always strive to uphold our kingdom's values, no matter the cost.

— LORD MYNIN JADIAR, FROM *THE COLLECTED SPEECHES OF THE GENERAL ASSEMBLY, FOURTH EDITION*

Assembly Hall's cavernous glass and steel entry was a bustle of nervous activity. The room echoed with voices, with sharp or polite laughter, with whispers, with a tension so thick you could carve a path through it. It was rumored that more deals took place here than in the official offices behind the entry hall, and Dressa didn't doubt it.

She chose a drifting path through the knots of Assembly members and their aides, through courtiers and city officials and business people and vloggers. A few camera drones drifted overhead.

Dressa and Lesander, who followed silently in her wake, passed more than one sound-dampened bubble, some dampeners even obscuring the visuals into blurred pools of light and shadow. Some even going so far as to puff out aggressively neutralizing scents, to help obscure the designer scents of the occupants within the dampening fields. Which Dressa thought was a bit too far.

As Lord Mynin Jadiar, Dressa nodded to whoever caught her eye, and smiled Mynin's self-ingratiating smile.

And she listened. Because comm chatter had caught up with her father's message from Hestia, and the news was everywhere now: the captain of the Melesorie's personal guard and a mid-level palace administrator had been attacked on Hestia. On the very same estate where Imorie Rhialden méron Quevedo had been staying—and that detail was also everywhere.

In Valon City, in these halls especially, nothing was ever seen as a coincidence.

"And what do you think about all of this, Lord Jadiar?" a young count called to her. "Our ruler becomes a magicker, and his own guard captain and palace administrator are attacked at nearly the same time. By the *Kidaa*, no less. Are the attacks all a farce to keep us from looking at the real problem?"

Which, Dressa guessed, would be that the ruler was a magicker.

She just barely kept herself from bristling. Of course this noble shit would be using the Kidaa attacks to fuel their own bigotry. It was *fashionable* at this exact moment to be against Green Magics on principle, and truth could be bent any way they wished and could get away with.

And anyhow, the Kidaa attack on her father hadn't been at the same time Iata was attacked. It hadn't been at the same time Iata had gained magics, either—but this count wouldn't know that.

But, well. The Kidaa attack had been very close in timing to the public announcement of Homaj Rhialden's magics. Close enough that the thought of it raised the hairs on Dressa's arms, an impossible part of the pattern. Her own nerves were screaming that it wasn't a coincidence, too.

"It is a sign, of course," Dressa said, her posture broad and arrogant. "Adeius telling us we should return to the holy mandates and curb the influence of these heretical beliefs. These magickers have gone entirely too far, and with our ruler among them, they might begin to rise even more above their stations."

Dressa wasn't bothered as much by what she said, ugly as it was—that was the role—but by the way those around her nodded in agreement. She'd thought she was being ridiculous to the point of parody. She'd expected them to give her disgusted looks. She'd hoped for that.

Did the anti-magicker sentiment run that strongly here? Fashionable positions were one thing, but these people believed what she was saying. She could see it in their eyes, in their body language.

There were no magicker members of the General Assembly. By precedent—though not yet law—magickers could not serve in any public capacity beyond their Green Magicker duties. And that was a problem for Iata, too. A really big problem. Because either he set a new precedent at the highest level, or...or...

Her throat was growing tight, and she had to consciously smooth it out again. She risked a glance at Lesander hovering quietly just beside her, tablet in hand to take notes or do tasks as asked. She could read the very subtle signs of Lesander's dismay, and knew it for what it really was.

Would they be able to sway the vote here at all? Was Iata's rule already over? And what about Iata's, and Imorie's for that matter, safety?

Dressa would have to rethink her tactics.

She suffered through another few minutes of conversation,

testing the waters and just how she might lever Lord Mynin Jadiar's ghastliness to her advantage. She was fairly sure she could bring some of the swayable Assembly members to Iata's side by demonstrating that any side *not* with Lord Jadiar on it was the better side.

She was about to make her excuses and move on when the same count asked, "Mynin, is this person borrowed from the palace?" This with a wave to Lesander, who was just now being extremely neutral.

"This? Oh, yes, this is Zara. She's on loan to me, I had need of an assistant—"

"Yes, but does she know Shiera Keralan?"

Dressa wanted to snap that they could just *ask* Zara if she knew, but she smiled Mynin's dashingly fake smile and turned to Lesander.

"Administrator Zara, do you, in fact, have any useful information about Shiera Keralan? Was she attacked on Hestia because of her association with the Melesorie?"

Lesander shifted uncomfortably, as Zara certainly would do, being pinned with an impossible question.

"I can't say, forgive me, my lords. I do not know Ser Keralan well."

"Pity," the count said. "And if you want to have a night of it sometime, here's my comm code."

Fucking hell. Dressa had to leave this group before she punched someone.

And maybe they weren't the majority. Maybe she was just stuck in the fringe here. Could she hope that? Dared she even hope?

She wasn't nearly as informed on the state of the General Assembly just now as she should have been, with her attention needed on everything else, and her own resources and networks as the Heir something she hadn't had time to fully build yet.

While Lesander tucked the offered comm card away with a politely fixed smile, she and Dressa finally made their exit.

Dressa breathed through each step, pushing her fury into kinetic motion.

This couldn't be the entire climate of the Assembly. There were level-headed people here, she knew that. Not everyone would suddenly decide to go crazy even if it *was* in fashion.

But among the crowd in the entry, the restless discontent was high. She'd need to go further into the building, into the quieter offices of the people who tended to avoid spectacle and gossip, to find the rationality she needed.

And now she wasn't sure she could stomach a whole day of Lord Mynin Jadiar being the disgusting boar that they were. She couldn't keep spreading that kind of blatant, manipulative hate. She was fairly vibrating now with her own self-disgust at going as far as she already had. It was a role, and it had a purpose, and she was playing the minor villain to try to bring about the greater good. But, *Adeius.*

She couldn't go to the Assembly members in her swayable zone, though, and sing Iata's virtues. Lord Jadiar was known to dislike and distrust magickers, and Dressa cursed Imorie for that crude bit of personality-building. Imorie hadn't been known to support magickers themself, before they'd become one.

These people acted like their ruler could just wave a hand and curse them all. Did anyone think to connect the fact that a curse was violence to the fact that magickers couldn't do violence without harming themselves?

But her own father had played up those beliefs after Imorie's engagement ball.

And then there were Imorie and Eti. Both magickers who were connected with deaths. Pardoned, yes, but still connected.

Dressa pressed her lips thin, trying to shove her growing frustration out through only her deliberate movements.

It wasn't working, and she knew her tension would show to those trained to see it. So she took a breath mid-stride and forced herself to sink deeper. Loathsome as that was.

She'd thought Lord Jadiar would be the best weapon for this mission. She'd already chosen her course, and there was little time to change it and come back again with a new plan. She'd just have to be the boar and use every bit of evaku she had to play to the members' dislike of Lord Jadiar's fringe, or even play on their greed. A stable kingdom meant a stable economy, and deposing the ruler just now might...

Adeius, but it might help the economy. She didn't want to think that. She didn't.

Could she convincingly argue that Iata should remain the ruler to anyone here?

Especially if she was questioning the wisdom of that herself, considering every other factor? Considering the level of paranoia playing out in the entry to Assembly Hall?

"Lord Jadiar."

Shit. Dressa recognized the voice of Denom Xiao before she turned, painting a wide smile on her face.

"Lord Xiao! Oh, it is so good to see you." She gripped Denom's damp hands, kissed both of his cheeks. Ugh, and he tasted like peach shaving cream.

"Same, Mynin. Are you well now? I was distressed to hear you've lately been sick, I hoped it wasn't—" He lowered his voice, making a show of looking around. As if he cared about keeping Lord Jadiar's secrets, the secrets of a lord he considered far beneath his lofty high house status.

"No, it's not," Dressa said, waving the comment off. Not the Bruising Sleep, they both meant. She offered Denom an edged smile, which he returned. Lord Jadiar was a boar, but certainly smarter than Denom Xiao.

"Good, good! What are you here for today? Have a meeting scheduled? If you don't have anything immediately, I would like to talk with you about one of the proposals I have for an upcoming session."

He raised his dark brows expectantly. And he looked more than a little like her father in that moment. An unsettling parallel.

Could she beg off of this invitation? *Should* she? Dressa knew there was no chance at all of swaying Denom to support Iata, but the information Denom had could be useful. It would be good to know what his tactics would be for the upcoming vote, and how he was handling everything now.

So she smiled. "Of course, Lord Xiao. I have a few moments."

39

TAKEN

My great-grandparent, Prince Malik Xiao, seldom left the Xiao homeworld in their later years and preferred to deal with Valon through their proxies. Many have criticized this handling of High House Xiao's affairs, saying that it led to a decrease in influence, but I think Valon was too painful for them to visit. Their favored child, my grandfather Jamir, was killed in Valon.

— ARIANNA RHIALDEN, MELESORIE X IN *THE CHANGE DIALOGUES*

The walk to Denom Xiao's office was short—he had conveniently managed to get prime office space on the first floor, with easier access. Which was a mark of his own pull in the General Assembly.

Denom waved to his admin staff as he breezed in, making a show of his easy authority. Was he trying to impress Lord Jadiar, or was he just always this way? Dressa had never felt a need to know her cousin from more than a distance, and maybe that had been a mistake.

She very firmly suppressed her eye roll. Lesander, trailing behind her and mostly unnoticed in the way that staff would be in these vaunted halls, said nothing, keeping her own body language sedate and contained.

"Well," Denom said, moving into his private office and shrugging out of his cream linen and silk day jacket. He slung it casually over a chair, as if it wasn't bespoke tailoring of the highest caliber. "We have a lot of work to do with the upcoming vote of no confidence against the Melesorie. I certainly could use your help in swaying some of the members who are hovering in the center, as if the choice was not blazingly obvious."

"I came here myself to do that," Dressa said. "There's a list of members I was going to talk to—this magicker threat must be stamped out now, before it spreads any further. If they already have overtaken our rulership—"

"I agree completely, Mynin," Denom said, pulling open a drawer on his desk. He glanced up, touched his desk controls, and Dressa felt the pop of a dampening field going up.

She looked back at Lesander, whose tablet was out and stylus hovering for notes.

"No notes on this one, Zara," Dressa snapped.

She turned back to Denom, bracing for the conversation ahead, but started.

He'd pulled out a breath mask and now held it over his mouth. He was glaring at her with a clear and obvious contempt.

Dressa felt the blood drain from her face.

What? What—no, she was still Lord Mynin Jadiar, she knew her performance had been excellent, or at least, as flawless as it could be without being Imorie to carry all the continuity. But she knew enough. She'd thought she'd known enough. Had she missed something, and where?

And why would Denom—

Adeius.

Dressa dropped to a crouch as she smelled the first hint of poisoned air. She identified the toxin and hit a light Change trance to nullify and purge it from her body, pushing it out of her sweat glands.

But there was more, so much more of it in the air, which was growing clouded.

Dressa shot another look to Lesander, who'd also crouched down, hunched and terrified.

Could she possibly think Lesander had outed her? Lesander had betrayed her family before. But Lesander had foresworn the Javieris. She had. Dressa had seen the sincerity in her wife's eyes.

And she saw the flash of hurt now as Lesander looked back at her and read enough of what she was thinking.

Dressa levered her glare back up at Denom, who was watching her, his eyes narrowed. He still held the breathing mask over his mouth and nose.

Looking far, far too much again in that moment like her father.

Had Denom planned this? How—why—and how had he known Lord Jadiar was coming? Dressa hadn't told anyone but Lesander what she was doing and why. There was no way, absolutely no way, Denom could have known without Lesander telling him, and she didn't think Lesander would. She just didn't.

Why would Denom want to poison Mynin Jadiar when he knew them to be on his side? Unless he knew that she wasn't Lord Jadiar? Was his command of evaku that great?

But her performance *had* been masterful, she knew that. She truly did. She didn't like Change, but that didn't mean she wasn't good at it.

Had it been those few moments where she'd been fighting

her rage, trying to get it under control? Had he seen something then?

Or had she'd missed something? Some vital detail that only Imorie would have known?

Dressa, her mind fogged with the trance needed to keep herself alert, tried to think through if she should attack Denom and find a way to turn off the gas, or run for the door, which would be locked.

But before she fully thought that through, she saw Lesander go still.

Adeius! Dressa crawled toward her. And maybe she was breaking character now, because Lord Jadiar wouldn't care about Administrator Zara.

But this wasn't a deadly gas, only known to knock people out in the right doses.

Okay, it could be deadly. But there were certainly better ways to kill with air than this drug.

Her thoughts were fogging again as she reached Lesander, felt at her neck, her own heartbeat spiking.

A back door to Denom's office opened. Not hidden, just discreet. Four people came in, all in Assembly security uniforms, gold piping on black.

And Dressa realized, belatedly, that if she wanted them to think that she wasn't in fact Truthspoken, if they didn't already know that for sure, that she had to pass out too. She had to let the gas take her. Had to let Denom do whatever he was trying to do.

Maybe he didn't know who she was, and she'd run afoul of something else entirely.

Dressa squinted up at the approaching guards and made a feeble show of struggling with them as two hauled her up, and the other two hefted up Lesander. But then, Dressa went limp. She slowed her heart-rate, slowed her breathing. Put herself, mostly, in trance—still dimly aware of her surroundings, but not immediately reactive.

One of the guards pressed an injector to Dressa's neck, and Dressa found herself now fighting a different sedative, one meant to last longer than the gas. And that one—that one she couldn't fight.

40

CAPTIVES

> *The high houses usually solve their problems through politics—an overt war between high houses is against the law, and most agree that a shadow war between houses is bad for business. The issue arises when the politics themselves are violent.*
>
> — EMRE PATEL IN *DECONSTRUCTING OUR TIMES: A PEOPLE'S PERSPECTIVE ON NOBILITY AND THE HIGH HOUSES*

Dressa coughed herself awake. Her mouth tasted like socks, her head felt—

In a rush of panic, Dressa delved into her body, trying to identify poison. She found traces of drugs, yes, and raked through herself only to find they were mostly expended. Still, she healed the drug hangover, healed any lingering damage, and came fully awake—

To find that she was sitting slumped in a wooden chair. Her ankles were cuffed to the legs, with a wire cord running from cuff to cuff through the rungs behind her so she couldn't slide the cuffs off the bottom. Shit. Her hands were bound tightly behind her with what felt like shock cuffs, with their rough contact pads pressing in on her inner wrists.

Oh fuck oh fuck—

She tried to scoot the chair, but craning around she found it crudely bolted to the floor in the back, the drill shavings still fresh on the carpet. Well, and she wouldn't have been able to slide the ankle cuffs off anyway. She could rock the chair a little, but she wasn't interested in falling over and having to stay that way.

Visions of what Iata described happening to Imorie flashed through her, along with every lesson her father had ever given her on what to do if captured or coerced. But those lessons had been so long ago. And—and Lesander was beside her, similarly bound and cuffed, still slumped forward. Changed black hair hanging in her eyes.

Dressa bit her lip to steady herself. Rechecked the bounds of her body, replayed every recent memory she could grab a hold of.

She was Lord Mynin Jadiar. Lesander was palace administrator Nin Zara. They'd been in Denom Xiao's office—Denom, the snake, she would find a way to destroy him. They'd been drugged, first through gas, then through directly injected sedative. If she'd been injected, she had to assume Lesander had been, too.

But...why? What had she given away, what would make Denom think Lord Jadiar was his enemy, not a sycophantic supporter? And he'd set this up beforehand—that gas and those sedatives hadn't come out of nowhere. The timing had been too on point. The people who'd injected her had been Assembly Hall guards, Adeius.

Truly, how had he known Mynin would be there? That didn't at all make sense, unless there were traitors at the palace, someone in the Palace Guard, maybe, who'd leaked that Lord

Jadiar had left from one of the underground garages. But the people who had access to that sort of surveillance were so very, very few, and all of them trusted.

Dressa tugged on her ankle bonds again, but she didn't want to test the stun cuffs yet. She wasn't really in the mood to have an electric hangover as well.

And where were they now?

The room was musty. Not unkempt, though—there was a decent older style white sofa against the far wall, a wall which had aging green floral wallpaper. The blinds were drawn on the room's two tall windows, but left in enough light, so it was still daytime. Stains mottled the faded blue carpet. The door to her left, which she could see clearly enough, had a handle, but no deadbolt that she could see. Was it even locked? Would it make a difference if Dressa couldn't actually get to it?

No one else was in the room, but she was sure it was under surveillance. Of course they were being watched.

Lesander stirred.

And would Lesander remember that she wasn't herself? Dressa's body spiked with adrenaline again, a sick hot wave going through her. She had no idea what training Lesander had in being captured by an enemy.

Mm, but possibly more than she had, if Lesander's entire life had been built around coming to infiltrate the Rhialden family as an illegal Truthspoken. Lesander might have expected to be caught at some point.

But Dressa wouldn't take chances.

"Zara," she said. She was close enough to Lesander that she could have nudged Lesander's leg with her foot—if her foot hadn't been bound to her chair.

Lesander coughed, gagged, and for a moment, Dressa thought she would be sick. Then Lesander went still a moment —tranced, certainly—and after a few heartbeats, took a long breath and sat up straight.

Would their captors know that Lesander had just tranced? Would they think Lesander was the Truthspoken, then— Adeius, what if the real Nin Zara had been the leak, knowing she'd be replaced by a Truthspoken? And so their captors had targeted Lesander, thinking she was Dressa? Was that a likely possibility?

That thought, knowing that she'd put Lesander in this danger, whatever this danger was, jangled Dressa's already frayed nerves.

Lesander looked around, cataloging the room. Her eyes stopped when she saw Dressa.

There was a moment of confusion, but only a moment. Recognition and remembrance lit in Lesander's now brown eyes.

"Lord Jadiar," she coughed, and grimaced, looking like she wanted to spit on the carpet beside her chair. But she didn't. "Sorry. My lord. It's—"

"Understandable," Dressa said, and tested her own bonds again, to demonstrate the point. She had no idea who'd be watching—Denom, or someone else, maybe, if Denom had only been the means to their capture, not the one behind it. Which Dressa was increasingly thinking was so. Denom was cruel, yes, and a narcissistic asshole, but not the sort to take the initiative on his own.

And come to think of that, had he even been spearheading the initiative to depose Iata? The entire rhetoric was like him enough, yes, but the way he was taking the lead on this—that wasn't quite in character.

"Where are we?" Dressa demanded, though of course Lesander wouldn't know.

But Lesander gamely said, "I'm not sure, my lord. If I had to guess, this looks to be a residential building. Probably not in Financial District anymore."

And maybe Lesander did know something. That was a good observation.

By the sounds coming from outside the windows, they were certainly still in the city. There was traffic outside, though maybe not as heavy as Financial might be, no. So they were not on a prominent street. And the sunlight was still bright, so it was probably still afternoon. They hadn't been out that long—just long enough to transport them and tie them up, apparently. Her hangover didn't feel intense enough for it to have been a full day. She'd ache a lot more if that was so, too.

"This is absurd," Dressa said. "I'm a supporter of Lord Xiao, and he repaid me with...with *kidnapping* me, cuffing me to a chair—"

She did try the stun cuffs now, because that would be in character for Lord Jadiar, and—*oh hell*—they worked. Dressa went rigid as the charge jolted her, leaving her breathless and panting. Not quite unconscious, but her vision came back slowly.

She dipped into as unobtrusive a trance as she could to soothe her body's responses, but she couldn't believably take them all away.

Lesander was staring at her, tight-lipped.

"Well?" Dressa croaked. "Do something! Try to get yourself free!" Then she took a breath, and did the most foolish thing she could think of, which Mynin Jadiar would absolutely do, and yelled, "Heeeelp!"

Lesander started laughing. And Adeius, no, that lack of control was dangerous. But, no, it was half a sob, wasn't it?

Stay in character, Lesander. Your life may depend on it.

And Dressa felt those icy threads of fear running through her veins now, too. She'd been captured by an unknown enemy, bound, and was being held prisoner. She wasn't herself. Her identity might have been compromised. The *palace* might be compromised. And she was with her wife, a Javieri illegal Truthspoken, who also wasn't herself. If Lesander was publicly exposed, Iata would have no choice but to bring down the full measure of the law.

She started to panic again and tempered it hard with another light trance.

But Lesander recovered from whatever lapse she'd had and started yelling with Dressa: "Help! We need heeeelp!"

After some minutes of this, when nothing happened, they both wound down.

And then after a few more minutes of trying to move at all beyond the bonds—Lesander had her turn with the stun cuffs, too—they both sat in frustrated, sweaty silence.

Dressa looked to Lesander at the same moment Lesander looked to her.

She opened her mouth—but what could she say? They were both other people.

And they *were* close enough that, if Dressa's arms hadn't been bound very uncomfortably behind her, she might have leaned far over and met Lesander's lips in the middle. And she thought, for a lingering moment, what that would taste like, Lesander being a different person just now, and was that hot?

Oh, yes. That was definitely hot. Dressa had lived all her life knowing that when she married or took a lover, it was possible she might be with them in different facets of her own body. As different people and personalities. But she'd never imagined at all that her lover could be with her that way, too.

And now, just exactly *now* Dressa's body decided with a fury that she was done being angry at Lesander, done being upset, done feeling betrayed, and she wanted her wife, right here and now, wanted to devour her, wanted to ground herself, wanted to not be afraid.

Then, and only then, when Dressa was ready to Change to try to get her wrists out of the cuffs to get to her wife, to get the hell out of here—and damn whoever saw her do it, and damn the shocks she'd have to suffer through, and damn if she could even keep herself conscious—only then did the door open.

A soft creak of hinges.

And the very last person Dressa might have expected stepped inside.

Tall, poised, every inch the high house prince with her red-brown hair short and spiky, tan skin flawless, red nova hearts in each ear and her left eyebrow. Her deep red jacket and pants tailored to devastating precision. She could have been Lesander's older sister, the resemblance was so prominent, though Lesander was paler, her own hair fiery red, and Lesander preferred her makeup to be more natural.

But no. This woman was not Lesander's sister. Prince Yroikan Javieri was Lesander's mother.

41

LOYALTIES

*I know who I am, and I know where I stand. That is
everything I will ever need to know.*

— PRINCE YROIKAN JAVIERI, AS QUOTED IN
THE CHANGE DIALOGUES

Dressa kept Lord Mynin Jadiar's personality wrapped
around her, but she already knew it was in tatters.
She wasn't Imorie. She wasn't her father—she wasn't
Iata, for that matter, who could so thoroughly lose himself in
another personality that it was absolutely flawless.

She was herself. She was a master at what she did, but she
was meant to be the second Truthspoken, not the Heir. Not
have to do missions like this, and confront people like...like *this*.

Prince Yroikan Javieri waited by the door while a person
dressed in Javieri guard livery carried in a padded folding chair,
unfolded it, bowed, and then left again, quietly shutting the
door behind them.

Yroikan gracefully sat down. Looked between them both
and smiled, then pulled a slim dampener out of one pocket and

clicked it on. Not the same level of security as the massive box Lesander had used in her guest suite, but adequate, likely, for this random building in a random part of the city.

"Well?" Yroikan asked. "You're not gagged." Her blue eyes were sharp and had an edge of cruelty Dressa had never seen in Lesander's. "Lord Mynin Jadiar. What do you have to say for yourself?"

Did Yroikan know who she was? Adeius, did Yroikan recognize Lesander, could she spot Lesander's tells? Dressa didn't dare look over at Lesander to see what state she was in. But if anyone would know her, it would be her mother. As a high house prince, Yroikan's command of evaku had to be robust. Dressa had to assume Yroikan was at least on par with Lesander there.

Dressa tugged against the ankle bonds again as safer to test than the wrist cuffs.

"Prince Javieri, why have you abducted me? Adeius, I was trying to help Lord Denom—"

"Ser Truthspoken," Yroikan said, and Dressa reared back.

"What? You think I'm—"

"Ondressarie."

Dressa stilled. Well. It had been worth a try.

Yroikan's gaze flicked to Lesander. "And my daughter, I see. Both of you, I suppose. Welcome to the family, Dressa."

No one knew Lesander and Dressa were married already but a select few in the palace, and they had sent word—heavily encrypted—to Yroikan on Ynassi III. That had been a risk, but a necessary risk.

Yroikan knew.

Dressa swallowed. And she suddenly and intensely felt the differences in Lord Jadiar's shape and body from her own. Felt the disconnect, and breathed through it.

Had she possibly thought she could *help* Iata by Changing and going on a mission of her own? How did she even think she could rule a Truthspoken kingdom if she couldn't manage this, this one thing that she hadn't thought would be overly challenging, going to the Assembly—

Yroikan pulled something else from her pocket—her comm. Dressa tensed, not knowing what else awaited her, especially with Yroikan having guessed her identity. Having guessed, or had she simply known? Had she known Lord Jadiar was a Truthspoken persona even before Dressa had chosen to use it?

Yroikan touched her comm screen, and a moment later, Dressa felt the stun cuffs click and drop to the floor behind her.

She gingerly pulled her arms back around, rubbing her wrists more out of reassurance than pain. She really wanted to rub her shoulders, sore from being held in that awkward position, but didn't want to give Yroikan the satisfaction.

Dressa found Lesander doing the same. And looking back at Dressa, her expression blank. Blanker, even, than the night when she'd attacked Iata. It was as if all the life in Lesander had just...gone away. Or been hidden, maybe, from this woman. Her mother.

Dressa wasn't overly fond of her own mother. Haneri could be cruel—usually was cruel—but she did care, in her way. She was certainly caring more lately, and Dressa thought the attempt was genuine.

But Yroikan? Dressa had watched Lesander's reactions when she'd talked about her family. She'd heard everything that night she and Imorie and Eti had debriefed Lesander, and then told her what she'd needed to know in return. Dressa had taken Lesander's vow of loyalty and renouncement of her family. There had been such grim determination in Lesander then. A coiled, knotted tension.

This woman here, Yroikan Javieri, was a monster.

"All right," Dressa said, leaning forward. "Release my ankles?"

"Mmm, I think not," Yroikan said. "Not yet, anyway, we do need to talk."

"Talk without consent is coercion," Dressa shot back. "Or interrogation."

Yroikan shrugged. "If you give me your word you won't leave this room, I won't believe you. So I'm at least being honest about it."

Dressa sat back, crossing her arms, one of Lord Jadiar's gestures. A shield. Adeius, she needed a shield.

"How did you know?" she asked.

"That you're Lord Jadiar? I've known for years that was a persona of Imorie's."

Dressa twitched. Shit. Shit and fuck. Yeah. And if Yroikan hadn't known for sure that Imorie had been Arianna, Dressa would have just confirmed it by her reaction now.

"And?" Dressa finally asked.

"It doesn't take much to follow lines of reasoning. That's not why I want to talk to you. I don't care that you're playing your little games—though I do care that you're trying to stop a legitimate vote of no confidence from happening in the Assembly. That's vote manipulation, and against the law—"

"You know how Truthspoken work," Dressa said. "You know the system. Be smart enough not to be manipulated, or you will be manipulated. That's how it works. Or would you care to tell me just *how* you obtained the information that Jadiar was Imorie? Can you tell me it was legally?"

Yroikan smiled. It was an eerie smile, genuine in every way, but absolutely off. It reminded Dressa in a weird way of Duke Koldari, and was there something there? Koldari had been associated with Windvale on Hestia, and so had the Javieris.

And there was so much, really *so much* that Dressa wanted to know from Yroikan too, but she had no illusions whatsoever that Yroikan would tell her the truth. Yroikan might be one of the few people who could lie to a Truthspoken convincingly.

"Mother," Lesander said. "Why are you here? You didn't tell me you were coming."

"I came to clean up your mess," Yroikan said. "First, the mess of your botched betrothal to Imorie—"

Yroikan knew, she even knew that Imorie was Dressa's older sibling's current chosen name, or she'd be using Ari or Arianna. Did she even know Iata had legally adopted them? Dressa had to assume.

"—and then your travesty of a marriage to the new Heir. And when I got here a few days ago, I found you already on a path to destruction, culminating in your ridiculous botched attempt on the life of the Seritarchus—forgive me, the *Melesorie*. My daughter, I trained you so, so much better than that."

The way Yroikan said "my daughter," the intonation, the exact phrasing around it—that was so close to how Dressa's father talked that it made her stomach drop. That had been deliberate, Dressa was sure. Was Yroikan trying to say her knowledge, her surveillance of the palace went that deep? Homaj Rhialden didn't often use that phrasing in public— though he had a few times, at least she thought he had.

And Yroikan had just confessed to multiple crimes in that one statement. Adeius. In front of Dressa. So she was absolutely sure Dressa wouldn't do anything with that information, and what did that mean?

Dressa's stomach churned, but she didn't dare give any of her concentration to calming it.

Lesander, too, gaped at her mother. Then, instead of answering, just looked down.

Yroikan turned back to Dressa. "I've said nothing you don't know. Yes, Lesander's Truthspoken trained—quite obviously so, as she's Changed right now. And you won't act on it, because you love her. Foolish as that is, I see it plainly. You love her. And I respect that."

That statement was not respect, it was a threat. When had Yroikan arrived on Valon? Before Lesander had tried to kill Iata? If so, Yroikan could have stopped Lesander, could have countermanded whatever order Lesander had received. Or—had Yroikan herself given the activation signal to Lesander? Dressa tried to think through the timing, and it might—just—have been possible if Yroikan had left Ynassi III as soon as she'd gotten word of their secret marriage and traveled at military speeds. Maybe.

"None of this," Yroikan said with a wave, "is what I actually want to talk to you about. Dressa, you are aware of the Kidaa attacks? Yes, of course you are. There was an attack on Ynassi III as well. And I see now there was an attack on the captain of the Seritarchus's personal guard and Maja Rhialden—"

Dressa jerked against her ankle cuffs. How the *hell* had Yroikan known about the attack on Maja, and that it was Maja at all—

But if Yroikan had somehow found out about Imorie being Lord Jadiar, was it such a stretch to think she knew some of the other Truthspoken personas, too? Shiera Keralan had been one of her father's personas for years. Her father was good, he was excellent at Change and evaku and personas—but apparently they'd all underestimated Yroikan's intelligence network. And her ambition.

And if Yroikan knew that Maja was Shiera Keralan, and on Hestia...

Dressa felt her limbs go numb, her ears ringing.

Yroikan knew about Iata. Yroikan knew that Iata, the man currently ruling as Homaj Rhialden, wasn't actually Homaj Rhialden. At least, he wasn't Maja, who was the one who'd actually been sanctioned by the Adeium to rule.

Yroikan had sent her daughter here to sow chaos. And it had worked, oh Adeius, it had worked.

"The problem," Yroikan said, "is that the Kidaa attacks are

only a fraction of the trouble we're about to see from them. My wife is from Sullana, a border world that has long had casual and unofficial contact with the Kidaa. Trade, even, in some circumstances. It's happening on half a dozen border worlds, which like their way of life enough not to report it, and the Navy only sends their border scouts through on a circuit. And one thing you must understand about the Kidaa—their minds aren't linear, like ours. They think in cycles, they think in eras and eons and patterns. And they're lining up with a pattern now that we won't like at all."

What?

Dressa looked to Lesander again, but Lesander's gaze was still on the floor. Did Lesander know what her mother was talking about? It felt like such a non sequitur after all the threats Yroikan had just leveled, after whatever pains she'd just gone through to kidnap them. Yroikan had brought them here to talk about the *Kidaa*?

Did Lesander know things about the Kidaa that she hadn't said?

But why wouldn't she have said something? No, Lesander couldn't have known whatever Yroikan was talking about now. Dressa was sure of that, too. The right body language cues weren't there.

"What do you mean?" Dressa asked, reluctantly, because this prince wasn't likely to give any information for free, or without bias or her own attempted gains.

"The Melesorie," Yroikan said, "is a magicker. That isn't by accident. Your fallen Heir is a magicker, and has the Bruising Sleep. Do you think that is an accident? My brother's wife was a magicker, manifested after they married. My wife has the Bruising Sleep—"

"What?" Lesander jerked upright. "What? Mama has—"

"She's had it for years, Lesander. Do you think we'd make

that public? It's managed well enough. She has long medi-
tations—"

"But—but I thought—her religion—"

"Is important, yes. But not that important." Yroikan waved it
away. And the gesture was so callous, so dismissive, when
Lesander was so obviously in shock and pain.

Dressa bit back her hiss. "Will you release Lesander, at
least? She's not going to go anywhere if I'm still shackled here."

Yroikan's eyes lit with an unholy fire. "Oh? You have her that
entwined, do you? Your few weeks with your wife have over-
ruled years and years and *years* of training? Of her loyalty to
her family, who gave her *everything?*"

Dressa braced against Yroikan's sudden rage.

No, not sudden. Well-hidden, and it had slipped now. And
that, she sensed, hadn't been something Yroikan had planned.

Could Dressa press that to her advantage?

Adeius, no. She didn't dare. Not when Yroikan seemed to be
holding far more cards than she did at the moment.

Than even Iata did.

And Yroikan had just said—she'd just said that Iata's gaining
magics wasn't an accident. Had she not known that Iata had been
a magicker for nine years now, not manifesting recently? Was
there one thing in this entire kingdom Yroikan did not know?

"So what are you saying?" Dressa asked. "We know there's
something else going on here. Do you know who's behind it,
then?"

Was Yroikan herself behind the Kidaa attacks? Was this
going to be a vid drama-worthy confession, complete with the
cackling monologue?

A chill went down Dressa's back, and she knew that no, it
wouldn't be that. And she knew, before Yroikan opened her
mouth again, that she wished it would be.

"It's the Kidaa. They gave the magics to your Melesorie nine years ago—and got the wrong brother, didn't they? They gave my brother's wife magics and my wife the Bruising Sleep. They're trying it again with Imorie, but this time, trying to get both in one person."

Did that make sense? Did that make any kind of sense, could it possibly be true?

"But...why?" Dressa asked, spreading her hands. "What purpose would that serve? What does it matter to the Kidaa if the Valoran ruler is a magicker? It doesn't impede his judgment, and with Imorie, yes, that has taken them out of succession, but it's still treatable. You said yourself your wife is in treatment."

Yroikan's smile, this time, was...tired. Which was more terrifying by far.

"It's balance and cycles. The Kidaa are obsessed with balance and cycles."

"Yes, but balance of what? Or a cycle of what? What in the world does making the ruler a magicker—or trying to, anyway —what does that balance out?"

Yroikan spread her hands. "We just know it is, we don't know why. The border worlds have had more contact with the Kidaa, but hardly more success in understanding them."

That...felt like a lie. But Dressa decided to let it go, for now. Because she needed to test everything Yroikan had just said again, test it against her reading of Yroikan's body language and expressions. And test it against the pattern she'd been holding in her mind of everything that was happening, everything that had felt, in some way, connected.

"And the Kidaa attacks?" Dressa asked. "Was that you?"

Yroikan smiled. "No." And, dammit, that felt like a truth. Dressa wasn't envious of Iata's magics, but in that moment she wished she had more than even her fine-trained Truthspoken senses.

"There's more than one faction of Kidaa," Yroikan said.

"And different factions have different ways of going about things. The faction that made those attacks is not in close contact with the faction that trades with Sullana. And the faction of my wife's homeworld is the one I'm most familiar with."

There, again, was more Yroikan wasn't saying. Dressa could feel that with cues she couldn't define, honed from a lifetime of evaku. There was much, *much* Yroikan wasn't saying. And some —most?—of what she was saying had her own personal slant attached to it. Her own agendas.

"Why are you giving me this information?" Dressa asked finally.

Yroikan's brows rose. "I would have thought that was obvious."

Dressa wasn't falling for that bait. She just stared back. And noticed Lesander had kept her head up, too, though she'd still been mostly silent for this conversation. Which wasn't like her.

"It's not," Dressa said.

"Well, then. I want Iata Rhialden out of the rulership. The Kidaa are moving, and whatever they intended with giving him magics, they've since moved on to other tactics. This kingdom right now needs a firm and steady rulership, and that can't be him, no matter if he's held the kingdom stable enough so far."

Adeius, how much *did* she know? Did she know Maja and Iata had been switching for years? It felt like that.

Dressa pressed her fingertips into her thighs. Grimaced as they met the resistance of Lord Jadiar's muscular build.

"You don't like magickers," Dressa said.

"No, I don't. They can't make decisions that will lead to violence, and those decisions might be necessary in the months and years to come. And this city, and the kingdom, is in an uproar over their ruler being a magicker, with all the powers inherent in both Truthspoken and a magicker. That is no way to rule a kingdom—he can't fight the threat without or within. He simply is not capable of it."

Dressa swallowed. Because she couldn't say those thoughts hadn't been churning in the back of her mind, too. And she hated that.

And more—if the Kidaa could *possibly* have given both Iata and Imorie magics...what was to stop them from giving magics to her as well? Or the Bruising Sleep, if Yroikan said that was from them as well, and—Adeius. She would have to think through that revelation, both of those revelations, later. If they were true.

Was this information sabotage? But Yroikan had just confirmed that the attacks were, in fact, from the Kidaa, and Dressa felt that at least, in this entire conversation, was true. Yroikan, master of evaku that she was, still wasn't quite the master Dressa was.

Dressa hoped, at least.

But it fit. It fit the pattern too well, connecting disparate threads. Even if she still didn't know the why of it.

Were the Kidaa, as Rhys had been worried about, as passive as they appeared? Yroikan didn't seem to think so.

And Yroikan's fear was also genuine. The lines taut beside her eyes, her lips pulled tight, the tension in her shoulders that she couldn't quite mask. And even, twice, her worried glances at Lesander.

Dressa had marked those—eye twitches only. Not voluntary. Could Yroikan possibly be concerned for her daughter, monster that she was?

"You're behind the vote of no confidence," Lesander said. It wasn't accusatory so much as tired fact.

Ah. Lesander had placed that before Dressa had. But that, too, fit all too well.

Yroikan sat back. "When I see something that needs doing, I get it done."

"So, what, you want to rule?" Dressa asked. "Is that what all of this is? Push the Rhialdens out, so the Javieris can move in? Because you have better information?"

"I do have better information. But, no. I don't wish to rule myself, at least. But you, my Truthspoken Heir, my daughter, happen to be married to my heir. Which I believe both your parents and myself agreed was an advantageous position for both of our families. No matter that you're not the Heir I originally agreed on. Or that I would never have approved of your secret union, I would simply have moved it up. Secrets create levers that people can move you by. But you would know that, Truthspoken."

The knot in Dressa's stomach, steadily growing, clenched.

Whatever was happening here, with Yroikan taking control of this situation, giving demands—that wasn't going to end, was it? Because Yroikan knew too much. And knew that Dressa knew that all of that information coming out publicly now, spun by Yroikan, would be the worst of all disasters. Would send the kingdom into utter chaos—and then Yroikan would win there, too. She could step into the vacuum of power and take over. She was absolutely placed for that, no matter what she said about not wanting to rule.

Or, Dressa could convince Iata to step down. She could take over the rulership. And she and Lesander—Yroikan was implying joint rule, wasn't she?—she and Lesander would rule the kingdom.

But they wouldn't, truly. Because they would always, absolutely always, be under Yroikan's shadow. Her will and her control.

And wasn't this scenario what her father had said he'd fought against at the beginning of his own rule? Against the people who'd been trying to control him?

Dressa met Yroikan's cold blue eyes. Nothing, absolutely nothing like Lesander's now.

Yroikan knew she understood the rules of this game. And that they weren't at all in Dressa's favor.

How many more information factories did the Javieris have, like the one that Imorie and Eti had shut down at Windvale? Shut down, and almost paid for with their lives?

How many spies, how many people bribed or blackmailed —how deep did the Javieri ties go into Palace Rhialden, the Assembly, the wider government at the planetary and provincial levels, the Navy, the Army—

Dressa swallowed hard.

Yroikan nodded. "So, then. This is the purpose of this meeting. You know that this kingdom needs stability. So you will go back to your Melesorie and tell him everything I've just told you. You will report, as Truthspoken do." A smirk at that, and Dressa didn't miss Lesander's twitch. "And he will decide what's best for the kingdom."

Dressa knew, she absolutely knew, that Iata would decide to step down. Because he had no other choice. No good choice.

And they'd all been quietly thinking it might come to that anyway, horrible as that was. His switch to a Melesorie rule had been desperate, maybe the right move in the moment, but the anti-magicker sentiments were still too high. The people's paranoia was high. She'd already seen today how deep it all ran.

Were the hatred and fear being stoked? Dressa wouldn't put that past Yroikan, either.

Dressa reached out beside her, without looking. And she felt Lesander's hand slipping into hers. Gripping tightly. Warm and hardly reassuring, but there.

In this with her. In this *with* her.

"Well," Yroikan said. She touched her comm again, and Dressa felt the ankle cuffs snap open.

Dressa took a breath. Because if Yroikan was letting her go... that meant Yroikan had her.

Dressa was not walking out of here because she'd won today, she was walking out because Yroikan wished it.

And if she ruled, it would be because Yroikan wished it.

Lesander had had a taste of Dressa's world—now, Dressa was about to learn Lesander's own hell. She'd married into this family, and this family was claiming her, body and soul and deepest will.

Lesander's mother, this person who'd raised her daughter to kill a ruler and set her up to fail, who'd tortured Lesander throughout the entire process, both physically and emotionally —*this person* was claiming her.

This person was claiming the Kingdom of Valoris.

And there was nothing Dressa knew that she could do about it.

Yet.

Dressa gripped Lesander's hand tightly, and they both stood together.

42

HERITAGE

Semlin ne Krata Javieri, wife and consort of Prince Niom Javieri, was killed today in an aircar accident outside of Javieri City, the capital of Ynassi III. She is survived by her husband of six months. Ceremonies will be held in the Adeium in Javieri City, to be presided over by Speaker Eridant and Prince Yroikan Javieri. A day of mourning shall be observed following the ceremonies, in which commerce will halt for Ynassi III and Javieri vassal worlds. Semlin will be mourned.

— ANNOUNCEMENT OF DEATH IN THE JAVIERI
CITY OFFICIAL FEED

I morie was asleep again in the cabin they shared with Eti —they'd only seemed to have enough energy to land on Kalistré, go to Eti's family's apartment, and little more. And now, on the second day of their three and change day trip to Ynassi III, Imorie had slept through most of the trip so far.

Eti had stayed near them some of the time, the rest of it hovering near his mother. He hadn't told his mother, at first, all that had happened. He hadn't wanted what had almost happened to him at Green Hall in Valon City to happen again —his mother was strong, yes, but far too sympathetic to his own emotions to hold him in place if he started to dissipate. He was terrified he'd take her with him.

He was absolutely galled that Iata had needed to hold him to existence. The *ruler* had held him together.

Eti could nearly hear his mother's fear screaming from every corner of the ship, tuned as he was to her emotions.

She was seventh rank, more powerful than he was—and he hadn't known until Doryan sealed him how powerful he was, too. Though...he had suspected. He hadn't thought it was entirely normal to share music with the trees.

And, he'd overheard Doryan saying to Farouk that his mother might be more powerful than the First Magicker Mariyit Broden himself. But she was largely self-trained, and Doryan said that was a problem.

She had taught Eti, and Doryan had said that was also a problem, because Eti would have the same inconsistencies and bad habits. So they'd both need heavy assessment, as high-ranking as they were. She could never be the First Magicker, though, not with her history as an unsealed magicker.

And Eti had thought, just a moment, if he hadn't been hauled off to Valon, if he hadn't been forced by the Javieris to work for them, if he'd been sealed a lot sooner...could he have one day been First Magicker?

But that thought went nowhere. Because none of that had happened.

And now, on the second day to Ynassi III, where his sibling was being held captive, his restlessness was driving him crazy.

Just what had Imorie sensed about his mother to throw them so off balance? He still felt that moment clearly, Imorie's shock, their ground-shaking shift in purpose that had just barely broken through his singular focus at the time, but was something he couldn't stop thinking about now.

He'd felt his mother's shift of emotions when she saw Imorie, too. She knew who Imorie was. But Eti didn't think that was all of why Imorie's center had moved so drastically.

And he couldn't ask them. Because they were asleep.

He'd been trying to wait until Imorie woke up, but—

But his mother might know. Probably did know whatever this was. And his sense of her was colored with more than a little foreboding in his direction. He didn't think it only had to do with the Javieris wanting him back.

Eti raked a hand through his hair, scratched at the stubble on his cheeks. He was shaving again, at least, and he needed to again. He couldn't stand for his beard to get any longer just now, it was too much sensation for his overtaxed senses.

He straightened the remains of Imorie's last meal—which he'd helped them prop up to eat—on the table beside their side of the bed. He lingered a moment, watching Imorie breathe.

His sense of them was...turbulent. They were not content in their sleep. They were almost distant, even. Not quite like they were dreaming.

Eti had a crawling feeling of being watched, and he whipped around, but no one was there. He still had half a thought focused on the strength of the ship—he'd paced Doryan for a few hours earlier—but he couldn't quite touch what he'd just sensed.

And then it was gone, and maybe it was the remains of his darkened aura, the things he would not—could not—think about.

Imorie stirred slightly, turning over. And Eti sighed and padded as quietly as he could out of the cabin they shared.

Out into the corridor, where he went to his mother's cabin and, steeling himself, knocked.

Eti waited, and after a minute, the hatch slid open, and his mother stood there, her smile tired but welcoming.

And it was so good to see her. Every time he saw her, it was good to see her. Even anxious for what he needed to talk about, he was still so very glad she was here.

He'd thought—gods, he'd truly feared—he never would see her again.

Eti's eyes stung, and they'd been doing that a lot, lately.

His mother stepped back. "Come in. I know we need to talk." And here—here, her smile turned sad. Bitter, even. He felt the apprehension from her as surely as if it was his own.

He was not used to seeing his mother haloed in green, her aura darker and deeper than Iata's had been at the palace. And he was certainly not used to seeing his mother's cheek marked with a magicker's seal, the holographic fractal pattern so dense it glittered. His own was dense, but not this dense.

It caught his eye and kept it there a moment, before she let out a soft sigh, and he shook himself, looking away.

His mother's cabin was smaller than the one he shared with Imorie, just one single bed, drawers and shelves built into the bulkheads, an adjoining washroom, a small chair stuffed into one corner. An outline in the wall that was probably a foldout desk.

"Sorry," he said, though he'd said it before. "We can switch cabins, truly—"

His mother smiled, because she knew his moods, and knew he sometimes repeated things when he was nervous. And made suggestions that weren't practical and that he'd regret later.

Eti carefully sat on the edge of the bed.

His mother sat beside him. Then she pulled a slim dampener out of the pocket of her loose pants.

Eti eyed it dubiously. Then this was going to be *that* kind of conversation, and he didn't like that at all.

Had he expected less, though? If whatever they needed to talk about had shaken Imorie so badly?

"Doryan gave it to me," his mother said. "Doryan's nice enough, and they knew we'd need to talk."

She clicked it on, and Eti's ears popped. He ducked his head, suddenly not wanting to say anything. Not wanting to ask.

Not wanting to know.

Because his mother's foreboding was building with a pressure that made him want to run. He wanted to back out and forget he'd come. To not ask Imorie anything, either.

He didn't want to know.

But he also *needed* to know.

His mother shifted, and he knew she felt his nerves, too. They were very much alike, they always had been.

"Eti, you've grown close to Imorie. Are you...involved with them?"

Heat rushed to his face, and he dug his fingers into the fleece blanket on the bed. Traced out patterns around him.

"No, not—not *with* them. They're ace, and I'm mostly ace, so...and it's not anything like that." He shrugged, squeezed his hands together in front of him, avoided her gaze. Scuffed the thick carpet with the toe of his shoe. "They helped me, and I helped them, and they helped me again."

Or was it the other way around? Or was that backwards—he'd betrayed them, and they'd...somehow seen fit to overlook that. Though his guilt there was still mostly just his own guilt, he already knew how Imorie felt. They weren't angry. At least, not at him.

His mother was quiet a moment, and he looked up at her.

Her hands were also folded on her knees, and he watched her slowly kneading her fingers.

When the silence stretched out, Eti said, "Mom, what—"

Just as she said, "Eti, I need to tell you about your father."

Eti blinked. "What?"

His mother shuddered. "Your father—not...not Graysen Rakorda."

That was the secret? "Mom, I know he's not my father."

She sat back. "But—"

"But I can hear when you're not telling the truth—"

"Fuck," his mother said, and passed a hand over her eyes. "Yes...yes maybe I didn't want to think about that."

Graysen Rakorda was the cargo master on a cruise liner that came through Kalistré's system three times a year. Graysen had been seeing Eti's mother during his week-long stays as long as Eti could remember.

And there was also the fact that Eti looked *nothing* like Graysen—Graysen had tan skin and light-brown hair, dark blue eyes. And yes, genetics could skew a lot, but nothing in Eti's mouth shape, eye shape, his build—*nothing* looked like Graysen. He'd just assumed his mother had commissioned his birth from the genetic banks, or had a fling and had to have the embryo transferred after the fact, something like that. It had never really bothered him. Graysen, when he came through, was amiable enough, but not someone Eti would want to call a father.

"Okay," his mother said. "Okay. Well."

She pressed a hand to her heart, and it was shaking.

Eti straightened, alarmed. "Mom—"

"I married Prince Niom Javieri when I was twenty-two. It was a marriage that our parents arranged, to bring mutual benefit to our families, and he was handsome enough, and sweet enough before I married him."

She grimaced.

Eti's ears started to ring. No. *No.*

"Mom—"

She held up a hand. "Let me finish before you ask, please. Because I'm only going to get this out once."

And he saw it, saw just how much saying anything was tearing at her insides. It was very nearly self-violence, and he half expected her to flicker.

But she didn't.

"Six months into our marriage," she went on, "I manifested Green Magics. And...I guess it all changed. We'd already started our first child in the incubator—that was you—and Niom wanted nothing to do with a child who might become a magicker, never mind that I'd manifested after you were started, and that should cut down chances of my child manifesting to the same as everyone else." She smiled tightly. "Turns out he was right, though, you did manifest. But we were already living on Kalistré by then, and I'd been declared dead in an aircar crash, and—"

Eti, who was vibrating with his world realigning, blurted, "You're Semlin ne Krata Javieri? That's you?"

He'd studied the accident in school, every child on Kalistré, every child on any Javieri vassal world, knew about the tragedy.

"Was," she said, and he felt her annoyance and shrank back.

She shuddered. "No, Eti, no—it's not you, this is just...hard."

She reached to pull him to her, but he scooted back. His mind was racing. Gods, he didn't know where to let his thoughts land.

Because an insistent horror was rising up, towering over everything.

"I'm...Javieri."

43

NOBILITY

> *There have, of course, been times when a child was commissioned and then not acknowledged by one or both of the parents. It's illegal for both parents to unacknowledge a child they started without a private hearing to discover the reasons, after which their petition may be denied, or granted and the child enters the adoption system. But if one parent chooses to do so, they may, under terms negotiated with the other parent. Of course, that doesn't account for parental negligence, which only truly has recourse in contractual procreation arrangements.*

> — EKANI NORS IN "BIRTH COMMISSIONINGS: A METHODOLOGICAL STUDY"

Eti's throat burned as he said the words. His muscles burned with revulsion. No, no no, this was a nightmare. This was—that couldn't be true.

He said it again to be sure: "I'm Javieri."

He felt the pulse of truth from his mother. And felt it echo in himself, with what he'd just heard, because it made sense.

He hated how much sense it made. Why would the Javieris single out his family? Yes, they were unsealed magickers, but why had his mother never been allowed to seal?

But, no, it didn't make sense. Why would the Javieris threaten them, hold them captive, take Geyl away—

"Is Geyl—"

"Geyl's second parent was a donor," she said. And didn't elaborate on that. And he wasn't sure he should ask.

Eti stood, took a lurching step toward the hatch, but he still had too many questions. Too much to process, and not enough to make sense of any of it.

He plopped back down again. And thought of Lesander Javieri in the palace on Valon, tall and regal, and he saw no resemblance there, either. He wasn't tall, he had never been particularly pleasant to look at, his features were in every way different.

"Lesander is—"

"You've met Lesander? At the palace? Did she...recognize you?"

New panic rose up. "No...?" He tried to think back through what his mother had said, just who exactly his father was.

No, no, he knew. She was Semlin ne Krata Javieri, so then his father was Niom Javieri, as she'd said, a prince—

Eti choked. "Am I a prince?"

"No. That, at least, you're not. The title only passes one generation in families not in the direct line of succession, unless the main branch of the family is, ah, removed. Your father's parent was the Prince Javieri—your father was merely *a* prince."

Eti didn't think that made him feel any better. "And Lesander?"

"Would be your cousin."

But he'd already worked that out.

"And my handlers? Your handlers? Do they know?"

"Yes," his mother hissed. She'd been watching him closely, intent on how he was taking this, but now she looked away. Pulled down the sleeves of the colorful sweater she'd borrowed from Iwan and huddled into herself. "Oh they very much know who we are. I didn't think it was something you needed to know, Eti, because your father would never take an interest in your life."

"But he has. If he's using me—"

"No, I don't believe that's him. At least, I don't want to believe that's him. I think we're either dealing with lesser family or Yroikan herself. Depending. What happened to you at Windvale, and I'm so sorry, Eti, makes me think it is Yroikan. And them taking Geyl—" Her voice caught, her face going harder than Eti had seen in a long time. No, as hard as it had been the day that he'd said he'd go with the Javieris, instead of her. And was that what they'd wanted all along? Him, and not her? Eti, who had Javieri blood in his veins?

"Them taking Geyl was certainly Yroikan," his mother said.

Eti shuddered. He'd seen Prince Yroikan Javieri plenty of times on the vids growing up, and even on Hestia. The Javieris and Delors had always been considered the highest houses beyond Rhialden, and they made news whenever they sneezed.

He'd never liked her, never liked the feel of her, even before the Javieris had taken him away.

And she was his aunt?

"She was your sister," he said, "by marriage?"

"Is," his mother said grimly. "Niom never officially divorced me. I'm dead, but that doesn't, by law, nullify a marriage, only makes it go legally dormant. It's possible for a person to be preserved in suspended animation after death for a few days, and sometimes resuscitated. But...I am still married to your father. Shitty as that is."

She rubbed the back of her neck, looked up at Eti, and her gaze sharpened. "What I need to know is, do you love Imorie?"

Eti stiffened. That wasn't something she needed to know, whether he did or not—

"I know it's not my place to ask," she said. "But in this instance, it must be. Eti—if you love them, if they love you, and even if it's not romantic love, if you care for them in any way, and I've seen that you do—then you become a lever the Javieris can hold over them."

"But Imorie's not—no one knows that they're—"

"That they were Arianna Rhialden? That they're still so visibly Truthspoken to a magicker it's painfully obvious the rumors about them are true?"

Eti opened his hands helplessly. She wasn't wrong, he'd found Imorie out just by looking at them at Windvale. Had found them out over and over again, no matter how much he'd tried to make himself forget. To keep them safe from him.

"I think it's one of the reasons the Javieris took Geyl. They want you, because you're now attached to Imorie. You escaped with Imorie. And your body language—I have enough rudimentary evaku training from growing up in a minor noble house to see that you react to each other. Much more now, even, than when the news footage was taken on Hestia. And that's dangerous, Eti."

"I—" He scrunched his hands into his hair, let go. "I don't know if I—"

He cared for Imorie, but he didn't know if that was love. No, it wasn't romantic, he was sure of that. But he knew that from the moment he'd seen Imorie on Hestia, vulnerable and sick, and vulnerable to him and his handlers, he had to protect them with all he was. He was still doing that, the best that he could.

And Imorie, in turn, was protecting him. Was holding him grounded and coherent, slowly helping him come fully back to himself.

Was that love?

He would easily give his life for them. He almost had. And that thought, and everything associated with it, made him hunch over stabbing pain in his gut.

His mother growled a curse that he was sure was a minor violence and braced a hand on his shoulder, pouring what warmth she could and her own love into him.

"Steady," she whispered. "Steady."

He shuddered and felt himself flickering, but kept breathing until it passed. And his mother was there, as she'd been throughout his childhood, holding him steady.

Eti had usually been the steadier one, where Geyl had high anxiety. He feared intensely for his sibling in the Javieris' custody. Geyl had always been sensitive, and they couldn't be taking any of this well.

And if he had to choose between protecting his sibling and protecting Imorie...

The thought left him cold, his limbs tingling. He couldn't make that choice. He couldn't.

That was his mother's point, wasn't it?

Eti's head turned in the direction of the cabin where Imorie was sleeping—but they were awake. He felt that, and their sleep-hazed panic at his deep distress. Adeius, had he wakened them? Were they both that strong in their magics, and that connected, that he could sense Imorie's emotions so strongly even from here?

Yes. And the depth with which he felt them, the depth of how their panic pulled at his, was more terrifying now that he knew he was a danger to them again. He'd hoped to never be a danger to them again.

Magickers paired up sometimes, he knew that, he'd seen magicker couples and triads a few times in the streets on Kalistré, and a few times in Racha on Hestia. But he didn't think it had ever been higher ranking magickers. He'd always thought that had been discouraged, to keep strong magickers from having even stronger children—something people might fear.

He felt Imorie approaching and rose, half-protesting their coming to him. A second later the door chimed, and Eti's mother, who was watching him carefully, said, "Come in."

The hatch opened. It was outside the dampener's field, so he didn't hear Imorie's entrance until they'd stepped within the bubble. But he felt them every step of the way.

Imorie's blue and violet hair was mussed, their cosmetics that little bit smudged from sleep. They hadn't been removing them except to reapply them again, and he understood—both for the way it obscured their recognizable features, and for the way it pushed them more masc.

They looked smaller, though they'd always been small, and vulnerable again, like that first day he'd seen them.

Eti was up and moving toward them without thinking about it.

He gripped their hand, something in him easing, and in them, too, as the connection of touch was restored.

Eti's mother watched from where she still sat on the bed, but didn't comment. And when Imorie turned, his mother smiled up at them.

"Imorie, you're welcome to join—"

"You've talked?" Imorie asked her, pulling Eti closer.

"Yes."

"And he knows?"

A sour smile. "He does."

Imorie sank down onto the bed, pulling Eti with them.

They rubbed at their reddened eyes, but didn't let go of him.

"I was thinking, as I drifted up—Adeius this need to sleep is frustrating—Eti, you need more protection than Koldari can give you. The Javieris absolutely can't have a hold on you, and Koldari, a rival house, is not enough. You are...you're blood, the Javieris do have a claim on you."

"Yes," his mother said flatly. "And you have a solution?"

Imorie nodded. "I want—" They stopped, turned to Eti, their gaze intense. Because everything Imorie did was intense. "I think you should marry me. Legally. I'm under the Seritarchus's protection, no matter which way you look at it, and you are, too, but this makes it so that if they do anything to you, they are also doing it to a member of the royal family. And if they know that, they might think twice."

"Will you reveal yourself to them, then?" his mother asked, leaning back on her hands on the bed.

"No, though I'm sure they'll have heard the rumors by the time we get there." They made a wavery motion with one hand. "But I'm legally the adopted child of the Seritarchus. *I* am, as Imorie Rhialden méron Quevedo. So Eti marrying me will give that protection."

Eti stared at Imorie, and they stared back. And the question...didn't actually surprise him. Maybe it had been hovering in the background this last day, in the moments Imorie had surfaced from their sleep to eat or use the washroom. Eti flowed into the idea as if it was natural.

Then his brow creased. "But would that hurt you, your position, because I'm not noble—"

Imorie squeezed his hand. "Yes, you are."

"But no one knows it," Eti's mother said.

"Then we'll tell them," Imorie hissed. "We'll tell everyone. If he is the son of a Javieri prince, the public's eyes will be on the Javieris about this, so they can't harm Geyl. It would be too public. And they can't harm us—that would also be too public. We'll tell them Eti is married to the adopted child of the Seritarchus—that's not public knowledge at all."

Imorie turned back to Eti. "And we should do this now, drop out of Below Space now. Doryan is a magicker, they can witness, or your mother can."

"A parent can't typically witness for their child," Eti's mother said, but nodded. "If you are willing, Imorie."

Eti bridled. And why wouldn't Imorie be willing?

Imorie let go of his hand and gripped his arm before he could take greater offense.

"Eti? What do you think about this?" they asked, and he could feel their trepidation in asking it, though their outward tone was confident. "It's a marriage in files only, no exclusivity clause, no obligations except the legal fact of it—"

"I—I want there to be," he said, and his throat closed around the words as they left his mouth. He felt his face heating, knew his toes were probably turning red in his shoes. "Not —not, I mean, not the traditional, uh, bedroom—"

"I know," Imorie said. "I know what you mean."

And they did. He knew they did. They knew him so well, so thoroughly well, as no one had ever known him before. They'd seen him, as no one had seen him before.

And he didn't want sex from them, if that wasn't what they wanted. He didn't want a romance. He wanted...a friend who would never leave his side. And he'd never leave theirs. He wanted to sleep beside them. He wanted their hands intertwined. He wanted to know them more and more, and them know him too.

Imorie studied him, brow just slightly furrowed, calculating all his nuances, he thought. But also, reading his emotions.

Imorie didn't need to list all the reasons why this might also be putting him in a hard position—he knew it would be. It was protection, yes, but it would make him a different kind of target.

He knew who and what he was aligning his course to. He *knew* them.

"I want this," he said again. "If you do."

He didn't really want the telling the worlds he was a Javieri part. Or even the marrying a royal part, officially adopted or not. He just wanted them. He wanted to be near them, and know they would be near him.

After a long moment, Imorie nodded.

And he felt their warmth, like a star blazing within.

They wanted to be near him, too. They weren't just asking about this for protection. And that warmed him all over, easing the tense places that hadn't relaxed in weeks. In years?

"Well," Eti's mother said, and she stood. "You two work out the details, then. I'll go talk to Doryan and see if Koldari can maybe call in some backup if we're going to drop into the Ynassi system guns blazing. And—" She sighed. "I'd best tell him who I am. If he hasn't already put it together. Can't have our allies going to battle without all the relevant data."

Eti straightened. Going to battle? "We're not going to fight the Javieris—" His stomach lurched at the thought.

"This marriage is a point in a war," Eti's mother said, her eyes hard. "Whatever else it is or will be, it will be that, too. Don't either of you forget who you are or where you come from. Because no one else ever will."

Eti's eyes met Imorie's. Who he was...who he was was still something he didn't want to think about. The Javieris were enemies to the Rhialdens—he'd heard every horrible thing Lesander's family had done to her in her training. What they'd intended for her to do with that training. Yroikan's first plan had been for Lesander to kill Imorie and replace them.

And he was a part of that family? The same family who'd kidnapped his sibling, and forced him to use his magics for them? Against Imorie?

He wanted to shimmy out of his own blood.

But he still felt Imorie's warmth, strong and clear.

They cared for him. They truly did, even knowing what he was.

It wasn't love, maybe.

Or maybe it was.

44

WE WILL MANAGE

We're roots growing together
always reaching
entangling
but never knowing sunlight.

— TERESA LIEPINS, EXCERPT FROM STARS
POEM "A SYSTEM OF REACHING"

They had, after all, been in Financial District, right on the edge in a mixed commercial and residential high-rise.

Lesander followed Dressa outside, staying close, staying bottled up inside. And Dressa knew they needed to get back to the palace, they needed to talk to Iata *now*, but her wife...

Her wife had just been kidnapped by her longtime abuser. And threatened, and coerced. Well, and so had Dressa.

But Dressa didn't have the history with Yroikan Javieri that Lesander did. Dressa could feel Lesander quivering beside her and trying not to let it show.

She sought and gripped Lesander's hand again as they

stepped out to street level, the air too exposed, too loud and busy with the background hum of city traffic, even on this less-busy street.

Lesander looked at her, but that deadness in her eyes was still there.

Dressa gripped her hand more tightly, then pulled out her comm and called an aircab. She was still Lord Mynin Jadiar, still not herself, though she was barely holding that pretense together. Lesander's persona had shattered entirely.

There was a safe house nearby—they could stop there, for a few minutes, to clear their heads before they took this monumental problem to Iata.

Monumental fuckup? But then, who had fucked up? They'd been thoroughly outmaneuvered, all of them. And it was far from being over. They were in the middle of a nightmare, and Dressa could hardly see the beginning, and didn't know the end.

The aircab descended, and they both climbed in, Lesander shivering by the time they were in the air. Dressa reached to touch Lesander's arm, to caress her face, to try to give some reassurance that she was here and Lesander wasn't alone in her own private hell.

But Lesander pulled back, arms wrapped tightly around herself, and Dressa let her be. Let her stare out the window as they traveled the short distance into Blue District toward the safe house.

Dressa wasn't interested now in parking a discreet distance away, getting out and walking, none of that. This safe house would have to be cleared out and sold. But then, that was partly what it was here for—a convenient, and temporary, refuge. It was as burnable as the comm Dressa had in her pocket.

Dressa didn't think they were in physical danger from Yroikan, not any more than they'd already been. Yroikan needed them both for her plans. But she didn't find that thought overly comforting.

The car let them out at a four-story brick building, and this was a mostly residential area now. Children played enthusiastically in the street, tossing a small ball among themselves.

Which sight felt...deeply and obscenely incongruous to everything Dressa had just experienced. It hit her so hard that for a moment she paused, her eyes filling with an emotion she couldn't name.

What was it like, could she even imagine what it was like, to grow up without any more cares than being a child of your parents, in your place in the world? Just that. Nothing else. Toss the ball, catch the ball. No one trying to control you or kill you or steal your kingdom out from under you.

Lesander was shaking now in whole body gusting tremors.

A few people gave them weird looks, one or two managing to actually look concerned, but Dressa shrugged out of her jacket and wrapped it around Lesander's shoulders, hustling her inside.

It wasn't cold out.

They rode the lift in silence, as they'd ridden the aircar in silence. It wasn't safe to talk.

In the corridor, Dressa, pausing long enough to Change her palm to her own DNA, pressed her hand to the scan plate beside the apartment door. The lock clicked open, and they stepped inside.

Dressa set Lesander down on a chair in the sitting room while she moved to the bathroom. Opening a drawer beside the sink, she plucked out a certain lip gloss from among a stash of them. She extracted the bug sniffer tube from the rest of the gloss and went back out to Lesander—she didn't say a word as she ran the tube scanner over first herself, then Lesander.

They pulled off two bugs each, stuck to their clothes with

nearly invisible tape. Yes, this safe house would definitely be unusable now.

Dressa went around the apartment with the tube, but the apartment, at least, was clean.

Just to be safe, she went back to the bathroom and rooted under the sink, coming back with a bulky gray military-grade dampener/scrambler combo. She set it down on the end table next to Lesander while she dragged a second chair over from across the room to sit beside her wife.

Lesander had found a blanket and wrapped herself in it, hunching down as far as she could go inside the folds of what looked like hand-crocheted yarn.

"I'm s-sorry," Lesander shuddered.

Dressa rocked in her chair, trying to bleed off her own tension. "Not your fault." And should she say Lesander's mother was, in fact, a monster?

But Lesander knew that. Lesander definitely knew that.

Lesander was crying. Long streams defeating what should have been a waterproof liner and mascara.

"Do you want to Change?" Dressa asked. She didn't know how to comfort Lesander. Yes, she knew what having shitty parents was like, but...not this. Her father and mother might be cruel in their own ways, but they'd never deliberately try to destroy her. She knew that.

And Lesander's mother had as much as ordered Dressa to give Lesander as much authority as Dressa herself would have as the ruler. That should have been a triumph for Lesander, but Dressa knew it was, in fact, the ultimate failure. Failure to do whatever Lesander had come to do on her own. Failure to secure this position for herself. Failure to do it without Yroikan's explicit promise of heavy-handed oversight.

And Dressa had failed, too.

She wasn't sure exactly how, but she had.

Or maybe, they'd just lost the game. And they hadn't made

wrong moves, just bad ones, because they hadn't known what they'd needed to know, and not even Truthspoken could know everything.

"The Kidaa," Lesander said. "My m-mother has been afraid for a long time, I think it's why she trained me, wanted me here. But she never told me. Never told me why. I promise, Dressa. I didn't know. I still—I don't know."

Dressa leaned forward and pulled Lesander to her, and with the chairs at corners to each other, it was awkward, but it was needed.

No, it *was* really awkward.

Dressa tugged Lesander up, wrapping the blanket back around her where it fell. She hefted the dampener under one arm, then gently led Lesander to the apartment's one bedroom.

The room smelled like dust and afternoon sunlight, the curtains drawn, nothing at all like their bedroom in the palace.

Lesander stiffened as they approached the bed, neatly made with an out-of-date floral print comforter.

"To get warm," Dressa said. "To be comfortable. So I can hold you."

And Lesander started to cry harder.

"I brought this on you!" she sobbed, clutching the blanket tighter around herself.

"No," Dressa said, with a fierce glare. "No. I asked you to marry *me*."

"Yes, but you didn't know—"

"I did. I *did*, Lesander. I knew you could be Truthspoken. Maybe I didn't let myself think through all of it, but I did know the possibility. I didn't know how bad you had it, but I did know your mother, and what she's like. Her ambitions."

Lesander's face twisted. "Her ambitions are all wrapped up in—in whatever she fears about the Kidaa. You can't separate them. It's obscene. She's trying to gain from whatever she thinks will save us."

Dressa swallowed. In everything else in that conversation with Yroikan, Dressa hadn't had time to fully process what she'd said about the Kidaa. It had been twisted and woven in with everything else Yroikan had wanted.

Yroikan had been scared, that much was clear, and Lesander had said as much, too. Not a new fear, apparently, but maybe growing more urgent. And what sort of threat would scare a woman like Yroikan? She'd said that what the Kidaa were doing now, what was about to come, they wouldn't like at all.

That was starting to feel, in the context of everything else, like a terrible understatement.

Dressa wet her suddenly dry lips. "Lesander, I didn't know any of what she said about the Kidaa. I don't know if it's true, but—"

"It feels true. True enough. I know. That's how she works. She doesn't threaten with lies. She omits, she twists, but she doesn't typically lie."

The defeat on Lesander's face, in her posture, in her voice, was a spike to Dressa's heart.

Dressa carefully set the dampener on the bedside table, trying not to make any quick moves or sharp sounds, and tugged back the covers. The room was a little dusty, but tidy. She kicked off the shoes she still had on, and Lesander did the same. They crawled into bed, scooting close together. Shoulder to shoulder, hand to hand.

And then Dressa moved so that she could surround Lesander, wrap her arms around her, and it was weird, because she was still Mynin Jadiar, still different proportions than she felt she should be, and Lesander's body had a different shape, a different feel, a different smell.

That didn't stop either of them from turning, slowly, their lips meeting.

The kiss wasn't passionate. Neither of them were up for that just now, and anyhow, it *was* weird. Maybe some day they could Change to their own special fantasy, whatever that would be, and find out what it was like to have mutually Changed sex. Yeah, that would be fun. But now?

Now, Dressa held her wife. Held her tightly, and needed her warmth as much as Lesander needed hers.

They didn't sleep. They didn't Change. They knew this moment wouldn't last longer than they needed it to. It was borrowed time already, but it was necessary.

"I love you," Lesander whispered in the muted sound of the softly humming dampener. In their bubble of protection, they couldn't hear any traffic outside the closed bedroom window. None of the sounds of the kids below screeching, or the ordinary buzz of the city. The silence made everything feel that little more lonely.

"And I'm sorry for it," Lesander went on, her voice breaking. "And I'm sorry you love me."

Dressa bit hard into her lip, baring her teeth out of Lesander's sight. "I'm not. I love you, too. I *love* you, Lesander. We will manage. We're playing for the kingdom, not the Rhialdens or the Javieris. The kingdom. And yes, your mother's a tyrant, and you had the most hellish childhood I can think of —and I've been through a lot—but I know who you are, Lesander. I know you, I've seen you, and you're nothing like them. Your mother's sins are not yours. We'll get through this, okay? Both of us."

Lesander was quiet a long moment, tense, as if she couldn't accept that. Couldn't accept anything but the harsh reality she'd been brought up in, anything but her mother's sadistic worldview.

But finally, she sighed out, and pressed her cheek into Dressa's shoulder. "Okay."

45

THE DECISION

If I said this was the end, would you believe me? And what if I also promised a new beginning?

— DENA OLEGANI IN THE VID DRAMA *NOVA HEARTS*, SEASON 10, EPISODE 8, "UNSTOPPABLE MOTION"

They were still Changed, still Lord Mynin Jadiar and Administrator Zara, when Dressa knocked softly on the panel door to Iata's study.

She didn't know if he'd be in there, but it was a safe bet with the amount of work he had to do. And if he wasn't there, Bettea or Pria would likely be.

It was Iata who opened the door, though, frowned at them, then stepped back to let them enter. He was mostly masc just now, cosmetics neutral, hair in a long straight tail.

Lesander had lightly tranced to clear the most obvious signs of having cried and washed her face at the safe house. Dressa had cleaned herself up, too, changing into a spare suit and coat at the safe house that mostly fit Mynin's bulky frame.

They'd had dirt scuffs and some light abrasions from being handled by Yroikan's people. Or maybe Denom's. Dressa had also quickly tranced and healed the most obvious signs of ill-treatment.

But even having cleaned up as best they could, she knew they both looked worn. They both were showing signs of stress that they couldn't—or weren't interested in expending energy to—conceal.

Bettea, who'd been working at a desk in the corner of the room, stood, coming over to them.

Fae looked far, far more Rhialden now, not like faer usual preferred appearance at all. And Dressa knew that was a deliberate choice. Because Iata, in the end, wasn't in a riches of heirs. And Bettea could rule, if fae had to.

Watching faer, Dressa's lips parted, and it was in her thoughts right then to abdicate herself. To take herself and Lesander completely out of the line of succession. To take Yroikan's grasp on them and throw it aside. She could do that.

But was that what was needed just now? Was an extra Rhialden showing up, after all the previous ones had fallen apart, going to be enough glue to hold a crumbling kingdom together? Would Yroikan just swoop in anyway?

She already had eyes and ears within the palace staff, and within the residence, of that Dressa was certain. Did she have bugs, could she possibly have bugs, in Iata's study?

Bettea's brow creased. "Dressa? What happened?" Fae was even moving with more authority. Moving with, Dressa saw, a lot of her father's mannerisms. As if fae could plausibly present faerself as Homaj's own child.

And she wished—Adeius, she wished—it could be that easy.

"Why are you Mynin Jadiar?" Iata asked. "That's Imorie's persona." But the question sounded rote, as if he'd already guessed it had something to do with the vote of no confidence. And he wasn't angry. And he wasn't happy. He was just...tired.

As they all were.

Dressa glanced at Lesander as they moved to the powder blue couch and sat, Iata settling across from them in her father's usual chair, now his. Bettea taking the chair beside him. None of them, not a one, who they actually were.

And Dressa gave her report. All of it, and every word Yroikan had said, verbatim.

Iata listened without interjecting anything, without asking questions. His aura flickered, once, when she reached the part about the Kidaa giving him magics, and giving it to the wrong brother. But still, he said nothing.

Dressa wound down, finally, with Yroikan letting them go.

And for a long moment, there was silence. The crackling of the hearth.

"That is just utter bullshit," Bettea finally said.

Iata snorted. Gathered a breath, reached up and unfastened the clip holding his hair. His masc mannerisms were rarer for Homaj Rhialden, but still part of Homaj's typical gender shifts.

It was weird, it felt like someone had broken into her home, to think that Yroikan knew about all of this. Who Iata was, who he'd partly been for all of Dressa's life.

Iata ran his hands through his hair, letting it fall loose, and he seemed to need the grounding as much as Dressa and Lesander had needed theirs.

Finally, he bound it back up again, in a loose knot this time, his body language shifting more toward femme. And Dressa wondered, after all these years, if he even realized he was doing it? Or was it simply natural now?

He sat back.

"They got the wrong brother," he said softly. In his own cadences, not Homaj's. "They were aiming for Maja, and got me."

"They weren't wrong that you were the ruler," Bettea shot back.

"Only part of the time," Iata said. "And not the greater part of that time."

Another pause.

He met Dressa's eyes. "I have to tell everything. We have to tell everything. It's the only way to step out of Yroikan's power. Otherwise—the kingdom is lost to us, anyway."

Dressa shifted uncomfortably on the couch. And if the kingdom crumbled from that telling? When Iata said tell everything, that would mean telling Iata's identity, that he'd ruled alongside his brother, that Dressa was already married to Lesander, that Lesander was the one who'd attacked him. Everything meant telling the entire kingdom that Lesander was also secretly Truthspoken.

"You can't," Dressa said, her voice raspy with strain. "Not about—" She looked to Lesander.

Iata's lips drew tight, but after a moment, he nodded. He glanced to Bettea, a long, long look, and Dressa knew he was making the calculations she had just made. About whether it was time for their entire family of Truthspoken to bow out, and hand it off to—well, Bettea was still their family. But not the family the worlds would have been expecting.

And Dressa didn't dare, didn't even dare, mention the heir that she'd already started in the incubator. Ready in six months' time.

Bettea braced faerself, as if fae would have to step into a maelstrom, as if that was, in fact, the fate that would be decided for faer. Dressa had the dizzying and skewing perspective that fae was just as scared as she was, caught up in this just as much as she was, forced into a position fae didn't want. Maybe fae had volunteered—Dressa couldn't see Iata ordering Bettea to assume this different, semi-legitimate Rhialden identity—but all the same, it was the start of a bad cycle all over again.

Dressa straightened. "We'll find a way around Yroikan. Or past her." She touched Lesander's leg beside her, gently, just a brush, trying to give some sort of reassurance. "Or we'll figure out how to bring her down."

Lesander gave a sharp, definitive nod.

"But I think," Dressa said, "I still need to rule."

Bettea sat back with sharp and obvious relief, but worry still clouded faer brow.

"Yes," Iata said with a sigh. "And I can't see a way forward that doesn't require my abdication to help settle the kingdom. I'm far too visible, far too strong a magicker—and, truly, it might not matter what strength I manifested at, they would have protested anyway." He shrugged. But his casual gesture didn't fool Dressa. He didn't want to abdicate. He didn't want to give up any of this. And he shouldn't have to.

"I'm sorry," Dressa said. "I don't want to usurp—"

He scowled. "Adeius, Dressa. You aren't." And his eyes shot to Lesander. "And this is *not* your fault. I am proud of you—I am proud of both of you, for how you handled this today. Thank you, truly, for working to help me and the kingdom. That this is the course we're set on now is...what it will be."

He reached out his hands and Dressa took one, and, after a moment, Lesander took the other.

Dressa was hit with a wave of...

Was that love? Love, like a meadow in summer. Love like sun clearing the storm. And pride, there was pride, and hope, and fear, and pain, and loss, and a coiled, screaming rage. But over it all, calming it all, love.

"Both of you," he said, looking between them. "You are my daughters, as much as you were ever Maja's, Dressa. As much as Bettea and Pria are mine. And Lesander, you are my family. You are my daughter, too. Dressa, you are ready. You will be an excellent ruler, and I know I won't be able to help directly, I'll need to retreat to Green Hall, or if that's not far enough, maybe offworld. But I'm going to try to stay near, for now. I think—I think that will be needed."

Dressa swallowed, a tight squelch in the pause.

She'd known she'd have to rule, but she hadn't truly thought through yet that she'd have to do it alone. She'd have to do this without his guidance, because he was too politically hot of a topic to be seen influencing her. To have even the appearance of being seen as that.

He squeezed her hand.

And if he had been Homaj for at least a fifth of Homaj's entire rule, had he been her father for at least a fifth of her life? Had he been as much a part of the heartache as the good times? Had he been just as shitty as he'd been good?

He smiled at her, a little sadly, and she felt regret pouring from him. But still beneath it that overriding, all-encompassing, love.

Was this what it was like to know, truly know, she was loved by her father?

She stared at his face, memorizing the details, and knew it wouldn't be his much longer. He would Change back to himself before he foreswore Change, or maybe Change to someone else.

And she was suddenly, overwhelmingly saddened by that. She swallowed again, her body rigidly trying to contain her emotions.

Iata's voice cracked as he said, "And when I'm myself, I still won't be less of your father. To all of you." He swept his shining gaze over them, settled on Bettea, smiled fondly.

Fae sniffed hard. Reached out and gently gripped his arm, and Dressa felt faer own turbulent emotions added to the fray.

"Okay," Iata whispered. And carefully, gently, let go.

46

WE WILL PREVAIL

I abdicated today, Uncle. This will be the last, I think, of these letters that I've never sent. And right now, I'm giving my permission, if any of my heirs ever find these, to do with them as you will. This life is so lonely. I have my family, I have my brother and my children. But do any of them know me? They should. I want them to. Maybe Zhang does, but Zhang still doesn't rule the kingdom. I wish I'd sent these letters, Uncle, because maybe you'd understand. I do hope, though, that things will get better.

— HOMAJ RHIALDEN, SERITARCHUS IX IN A
PRIVATE LETTER, NEVER SENT; PUBLISHED IN
THE CHANGE DIALOGUES

In the Reception Hall, Iata leaned on the table in front of him. His whole body still. His entire spirit quivering. He knew it showed in his aura, and he couldn't help that. Let them think what they would. He would use it, he'd spin it, everything he could to propel this kingdom favorably forward into the maelstrom it was about to face. Through the maelstrom it was already facing.

They all watched. Even more silent than the day he'd declared himself the Melesorie.

And he'd thought over how to handle this. He'd run so many scenarios in his head—until he'd realized that was what a Seritarchus would do.

And then he'd just...blanked out for a while until he'd gotten sick enough of that to start moving again. The result of that movement was...this.

Iata glanced at Laguaya beside him. Their passive expression didn't quite hide their stress.

He held out his hand, and they met his eyes, searching, but took it.

He hadn't told them what he was about to do, only that he needed their support at this meeting.

"Witness my truth, please, Admiral of the Fleet Dassan Laguaya."

Laguaya stiffened as their hand touched his. If they couldn't sense his exact thoughts, they surely knew the sense of finality that was settling into his marrow. But they didn't let go. They gave him a penetrating look before they also gave the smallest nod.

He and Laguaya might never have been friends, but he did trust them. And they, apparently in this moment, trusted him.

The camera drones whirred closer, smelling blood. Those in the audience here, nobles and palace administrators and foreign dignitaries, all leaned a little forward.

"A few days ago," Iata said, "you asked me to be your First Magicker. And I accepted that honor and that duty. But one of the utmost duties of the First Magicker is to always uphold the truth. So, I have some truths I must uphold with you now, while we're facing Kidaa attacks, and unfortunate unrest in our economy and throughout the kingdom. I will give you, my people, the knowledge that you need to move forward."

If someone coughed into the silence just now, he was sure everyone would jump. But no one coughed. Even the palace air system, for once, was silent. He could hear the faintest hum of the overhead lights.

Iata spread his free hand carefully over the table, a casual motion. He hadn't worn all of his usual rings as Homaj today, only the spare band of the Palace Guard ring comm, and his ruler's signet ring. He drew deliberate attention to that lack, then settled his hand palm down. The other hand, ringless, Laguaya held in a tightening grip.

"My name is Homaj Rhialden. My name is *also* Iata Rhialden."

He waited, but there was still silence.

"I have three full siblings, all children of Anatharie Rhialden and Jamir ne Xiao Rhialden. Of the four of us, I was the third, and my brother, Maja, the fourth. And when our parents were assassinated, I did what every bloodservant should—I protected my Truthspoken with the shield of my life."

The crowd stirred. People looking at each other, trying to gauge if any others among them knew. Trying to parse out what it actually *meant*.

He went on before the uproar could start. "My duty did not end when Maja successfully ascended to the rulership. Because I *also* ascended to the rulership. There is only one Truthspoken ruler, and that is Homaj Rhialden. But Homaj Rhialden is one person shared by two lives. He has been since before he ascended—"

He was drowned out by the uproar, nobles and business people and courtiers and heads of high houses and their representatives, all shouting, some screaming, just—utter chaos.

Laguaya sat back. They still held his hand, and he could feel their deep dismay as they looked at him.

He smiled at them.

He could almost hear them saying, "You fucking bastard, you actually did it." With admiration, sure, mixed in with the incredulity.

He stood, pulling Laguaya up with him, and it did nothing to calm the crowd.

He looked to Dressa on his other side—she stood as well.

"The same," she said, in a voice pitched to carry, "is not true for me. But it could be. It's why we have bloodservants—so we don't have to rule the kingdom alone."

"But there should only be three!" someone shouted, Iata didn't see who, couldn't tell the voice among the uproar.

"Yes," Dressa said. "And there only are. Homaj Rhialden is one person, not two. Such is the nature of Truthspoken that this can be true—"

"That's just an excuse to—"

Iata let go of Laguaya's hand, settled his nerves—which wasn't easy—and reached into the air around the room. He drifted into the feel of life around him, agitated and volatile.

The life was the storm. It was the peace, it was the space between worlds, it was the seething chaos on every world, it was beauty and it was destruction—all of it. Iata shuddered, because he'd never been this open before. He'd never let himself be this tuned to the energies around him, the feeling of...everything.

It was so much. And it was above everything else going on. It was absolute, utter calm.

And his people needed to know. They needed to know that this, *this* was their strength. Not their fears, not their bigotries, but the life that connected all of them. It was how they'd stand against what was coming, with the Kidaa, with the high houses, what they were facing now.

Even if it cost him all he had, he would do this, he would show them this truth, his parting gift.

He extended all that he was into the calm.

Silence fell in a startled wave of calm. And he knew, wherever this was watched, no matter the distance or comm lag, there would be calm. Possible or not, he knew there would be.

Maybe that should have terrified him just now, but he couldn't reach that place of fear. He only felt *life*.

"I'm telling you now," Iata said into the hush, "because I don't think this kingdom is best served just now by my continuing to be the ruler. I, Homaj Rhialden, and Iata Rhialden, therefore abdicate—"

"You can't abdicate for Homaj—"

Denom Xiao, and of course it was Denom Xiao, fighting through Iata's blanket of calm.

But Iata was too enmeshed in the life around him to be bothered by it.

"Cousin," he said. "I *am* Homaj Rhialden, haven't you been listening?" He paid for that very small violence in a loss of concentration, a shudder that rippled through the crowd.

And he couldn't hold them.

And maybe they weren't his to hold. They never had been.

And maybe, just maybe, trying to hold them, imposing his calm, had also been a violence.

He slowly eased back on his projected calm, the immense sense of life around him fading.

Iata blinked rapidly. Adeius. Had he done that? *Why* had he thought that was a good idea?

He hadn't thought at all, he'd only acted on an instinct he couldn't name. And he was rattled that it had even worked. He was rattled by what he'd felt, and what he'd known to be true. That effect *would* reach anyone who saw this broadcast, and that he knew that to be true was something he couldn't examine just now.

There would be hell to pay.

"You used your magics on us!" Denom cried. "Adeius, Truthspeaker, you cannot condone this!"

But Ceorre, beside Lesander, remained silent and stoic, staring Denom down.

"I abdicate my position as ruler," Iata went on, fighting to keep the shake from his voice, "as Homaj Rhialden, for the both of us. Maja has already abdicated on his own. It is done. Truthspeaker—witness, please."

"I witness, under the eyes and in the will of Adeius. It is done." And he felt from Ceorre the absolute necessity of that abdication, especially after what he'd done just now. She was not happy with what he'd done. But then, neither was he.

Another heartbeat of silence.

And into that came a new voice.

Iata had been almost certain it would be coming. He'd known. Dressa had, at least, given him warning of all of this, a warning that Yroikan had given herself. If feeble warning and far too late it was.

"Abdicate in favor of whom?" Prince Yroikan Javieri asked. He'd noticed her come in. She'd made her quiet entrance when he'd had everyone in his calming grip.

Adeius, that had been a *mistake*.

Heads swiveled in her direction, hearing power in their midst. A dawning sun when his was setting.

"When you've just said that the Rhialdens have been lying to us all for decades?" she said. "That you've broken the laws—"

"Yroikan," Iata said, as calmly as he could manage, "if you would like to talk about breaking the law, we can have a conversation about—"

He knew she wouldn't let him get that far, but still it hurt him like a strike to bring Lesander and her training into this. Because that was gambling with Lesander's life, too, and he'd told Dressa he wouldn't do that.

But he found himself stuttering off, because Yroikan didn't stop him. She just nodded. Her spiked red hair glimmering in the overhead lights. Red lips curling up.

She would give up her daughter for this? Even if he exposed her as plotting against the Truthspoken? As illegally training her daughter to be Truthspoken? The Javieris would be cast out, open to censure.

No. No, but in this very primed moment, she would paint herself the hero, the one person who had almost brought the Rhialdens, the deceitful Rhialdens, down. Who'd had the foresight to train a Javieri Truthspoken to rule.

He shut his mouth. And her smile widened. Because she knew that he wouldn't give up Lesander to that. To her ultimate and unyielding control.

"Rhialdens have seen this kingdom through every storm for centuries," Iata said. "You, more than anyone, should know that what's happening with the Kidaa is a storm we must weather together. I abdicate in favor of Ondressarie, my Heir, with Lesander Javieri as her consort, because they will both see us through."

He turned around, met Dressa's eyes. "From this moment, she is Ondressarie Rhialden, Ialorius X. She will not let any who seek to harm us get a hold."

Dressa's eyes burned, and he saw the flare, the rising fire in her soul. Yes. Yes, keep that, Dressa. You will need it.

He turned back to the crowd. "I sought to keep us thriving by declaring myself as a Melesorie, but that's not what this kingdom needs. We need the fluidity and adaptability of an Ialorius to see us through our trials now and what's to come."

"Do we?" Yroikan asked, breaking his flow.

"Yes," Laguaya said, finally stepping up. "Yes, we do. Yroikan, I know you're trying to pull this situation to your own political gain. But the Navy is out there, facing perhaps the greatest threat we have ever known. I witness the truth of

Homaj and Iata Rhialden. He is both, as he says, and can speak for both and the rulership. He's never been my friend, but he has my respect. And yes, I did know."

No. No, Laguaya, don't take that blame on yourself.

He wanted to say that they'd only known for a few days, but they pinned him with a hard glare.

Because now that Laguaya had said they were in on the deception, and they had many supporters among this crowd, how could their supporters reject Iata's deception but embrace theirs?

Ceorre slowly stood. "I also knew, and approved. The will of Adeius is channeled through whichever person is at the pinnacle, and if the kingdom is best served by that person being inhabited by two souls, then that is the will of Adeius."

A staggering challenge. There would be, of course, those who wouldn't believe a word of that in this crowd, who'd find a way to twist the holy mandates or quote the heretical texts to their purpose. But how much face would they lose if they directly challenged the Truthspeaker, the head of the ruling religion of Valoris?

Ceorre's voice hardened. "This man is giving you the gift of not tearing us all apart by you demanding that he abdicate— he's doing it himself. And telling you why. If he ruled by the will of Adeius, then he now sets that aside by the will of Adeius, to take up the other mantle given to him."

She turned to him. Gave a slight, just a slight, nod. Not her usual deference, as he would give to her in return. They were not co-rulers any longer.

And that hurt, oh Adeius it hurt, but it was what it needed to be. She was doing what she needed to do.

"First Magicker," Ceorre said, "the Adeium continues to acknowledge you in your position."

Iata bowed, much more deeply than he ever would have as

Homaj, or even Iata, in return. He did not have a place here anymore. Not at this table, not, truly, in this palace.

"Truthspeaker." He turned to Dressa and bowed even deeper. "Ser Ialorius."

And he watched Dressa expand, her posture taking on the mantle of command, chin tipping up, shoulders back, eyes still blazing.

"I am your Ialorius," Dressa said to the restless crowd. "And I'm telling you, we will get through these trials together. We will prevail."

47

THE STORM

Sometimes, when I dream in Below Space, it feels true. Reality bleeds over, and it's like I can see beyond the walls of the hull, beyond the metal, beyond the tumult —or maybe the nothing—outside. I hear whispers.

— OWAM, IN AN INTERVIEW ABOUT THE
SOURCE OF THEIR POETIC INSPIRATION

"Coming out of Below Space in thirty seconds," Onya Norren said. "Let's hope we're in the right system this time."

They'd traveled to where *Occam's Storm* was supposed to be on its filed schedule, an uninhabited border system with no hospitable worlds, but had found nothing more than a few drones monitoring the system.

Maja hadn't panicked. A schedule delay for a border scout ship could mean any number of things, and it wasn't necessarily a disaster.

So they'd backtracked.

But that rune. Storm. That rune had been carved during an

attack. And his feeling of being watched had only gotten stronger every moment of the six and a half day trip to the border. Onya had been pushing their speed hard and was grumpy the last two days in particular, claiming his thoughts were keeping her from sleeping much at all. He was hardly sleeping himself.

His palms were damp now as he touched the controls, readying the scanning systems for when the ship emerged back into normal space.

He'd Changed two days ago to Captain Kian Temir, his persona among his—well, now Iata's—personal guards, and the other person listed aboard this ship. He wasn't even trying to hold the persona just now, though.

Zhang, behind him in the observer's seat, leaned forward, trying to get a good view of all the displays. Her crutches were propped next to her, and he wondered if he should say something, because they would fall if there was trouble. Zhang was strapped in, all of them were—that, at least, was habit.

And would there be trouble?

He had a gut feel, a deep, deep foreboding. Whether it was a sense of the patterns around him that his mind hadn't put together yet or...something else...he didn't know. But he'd learned not to ignore his gut.

"Zhang," he said, nodding to her crutches.

She turned, levered them to slide onto the deck. He'd have to mark the tripping hazard, but—later.

"Five seconds," Onya said.

He waited through the last pause. Tensed for...what?

Then the front screens shimmered and resolved into stars again. He might have breathed easier, because the blur of Below Space had really started to freak him out, and maybe that had been most of what was getting to him, but an alert started blaring.

He checked the scans as one of the system buoys updated

the sensors with a current in-system configuration. Everything near the buoys would be tagged, with trajectories calculated for everything further out where it would produce light lag. This wasn't a populated system with a full Below Space comm lace.

He blinked at the indicators, leaned closer.

Kidaa ships. *Three* Kidaa ships, decently close, and yes, there was the *Storm's* beacon tag on the scans, but—

"Fuck!" His heart leaped into his throat. The *Storm's* tag was right on top of one of the Kidaa tags. Were those ships overlapped?

He zoomed in on the screen to make sure he was actually seeing what he was seeing. That it wasn't some buoy glitch, or a factor of distance.

"Zhang," he said, and she was levering up beside him, crutches out of reach, dammit, leaning heavily on the back of his chair to take the weight off her still-healing ankle.

Visuals resolved and enhanced, and he threw them up above the controls.

One Kidaa ship, farther forward than the others, had *swallowed* the *Occam's Storm*. There were a very few edges in the rear of the *Storm* poking out beyond the bulky, angular shape of the much larger Kidaa ship.

"They're overlapped," he said.

"I see it," Zhang said.

"Onya? What do you sense? Can you sense anything at this distance?"

Onya, who'd been sitting pilot to his copilot for this part of the trip, sat back in her seat with a tense sigh, closing her eyes. Her aura brightened, just a little.

He left her to her sensing as he went back to surveying all of the information in front of him. Much of which he wasn't sure what to do with. Like how to handle the Kidaa overlapping the ship they'd directed him to. Should he board the *Storm*? Could he even board the *Storm*—but it looked like it was the Kidaa ship that was intangible, not the Valoran ship. On the visuals, he could faintly see the pinpoints of stars through the Kidaa ship. And that was damn spooky.

Maja cupped a hand over his mouth, transferring pilot's priority to his controls. He maneuvered their ship onto a parallel course with the Kidaa ships and the *Storm,* though he didn't move any closer.

And they weren't far.

Maja checked the nav displays—Onya had calculated to come out at a conservative system entry point, not near any of the system's planets or asteroids. The odds of them coming out here, so close to the Kidaa ships, were...were...

And were they in any danger? The Kidaa would certainly see them. And then what? Would the Kidaa...attack?

"There are two magickers on *Occam's Storm,*" Onya said. "I know one, the other I don't. There should be only one on that ship, though, so someone's manifested. Or someone's boarded."

Maja looked at her askance. He wasn't going to ask why she knew about the disposition of magickers on Navy ships if she was no longer the First Magicker. And never mind that she'd gathered that much detail with her magics at this distance yet.

"So does that mean anything?" he asked.

"Maybe."

"We could just hail them," Zhang said.

Maja's breath went out in a humorless laugh. Well, leave it to Zhang to find the simplest solution.

But did he dare disturb whatever was happening there?

"Is the Kidaa ship moving at all, relative to the *Storm?*" he asked, even though he could see it wasn't.

He pinged the system buoys for back data up to a day, and then waited the few heartbeats for that to sort itself in the ship's systems into useable information.

The data, when it painted its picture, was appalling.

"They've been overlapped for more than a day," Zhang said, her voice rising in alarm.

Maja shared a look with her. Had he come too late? Had they not found the *Storm* in time? But then, they couldn't have come sooner. They'd come as fast as possible through any means or magics, and they'd had to backtrack even then.

His chest thrummed again with foreboding.

Then the comm crackled. "Unknown ship, this is the *V.N.S. Occam's Storm*. Be advised there are Kidaa in-system, proceed with caution. Please state your business in-system."

Rhys. That was Rhys, *that was Rhys.*

Maja shuddered with a relief that he hadn't known he needed to feel. Because that ship in that position was terrifying.

He reached for the comm, but Zhang grabbed his hand.

"How are we playing this?" she asked.

He was Captain Temir just now, and they were nominally the same rank. But Zhang, as captain of the Seritarchus's personal guard, definitely had seniority over Temir, an auxiliary intelligence officer. He couldn't take point.

Officially, Shiera Keralan had been left on Hestia to board another ship back to the capital, so he couldn't be Shiera here without burning an identity he cherished. And there wasn't time to Change. And Zhang would still be senior anyway.

As Temir, his build was taller than his own and willowy, blade of a nose, shoulder length brown hair braided back tightly in a no-nonsense style. His maroon and silver Palace Guard uniform was crisp, his cosmetics heavy and unartful. Applied by Zhang, because she said she'd best be able to make it look like a working guard's makeup.

He'd planned, if needed, to use Iata's persona if absolutely necessary, but he still didn't want to spread around that blood-servants could Change any more than he had to. General Kim had been enough of a risk already.

Never mind that it would be blown into the open soon

enough, when he publicly abdicated and Iata became the ruler in his own right. If that still happened, with everything else going on.

"Take point," he said. Because he had to. And because maybe it was the right choice anyway.

Zhang nodded and reached for the comm controls. "*Occam's Storm,* this is Captain Vi Zhang of the Valon City Palace Guard, on the ship *Open Hand* in from Hestia. We came to find you. Please advise of your status. Are you in need of assistance?"

A pause. Which turned into a longer pause, and Maja wondered if there was an argument happening on the other side. Or panic?

Finally, the comm crackled again. He'd expected the captain this time, but it was Rhys again.

"Captain Zhang, you said you were in from Hestia? Did you get my—our—message?"

"Message?" Maja mouthed.

Onya was sitting forward now with her eyes narrowed. Maja didn't like the tension written in her posture at all. It was more than just an immediate sense of danger.

"We've had no word from *Occam's Storm,*" Zhang said. "I am traveling with Captain Temir of the Palace Guard and a magicker."

Another pause.

Zhang leaned hard on the console. "This is Lieutenant Petrava?"

"Yes," Rhys said tightly, immediately.

"Lieutenant, please advise us of your status. Because from what we're seeing, we don't know how to proceed."

"A moment, Captain. I need—I need to try to get the Kidaa to back off so you can dock."

There was something off in Rhys's tone. Something scared, something heavy. Like they were carrying the weight of whatever was going on here.

And maybe they were. Iata had given them the Seritarchus's seal. Rhys shouldn't be the officer on point here, they were a junior lieutenant, but they were the one who'd answered the comm. They were the one who'd been researching the Kidaa.

And the Kidaa had called *him* to the *Storm*.

Should he say he was Iata now? Take charge of this situation, whatever it was? As a bloodservant, Iata would have that authority—he'd outrank everyone here, at least. He knew Rhys well enough to know they'd be giving this their absolute all. But whatever this was, Rhys was way, way in over their head.

Maja had decades of ruling a kingdom, and he was still in over his head. They all were. Every single person was.

He still didn't know what was happening to those two ships.

Maja opened his mouth, started to say something, started to shift his posture and his thoughts to Iata's cadences, when Onya made a noise.

He turned, and he saw she'd brought up the beacon news.

No—no, this was something different, from a private channel. From the other ship. He couldn't quite make out the words from his station. Something Rhys had wanted them to know?

Onya reached to mute the comm. "Maja, I feel you shifting personalities, you'd better stop right now." And there was a terror in her voice that made every cell in his body go on alert. The last time he'd seen her this upset, she'd just witnessed what no mother should ever witness.

He made a give-to-me motion, and she threw the text to his station.

"I'll take the controls," she said, "you'll want to read this."

He released pilot's status back to her, then expanded the window, swallowing on a dry throat.

The message was an urgent order from Admiral of the Fleet Laguaya. It was the news that Iata had been attacked by—well, he hadn't been attacked by himself. Something more had happened. He was a magicker now, publicly. *Homaj* was a magicker publicly.

And Iata had an arrest order, with a kill order attached, on his head.

Homaj let out a slow breath, pulling a light trance around himself, but his trance stuttered, was interrupted as the two Kidaa ships traveling behind the other started to move forward. To flank the central ship on either side.

The comm crackled. And why couldn't Rhys show visuals, show a holo? Use, even, a better quality channel?

He had a sudden need to know they were okay. This brilliant child who'd come into his home, who he hadn't raised, exactly, not in a direct way—that would be overstepping social bounds and painting a much greater target on Rhys than there already was. But Rhys had been with his own children from their early teens, had played training games with them, had learned evaku from their games, had learned the technicalities of Change if not the means itself.

Rhys navigated palace life with ease, had learned to segment their public and private personas just as surely as Imorie and Dressa had. And Maja had watched, not allowed to officially care for this child who Hancri had never looked after herself, not willing at all to abandon them to the confines of his wife's austere household. Not able to deny, either, that he might need to use Rhys someday, that having another person who was as trained in evaku as any Truthspoken would be a good asset to the kingdom. And Rhys was so flawless that people seldom saw them as the threat they actually were.

Was Rhys in this situation now because of that training? Because he'd allowed it, and encouraged it, even?

Maja had been summarily *summoned* to this ship, right now, and while he'd had his doubts on the rushed trip here, doubts that he'd been reading that right, he had no doubts now. Whatever was happening with the Kidaa, with the attacks—this was the center right here.

"Captain Zhang," Rhys said, "this Kidaa ship will remain overlapped, but you will be able to pass through the ship to the starboard airlock. Your ship's not small enough to fit into our bay, unfortunately." A small hesitation. "You'll all want to board. We're preparing quarters as well."

"Thank you, Lieutenant." Zhang didn't ask, this time, about what was happening here. Because if Rhys wanted them to know, or could tell them, they would have already said. That they hadn't said anything yet told much.

Zhang muted the comm again. "Onya, ETA?"

"Twenty minutes. I don't want to come in too quickly."

Zhang nodded and opened the comm.

"I estimate, then, that we'll dock in twenty minutes. Is it safe to pass between the Kidaa ships?"

"It's safe," Rhys said. Another pause. "They're waiting for you to arrive."

Maja shivered, glanced to Onya, who didn't look any less distressed now than she had before.

"Understood, Petrava," Zhang said, though it was far, far from understood what was going on here. "Zhang out."

She straightened from the console to lean on his chair.

"Maja, I don't like this."

He'd been applying treatments to her broken ankle three times a day, and it was healing quickly, but she wasn't Truth-spoken. She couldn't heal like he could. He deeply wished he'd been the one to have the break, not her.

"I don't like it, either," he said. "But it's what we have. Onya? Are you good to take us in?"

But Onya had already plotted a course, logged it with the *Storm,* and synced navigational data.

"Yes," she said. Then, "Maja. I've never felt the Kidaa before.

I've never been to the border—and I should have. Because they can sense me back, sure as anything."

"You've read reports of magickers sensing the Kidaa," he said, because he had, too. "They don't have magickers like we do."

"No," she agreed. But the tension in her shoulders didn't ease.

With a careful hand, she took their ship in to dock with the *Storm*.

Thanks so much for reading, and I hope you enjoyed *The Nameless Storm*!

Read along as I write the next book, *The Second Ruler,* in early access on my Patreon!
https://www.patreon.com/novaecaelum

Want to stay up to date on the latest books? Sign up for Novae Caelum's newsletter.
https://novaecaelum.com/pages/newsletter

THE CAST

Note: Because this future universe has full gender equality, binary gender characters (male, female) may be cis or may be trans. I've only stated if they're trans if it comes up within the story itself.

Imorie Rhialden méron Quevedo (formerly Ari Rhialden): Second Truthspoken heir of the Kingdom of Valoris and would really like to change that. Hates when things are out of their control. Has a chronic illness. Agender, ace/aro. they/them

Ondressarie Rhialden (Dressa): The Truthspoken Heir of the Kingdom of Valoris, coming into her own. Former court socialite. Married to Lesander Javieri. Female, lesbian. she/her

Rhys Petrava méron Delor: Lieutenant in the Valoran Navy. Half-sibling to Imorie and Dressa. Has phosphorescent hair. Likes to research the alien Kidaa. Nonbinary, pan. they/them

Maja Rhialden (Homaj): The former Seritarchus. Trying to find his way back to himself. Genderfluid, pan (mostly gay). he/him and sometimes she/her

Iata Rhialden (Yan): Former bloodservant to Homaj, now the Seritarchus in Homaj's identity. Far kinder than he has a right to be. Male, gendernonconforming—it's complicated. he/him

Etienne Tanaka (Eti): Former gardener on the resort world of Hestia, now adrift. Trans male, ace, pan. he/him

Lesander Javieri: Secret Heir Consort of the Kingdom of Valoris. Tall and gorgeous. Secret Truthspoken. Married to Dressa Rhialden. Has a crappy family. Female, bi. she/her

Vi Zhang: Captain of the Seritarchus's personal guard. Closest friend and sometimes lover to Maja. Female, gray ace. she/her

Misha Moratu: Ensign in the Valoran Navy. Green Magicker. Has some secrets she's doing a good job of hiding. Has phosphorescent *green* hair. Female, pan. she/her

Kyran Koldari: Duke, royal PITA. Handsome and likely up to no good. Male, pan. he/him

Bettea byr Rhialden (Jis): Bloodservant to Imorie. Takes no BS. Genderfluid, aego. fae/faer

Ceorre Gatri: The Truthspeaker, aka the only person who can boss the Seritarchus around. Religious leader of Valoris. Takes no prisoners. Female, bi. she/her

Haneri ne Delor Rhialden: Seritarchus Consort, aka Imorie's, Dressa's, and Rhys's mother. Has seen some things, will see some more. Demigirl, pan. she/her

Yroikan Javieri: Prince of High House Javieri. Pretty sure she should be the ruler instead. Female, pan. she/her

Dassan Laguaya: Admiral of the Fleet of the Valoran Navy, tough as nails, loyal to the kingdom. Nonbinary, ace. they/them

Ira Nantrayan: Captain of the *V.N.S. Occam's Storm*. Likes to be in control. Female, hetero. she/her

Gian: First officer of the *V.N.S. Occam's Storm*. Caustic, a stickler for rules, not a big fan of magickers. Male, bi. he/him

Doryan Azer: Green Magicker. Healer. Will stand up to anyone for those in need. Nonbinary, pan. they/them

Rivan Tanaka: Eti's mother. A powerful magicker, not a big fan of the Javieris. Female, pan. she/her

Mariyit Broden: First Magicker of the Green Magickers. Kindly, but doesn't take slack. Male, gay. he/him

Jalava: Commander of the Palace Guard. Harried, loyal, usually right. Genderqueer, pan. they/them

Farouk: Personal guard to the Seritarchus, solid and steady, hides a mischievous streak well. Male, pan. he/him

Orilan Chadrikour: Personal guard to the Seritarchus, now captain of his personal guard. Loyal as they come. Female, pan. she/her

Onya Norren: Former First Magicker. Wise and irreverent. Flies like she has a death wish. Female, hetero. she/her

Iwan ko Antia: Partner of Kyran Koldari. Upbeat and effusive. Knows more than they let on. Nonbinary, pan. they/them

THE FACTIONS

Kingdom of Valoris: 187 worlds of theocratic goodness. Ruled by the Seritarchus. Bickered over by the high houses. Shares a border with Kidaa space.

The Kidaa: A species of quadruped sentients. Organized into clans, occupy a large portion of space. Far more technologically advanced than Humans. Hard to talk to. Pacifists (theoretically).

The Onabrii-Kast Dynasty: Former territory of Valoris, now their own empire. Also share the border with the Kidaa. Not super interested in sharing anything else.

Green Magickers: Organized sub-culture of people who manifest the ability to use Green Magics. Marginalized. Can't do violence.

The Adeium: Religion at the heart of Valoris. Genderfluid god. Oversees the Truthspeaker and the Truthspoken.

The High Houses: Fourteen families that include the Rhialden rulership, five princedoms, and 8 dukedoms that together rule the majority of the 187 worlds of the Kingdom of Valoris in an ever-shifting hierarchy.

The General Assembly: A parallel governing body to the rulership comprised of lesser nobility, business people, and common people. Has voting power, but no real teeth.

Valoran Navy: Valoris's space military organization whose purpose is to deter interstellar crime, hold a military presence against grabby neighbor nations, and monitor the border with the Kidaa.

ACKNOWLEDGMENTS

Thanks, first and foremost, to my patrons for your support while bringing this book into the world! <3 It truly means the world!

A big thanks to everyone who's read the series in the last months, you all have truly changed my life.

To my writer pals in my favorite servers and forums, you all are so much of why I'm sane.

Thanks always to Laterpress! You all are absolutely awesome.

And to everyone at Robot Dinosaur Press, thanks for being excellent publishing pals.

To all my friends and family who've supported me through all the ups and downs and cheered me on, you have all my love.

ABOUT THE AUTHOR

Novae Caelum is an author, illustrator, and designer with a love of spaceships and a tendency to quote Monty Python. Star is the author of *The Stars and Green Magics* series, which was a winner of the 2022 Laterpress Genre Fiction Contest Fellowship, *The King's Weaver*, and *Magnificent*. Stars short fiction has appeared in *Intergalactic Medicine Show, Escape Pod, Clockwork Phoenix 5,* and Lambda Award winning *Transcendent 2: The Year's Best Transgender Speculative Fiction*. Novae is nonbinary, starfluid, and uses star/stars/starself or they/them/their pronouns. Most days you can find Novae typing furiously away at stars queer serials, with which star hopes to take over the world. At least, that's the plan. You can find star online at novaecaelum.com

ALSO BY NOVAE CAELUM

The Stars and Green Magics

The Truthspoken Heir

The Shadow Rule

A Bid to Rule

Court of Magickers

The Nameless Storm

The Second Ruler (early access)

The King's Weaver

The King's Weaver

Lyr and Cavere

Good King Lyr: A Genderfluid Romance

Borrowed Wings

The Space Roads

The Space Roads: Volume One

Standalone

Magnificent: A Nonbinary Superhero Novella

The Throne of Eleven

Lives on Other Worlds

Sky and Dew

Visit Novae Caelum's website to find out where to read these titles direct from the author!

https://novaecaelum.com